MY LIFE WITH THE WALTER BOYS

ALI NOVAK

sourcebooks
fire

Published by Sourcebooks Fire, an imprint of Sourcebooks, Inc.
P.O. Box 4410, Naperville, Illinois 60567-4410
(630) 961-3900
Fax: (630) 961-2168
www.sourcebooks.com

Library of Congress Cataloging-in-Publication data is on file with the publisher

Printed and bound in the United States of America.
VP 10 9 8 7 6 5 4 3 2

In loving memory of my father whose unbelievable strength still inspires me. Dad, during our last Christmas together I promised you I would never give up on my dream. Here it is.

Prologue

I never felt bad for Romeo and Juliet.

Don't get me wrong. The play's a classic, and Shakespeare was by all means a literary genius, but I just don't understand how two people who barely knew each other could give up their lives so willingly.

It was for love, people argue—true, everlasting love. But in my opinion, that's a load of garbage. Love takes more than a couple days and a secret, shotgun marriage to develop into something worth dying for.

I'll admit that Romeo and Juliet were *passionate*. But their passion was so intense, so destructive, that it got them killed. I mean, the entire play is driven by their impulsive decisions. Don't believe me? Take Juliet, for example. What girl's first thought would be to marry the son of her father's mortal enemy after she catches him spying outside her bedroom window? Not mine, that's for sure. So that's really why they lost my sympathy vote. There was no preparation—or even thinking, for that matter. They just *did*, regardless of the consequences. When you don't plan ahead, things get messy.

And after what happened three months ago, after my life was completely thrown off course, a messy love life was the last thing I needed.

Chapter 1

I didn't own a single pair of jeans. It's crazy, I know, because what sixteen-year-old girl doesn't have at least one pair, maybe with a tear in the left knee or a heart doodled across the thigh in Sharpie?

It wasn't that I disliked the way they looked, and it had nothing to do with the fact that my mother had been a fashion designer, especially considering that she used jeans in her collections all the time. But I was a firm believer in the phrase "dress to impress," and today I was definitely going to need to make an impression.

"Jackie?" I heard Katherine call from somewhere inside the apartment. "The taxi is here."

"Just a minute!" I scooped a piece of paper off my desk. "Laptop, charger, mouse," I muttered, reading off the rest of the checklist. Opening my satchel, I searched for my possessions to make sure they were safely tucked inside. "Check, check, check," I whispered when my fingers brushed against all three things. With a bright red pen, I marked an X next to each of them on my list.

There was a knock on my bedroom door. "You ready, honey?" Katherine asked, poking her head inside. She was a tall woman in her late forties, with golden hair that was cut into a mom bob and starting to gray.

"I think so," I told her, but my voice cracked, revealing otherwise. My gaze snapped down to my feet because I didn't want to see the look in her eyes—the sympathetic one that I'd seen on everyone's faces since the funeral.

"I'll give you a moment," I heard her say.

When the door clicked shut, I smoothed down my skirt as I glanced in the mirror. My long, dark curls were straightened and tied back with a blue ribbon like always, not a single strand out of place. The collar on my blouse was crooked, and I fidgeted with it until my reflection was seamless. I pursed my lips in annoyance at the purple circles under my eyes, but there was nothing I could do to fix the lack of sleep that was causing them.

Sighing, I took one last look around my room. Even though my entire checklist was crossed off, I didn't know when I would be returning, and I didn't want to forget anything important. The space was strangely empty, since most of my possessions were on a moving truck bound for Colorado. It had taken me a week to pack it all, but Katherine had helped me with the huge task.

Clothing had filled most of the boxes, but there were also my collection of Shakespeare plays and the teacups my sister, Lucy, and I had collected from every country we had ever visited. As I glanced around, I knew I was stalling; with my organizational skills, there was no way I'd forget anything. The real issue was that I didn't want to leave New York—not one bit.

But I didn't have a say in the matter, so with reluctance I grabbed my carry-on. Katherine was waiting for me out in the hall, one small suitcase sitting at her feet.

"Have everything?" she asked, and I nodded my head. "All right, let's get going then."

She led the way through the living room and toward the front door, and I trailed slowly behind her, running my hands over the furniture in an attempt to memorize every last detail of my home. It was hard, which was strange considering I'd lived here my entire life. The white sheets thrown over the furniture so dust wouldn't frost the fabric were like solid walls, holding my recollections at bay.

We stepped out of the apartment in silence, and Katherine paused to lock the door. "Would you like to look after the key?" she asked.

I had my own set tucked in my suitcase, but I reached out and took the small silver piece of metal from her hands. Unfastening my mother's locket, I let the key slip down the delicate chain so it could rest against my chest, right next to my heart.

• • •

We sat on the plane in silence. I was trying hard to forget that I was currently moving farther and farther away from my home, and I refused to let myself cry. For the first month after the accident, I never left my bed. Then came the day where I miraculously pulled myself out from underneath my comforter and got dressed. Since then, I'd promised myself that I would be strong and composed. I didn't want to go back to that weak, hollow person I'd become, and that wasn't going to change now. Instead, I focused my attention on Katherine as she clenched and unclenched the armrest, her knuckles going white each time she did.

I only knew a few things about the woman sitting next to me.

First was that she was my mother's childhood friend. They grew up in New York and attended Hawks Boarding School together, the same school my sister and I had been enrolled in. Back then, she was known as Katherine Green, which brought me to the second thing I knew about her. During college she met George Walter. The two married and moved to Colorado to start a horse ranch, George's lifelong dream. Finally, the third and most noteworthy piece of information I knew about Katherine—she was my new guardian. Apparently I'd met her when I was little, but it was so long ago that I couldn't remember. Katherine Walter was a complete stranger to me.

"Afraid of flying?" I asked, as she let out a deep breath. Honestly, the woman looked like she was going to be sick.

"No, but to be completely truthful, I am a bit nervous about—well, taking you home," she said. I felt my shoulders tense up. Was she afraid that I was going to go off the deep end? I could assure her that wasn't going to happen, not if I wanted to get into Princeton. Uncle Richard must have said something to her, something about me not being okay, even though I was perfectly fine. Katherine caught my look and quickly added, "Oh no, not because of you, honey. I know you're a good kid."

"Then why?"

Katherine's smile was sympathetic. "Jackie, honey, did I ever tell you I have twelve kids?"

No, I thought as my mouth dropped open, that definitely wasn't mentioned. When he decided that I was moving to Colorado, Uncle Richard did say something about Katherine having kids, but twelve? He'd conveniently left that little detail out. A dozen kids. Katherine's household must be stuck permanently in a state of chaos. Why would anyone even *want* to have twelve children? I could feel the tiny wings of panic fluttering inside my chest.

Stop overreacting, I told myself. After taking a few deep breaths in through the nose and out through the mouth, I pulled out a notebook and pen. I needed to find out as much as I could about the family I was going to live with, so I could be prepared. Sitting up in my seat, I asked Katherine to tell me about her kids and she agreed enthusiastically.

"My oldest is Will," she began, and I started writing.

The Walter Boys:

Will is twenty-one. He's in his final semester at the local community college and is engaged to his high-school sweetheart.

Cole is seventeen. He's a senior in high school and a talented auto mechanic.

Danny is seventeen. He's also a senior in high school and the president of the drama club. He's Cole's fraternal twin.

Isaac is sixteen. He's a junior in high school and is obsessed with girls. He's Katherine's nephew.

Alex is sixteen. He's a sophomore in high school and plays way too many video games.

Lee is fifteen. He's a sophomore in high school and a skater. He's also Katherine's nephew.

Nathan is fourteen. He's a freshman in high school and a musician.

Jack and Jordan are twelve. They're in seventh grade and

twins. They believe that they will be the next Steven Spielberg and always have a video camera with them.

Parker is nine. He's in fourth grade. He looks innocent but loves tackle football.

Zack and Benny are five and are in kindergarten. They're twins and crazy little monsters with potty mouths.

I looked over what I wrote, and my stomach dropped. This was a joke, right? Katherine didn't just have twelve kids, but twelve *boys*! I knew nothing, absolutely nothing, about the male species. I went to a private school for girls! How was I ever going to survive living in a house full of boys? Didn't they speak their own language or something?

As soon as the plane landed, Uncle Richard was going to hear an earful from me. Knowing him, he was probably wrapped up in an important board meeting and wouldn't be able to take my call, but I couldn't believe him! Not only was he pawning me off on some woman I didn't know, but he also was dumping me with a pack of boys. He said he was doing what was best for me, especially since he was never home, but over the past three months, I'd gotten the feeling that he just didn't feel comfortable being a parent.

• • •

Richard wasn't my real uncle, but I'd known him since I was a little girl. He was my dad's college roommate, and after graduating, they became business partners. Every year on my birthday, he would bring me a bag of my favorite jellybeans and a card with fifty dollars in it.

In January, Richard became my guardian, and to make the situation more bearable for me, he moved into the penthouse on the Upper East Side where my family lived. At first it was weird with him in the house, but he kept to himself in the spare bedroom and soon we fell into a comfortable routine. Normally, I only saw him at breakfast since he always worked late into the night, but last week that all changed. When I came home from school, the dinner table was set with what must have been his best attempt at a home-cooked meal. Then he told me I was moving to Colorado.

"I don't get why you're making me leave," I told him after ten minutes of arguing.

"I explained this already, Jackie," he said, his face pained as if this decision was ripping *him* away from the only home he'd ever known and not me. "Your school therapist is worried about you. She called today because she doesn't think you're coping well."

"First of all, I never wanted to see that stupid therapist," I argued, slamming my fork on the table. "Secondly, how can she even suggest I'm not coping well? My grades are excellent, if not better than first semester."

"You've done a fine job in school, Jackie," he said. I could hear the *but* coming. "However, she thinks that you're throwing yourself into your work as a way to avoid facing your problems."

"My only problem is that she has no clue who I am! Come on, Uncle Richard. You know me. I've always been studious and hard-working. That's what it means to be a Howard."

"Jackie, you've joined three new clubs since the start of the semester. Don't you think you're spreading yourself a bit thin?"

"Did you know that Sarah Yolden received a scholarship to go study an endangered species of plants in Brazil over the summer?" I asked instead.

"No, but—"

"She got to publish her findings in a science magazine. She's also first chair for violin and got to perform in Carnegie Hall. How am I supposed to compete with that? I can't just have good grades if I want to get into Princeton," I told him coolly. "My application needs to be impressive. I'm building it up."

"And I understand that, but I also think a change of scenery might be beneficial for you. The Walters are wonderful people and are happy to take you in."

"A change of scenery is relaxing on the beach for a week!" I exclaimed, rocketing out of my seat. Leaning over the table, I glared at Uncle Richard. "This is cruel. You're sending me across the country."

He sighed. "I know you don't understand right now, Jackie, but I promise this is a good thing. You'll see."

• • •

So far, I still didn't understand. The closer we got to Colorado, the more nervous I became, and no matter how many times I told myself that things would be fine, I didn't believe it. I chewed my lip until it was raw, worrying over how difficult it would be for me to fit into the Walters' lives.

When the plane landed, Katherine and I made our way through the airport to find her husband.

"Now, I told the kids last week that you're moving in, so they know you're coming," she chattered as we pushed through the crowds. "Also, I have a room for you. I just haven't been able to clean it out yet, so—oh, George! George, over here!"

Katherine jumped up and down, waving to a tall man in his early fifties. I could tell Mr. Walter was a few years older than his wife because most of his hair and scruff were completely gray, and age lines were starting to streak across his forehead. He was wearing a red-and-black flannel shirt with ripped jeans, heavy work boots, and a cowboy hat.

When we reached him, he pulled Katherine into a hug and stroked her hair. It reminded me of my parents, and I cringed and turned away. "I missed you," he told her.

She pecked him on the cheek. "I missed you too." Pulling away, she turned to me. "George dear," she said, taking his hand. "This is Jackie Howard. Jackie, this is my husband."

George looked uncomfortable as he sized me up. After all, how exactly do you greet someone who just lost her entire family? Nice to meet you? We're happy to have you? Instead, George held out his free hand for me to grasp and muttered a quick hello.

Then he turned back to Katherine. "Let's get the luggage and go home."

• • •

Once all of my suitcases were packed into the bed of the truck, I climbed in the backseat and dug my iPod out of my jacket. George and Katherine were chatting quietly about the flight, so I pulled on my headphones, not wanting to hear any more of their conversation. As we drove farther away from the city and deeper into

ALI NOVAK

the country, I became more upset. We were surrounded by green fields and hills that dipped up and down along the pavement, but without the tall, proud buildings of New York City, I somehow felt exposed. Colorado was beautiful, but how was I ever going to live here?

Finally, after what seemed like hours, the truck pulled onto a gravel road. In the distance, I could see a house at the top of a hill, but just barely. Was all of this land really theirs? When we got to the top, I realized that it wasn't a single house; it looked more like three homes put together. I guess you need a lot of space for twelve boys.

The grass desperately needed to be mowed, and the wooden front porch could have used a paint job. The lawn was covered in toys, probably the younger boys' handiwork. George hit one of those small clicker-thingies that was clipped onto the visor, and the garage door started to open. A bike fell over, followed by a few more toys, which blocked the truck's way into the parking spot.

"How many times do we need to tell them to clean up after themselves?" George grumbled to himself.

"Don't worry, dear. I'm on it," Katherine said as she unbuckled her seat belt and slid out of the car. I watched as she moved the mess so her husband could pull in. When the car was finally parked, George let the engine die, and we sat in the dim silence. Then, he turned around in the front seat to face me.

"You ready, Jackie?" he asked. He looked me over and frowned. "You're looking kind of pale."

Of course I looked pale! I had just flown halfway across the

12

country with a woman I didn't know because my family was gone. On top of that, I was going to have to live with twelve kids, all of whom were boys! This wasn't exactly a top-ten day for me.

"I'm fine," I said, muttering my automatic response. "Just a little nervous, I guess."

"Well, the best piece of advice I can give you 'bout my boys"—he began while unbuckling his seat belt—"is their bark's worse than their bite. Don't let 'em scare you."

How was that supposed to be reassuring? George was watching me, so I nodded my head. "Um, thanks," I said.

He gave me a small nod and then got out of the car, leaving me alone to compose myself. As I stared out the windshield, quick images started to flash before my eyes like the pages of flipbook: my parents in the front seat of our car teasing one another, my sister in the backseat singing along with the radio, the flicker of another car, and the wheel spinning out of control. Then twisted metal, red. It was the nightmare that had been keeping me up since the day my family died. Now, apparently, it was here to haunt me during the daylight hours as well.

Stop! I screamed to myself and squeezed my eyes shut. Just stop thinking about it. Gritting my teeth together, I opened the door and hopped out of the car.

"Jackie!" Katherine called. Her voice drifted through an open door at the back of the garage, which led to what must have been the backyard. Slinging my carry-on over my shoulder, I emerged into the sunlight. At first, the only thing I saw was her standing on a pool deck, waving at me as the sun glared into my eyes. But then I saw them in the water. They were splashing and goofing around—a completely shirtless bunch of gorgeous guys.

"Come here, honey!" Katherine said, so I had no other choice but to join her on the deck.

I climbed up the wooden steps, hoping that my clothes weren't rumpled from the flight, and unconsciously moved my hand up to smooth out my hair. Katherine was smiling at me as two young boys stood next to her, clinging to her pants. Must be the youngest set of twins, I decided before turning to face the rest of the group. Much to my discomfort, everyone was staring at me.

"Boys," began Katherine, breaking the silence, "this is Jackie Howard, the friend of the family your father and I told you about. She will be staying with us for some time, and while she's here, I want you all to try your best to make her feel at home."

That seemed like the opposite of what they wanted. All the boys were staring at me like I was a foreigner invading their own personal country.

The best thing to do is to make peace, I told myself. I slowly raised my hand and waved. "Hi, guys. I'm Jackie."

One of the older boys swam forward and pulled himself out of the pool, making the muscles in his tan arms bulge. A spray of water flew in all directions as he shook his messy bangs out of his eyes, just like a wet dog would, only sexier. Then, to finish it off, he ran his fingers through his sun-bleached blond hair, combing it back into golden white streaks. The boy's red swim trunks hung dangerously low, flirting between inappropriate and just enough room for imagination.

I took one look at him and my heart fluttered, but I quickly pushed the stirring feeling away. What is wrong with you, Jackie? I screamed at myself.

His gaze flickered over me casually, and the water droplets caught in his eyelashes sparkled in the sunlight. He turned to his father. "Where's she going to stay?" he questioned, ignoring me as if I weren't there.

"Cole," George responded in a voice that was meant to reprimand his son. "Don't be so rude. Jackie is our guest."

Cole shrugged. "What? We're not running a hotel here. I, for one, am not sharing a room."

"I don't want to share either," another boy complained.

"Me either," someone else added.

Before a chorus of complaints rang out, George held up his hands. "Nobody is going to have to share or give up their room," he said. "Jackie will have an entirely new room."

"New room?" Cole asked as he crossed his arms over his bare chest. "Where's that?"

Katherine shot him a look. "The studio."

"But, Aunt Kathy!" one of the other boys started to say.

"You did have a bed moved in there while I was gone, right, George?" she asked, cutting off one of her nephews.

"Of course. Not all of the supplies have been moved out, but it will have to do in the meantime," he told his wife. Then he turned to Cole and gave him a look that said "knock it off." "You can help Jackie move her things," he added. "No complaining."

Cole turned back to me, his gaze unnerving. My skin blazed like a bad sunburn where his eyes touched my body, and when they lingered too long on my chest, I crossed my arms in discomfort.

After a few tense seconds, he shrugged his shoulders. "No problem, Dad," he said.

Cole cocked his head and offered me a smirk that said "I know I'm hot." Even with my limited knowledge of boys, a twisting in my stomach told me this boy in particular was going to be a problem. Maybe if I could learn to deal with him, the rest wouldn't be as bad. I risked a quick glance at the other boys and my shoulders slumped. The scowls plastered across most of their faces were not a good sign. They seemed to want me here as little as I wanted to be here.

Katherine and George disappeared into the house, leaving me to the wolves. I waited awkwardly on the deck for Cole to help me with my luggage. He was taking his time, slowly drying off with a towel that had been flung over one of the many pool chairs. I could feel the boys watching me, so I kept my eyes focused on one of the swirled knots in the wooden deck. The longer Cole took, the more intimidating the staring became, so I decided to wait for him in the garage.

"Hey, wait," someone called as I turned to leave. The screen door slid open, and another boy stepped out of the house. He was the tallest of them all and probably the oldest too. His golden hair was pulled back into a short ponytail, and the few strands that weren't held back had curled up around his ears. His strong jawline, thick chin, and long, straight nose made the glasses he was wearing look small compared to the rest of his face. His forearms were toned and his hands looked rough, most likely from years of working on the ranch.

"Mom said I needed to introduce myself." He crossed the deck in three long strides and held his hand out for me to shake. "Hi, I'm Will."

"Jackie," I said and slipped my hand into his. Will smiled at me, and his tight grip crushed my fingers just like his father's had.

"So you'll be staying here for a while? I just heard," he said, jabbing a finger over his shoulder and gesturing at the house.

"Yes, it seems so."

"Cool. I don't actually live here anymore since I'm in college, so you probably won't see me much, but if you ever need anything, just let me know, okay?"

By now, all of the boys had climbed out of the pool to dry themselves off and someone snorted at Will's comment.

I did my best to ignore it. "I'll make sure to remember that."

Will, on the other hand, did not. "Are we all playing nicely?" he asked, turning toward his family. When no one responded, he shook his head. "Have you idiots even introduced yourselves yet?" he demanded.

"She knows who I am," Cole said. He was sprawled in one of the plastic lounge chairs, hands tucked casually behind his head. His eyes were closed as he basked in the sun, a smug smile playing on his lips.

"Never mind him. He's an ass," Will said. "Over here is Danny, the ass's twin." Although there was no mistaking they were brothers, Cole and Danny were far from identical. Danny closely resembled

Will, especially in height, but he was much skinnier and his chin was covered in scruff. He looked rougher than Cole, less pretty boy.

"That's Isaac, my cousin," continued Will, pointing to a boy who stood out due to his midnight black hair. He had the same facial features as the other boys, but was clearly from different parents.

"This is Alex." A younger-looking version of Cole pushed his way to the front of the group. Since getting out of the pool, he had pulled on a baseball cap, his blond hair curling over the edges, but he was still without a shirt and was sporting a horrible farmer's tan. I gave him a nervous nod, and he nodded back.

"Lee, also my cousin, is Isaac's younger brother." Will gestured to another boy with curly black hair, which desperately needed to be cut. His face was blank, but his dark eyes flashed with anger when I acknowledged him, so I quickly looked away.

Next, Will introduced me to Nathan. He was a scrawny teen, but I could tell that when he grew, he would be just as attractive as his older brothers. His sandy blond hair looked brown since it was wet, and hanging from his neck was a guitar pick on a silver chain. Then there were Jack and Jordan—the first set of identical twins. They were both wearing the same green swim trunks, which would have made it impossible to tell who was who, except that Jack was wearing glasses.

When Will introduced Parker, I realized that I wasn't alone. *She* stepped forward, and I understood why I hadn't realized there was another girl before now. Parker was wearing an orange T-shirt and swim trunks, both heavy with water and clinging to her skin. Her hair was cut into a short bob—nearly as short as some of her brothers. I thought back to the list I made on the plane and remembered that Parker liked tackle football. Maybe that was why I'd assumed she was a boy.

"Hi, Parker," I said excitedly and offered her a big grin. It was nice to know that there was another girl in the house.

"Hi, *Jackie*." Parker said my name as if it was something funny and the smile slipped off my face. She leaned down and whispered something to the two boys I had yet to meet—the youngest set of twins. A wicked grin crept onto both of their faces.

"And finally we have—" But before Will could finish introducing me, the pair shot out from the line of Walters and bulldozed into me like I was football player. I thought I would be able to keep my balance, but my knees buckled and I fell back—straight into the pool. I paddled back up to the surface, sputtering and gasping for air. I could hear most of the guys laughing.

"Got ya!" cried one of the twins as he stood at the edge of the pool. He was a cute little kid who still hadn't lost his baby fat. Freckles covered his face and his yellow hair curled all over. "I'm Zack and that's my twin, Benny!" When he pointed next to me, I looked over to see an exact replica of the smiling kid break the surface of the water.

"Zack, Benny! What the hell is wrong with both of you?" Will demanded. "Someone get Jackie a towel!" He stuck out a hand to help me up, and soon I was dripping on the side of the pool. It was too early in spring to be swimming. How are they not freezing? Someone handed me a red Power Rangers towel, and I quickly wrapped it around myself to cover the now see-through white blouse I was wearing.

"I'm really sorry about that," Will said, before shooting the youngest twins a glare.

"The only thing I'm sorry about is that he gave her a towel," someone said. I whipped around to see which boy it was, but they were all standing together silently, trying to keep the grins off their faces. Taking a deep breath, I turned back to Will.

"It's fi–fine," I said, my teeth chattering, "but I'd like to change into something dry."

"I can help with that," another voice joked. This time the boys couldn't contain their laughter.

"Isaac!" Will snapped. He glared over my shoulder at his cousin until the boys quieted down. Then he turned back to me. "Your bags are in the car?" he asked. Shivering from the cool spring air, I was only able to nod my head. "Okay, I'll start unloading and someone can show you to your room."

As Will retreated off the deck, I felt myself shrink. My only friend so far had just left me with the enemies. Taking a deep breath of air, I gulped and turned back around. The Walter boys looked at me, their faces vacant. Then, everyone started to grab their towels and clothes lying around on the deck before heading back into the house without another word to me.

Only Cole was left. An awkward thirty seconds passed before his mouth jerked up into a half grin. "Are you just going to stare at me, or do you want to go inside?" he asked. Cole was hot—his damp hair had dried in a dreamy, I-just-had-sex kind of style—but his overconfident attitude made me clam up.

"I want to go inside," I mumbled quietly.

"After you." He flourished his hands and bowed.

Taking a deep breath, I gazed up at my new house. With its yellow shutters and rude additions that must have been added onto the house with each new Walter child, it was nothing like the penthouse back in New York. Throwing one last glance at Cole, I sucked a mouthful of air into my lungs and stepped inside. This might be where I have to live and I'm going to try to make the best of it, I thought, but it will never be my home.

Chapter 2

About earlier," Cole said as he led me through the cluttered house. "This whole you-moving-in thing kinda came out of nowhere. Caught me off guard."

"I get it," I told him. It wasn't exactly an apology for his unfriendly behavior, but hopefully it was the reason behind most of the boys' unenthusiastic reactions toward me. "You don't need to explain."

"So my mom said you're from New York." He paused at the bottom of the staircase to look at me.

"Yeah," I answered, and suddenly my stomach bottomed out. What else did he know about me? The accident…had he heard? If there was one good thing about moving to Colorado, it was that nobody knew who I was. I could go back to just Jackie, not the girl whose family died. I didn't want the boys to know. What if they acted funny around me? "Did she tell you guys anything else?" I added, trying to sound nonchalant.

He paused then, and it was all the confirmation I needed. One small moment of hesitation, and I knew he knew about my family.

"Not much," he recovered quickly, and a smile slipped onto his face with such ease that the upward curve of his lips almost looked genuine. "Just that the daughter of her friend was moving in. You're pretty much a mystery girl."

"I see." The thought of all the Walter boys knowing about what happened made my mouth dry, but at least Cole was making the effort to act normal.

"Now that I think about it, I don't even know how old you are."

"Sixteen."

"Are you always this shy?"

"Shy?" I echoed in confusion. What did he expect? It wasn't like he had been the president of my welcoming committee. Besides, the fact that he practically had abs down to his toes didn't help calm my nerves.

"Never mind," he said, laughing, his eyes dancing in amusement as he shook his head at me. "Come on. I'll show you upstairs."

We started up the steps, which was more difficult than it sounded. Stacks of books and board games, dirty clothes, a deflated basketball, and a pile of movies made reaching the second floor without knocking anything over harder than completing an obstacle course. Next was the maze of hallways that I knew I would get lost in. They seemed to twist and turn in strange places as if there was no real floor plan. When we reached the farthest corner of the house, Cole finally stopped.

"This is where you'll be staying," he said, pushing open a door. Putting my hand on the wall, I searched for the light switch. We found it at the same time, our fingers fumbling over each other's in the dark. The contact sent a pulse down my arm, and I ripped my hand back in shock. Cole chuckled, but the lights flickered on and a warm glow lit up the room, making me forget my embarrassment.

"Oh wow."

Every inch of the wall was painted in vivid colors. A mural of a tropical rain forest started on one end of the room, and by the time it wrapped around to the other side, it transformed into an ocean filled with sea creatures. One half of the ceiling was painted to look like the night sky and the other daytime. Even the wooden panels on the ceiling fan had been decorated. I stood, mouth open, and gaped at my new room.

"This was my mom's art studio," Cole said.

A large desk was painted as brightly as the rest of the room. On top was a collection of glass jars and coffee mugs that were filled with paintbrushes, charcoal pencils, and markers. A sketchbook was open to a rough-draft sketch of the painting on an easel in the middle of the room. Light brushstrokes covered the canvas, depicting a scene that I recognized from my drive from the airport—the rolling hills of Colorado.

"It's amazing," I said, brushing my hand over the edge of the canvas.

"Yeah, she's kinda awesome with art stuff." There was an edge to his tone.

Then I noticed a small shelf holding more art supplies that was pushed over to the edge of the room so my single bed could fit inside, and I realized why the boys were upset when Katherine mentioned my sleeping arrangements.

"I'm taking her space."

"She doesn't have much time to paint anymore," Cole said, stuffing his hands into the back pockets of his trunks. "Twelve kids and all."

In other words: yes, I was.

Before I could respond, Will dropped one of my suitcases onto the floor, surprising both of us with a thud. "Come on, Cole," he said and straightened back up. "Jackie's got a ton of bags that we need to bring up."

"I'll help as soon as I'm done changing," I offered, not wanting them to do all of my work.

Will dismissed me with a wave of his hand. "Just make yourself at home."

When they were gone, I shut the door to change, dropping the wet towel that was still wrapped around my shoulders to the floor. This morning I'd made sure an extra set of clothes—tailored pants and a pink shirt with a simple collar—was packed in my carry-on in case of an emergency. After changing, my hair came next. It took me nearly ten minutes of battling with my comb to detangle the knots.

"Hey, you alive in there?" I heard Cole ask as he knocked.

"Give me a moment," I called and patted down my hair one last time. With my straightener packed away, there was nothing to do about the curls, so I grudgingly let them hang down in dark waves after fastening my blue ribbon back in place. "Yes?" I asked, pulling back the door. My luggage was now piled outside.

"Just checking," Cole said as he leaned against the doorframe. "You were in there for a while."

"I was changing."

"For fifteen minutes?" he asked, his eyebrows scrunching up. "And what the heck are you wearing?"

"What's wrong with my outfit?" I asked. Sure the outfit was a bit casual, but I hadn't planned on being thrown into a pool.

"It looks like you're going to an interview," Cole said, trying not to laugh.

"If I were going to an interview, I'd be wearing a business suit."

"Why would you wear guys' clothes?"

I scoffed. "Business suits aren't only for men." Hadn't his mother taught him *anything* about fashion?

"Okay, whatever, but I wouldn't wear that nice top to dinner tonight. We're having spaghetti."

What was that supposed to mean? I didn't eat like a caveman. "If we're having dinner, shouldn't we wear something more…appropriate?" I countered. Cole was still shirtless, and I purposely kept my gaze glued to his face so I wouldn't stare. With his sun-bleached locks and chiseled abs, he looked like a Greek god. How was I ever going to live with this boy? Everything about him made me self-conscious and uncomfortable.

"I don't know how you guys do things in New York, but we don't dress up for dinner around here. I'll be fine in this." He smiled a slow, arrogant grin that made me squirm. "Anyway, I'll give you time to unpack," he said before I could respond.

Cole pushed himself off the doorframe, his arm muscles flexing. Holding my breath, I watched him leave without the ability to tear my eyes away. He finally disappeared around the corner in the hall, breaking my trance, and I collapsed on my new bed. I had survived my first encounter with the Walter boys.

• • •

Katherine's kitchen was a sight I had never seen before. The place was loud and cluttered, but warm and cozy at the same time. Her artistic hand had definitely taken part in decorating the kitchen. All of the walls were painted to be one huge mural of a vineyard, and almost every chair around the table was a different color. It was the opposite of my mother's clean-tiled, sparkling steel, half-a-million-dollar kitchen. At home, I felt like the kitchen was just there to look pretty and if I made a mess, I was in big trouble. This room looked lived in and, for some strange reason, I liked it.

When I walked in, Katherine was standing at the stove, stirring a pot of something boiling and shouting orders at Isaac, who was helping her. Two dogs were running around the room chasing each other, making it hard for everyone who was trying to set the table for dinner. George almost dropped the salad bowl when he tripped over a dog running between his legs.

Zack and Benny, the youngest set of twins, were sitting on the floor three feet apart playing some type of handheld video game with a cord connecting each boy's device. I nearly choked when Zack yanked Benny's away from him and yelled, "You lose, shithead!"

A deafening cheer erupted from the den that was connected to the kitchen, and I turned to see the rest of the guys watching a basketball game on TV. My eyes instantly found Cole, who jumped up out of his seat, pounding his fist into the air. Since I'd seen him last, he'd pulled on a fitted black shirt that emphasized his broad shoulders and contrasted with his fair hair, making it look platinum.

"Stop staring," said Lee as he rode his skateboard into the kitchen

from behind me. I remembered Lee because we were both sopho-
mores in high school, and when Will introduced him, he had given
me the most chilling look. I turned away from the den, embarrassed that he had caught me watching his cousin.

"Lee! How many times do I have to tell you not to ride your
board in the house?" scolded Katherine as he crashed into one of
the kitchen chairs, knocking it over. It fell on Benny's head, and he
immediately started screaming bloody murder.

"Only a thousand times more, Aunt Kathy," he said before kneeling next to his little cousin to see if he was okay.

I rubbed my temples, trying to make my headache go away. This
place was maddening. And then, in the midst of it all was one
boy. I couldn't remember his name, but he was sitting at one of
the kitchen chairs, guitar in his lap, music sheets spread out on
the table in front of him. Thinking back to my list, I guessed that
this was Nathan—the fourteen-year-old musician. I watched as he
strummed a few notes on the instrument that I was unable to hear.
Shaking his head, he grabbed the pencil from between his teeth
and crossed something out. I wondered how he could concentrate
with everything going on around him.

"Jackie, honey," said Katherine, finally noticing me. She was
straining the water out of a huge pot of noodles. On the counter
next to her was an economy-sized jar of spaghetti sauce. "I'm so
glad you didn't get lost on your way to the kitchen. This place is
so huge, and your room is the farthest away. I asked Cole to go get
you about ten minutes ago, but it looks like he got wrapped up in
the game." She smiled at me, and I went over to help her.

"It's okay. It wasn't very hard to find," I said, popping the lid off the jar. "I just followed all the noise."

Katherine laughed, took the jar from me, and emptied it over the noodles. "It's always loud in here. That's what happens when you have twelve kids." She paused for a moment and gave me a small smile. "Make that thirteen."

I looked at my feet and whispered, "Thanks, Mrs. Walter."

"Anything for you, dear. And please, don't call me that. I'm Katherine," she said and pulled me into a hug.

"Boys!" bellowed George. "Grub's on the table. Turn that stupid thing off."

Katherine let me go, grabbed the bowl of spaghetti, and set it next to the other dishes of steaming food. I followed her over to the table and sat down in the nearest chair.

"You can't sit there," said one of the boys from the middle set of twins. Once again, both of their names slipped my memory.

"Sorry," I said, sliding into the next chair.

"Not there either. That's my chair," said the other twin.

"Boys, why doesn't one of you go get a chair from the dining room and bring it in here for Jackie to sit on?" asked George. One of the twins looked like he was about to protest, but then his double elbowed him in the side.

"Okay, Dad. Be right back," he said, smiling sweetly.

A minute later, he came back, dragging a chair behind him. After it was pushed up to the table, I sat down and George began grace. About halfway through his prayer, I felt movement on my leg. Reaching beneath the table, I grabbed something thin and smooth.

When I pulled it up, I screamed and flung the yellow reptile away from me. The table burst into commotion.

"Snake!" roared Benny as he jumped away from his seat. As he did so, he stepped on one of the dogs. The poor thing yelped and launched itself away from him. Alex, who pushed away from the table in shock, tripped over the wild dog and crashed into Isaac, who was sitting next to him. George was trying to calm Benny down but managed to slip in a puddle of milk that had somehow spilled onto the floor in all the frenzy.

As he fell, George grabbed the tablecloth in an attempt to regain his balance, but instead he brought all of dishes down with him. When the bowl of spaghetti hit the ground, its contents flew in every direction and covered us all with tomato sauce.

"Jordan!" George bellowed at his son. "You're beyond grounded!"

• • •

Dinner had been a disaster, and it was entirely my fault. After George and Katherine calmed down the mayhem, everyone was given a job to clean up the mess. That was, everyone except me. Katherine apologized profusely for her sons' behavior, and sent me off to clean myself up even, though I pleaded to help.

Turning off the hot water, I stepped out of the shower. It felt good to wash off the chlorine from the pool and the spaghetti from dinner, but no amount of shower time would ease the dread that was swirling around in my stomach. To add to my discomfort, a stab of irritation shot through me when I spotted my shirt on the floor, covered in sauce. Cole had been right—now it was completely ruined. I was already making a mess of living with the

Walters, as I could tell from the way most of the boys threw me dirty looks when I left the kitchen.

As I wrapped a towel around myself, I wished I'd worn flip-flops to the bathroom. The floor was a minefield littered with dirty boxers and used tissues that had missed the garbage, not to mention that tile looked like it hadn't been scrubbed since the Walters moved into the house.

I also had to be extra careful not to lean against the counter as I washed my face. Globs of toothpaste speckled it like bird poop, along with pieces of hair and bright blue shaving cream. Most of the boys tossed their toothbrushes next to the sink, as if the damp countertop wasn't a cesspool of mystery toxins. There was no way I'd be keeping mine in here.

Pulling back the door, I poked my head out into the hallway to make sure no one was around. I didn't want any of the boys to see me in a towel. Next time I showered, I'd remember to bring my clothes with me. As I crept back to my room, I imagined this was how a wild teenager felt as he or she carefully slunk out of the house in the middle of the night. I myself had never done anything that crazy.

I successfully reached my new room without encountering one of the boys and slipped inside, sighing with relief.

"Nice towel, Jackie."

"Oh!" I squeaked, almost dropping the fluffy fabric when I spotted Cole sitting on my bed. He was still covered in tomato sauce, but was eating out of a takeout Chinese carton. Two more steaming cartons were sitting on the desk waiting to be eaten. A smile eased across his face as he looked me up and down.

My face flushed as red as the stains on his shirt, and I yanked the towel tighter around my figure. "What in the world are you doing in my room?"

"Dinner. Want some?" he asked, holding up the carton of food.

"Yes, but can you please leave?" I asked, mortified that this was actually happening. "I need to change."

"Don't worry. I'll close my eyes."

"I'm not changing with you in the room."

"That's fine. I won't mind if you eat in the towel."

"Cole, get out!" I finally snapped.

"Damn, woman, don't get your panties in a bunch." He got up from the bed, springs squeaking, and set his food next to the other cartons. "Although, that's not really possible right now, is it?" Cole chuckled to himself as he stepped outside. I slammed the door behind him and turned the lock for good measure.

After quickly pulling on a pair of pajamas, I unlocked the door and let Cole back inside. He brushed passed me and flopped down on the bed before grabbing his takeout. I flinched as he shoveled a bite into his mouth. I never ate in my bedroom. It was unsanitary.

Once he noticed me watching him, Cole stopped chewing. "What?" he asked, his mouth full.

"Do you have to eat on the bed?"

"Why, you wanna do something *else* on the bed?"

"No, Cole," I said, trying my best to ignore the comment. "I just don't want food in it. I have to sleep there."

"A few pieces of rice gonna keep you awake, princess?" Cole glanced around the room. "Besides, where else will we sit?"

Of course, he was right. My suitcases were taking up all of the floor space, and Katherine's art supplies occupied everywhere else. And there was no way I was going back to the kitchen to eat. Cautiously, I sat down on the edge of the bed and he handed me some chopsticks. For the next few minutes we sat in silence eating sweet chicken, and surprisingly it was peaceful sitting with Cole. But when the food disappeared, he ruined one of the only relaxing moments I'd had since arriving in Colorado.

"I enjoyed the dinner show tonight," he said, setting an empty container down. I turned away from him and halfheartedly poked at a piece of broccoli. Cole laughed. "Come on, Jackie. It was just a joke. To be honest, that stuff happens *all* the time in this house."

Putting my food aside, I propped myself up on my elbows and looked at Cole. "Really?" I questioned.

"Well, it's not always that dramatic, but at least tonight was funny. You should've seen the look on your face when you pulled Rumple out." He let out a wholehearted laugh again.

"Rumple?" I asked in confusion.

Cole stretched and scooted closer. "Rumplesnakeskin. He's Jordan's snake."

"Any other dangerous pets I should know about?" I grumbled.

"Nope," he said with a laugh. "Just Isaac."

"I'm not really an animal person," I said as the floorboards outside my room creaked. "Especially not snakes."

The door banged open. "Corn snakes aren't dangerous," Jordan said as he barged in. His double, Jack, followed behind him with a video camera in hand, and a green flashing light let me know that he was recording.

Jack nodded his head. "We wanted a python, but Mom won't let us get one."

"Yeah, my friend's older brother Nick has a python," Jordan said excitedly. "He told me this one time, the tank broke. Snakes are ectothermic, and he needed to keep it warm, so at night Nick put the python in his bed and used his body heat. Instead of curling up like it normally did, the python straightened itself out on the bed. It wouldn't eat either, so Nick thought something was wrong with it. He brought the python into the vet, and they said it was stretching itself out so it could eat him! How awesome is that?"

I gaped at the twins in horror. Apparently my definition of "terrifying" was equivalent to Jordan's for "awesome."

"If I had a snake," Cole started, "I'd probably let it eat you, Jo. You obviously don't know anything about knocking."

"Dad sent us up here to tell you that if any of us are alone in a room with Jackie, the door has to stay open. Therefore no knocking is required, dickwad," Jordan replied, crossing his arms over his chest in defiance.

"Fine. That doesn't explain why you're still here. You told us about Dad's stupid rule. Now leave."

"I wasn't done. We also came up to inform Jackie that she's our new subject."

"Subject?" I asked.

Cole rolled his eyes. "These two morons think they're going to be film directors one day. They're always trying to find interesting subjects for what they think will be the documentary of the century."

"It will be award winning," Jack added, turning to me. "Jordan and I realized at dinner that you'd be perfect. Too bad I didn't have our camera then. We were hoping we could reenact the scene."

"Fat chance that will happen. What will you say? 'Hey, Mom, do you mind if we destroy the kitchen again? We promise we'll clean up all the spaghetti sauce.'"

Ignoring Cole, I responded to the twins. "I'd prefer if you didn't film me at all. I don't really care to be your next film subject."

"But you don't understand," Jordan said. "You're the first female in the Walter house. This is monumental."

"You do remember that you have a mother and a little sister, right?" Cole pointed out.

"Mom doesn't count because she's, well, our mother. And Parker doesn't even have boobs yet."

A knock on the door interrupted the conversation. One of the older boys was standing outside the bedroom as if he was afraid to come in. "Um, Cole?" he asked, barely looking at me.

"Yeah, what's up, Danny?"

When Cole said his brother's name, it clicked. Now I remember, I thought, as I looked him over and noticed the facial hair. Danny was Cole's fraternal twin.

"Erin is here for you," he mumbled, "waiting at the front door." When he finished delivering his message, Danny spun on his heels and left.

"That's my cue." Cole stood up from the bed. "Come on, you

two," he said, pushing his younger brothers toward the door. "Leave Jackie alone for now. She's had a long day."

"Fine," Jack grumbled. "We can discuss your contract in the morning, Jackie. Jordan and I have been pooling our allowances for a while now, and we can pay you handsomely." Without another word, the pair ran off, leaving me alone with Cole.

"I really don't want to be in their movie," I repeated with a sigh.

"If you ignore them long enough, they'll move on to something else."

"I guess, but your family is really overwhelming, and I just want everyone to forget about dinner."

"Tomorrow will be easier, okay? I'll see you in the morning before school."

"Oh, great," I moaned and flopped back onto my pillow. "School." I was so caught up in the dinner disaster that I almost forgot that I would be going to a public school for the first time in my life.

"Don't worry," he said with a yawn. Griping his elbow, Cole stretched his arm out over his head and I quickly looked away from his rippling muscles. "It will be a breeze."

"Easy for you to say," I said, tugging my mother's locket back and forth across the chain. "I've gone to the same boarding school since I was eleven. The thought of a public school scares me."

"I promise you'll do fine." Cole chuckled as he stepped out into the hall. "Night, Jackie."

"Good night, Cole," I responded. Suddenly, a thought ran through my head.

"Wait," I called just as he was about to shut the door. "Who's Erin?"

Cole paused before responding. "Just a friend."

When he shut the door, I held my breath and listened to him leave. A few seconds later, I heard his feet pound down the stairs.

Then, "Hey, Erin."

I was so surprised to hear Cole again that I nearly fell out of my bed.

"Cole," a girl responded, her voice smoky. "You said you were going to call me."

I glanced around the room, looking for the source of the voices. There were three windows, and I realized why Katherine had picked this room for her art studio. It gave her a handful of different views to paint. The window on the front side of the house was pushed open.

"Yeah," Cole said. "Something came up. Sorry."

Pushing back the curtain, I looked down and saw Cole standing on the front porch. The front door was still open, and the light from inside poured into the night, outlining his body in a yellow glow.

"Are we still on for tonight?" asked Erin. She was standing a few steps down, and with her back to me, all I could see were long legs and a high ponytail.

Cole paused. "It's late."

Erin crossed her arms. "Fine, but no excuses tomorrow. You can't keep bailing on me. I miss you."

"Okay."

"You promise?" she asked. Cole nodded his head. "Good. I'll see you tomorrow."

Cole stood on the porch and watched as Erin walked to her

car. When the headlights disappeared down the dark driveway, I expected Cole to go back inside. Instead, he stepped off the porch and made his way across the front walk. He was heading for what looked like a shed.

When he unlatched the lock and pulled back the double doors, I realized that it was a second garage. After flipping on a light switch, he shut the doors. I waited for a few minutes, but he didn't come back out. Finally I gave up and crawled into bed, but I couldn't stop wondering. What the heck was Cole doing out there?

Chapter 3

I was in the car with my family. My dad and mom were in the front seat, and Lucy was sitting next to me in the back. We were sharing a set of headphones and jamming out to one of our favorite songs. When it came to an end, I smiled and looked out the window. It was one of those crisp, sunny spring days that let you know that winter was almost over. A small green haze that was almost invisible surrounded the tree branches as new buds started to push forth.

I looked down in surprise as my seat belt suddenly slid off. "What the...?" I muttered to myself and clicked it back in. A sinking feeling formed in my stomach when the buckle clicked undone again. Before I could push it back in, an invisible force yanked me from the car.

Now I was standing on the concrete. The trees on both sides of the road had shriveled up, and the sky darkened to an ominous gray. Our car sped by, and I caught a glimpse of Lucy staring out the back window at me.

"Wait, stop!" I cried and started to sprint down the street.

But the car didn't stop. I watched in horror as a mile down the road the pavement started to crumble apart. When the road split in two, our car drove right off the edge and the earth swallowed my family up.

Panting, I sat straight up in bed with a thick layer of sweat covering my body. As my vision adjusted to the dark, dread built up inside me at the sight of unfamiliar surroundings. I kicked the covers off and stepped onto the cold, hard floor. For a moment, I was confused because my room didn't have a wooden floor. Where was the carpet?

I searched in the dark for the light switch, and when I flipped it on, the mural on the walls lit up around me. The shock of reality hit me so hard that my knees buckled and I crumbled to the ground in a heap. I wasn't at home in New York. I was in Colorado.

It was a dream. I had only been dreaming about the accident.

When it happened, I wasn't with them. Instead, I had been lying on the couch, sick with the flu. I remember being tucked into a cocoon of blankets, trying to sleep away the shivers. As the morning slipped by, I drifted in and out of consciousness, and my family must have disappeared from existence sometime then.

At some point, the phone started ringing, but I felt too awful to answer. It continued to ring all afternoon long, until finally there was a knock on the front door and I was forced to get up. When the police officer told me what had happened to my family, my stomach reacted before I could process anything. I bent over, hands to my knees, and emptied onto the floor the small amount of hot chocolate I'd been able to sip that morning.

I didn't understand how Lucy could be gone. She had always gone a step beyond being an older sister. The night before, when I came down with the flu, she'd held my hair and rubbed soothing circles across my back as I cried into the toilet. And my mother—she had been the strongest woman I knew. At the time, it didn't make sense that she was dead.

But she was. They all were.

Ever since that day—ninety-four days, to be exact—I'd been dreaming about them. My father was the famous CEO of Howard Investment Corporation, so their car accident played on the news in loops, a constant reminder that they were gone. I still couldn't get the image out of my head of our car, which had been crunched up into a ball as if it were nothing more than aluminum foil. It was as if every detail was seared into my brain, like when you look away from the sun after staring too long and it starts multiplying across the sky in vivid colors.

Minutes passed as my chest heaved up and down, until finally I was able to gain control of my breathing. I picked myself up and glanced at the clock—5:31 a.m.

I wouldn't be able to fall back asleep, so I went to my dresser. After finding my workout clothes, I pulled on a pair of athletic shorts, grabbed my running shoes, and unhooked my iPod from its charger. It was early and I was exhausted from my nightmare, but I needed a distraction.

Normally I worked out on one of the treadmills in our family's gym, but the Walters didn't have a gym—or even a treadmill, for that matter. Running outside would have to do. The sun was creeping into the sky, and a cool breeze swept across my neck as I stepped out onto the rickety, wooden porch. The morning dew sparkled on the lawn as I sat down to tie my shoelaces before stretching.

As I stretched, butterflies knotted up in my stomach. I couldn't tell if they were left over from my nightmare or if I was nervous about my upcoming day. The prospect of going to a new school made me feel sick. I had only been in the Walter household for a day, and so far it was awful. I couldn't imagine going to a public school with hundreds of boys—eleven plus Parker was bad enough.

It was already nearing the end of the school year, and I was positive that I wouldn't make a single friend. I found myself wishing it were already three in the afternoon, so I could shut myself in my room and curl up under the covers.

Just as I was about to take off, the screen door screeched open as George stepped out. Will and Cole were right behind him, and they were all dressed in work clothes: jeans, old T-shirts that had faded from white to cream, boots, and hats to protect them from the sun.

"Morning, Jackie," George said and tipped his hat at me. Will waved and offered me a friendly smile.

"Morning, Mr. Walter, Will," I replied.

"You're up early," Cole grumbled as he rubbed the sleep from his eyes.

"I could say the same to you."

Cole scowled. "Chores," was all he said.

"The boys have some work on the ranch to get done before they head off for the day," George told me. "If you're going for a run, you might want to wait for Nathan. He'll be out in a second."

"Okay, thanks," I said as the three stepped off the porch.

As I waited for Nathan, I watched them head in the direction of a barn that was barely visible in the early morning light. At one point in their walk, Will playfully shoved Cole, who tripped and fell over into the grass. I covered the smile on my face with my hand.

The screen door screeched again, and Nathan stepped out. When he saw me, he beamed. I was trying to remember which boy he was when I noticed the guitar pick necklace. Right, the musician.

"You like to run?" he asked me excitedly, without a good morning.

"I like keeping in shape," I told him. "I wouldn't necessarily say I enjoy running."

"Okay," he said and laughed. "Do you want to join me on my attempt to stay in shape?" He seemed genuinely eager about it.

"Sure, I don't mind," I said. "Actually, I'm surprised that you want me to come with you. Everyone seemed pretty mad at me last night." I felt my cheeks burn at the memory of the spaghetti flying through the air, but Nathan just grinned. He was going to look so much like Cole when he was older, but he wasn't anything close to being as intimidating.

"Of course I want to run with you! And besides, I thought it was funny. Don't let Jordan get to you. He's just a prankster."

"I'll try to keep that in mind," I said as we headed down the steps.

"Want to follow my normal route?" Nathan asked me.

"Lead the way."

• • •

After my run, I went to the kitchen to get some breakfast before anyone else woke up. I thought it was the perfect way to avoid another catastrophe. Of course, my plan backfired. Katherine was sitting at the table in a pink, fuzzy bathrobe, drinking coffee and reading a book. To make matters worse, Katherine's oldest nephew was there too. He was standing at the kitchen counter and eating a bagel *in his boxers*. Good morning, six-pack! The only thing I could do was stand there and gawk like an idiot.

"Morning, Jackie!" he exclaimed through a mouthful of bagel. Once again, I felt warmth creeping into my cheeks. Why did every one of these boys have a perfect set of abs?

"Um, hi," I greeted stupidly. Katherine looked up with a start at the sound of my voice.

"Isaac!" she scolded, jogging my memory. I remembered that we were the same age, sixteen, but he was a year above me in school. "Go put some clothes on, for God's sake! There's a girl in the house now."

"But you're a girl and you've never had a problem with it before," he countered. "Besides, Jackie doesn't mind. Do you, Jackie?" He turned to face me.

What the heck was I supposed to say to that? *Oh yes, Isaac. I love staring at your half-naked body?* Instead, I answered like any smart girl in my situation would do. "Um…" I trailed off, looking back and forth between the two.

"See, Aunt Kathy? Jackie said she doesn't care," he told his aunt.

Funny, I didn't remember saying anything along those lines.

"No, she didn't, young man," countered Katherine, placing her hands on her hips. "Now go get dressed before I drag you upstairs!"

Just then Alex entered the kitchen, still rubbing away his sleepiness. He was also wearing nothing but his boxers. Unlike Isaac, he slid to a halt when he spotted me. For a moment he stood frozen, his eyes wide, but then he spun around and dashed down the hall.

"See!" Katherine said when her son was gone. "That's exactly how you should be acting in the presence of a beautiful girl—embarrassed!"

"Aunt Kathy, Jackie might be hot, you know, in a preppy, Goody Two-Shoes sort of way, but I could never be embarrassed about this," Isaac said and pointed down at his body.

"Isaac Walter!" she said, shaking a finger and taking a step toward him. Laughing, Isaac exited the kitchen, but not before winking at me. I don't know exactly why I blushed. It might have had something to do with Katherine complimenting me, or maybe it was because Isaac had agreed.

• • •

"What do you think you're doing?" Lee demanded as I waited outside the bathroom in my robe. I was still sweaty from my run with Nathan and needed to shower before school. This time I remembered to bring shower shoes and my clothes, and was mentally preparing myself for the disgusting war zone inside.

"Waiting for the bathroom," I answered. "I believe Cole is inside."

"I know Cole's inside. It's his scheduled time to be in there," Lee said, pointing at a piece of paper taped next to the bathroom door. He flicked his dark hair out of his eyes as he glowered at me. "I'm up next, so get lost."

"There's a schedule to use the *bathroom*?"

"Only in the morning," Nathan said, coming out of his room already showered and dressed. "With all of us trying to get ready before school, it's kind of hectic."

Cole opened the bathroom door, and a wave of steam rushed out into the hall. He only had a white towel wrapped around his waist, and water droplets still clung to his sculpted shoulders and abs, making his skin sparkle.

"If we didn't have an allotted time," he said, trying to shake some water out of his ear, "Danny would be in there for hours trying to make himself look pretty." Then he pushed past Lee, Nathan, and me, calling over his shoulder, "I myself don't need much time because I was gifted with being naturally pretty."

"Is there any way I can squeeze in?" I asked as I glanced over the schedule. The twenty-minute increments were booked all the way up until we had to leave for school.

Isaac poked his head out of the room he shared with Lee. "Has anyone seen my leather jacket?"

"It's in your closet, idiot," Lee told his older brother.

"Like on a hanger? How the heck did it get there?"

"Guys?" I asked.

"Your crap was all over the place and I couldn't find my board."

"Next time you decide to do a bit of spring cleaning, do me a favor—don't touch the jacket."

"Hello? Is anybody going to answer me?" I demanded, putting a hand on my hip. "I need to use the shower too."

"Should have said something earlier, babe," Isaac said. "We could've shared my shower time." He grinned at me before vanishing back inside his room.

Lee laughed at his brother as he slipped into the bathroom and slammed the door in my face.

"Try the one downstairs next to the little kids' rooms," Nathan suggested. "They take baths at night, so there shouldn't be anyone in there. Just watch out for all the bath toys. I've tripped on them before."

• • •

Once everyone showered, ate breakfast, and hurried to finish their homework at the last minute, Katherine pushed us all out the door.

"Lee, leave that skateboard at home. If you ride it in the school halls again, you'll get a suspension."

"But, Aunt Kathy—"

"No buts. Alex, you got an F on your history paper. Star Wars does not count as a valid topic for most significant war in history. Apologize to your teacher and tell him you'll rewrite it. Isaac, the women's volleyball coach called and said if she catches you trying to sneak into the girls' locker room one more time, she'll make sure you fail gym class. Now get going," Katherine shouted from the porch. "Jackie better not be late for her first day of school, or I won't be very happy!"

The guys dumped their backpacks into the bed of the old pickup truck and started piling in. I stared at them from the side of the driveway, feeling like I was watching a picturesque scene from a movie. Everyone had so much personality, and I felt like I didn't belong. Even the truck had character. It had probably been a bright crimson color when it was brand new, but age and weather had worn it down to a dull red. One of the side mirrors was missing, and a headlight had been smashed in. I wondered how it was possibly roadworthy.

Danny, who had taken more time than anyone getting ready, ran out the front door, trying to avoid his mother's scolding. He threw the car keys at Cole, who climbed into the front seat. It didn't take a genius to work out that he was the designated driver. Soon, everyone else had settled into their usual seats, and I realized that the truck was full. Danny, Isaac, and Alex sat in the back, while Cole, Lee, and Nathan sat in the front.

"Um," I began awkwardly, still standing on the grass, "where should I sit?"

"You could always walk," Lee replied sarcastically.

I fought the urge to stick my tongue out at him, but thankfully Nathan came to my rescue. "Don't worry, Jackie. You can squeeze in up front. We'll make room." He smiled warmly from the passenger window.

"If that doesn't work, we can always strap Alex to the roof. Nobody will care," Cole offered as he started up the car.

"If anyone is going to be strapped to the roof," Alex shot back, "it should be you, Cole. You take up the most room."

"Nobody asked your opinion," Cole said, glaring at his younger brother in the rearview mirror. "Now come on, let's go."

Lee grunted in annoyance but scooted closer to Cole. He didn't look too happy about sharing the front with me, but I opened the passenger door and slid in anyway once Nathan made some room.

During the twenty-minute drive to school, I received a crash course in Boys 101 and decided that maybe the male species wasn't so different from females after all. To sum it up, the Walters gossiped worse than the girls at my old boarding school. At first the car was silent, which was probably due to my presence, but soon the boys relaxed and carried on as if I wasn't there. They talked about who was going to make track team this spring and who wasn't. They discussed what they should wear to a party on Friday night and who was going to be there. But most of all they talked about girls: who was cute, which girl wore the perfect perfume, and who had the prettiest hair.

When they started talking about a girl named Kate who, to use Isaac's words, had "the perkiest pair of tits in the world," I felt uncomfortable. Trying to tune the conversation out, I shrunk back into my seat and stared out the window. *Please let us be there soon. Please be there soon!*

But as the truck sped into the school parking lot, Cole laughing like a little boy when the wheels screeched, I instantly regretted my silent prayer. Valley View High was three times the size of my old school. Instead of the green lawns and bricks covered in crawling ivy that I was accustomed to, it was an ugly, cement block building that looked like it was straight out of the '70s. A banner hanging over the front entrance read: Home of the Tigers!

Staring at my new school, I decided that the sheer number of kids was making me nervous. A stream of students made their way toward the front steps, backpacks slung over their shoulders. Other people lingered in the parking lot; there was a group of guys tossing around a football, couples making out against cars, and friends talking in big groups.

"Out," Lee demanded, even though Cole was just swinging the truck into an empty spot. As soon as Nathan and I slid out, Lee dropped to the pavement and tore off into the crowd. I tried to follow him with my eyes, but he disappeared in a matter of seconds. How was I ever going to find my way around this place?

The back doors slammed shut, and the guys grabbed their bags from the bed of the truck. I hung back, hoping someone would offer to show me around.

"Let's get out of here before the fan club arrives," I heard Alex whispering to Danny as they brushed by me.

Isaac shrugged on his leather jacket and pulled a lighter out of his pocket. "Enjoy your first day as the new girl," he called over his shoulder, a smoke already pressed between his lips.

My stomach did a flip. His words made me feel even more nervous. I didn't want to be the new girl—I didn't know how! I had been attending Hawks since sixth grade, where I'd shared the same dorm room every year with my best friend, Sammy, and hung out with the same group of girls that I'd known since preschool. My eyes welled up as I thought about home.

"You okay?" Nathan asked. He must have noticed the worried look on my face.

"Fine," I muttered, blinking away the tears.

"You sure?"

"I'm fine, I swear."

"Okay. Well, how about I show you where the office is?" he asked as he strapped his guitar onto his back.

"You'd do that?" My voice jumped up in hope.

"Sure thing," he said and smiled. "Can't have you getting lost on your first day."

The breath I'd been holding in hissed out through my lips. "I'd really appreciate it, Nathan. Just let me grab my stuff."

At the back of the truck, Cole was sitting on the tailgate as if he was waiting for something. "So, New York," he said and handed me my bag. "Whad'ya think?"

"About your school?" I asked. "It's, um—big."

Cole laughed. "You've been sheltered in a boarding school since junior high, and all you have to say about your first impression of the real world is that it's big?"

I hate it, I thought. But that answer wouldn't do. "It's very different from my old school," I said slowly. "For example, I don't have to wear a uniform."

"You wore uniforms?"

"Yes," I replied. "It was a private school, so they were a requirement." Thinking of my old, lumpy-looking sweater, tie, and matching plaid skirt, I heaved a sigh. Yes, my uniform was ugly, but there was always something comforting about pulling it on in the morning. Today, I'd had no clue what to wear. After Cole made fun of my outfit yesterday, I realized I didn't know how kids at public schools dressed.

"And you went to an all-girls' school? Man, that must have been a sight. Schoolgirl outfits are hot."

"Sorry?"

"You know, like Britney Spears?"

I gave Cole a pointed look. "Our skirts came down to our knees."

"Shame," he said, shrugging his shoulders. "But, I bet you made it look cute."

His compliment caught me off guard. "I—um," I stammered.

"Coley!" someone squealed, saving me from my embarrassment. A small girl with chestnut hair and poison-green eyes flung her arms around Cole's neck and slammed her lips into his. I looked away when I saw a flicker of tongue.

"Olivia," Cole said, finally breaking away from their kiss, "what did I tell you about calling me that? It's not manly." He peeled Olivia's arms off his neck, but stood next to her and slung an arm over her shoulder.

"Sorry," she responded without an ounce of humiliation, "but you know how happy I get when I see you. Sometimes I can't contain my excitement."

"Yeah, I know, babe," he said and guided her toward the front entrance. He was halfway across the parking lot when he swung back around. "Good luck today, New York!" he called.

"Typical Cole," Nathan said as he shook his head.

"Is she his girlfriend?" I asked as I stared after them, unable to take my eyes off Olivia. It didn't surprise me that Cole had a girl who looked like a supermodel. Together they were a picture-perfect couple.

Nathan snorted. "She wishes."

"Huh?"

"Cole doesn't date," he explained as we started walking in. "He has lots of girls that he hooks up with, but never anything more."

"The girls? They're okay with that?"

"I guess," Nathan said with a shrug.

I frowned as we climbed the steps to the school. "That's disgusting."

"The thing you need to know about Cole," Nathan said, holding the door open for me when we reached the top, "is that he runs this school. All the girls want him, and all the guys want to be him."

"But if all the girls want him, why doesn't he just pick one?"

He shrugged. "Why pick one if he can get away with sampling every flavor?"

"Sampling every flavor?" I gasped. "I can't believe you just said that!"

"Look, Jackie," Nathan said, laughing. "I'm not saying I agree with how Cole behaves. I'm just trying to explain the way he thinks."

We stepped inside, and I realized how very different attending a public school was going to be. Just thinking about it made my head spin. Did guys actually think like that? Maybe Boys 101 hadn't been as informational as I thought.

"Fine," I said, shaking my head in disbelief. "But I don't understand how any girl would be okay with a guy treating her like that."

"Trust me," Nathan said as a bell overhead rang, "I ask myself that same question all the time. That was the first bell. Let's head down to the office so you aren't late."

After helping me find the office so I could pick up my schedule, Nathan walked me to my first-period class, which happened to be anatomy.

"Here you go—Room 207," he said, escorting me into the room. "Hey! Looks like you have a class with Alex." Nathan pointed out his brother, who was hiding in the back corner of the room with his nose buried in a book. "Let's go see if you can sit with him."

"Wait, no," I started to say, but Nathan was already strolling into the classroom. Sighing, I followed him.

"Hi, Alex," Nathan said when he reached the back of the room.

"What's up, Nate?" Alex asked without looking up from his page.

"I was just walking Jackie to class, and she happens to have anatomy with you. Mind if she shares your table?"

Alex looked up sharply when he heard my name. "Um…" he started to say. He trailed off as something caught his attention over my shoulder.

A high-pitched giggle filled the room, and I turned to see a beautiful girl with curly blond ringlets. She had a perfect button nose that crinkled up in delight as she laughed, and her blue eyes sparkled. Her arm was locked with another girl's as they walked into class, joking.

I turned back to Alex and noticed his eyes were locked on the girl. He pressed his lips together, and for a moment I thought he was going to tell Nathan no, but then he cleared off the space next to him.

"Awesome! Thanks, Al," Nathan said.

"No problem," Alex said and returned to his reading.

"Well, I better get to class. Have a good first day, Jackie."

"Bye, Nathan. I really appreciate all your help this morning."

"It was my pleasure," he said. "See you both later."

When Nathan was gone, I hovered at the edge of the table. "I can move if you want to sit by one of your friends," I told Alex quietly, and by friends I meant the girl. "I'll be fine by myself."

"Huh?" He looked up from his book again. "Oh no. It's totally fine. Sit down," he said, pulling out the chair for me.

Relief washed over me. "Okay, thanks."

Alex's eyes darted back to what he was reading, but then he pulled out a marker, jammed it between the pages, and shut the book.

"Don't stop on my account," I said, unzipping my schoolbag and pulling out a notebook.

"No, I was being rude before," Alex said and offered me a smile. "You just caught me at my favorite part."

"Oh, so you've read it before?" I asked, tilting my head to read the title. "What's it called?"

"*The Fellowship of the Ring.*"

I stared at Alex blankly.

"Tolkien?" he asked, shaking his head in disbelief. "You're joking, right? You've never heard of *The Lord of the Rings*?"

"Oh, like the movie?"

Alex groaned and banged his head on the table in frustration. "Why don't girls ever *read* good fantasy?"

"What are you talking about? I thoroughly enjoy fantasy. What about *A Midsummer Night's Dream*?"

"Is that some girly crap like *Twilight*? That doesn't count as fantasy."

"Shakespeare doesn't write about sparkly vampires," I scoffed.

"Oh, I know now! Isn't he that super-old dude who wrote plays? I've read his stuff in English class."

I knew he was only joking, but I scoffed and said, "You don't know who Shakespeare is but laugh at me for not knowing Tonkin or whatever his name was?"

"Tolkien," Alex corrected me, "and he wrote the greatest fantasy series of all time."

"Yes, but Shakespeare could be considered the greatest literary figure of all time."

Before Alex could respond, a young man appeared in the front of the room.

"Good morning, class," he began. "Today we have a new student. Jackie, is it?"

When I heard my name, I instantly froze up. The entire class turned to look at me.

"Um, yes?"

"All right, then," the teacher continued enthusiastically. "Welcome to Valley View. I'm Mr. Piper, and I teach most of the science classes here. Why don't you stand up and tell us something about yourself?"

He wanted me to stand up, like in front of everyone? I could feel my face burn.

"Jackie?" Mr. Piper prompted me.

I heard my chair scrape back and then I was standing. My hands shook and I quickly tucked them behind my back. "Um, okay. Hi, I'm Jackie Howard and I recently moved here from New York." I announced my short greeting in a rush and sat back down. If I had to do this in every class, today was going to be a nightmare.

"Thank you, Jackie," Mr. Piper said, rubbing his hands together. "Moving on. Please take out your books. Today we're going to start working on our skeletal unit."

"Not much of public speaker, huh?" Alex whispered. A lazy grin covered his face, and for a moment I was taken aback at how similar he looked to Cole. They had the same strong jawline, the same sun-kissed skin, and the same blue eyes surrounded by thick lashes that any girl would kill for. But as I studied his face, subtle differences started to emerge: a nearly invisible sprinkle of freckles dotted his nose, and his eyes were a slightly darker shade of blue with flecks of gold that I noticed only because we were sitting so close.

When I realized that I was staring, I shook my head and looked away. "No, not at all."

"Me neither," Alex told me. "Just thinking about it makes me itch." He pushed his textbook into the middle of the table. "You don't have a book yet, right? We can share." I smiled to myself. It seemed that I made another friend in the Walter house.

Mr. Piper dove into his lecture, and I focused my attention up front. It was then that I noticed the blonde from before. She was sitting across the room, glaring daggers in my direction.

• • •

Once anatomy was over, I had art. I got lost finding the room, and when I showed up late, the class had already started working on their project. Mrs. Hanks, the art teacher, was a short lady with red glasses and copper hair that curled in every direction. She told me the class was finishing up a project and would be starting something new tomorrow, so I could take a free period.

Glancing around the room, I failed to spot the bright blond of any of the Walter boys, so I found an empty table near the back. As I sat down, a girl with red hair smiled at me before returning to her project. Maybe the people here won't be so bad, I thought to myself and pulled out *The Lord of the Rings*. Alex had lent it to me when our class finished, and I told him I would read it on the condition that he brush up on his Shakespeare. The thick book was daunting, but after only a few pages I was so absorbed that I jumped in my seat when the bell rang signaling the end of class.

The rest of the morning flew by until I only had one period left before lunch. When I walked into the math room, I noticed that many of the students looked older than me. My private school education put me ahead of most of the public school kids, so I was enrolled in advanced calculus, which was a senior class.

About ten minutes into class, Cole came strolling in with a grin on his face.

"Hey, teach, sorry I'm late," he said like it was no big problem. Then he spotted me. "Hey, Jackie! I didn't know you were in any of my classes!"

Everyone turned to look at me. Glancing down, I kept my eyes on my notes and hid behind a curtain of hair.

"Mr. Walter! Will you please take a seat and stop interrupting my class?" the teacher asked.

Cole saluted him before taking the only seat left, right in the front row.

When we were finally dismissed, I began packing up my stuff. I was shoving my new textbook into my bag when Cole came up and sat right on top of my desk.

"'Sup, Jackie?" he asked, grabbing one of my notebooks and flipping through it. "Whoa, you actually use this thing?" he asked when he spotted the notes I took.

"Um, yes, that's what it's for," I responded with a *duh* tone.

"Who takes notes these days?" he questioned. I took my notebook from him, tucked it away, and zipped up my satchel.

"Me." I threw my bag over my shoulder and headed toward the door.

"Yeah," he pestered, following me out of the room, "losers like you."

"I am *not* a loser," I opposed, stopping to frown up at him.

"Are too," he teased.

"Am not," I argued, starting to get angry. "There's a big difference between being a loser and a good student." I wasn't sure why I couldn't stand his teasing. Maybe it was because I was still upset about what Nathan had said about him this morning.

"Relax, Jackie. I'm just joking," Cole told me.

"What's so funny?" I asked, still frowning.

"You get really red when you're angry," he said and poked my cheek.

"Where's the lunchroom?" I snapped and brushed his hand away. I was fed up with Cole.

He laughed and pulled me to his side. "Chill out, Jackie." I inhaled sharply as his hand touched my bare arm. Cole continued to talk as if he didn't notice. "I'll walk you down there and even show you the best table to sit at."

Since I didn't know where I was going, my only choice was to let him lead me toward the cafeteria. I planned on ditching Cole when we arrived, but as we stepped into the loud room, I felt my stomach drop. There were so many people, and I knew nobody. The thought of sitting by myself was terrifying, so I followed him without complaining. He pulled me through the crowds toward the front of the lunch line, and as we went, I could feel the stares of curious students. Instead of looking back, I kept my gaze glued to the back of Cole's head.

After grabbing a tray, he scooped up two bags of pretzels.

"You like turkey?" he asked. I nodded, and he dropped two sandwiches on the tray. "An apple to keep the doctor away," he muttered to himself as he picked up two pieces of fruit. "And milk for strong bones. There you go, a Cole Walter certified lunch. Hold the tray while I pay for this."

"I have money," I told him as he dumped the tray into my hands.

Ignoring me, Cole dug out his wallet and handed the lunch lady a bill. He pocketed the change and put his hand on the small of my back. "This way," he said and guided me toward the middle of the lunchroom.

The table we arrived at was mostly full—guys wearing letter jackets and girls in cheerleading uniforms—and I immediately felt out of place. Cole sat down next to a tall girl with long auburn hair. Her lips were rosy pink, and they parted into a smile when she saw him.

"Where have you been all day, Walter?" she asked, running her manicured nails through Cole's hair. "Not off with that floozy Olivia, were you?"

"Nice to see you too, Erin," Cole said. "For your information, I was getting lunch with Jackie."

"Jackie? Who's she?"

"My friend," Cole said and gestured to me, "so scoot over and give her some room."

"It's a little cramped at the table for an extra person, don't you think?" Erin asked as she looked me over.

"Then leave," Cole suggested.

Erin mouth's dropped open in shocked surprise. "Are you serious?" she demanded. Cole stared back at her with cold eyes, so she pressed her lips together in a tight line and moved over without another complaint.

When I set the lunch tray down on the table, the look of loathing on Erin's face nearly made me leave. Cole, however, patted the now empty space next to him. "What are you waiting for?" he asked, the warmth returning to his face with a beam. Swallowing my nerves, I forced myself to sit down.

Chapter 4

The rest of the day passed in a whirlwind of new classes and unfamiliar faces. It was actually a relief to see the Walters' rickety house when the truck pulled into the driveway after school.

"We're home, Aunt Kathy!" Lee shouted as soon as he walked through the door. "What's for dinner?"

Danny, Lee, and I had to step over a pile of boxes in the front hall. We were the only ones who actually left school at three o'clock. Alex had baseball practice; Cole caught a bus to his job at a local auto-repair shop; Nathan stayed in the music room; and Isaac never showed, which apparently was normal because we left after only a five-minute wait. I planned to join a few after-school clubs, but I decided it could wait until next week when, hopefully, I didn't feel so weary.

"Hello to you too," I heard Katherine call from the kitchen. The smell of something amazing was drifting down the hall. We found her standing at the counter cutting open a huge pile of buns.

"Hell, yeah," Lee said when he lifted the top of the slow cooker. "I love me some sloppy joe."

"What's sloppy joe?" Whatever it was, it sounded disgusting.

Katherine, Lee, and Danny all stared at me like I was speaking an alien language.

"You're never had a sloppy joe before? What kind of crazy planet are you from?" Lee asked.

"Lee, be nice," Katherine scolded, pointing the serrated knife she was using to cut buns in Lee's direction. "A sloppy joe is a ground-beef sandwich," she explained to me. "We're having them for dinner and you can try one then. The rest of your things arrived today, so in the meantime, why don't you work on moving into your room? I cleared out all of the art supplies, and Danny can help you bring the boxes up and unpack."

"Why can't Lee help?" Danny asked.

"Because he's going to help Parker with her math homework."

"I am?"

"Would you rather carry boxes up to Jackie's room?"

"Right. Two plus two. I'm all over that shit," Lee said and left the kitchen before Katherine could change her mind.

"All right, you two," Katherine said, picking up another bun. "Why don't you get started? I want those boxes out of the front hall by the time everyone else gets home."

Twenty minutes of tense silence passed as we moved my things to my room. While we worked, we hurried by each other on the stairs, trying to avoid bumping into one another or making awkward eye contact. Finally, I collapsed on my bed feeling sore and sweaty as Danny set the last box on the floor.

"Thanks a bunch for your help. This would have taken forever without you."

Danny nodded his head and quickly turned to leave without a word, but my room was now a maze of cardboard towers. His foot connected with one of the piles, and the box teetering on the top crashed to the floor. My Shakespeare collection spilled out, and Danny dropped down to pick it up.

"Sorry," he mumbled and scooped the books back into the box.

"Don't worry about it," I said, jumping off my bed. "I can take care of it." I spotted *A Midsummer Night's Dream* and wanted to grab it for Alex. By knocking over the books, Danny actually did me a favor because I wouldn't have to search through all the boxes to find them. I plucked the play off the floor, and Danny stopped to examine what was in his hands.

"*Romeo and Juliet?*" he asked, reading out the title. The rise in his voice revealed his surprise. "You like drama?"

"Of course, I'm a New Yorker! I've been attending all types of different performances since I was little. I have a personal soft spot for Shakespeare, but I also admire Shaw and Miller's work." When I responded, Danny clamped his mouth shut as if he just realized that he had spoken to me.

"Oh, cool." He shoved one last book back into the box and shot to his feet. "I'll see you later." He was out the door before I could mutter a good-bye.

Running my hand over the cover of my favorite play, I grinned to myself. My encounter with Danny could have gone a little better, but at least now I knew we shared a similar interest. Maybe I would make more friends in the Walter house than I had originally thought. Apparently I just needed to tackle the boys one at time.

• • •

At dinner I tried my first sloppy joe ever, and I immediately understood the reason behind the name. It was impossible to keep the meat on the bun. It oozed out every time I took a bite and splattered against my plate. My fingers and face were disgusting by the time I finished. I thought it made more sense to put the slop in a bowl and dip the bun in, but the Walters seemed to enjoy diving in face-first.

When everyone was full, we all had to help clean up the table, but afterward we were allowed to do whatever we wanted. Parker and the little twins rushed to the living room and battled over the remote. Jack and Jordan went to edit the footage they got of me eating my first sloppy joe. Isaac challenged Alex to a pickup game of hoops, while Lee and Nathan disappeared into their rooms. The freedom felt strange. At boarding school I was used to a strict schedule of dinnertime, homework, and lights out at nine.

Trying to keep some normalcy in my life, I climbed the stairs toward my room to do schoolwork. Although I wasn't assigned anything in particular, I knew I was behind in English. The class was already halfway through reading *Moby Dick*, which was thicker than any of the textbooks I'd received throughout the day. Five pages in, I shut the book in irritation and pulled out Alex's copy of *The Fellowship of the Ring*.

Someone knocked on the door.

"Jackie?" Cole asked, poking his head inside. He hadn't been at dinner, and judging by the Tony's Auto Repair jumpsuit he was wearing with his name stitched onto the breast, he'd just gotten back from work.

"Mmm-hmm?" I sat up in bed. Glancing at my clock, I realized that two hours had vanished since I started reading.

"Everyone's out in the backyard. We're going to play some night games. You want in?" He was wearing a baseball cap backward to hide the fact that his bangs were plastered to his forehead and there was a smear of grease across his nose, but somehow just one glance at him made my pulse surge.

"What's a night game?" I asked, trying to keep my voice even.

"Games you play outside in the dark. You know, like kick the can, cops and robbers, ghost in the graveyard…" Cole trailed off as he waited for me to catch on.

"Sorry, but I've never heard of those."

"What the heck did you do for fun when you were growing up?"

"I've been to my fair share of Broadway shows, and my family has memberships to most of the museums." As soon as the words were out of my mouth, I realized my mistake. My family *had* member-ships to most of the museums.

"Sounds awful," Cole said. "How about we show you what real fun looks like?"

As nice as it was that Cole was inviting me to do something with the rest of the guys, I couldn't bring myself to accept. The thought of hanging out with all the Walter boys was intimidating. Besides, thoughts of my family were now swirling around in my head, and I knew I would only be able to hold back the tears until Cole left. I didn't want him to see me crying.

"I've got some catching up to do in most of my classes. Maybe another time?"

"Come on, Jackie. It's not like your teachers expect you to know everything you've missed by tomorrow."

Pulling my knees up to my chest, I blinked my eyes, trying to keep them from watering up and my feelings from spilling out. "Sorry, Cole, but it's been a long first day."

I thought he was going to continue arguing, but he must have sensed that something was wrong. "Okay. In any case, you know where to find us if you change your mind."

Cole shut the door. I sat unmoving, staring at the swirling blue of the ocean waves that Katherine had painted on the wall. It reminded me of my childhood summers—warm, sunny days spent at the beach house in the Hamptons, where Lucy and I would munch on fresh picnics spread out on our beach towels and suntan on the seashore, occasionally dipping our toes into the cold water to cool off.

I needed to hear a familiar voice, someone who could comfort me. Grabbing my cell phone off the desk, I dialed a number I knew by heart.

Sammy picked up on the first ring. "*Hola, chica*, what's up?"

At the sound of my best friend's voice, my lips started to tremble, and I could only manage a measly greeting without bursting into tears.

"Oh my God, Jackie. What's wrong? Is Colorado, like, horrible or something?" she asked.

"Sammy, it's worse than horrible. I'm on a ranch in the middle of nowhere. Katherine Walter has twelve kids, and I haven't seen a Starbucks since leaving New York."

"Holy cupcakes! That string bean of a woman pushed twelve people out her who-ha?"

I managed a half smile. "Only ten of the boys are hers. Two of them are nephews."

Sammy gasped. "Did you just say boys plural, as in *all* twelve kids have a Y chromosome?"

"Parker's a girl, but she doesn't act like it."

"That's still pretty good odds, if you ask me. Any hotties?"

"Sammy," I groaned. The Walters were the last thing I wanted to talk about.

"What? That's a completely reasonable question. My best friend is completely isolated from civilization, so it'd be nice to know if she at least has some eye candy to cheer her up."

There might be one or two drool-worthy guys. As soon as the thought crossed my mind, I felt the guilt twisting in my stomach. How could I be thinking about cute boys when my family was gone? "Can we please talk about something else?" I muttered into the phone.

"Talking about delicious boys is my version of therapy."

"You're not cheering me up."

"That's totally what I'm doing. Now spill! What's his name?"

I paused, not sure if I should tell her. One little name won't hurt, I decided. After all, it didn't mean anything. A sigh escaped my lips. "It's Cole." His name came out in a whisper, as if I was giving away a secret.

"Hmm. I guess that's hot. I mean it's no Blake or Declan, but Cole has a nice ring to it. Okay, now give me details. What does he look like?"

I buried my face in my pillow. "This is not how I envisioned our conversation going."

"You're making the whole process difficult with all the stalling."

"Fine," I said quickly. "He's tall, blond, and from the sound of things, a complete pig. Besides, I can't even think about boys right now. I just want to come home, okay?"

"Oh, Jackie," Sammy said, her voice soft. "I wasn't trying to upset you. I just wanted to take your mind off the bad things."

"I know," I responded, feeling bad that I'd snapped. "It's just, all my stuff arrived today, and I can't bring myself to unpack it. It would make everything feel so permanent."

"I totally feel you, sister. My new roommate moved in last night. It was so weird seeing someone else's stuff on your side of the room. And don't even get me started about French class. Like, I had to sit by myself."

The cord around my heart tightened as I thought about my old school, old dorm room, and old classes. The move to Colorado had cut me off from my old life and everything that was familiar to me, and the only remaining link to that world was my best friend. "Sammy, you don't know how good it is to hear your voice. I miss you so much. I wish—I wish…"

"Jackie," Sammy said slowly and deliberately. "Everything is going to get better, okay? Just promise me you'll make an effort to settle in. It will help. I know it."

"Okay," I told her even though I didn't want to.

We stayed on the phone for the next hour. Talking to Sammy made me feel a little better, but as I curled up under the covers of my bed, a feeling of complete and utter loneliness kept me wide awake.

• • •

The next morning, getting up to run with Nathan was nothing short of torture. No matter how many times I rubbed my eyes, I couldn't shake off the blanket of drowsiness that was draped over my entire body. Then I caught Olivia sneaking out of Cole's room. It was such a shock, seeing her standing in the hallway with rumpled hair and wearing one of his shirts, that I was instantly snapped awake. We both stared at each other with the same deer-in-the-headlights look, and then Nathan stepped out of his room, making the situation even more awkward. Even worse, we all had to walk down the stairs together.

"So…" I said once Olivia's car had pulled out the driveway. We were sitting on the front porch, stretching before our run. "Does Cole normally have *friends* stay over?"

Nathan pulled his ankle back behind him, focusing on his hamstring. "Occasionally, but not too often. I suppose he doesn't want to get caught."

"Why?"

"Because," he said, looking at me as if I was acting stupid, "our dad would kill him."

"I get that," I said, pulling my hair back into a ponytail. "I mean, why is he such a—"

"A guy?"

I must have tugged my hair tie too tight, because it snapped and my bangs tumbled down into my face. "You know that's not what I meant," I said, sighing in frustration. "You're a guy. I don't see you sleeping around."

"I guess he wasn't always this way," he said with a shrug. "But Cole's never been one to share his feelings."

"So what changed?"

Nathan paused and gave me a wary look. "If I tell you, you can't repeat any of this to Cole, all right? He's kind of touchy about the subject."

"Okay."

"He lost his football scholarship last year."

"How did he manage that?" My mind immediately jumped to negatives—drugs, drinking, horrible grades—so I was surprised by Nathan's response.

"During a game. He was the best receiver in the state until he got tackled wrong and broke his leg," Nathan said. "Obviously his leg got better, but I don't think he was the same after that. Didn't even go to tryouts this year."

"That's horrible," I said, feeling guilty. Maybe there was more to Cole Walter than girls and sex.

After our run, I went to shower, cranking the handle to cold in an attempt to cool off. The water did its job, and when I was done washing my hair, I hopped out with new life. Standing on the shower mat dripping wet, I looked around. The hook where my towel was supposed to be was empty. What the heck? I'd hung it up only moments before stepping into the shower.

A sudden thought crossed my mind, and I glanced at the counter. My heart hammered against my chest as dread surged through me—the pile of neatly folded clothes was missing. Someone must have snuck into the bathroom while I was showering and stolen my towel and clothes!

I flung open the bathroom cabinets in hopes that I would find something, *anything* I could use to cover myself up, but I knew that my search would be useless. The shelves were filled with toilet paper, soap, and washcloths, but nothing that could help me.

"No, no, no!" I muttered to myself. "This can't be happening." How in the world would I get to my room without one of the boys seeing me?

"Everything okay in there, Jackie?" Isaac asked, knocking on the bathroom door.

"Um, not exactly," I said, my cheeks flaming. "There are no towels in here."

"Why didn't you bring one in with you?" he asked, trying to contain a snicker.

"I did! Someone took it. Do you mind running upstairs and grabbing me one?"

"I don't think so."

"Why the heck not?"

"Because I bet Cole five dollars that you'd rather miss school than streak through the hallways. I don't want to lose a Lincoln, now do I?"

What a complete pervert!

Although I wanted to avoid stepping on the boys' toes so I could fit in more easily, there was no way I was going to let Isaac get away with this. "KATHERINE!" I screamed at the top of my lungs. With any luck she would hear me from the kitchen. "ISAAC STOLE MY TOWEL!"

"Sorry, Jackie, but my aunt took Zack and Benny to a dentist appointment, so she won't be able to help you. Besides, I never said *I* took your towel. I just said I won't be providing you with another one."

"Please, Isaac," I begged, my voice jumping up in desperation. "I don't want to miss school."

"Hey, I'm not stopping you. We're leaving in ten, so you better hurry up."

"Isaac!" I shouted, pounding on the door. "This isn't funny." When there was no response, I knew he'd left me stranded in the bathroom.

I slammed my fist into the door one last time before letting my forehead rest against the smooth wood in frustration. School was important—in fact, it was my life—but there was no way I would ever run through the Walters' house completely nude. I was going to have to wait for Katherine to come home from the dentist, and by then the boys would already be at school.

Goose bumps swept up my arms as I stood in a puddle shivering. It looked like I was going to be stuck in the bathroom for a while, so I decided to step back into a hot shower to keep warm. I started to pull back the shower curtain when an idea came to me. The curtain had two parts: an inner layer of clear plastic to keep water from getting on the floor, and the second, a dark blue piece of fabric for privacy. Unfortunately, little silver rings were holding the fabric up. If only I could separate the fabric from the rest of the curtain. Maybe if I tugged hard enough…

Gripping the material in my hands, I yanked with all my strength, but instead of ripping down what I wanted, I felt the entire pole above the shower topple onto my head.

"Dang it!" I cursed as it clattered against the floor. Even though my head was throbbing, I quickly scooped the pole up and slid the curtain off. Then I tore the plastic section away from the rings and used the remaining blue fabric to form a makeshift towel. Since it was in the little kids' bathroom, a hideous pattern of monkeys and bananas covered the curtain, but it would have to do. Hopefully Katherine won't be mad at me, I thought, looking down at the mess I'd made. I could always replace whatever I'd ruined.

Instead of peeking into the hall to make sure the coast was clear, I threw open the door and rushed toward the stairs.

"Isaac, the pigeon has flown the coop! Repeat, pigeon flown coop!" Glancing over my shoulder, I saw Jack with a walkie-talkie. Next to him was Jordan with the video camera in his hands, green light blinking.

"She was supposed to be naked," Jack said as if I'd caused him some type of inconvenience.

Not bothering to stop or even yell at the twins, I started taking the stairs two at a time, wanting to get to my room before someone else spotted me wearing the shower curtain. Isaac appeared at the top of the landing, the second walkie-talkie in hand and a wicked grin on his face.

"I didn't think she'd actually—" He stopped when he saw me. "Oh, aren't you clever? I didn't even think about the shower curtain."

"Move," I said and shoved past him.

"Jackie, wait!" Jordan called, chasing me with the camera. "Can you answer a few questions for our film? For starters, do girls ever play with their boobs?"

The twins followed me down the hall to my room, bombarding me with ridiculous questions until I slipped inside and locked the door. Leaning against the wood, I closed my eyes and slid to the floor.

"Can you explain girls' obsession with shoes?" I heard Jack saying from the other side. "Why do you need so many?"

"Ask the bathroom question. That one's good."

"Yeah, it is. Jackie, why do girls always go to the bathroom in groups?"

I realized then that I was never going to have a moment of peace again.

• • •

"All right, people, listen up. I need you to partner with two friends," said Mrs. Hanks.

I looked around the room, biting hard on my lip. We were starting a new group project in art class, and friends were a commodity I was currently lacking. Chairs scraped across the floor, and everyone moved toward someone they knew. Knowing that no one was going to want to partner with me, I stayed in my spot, wondering which unlucky group the teacher would stick me with. I noticed the redheaded girl from the day before as she stood and made her way across the room. When she waved, it took me a second to realize that she was waving at me. I lifted my hand in a small greeting as she came to a stop at my table.

"Howdy, Jackie. My name's Riley," she said in a thick Southern accent. "Would you like to join my group?"

"You know my name?" I asked in surprise.

She smiled. "Everyone knows your name. You're the new girl who sat with Cole Walter on her first day here." Riley pulled out the chair across from me and sat down. "So how about it? Partners?"

Thank you, Cole Walter! Apparently he was useful for something other than making me feel nervous. "Yes, please. I was thinking I might have to work alone."

"Oh, don't be silly. Heather and I never would've left you by your lonesome," Riley said, mentioning a girl I had yet to see. "She'll be joining us soon. Probably late because she's flirting in the halls."

On cue, a girl with long sandy hair twisted up in a bun hurried into the room and headed straight for Riley.

"You will never believe what I just found out," she exclaimed, pulling out the chair next to her friend. "You know that new girl Jackie who was sitting with Cole the other day? Apparently her dad was some New York businessman worth billions and her mother was a famous fashion designer. Her whole family just died in a car accident—"

"Heather?" Riley hissed, trying to cut her off.

"—and there was a whole article about it on that one gossip website I like. You know, the one that posted nude pictures of that hot British actor I was telling you about? Anyway, can you imagine being that rich?"

"Heather!" Riley said again, this time with more force. She pointed in my direction.

Heather followed Riley's finger with her eyes. "Holy heck," she said when she noticed me.

"What she means is, 'Sorry,'" Riley said, giving her friend a look. When Heather said nothing, Riley elbowed her in the side.

"Oh, right! I'm super sorry. That was so tactless of me. I didn't realize you were sitting there." Heather didn't look the least bit sorry. Her lips twitched as she tried to contain a smile that was threatening to break across her face. Instead of embarrassed, she looked thrilled to see me.

"It's fine," I responded, my shoulders stiffening.

A minute of uncomfortable silence passed as Heather danced on the edge of her seat. The girl looked like she was about to explode, and finally she couldn't contain her questions any longer.

"So how do you know Cole? Are you related or something?" The words burst from her mouth, the last part sounding hopeful.

"No, we just met a few days ago."

"And he just invited you to sit with him?" Heather's forehead crinkled in disbelief.

"Yes."

"Ugh, I'm so jealous."

"Why would you be jealous?"

"Because," Heather said, rolling her eyes, "Cole doesn't let just any girl sit with him at lunch. Only girls he's *interested* in."

Cole was the furthest thing from being interested in me. In the parking lot this morning, he'd snatched Olivia by the waist and swirled her around before dipping down into a kiss. Nothing says "I want you" like being romantic with another girl, right? But then Nathan's words came back to me in a rush, about how Cole liked to bounce from girl to girl. I laughed nervously. "You're wrong. He's just being nice."

"Oh my lord, you are so toast," Riley said, sounding sympathetic as she shook her head. "Cole Walter doesn't do nice unless he's getting something out of it. That's boy's gonna eat you alive, and you won't see it coming."

"I wouldn't mind if he ate me alive," Heather said, her eyebrows waggling.

"Would you keep your dirty thoughts to yourself?" Riley wrinkled her nose in disgust. She turned back to me. "Jackie, you should sit with us at lunch today. We'll fill you in on everything you need to know 'bout that boy."

I nodded eagerly. Riley was sweet, and I could use as much education as possible about Cole Water if I was going to figure him out. On top of that, it was the perfect excuse to avoid Erin and her hateful glares. "That sounds great."

Heather squealed and clapped her hands. As brazen as she was, I decided I liked her. She reminded me a bit of Sammy and somehow that made me relax, even though I wasn't completely comfortable.

"Perfect," Riley said, leaning forward on the table. "I can't wait."

• • •

Just like the day before, Cole walked me to the cafeteria after math class. This time when we reached the front of the lunch line, I grabbed my own tray. After paying for my food, I stood on my tiptoes, scanning the tables for Riley, and finally spotted a flash of bright red hair.

I started off in her direction, but Cole reached out and grabbed my shoulder. "Hey, where you going, Jackie? The table is this way." He pointed to where we sat yesterday, and I noticed Erin watching me.

"Sorry, Cole. I promised my new friend Riley that I would sit with her."

Cole hesitated, almost as if he was surprised. "Okay then, Miss Popular, but you have to promise you'll join me tomorrow."

"Maybe I can pencil you in," I joked.

"Fine," he said, laughing. "At least let me walk you to your table."

"Sure."

I led the way through the crowded room, Cole following me. The rows between the tables were so congested that sometimes Cole's elbow bumped into mine as people shoved by us, sending goose bumps up my arm.

"Hey, girls," I said and set down my tray. Riley and Heather both stared up at Cole without responding.

"See you after school, New York," Cole told me. He nodded in Riley and Heather's direction. "Ladies." He flashed them a grin before walking away.

As soon as he was out of earshot, Riley began to babble. "Oh, my word! That boy just walked you to lunch. I can't believe it."

"Can't believe what?" I asked.

The two girls looked at me like I was clueless, which I probably was, but it was only my second day. They needed to give me a break.

"The god of all guys is flirting with you," interjected a boy who appeared out of nowhere and dropped his tray on the table. "And not just casual flirting. More like *I want you in my pants* flirting."

The new boy was wearing a crisp blue shirt with a red bow tie. His flawless blond hair was combed to the side, and by flawless I mean like Fabio, *Baywatch*, or Ford models. "You must be Jackie," he said. "I'm Skylar, Valley View High's fashion expert. I run the style blog for the school newspaper. If you're interested in an editing position, I'd love to work with you. Your East Coast look is so chic."

"What? No business card?" Riley said, laughing.

Skylar rolled his eyes and turned to me. "She loves making fun of me, but at least I don't look like a hick," he mocked in a terrible Southern accent.

"Would you two stop?" Heather said as she flipped the page of the *People* magazine in front of her. "I wanna hear juicy details about Cole."

Everyone turned to me.

"What?" I asked, looking back at them. I hadn't realized they were expecting something from me. I barely knew the guy.

"So?" asked Skylar. "What happened?"

Why did everyone care so much about Cole? He was just one guy.

"He's in my class before lunch, so he walked me to the cafeteria," I responded, not knowing what else to tell them. I wasn't good with all this boy gossip, and I could tell right away that Heather wasn't happy with my answer.

"But what did you guys talk about?" she demanded. To show she was dedicated to the conversation, she pushed her magazine off to the side. "Did he compliment you? Maybe he touched your arm?"

"Are you talking about Walter *again*?" asked another girl who plopped down onto the bench next to Skylar. "Sorry I'm late. I got caught up in the computer lab."

"This is our pet nerd, Kim," Riley said, introducing her to me. Kim was a slender girl whose long, flowing hair and flawless skin reminded me of an elf. "As long as you don't make fun of her little computer game or whatnot where she battles mythical creatures, she won't bite."

"It's called a massively multiplayer online role-playing game, Riley." Kim flipped her hair over her shoulder. "Besides, I don't battle mythical creatures. I *am* a mythical creature. My avatar is a dwarf."

"Avatar?" I couldn't follow anything Kim was saying.

"It's a graphic representation of my character, a reflection of my personal self," she explained for me, even though I didn't understand a word. I wasn't quite sure how a three-foot-tall creature could symbolize her tall, willowy frame, but I nodded my head like it made sense.

"Hi, you must be Jackie." Kim extended a hand to me across the table.

"Wow, does everyone already know my name just because of Cole?" I asked.

She shook her head. "Actually, I'm a friend of Alex Walter. He mentioned you just moved in."

Heather's spoon fell from her hand. "What did you just say?"

"That Alex and I are friends? You already knew that," Kim said, frowning at Heather.

"No, the other part," Heather said. Her spoon was back in her hand, and she was waving it wildly. "About moving in."

"Oh," Kim said, pulling a soda out of her paper-bag lunch. "Jackie just moved in with the Walters. Right, Jackie?"

Three heads whipped around to look at me.

"Um, yes. I live with them," I said uneasily, afraid of how the group would react.

"How in heaven's name did you forget to mention something like that?" Riley gasped, her mouth hanging open in surprise.

"Oh my God!" Heather squealed. "You are like the luckiest girl in this whole school."

"Debatable," I mumbled to myself. What was so cool about living with a bunch of wild, crazy, childlike boys? Besides, it's not like I wanted to be living in Colorado. Had Heather already forgotten the gossip she told Riley about my family's accident?

"She did *not* just say that!" Heather cried, turning to Kim.

"Jackie, Jackie, Jackie," Riley said, shaking her head. "Haven't you noticed that the Walter boys are just perfect?"

"No, they're better than perfect. They're gods," Heather said, dreamily staring off into space.

"That did not just come out of your mouth," Kim scoffed. "That's so creepy."

"Is not! It's the truth. Jackie has crash-landed in boy heaven. I mean, think about it. It doesn't matter what type of boy she's into because there's one of everything. First there's Danny, who has the whole mysterious brooding thing going on. Isaac is the classic, sexy bad boy. Next is Alex, your typical geeky, shy guy." Heather was ticking off the boys on her fingers. "Nathan is the laid-back musician. Lee's the edgy skater, and then there's Cole—the golden boy."

Everyone sighed and nodded in agreement when she said his name.

"I don't get it," I said, looking across the cafeteria to the table where Cole was eating his lunch. Erin was sitting in his lap and playing with his hair. "There are plenty of guys who are good looking. What makes him so special?"

"If he isn't so special, then why can't you take your eyes off him?" Skylar asked, his eyebrow arching up in question.

"I can too," I said, quickly looking away. "Besides, I'm not looking for a boyfriend. I need to concentrate on my schoolwork."

The entire table started to laugh at me, and when they finally started to calm down, Skylar said, "Sure, whatever."

"Look, I'm just trying to understand it," I said, frustrated. If I could figure out what made Cole so special, then maybe I could eliminate the twisting in my stomach every time I saw him. "I mean, look at her. What *makes* her do that?" I said and shook my head at Erin. She was diligently hand-feeding Cole grapes.

"There's just something about him," Heather said with a shrug, as if that explained everything. "Some extra aspect that no sane girl can ignore."

"What is it?"

"You can't define it, Jackie." She leaned across the table toward me, hair spilling out in front of her as if she were revealing a trade secret. "It's what I like to call the Cole effect."

"But if everyone likes him, there has to be some common variable," I said, trying to think logically.

"That's my point—there isn't! The fact that you can't put your finger on it, whatever it is, is what makes him so swoon-worthy."

"That's ridiculous."

"And yet you feel it, don't you?" Heather said with a knowing smile.

"Don't feel embarrassed, Jackie," Riley said, and when I glanced at her a little too sharply, she added, "We've all been swept away by a Cole Walter crush."

"I don't like him," I said firmly, as everyone rolled their eyes. "I'll admit he's attractive, but that's it. I hardly know him."

"Deny it all you want, girl," Riley said, putting a hand on my shoulder. "But I know a lovesick puppy when I see one."

I wanted to argue again, to let Riley know that she was wrong. I knew I wasn't lovesick, and yet I kept my mouth closed. The nausea burning inside my stomach held me back. Heather and Riley made it sound as if no girl had the ability to resist Cole, which made my lack of experience with boys that much more disconcerting.

How would I stand a chance? I couldn't fall for him. Not after what Nathan told me, and especially not after what had happened to my family. It wouldn't be right. It was too soon. I needed to do well in school so I could follow in my dad's footsteps.

I couldn't do that with a boy like Cole Walter distracting me.

Chapter 5

After school, I locked myself in my room and set to work unpacking, determined to keep my promise to Sammy. I would settle in and make the most of my situation. On my bed was a checklist so that as I unpacked, I could make sure all my belongings were here and organized.

Even though it was only spring, the house was hot. The Walters didn't seem to understand the benefits of air-conditioning, so I had my window shoved up all the way to let what little breeze there was inside. I'd been at it for almost an hour, moving my clothes from boxes to the dresser that Katherine had managed to squeeze into the room, when I heard voices drifting up from the backyard. There was a splash of water, then another. Wiping the sweat from the back of my neck, I peered out the window and spotted two people in the pool.

"You look so sexy when you're dripping wet. I just want to run my hands all over you."

It was Erin speaking. She was treading water, her long auburn locks swirling out behind her like mermaid hair. Her fingers worked back and forth as she rubbed someone's shoulders. He wasn't facing me, but I recognized his red swim trunks immediately.

"Sexy, huh?" Cole drawled. "Tell me more."

"Really, guys?" another voice said, and Alex stepped into view on the deck, also wearing swim trunks. He kicked off his flip-flops. "I don't want to barf in the pool."

"The chlorine will kill it. Stop being so prissy," Cole said, but he untangled himself from Erin.

Giving his brother the finger, Alex stepped up to the side of the pool and curled his toes over the edge.

"Alexander James Walter!" Katherine called from somewhere out of sight. "Shouldn't you be rewriting that history paper?" It wasn't a question. Alex looked up at the sky as if to ask "Why me?" before slowly turning away from the pool.

"On it, Mom. No need to cool off. It's only like a hundred degrees inside," he said sarcastically.

"Good, and when you go upstairs, ask Jackie what type of dressing she likes on her salad. We're eating dinner in half an hour."

Slipping his sandals back on his feet, Alex headed toward the house, and a few seconds later I heard the screen slide shut.

"Alone at last," Cole said, his voice low. He swam over to Erin and folded her in his arms.

"Jackie?" she said, pushing away from him. "That girl who sat with us at lunch yesterday? What's she doing here?"

I froze at the sound of my name.

"Yeah, her," Cole answered. "She's living with us."

"Un-flipping-believable," Erin said loudly, her face twisting in anger. "That's why you've been spending time with her. You like her, don't you?"

Cole didn't answer. The following silence was static and uncomfortable, unbearable even, and I stared at Cole, willing him to answer.

"I barely know her," he said eventually.

"You obviously know her well enough to invite her to sit with us at lunch."

"You know me," he said back. "It's no big deal."

"Not a big deal? Are you serious? She's living under the same roof as you," Erin hissed.

"Yeah, I'm completely serious. Why are you overreacting? It's not like you're my girlfriend."

It was the wrong thing to say. With a splash, Erin swung around and swam to the edge of the pool. When she started climbing out, Cole groaned and chased after her.

"Babe, are you really going to act like this right now?" he asked, trying to pull her back into the pool.

Erin shook his hand off. "Until you starting *acting* like my boyfriend, don't call me that. I'm leaving." She plucked a purse off one of the pool chairs and stomped down the deck steps into the backyard before disappearing around the side of the house.

There was silence again, and in that moment, I realized that Nathan might be wrong about some of the girls at Valley View High. Erin didn't seem very accepting of Cole's player behavior. Maybe I stood a chance after all.

Cole slapped the surface of the water before raking his fingers through his hair. Even from a distance I could see his lips curl in anger, and as if sensing me, he looked up at my window. I barely ducked in time, and with my heart racing against my chest, I retreated toward my bed and out of view.

• • •

Peering down into the box, I discovered that I was finally done unpacking. There was only one item left inside to give a new home to, and I knew exactly where to put it. The picture frame was a shimmery gold, and the metal edges swirled like lace around the photo of my mother and me. I positioned the picture of us on top of my dresser next to all the other frames I'd set up—and took a step back.

Ever since I was young, people had said how similar we looked, even if I couldn't see it. It's the hair, I would tell them. We have the same hair. My mother laughed at the comparison, not because she didn't think we looked similar, but because to her, we were nothing alike.

And we weren't.

Growing up, it didn't take long for me to realize how incredibly different my life was compared to the rest of the world. Most people had one house, not four vacation homes in different locations around the world, two beach properties—one on the East Coast and the other on the West—and one luxury penthouse on the Upper East Side of Manhattan.

In the first grade, I visited a classmate's house to work on a science project and was shocked to find out that she did chores. I always had maids to clean up after me, to fold my clothes and put away my dishes. Chauffeurs didn't drive every car on the road— most people drove their own. And owning a private jet? That wasn't normal either. My dad was the definition of successful, and it was a lot, maybe even too much, to live up to.

I tried anyway. I had to for my mom. In school, not only did I have the highest GPA in my year, but I also became the student council president and head of the yearbook committee as a freshman. During the summers, I interned at my dad's company, while at the same time helping my mother plan her autumn charity ball.

My life was busy, but never in a hectic, out-of-control way. I organized my time, every minute of every day, within the confines of a little black day planner. What drove my mother crazy were the lists. Every task I ever needed to complete—whether redecorating my room or doing my nightly homework—was tackled using an orderly to-do list. The most important business went on the top, and by the time I reached the bottom, I could be safe in knowing that I hadn't forgotten anything. Because after all, those were the worst surprises, weren't they? The stuff you didn't plan for—or didn't plan *enough* for—that made everything less…perfect.

So where I was cautious, aiming for perfection, some impossible abstraction, my mother was the opposite: wild, spontaneous, carefree. There was a reason why Designs by Jole & Howard was one of Manhattan's most popular fashion houses—Angeline Howard was willing to take chances, to leap without looking. Jackie, she would say, you can't control everything. Roadblocks, little unexpected bumps, they're all part of living.

I disagreed. Everything could be accounted for. All it took was some preparation. Why would anyone choose chaos when they could live in control?

"Hey, Jackie?" someone asked, interrupting my thoughts. The door opened a sliver, just enough for me to make out Alex in the hallway.

"Yes?" I asked, pulling it open all the way.

"Um, my mom wants to know what type of dressing you like on your salad."

"I'm fine with whatever."

"Okay, thanks. Dinner should be ready in ten," he said, turning away.

"Wait. Before you go!" I spun around and grabbed the Shakespeare play off my bed. "Here," I said, handing it to him. "Take it."

"What's this?" he asked, looking down at the cover.

"*A Midsummer Night's Dream.* Remember? I read yours and you read mine?"

"Right," he said, grinning up at me. "Book swap."

• • •

"So, boys," said Katherine, unfolding her hands after George led grace. We were all seated for dinner, with the exception of Will who had returned to his apartment the day before. "Who wants to fess up for wrecking the shower curtain?"

I almost dropped my plate, which I was holding up so Nathan could scoop a serving of mashed potatoes onto it. Somehow, over the course of the day's events, I'd forgotten about this morning. Most of the boys snickered, and I knew that they knew. Jack and Jordan must have shown them the footage of me rushing out of the bathroom. I could picture them in my head, all crowded around the small device, laughing as I shrieked on-screen.

"Don't anyone try to blame this crime on Zack and Benny like the noodles-in-the-washing-machine incident. Since they were at the dentist with me, they have an exceptional alibi."

"I know who did it," Lee said, words spurting past his lips, almost as if he had been waiting for her to ask.

When he didn't respond immediately, Katherine pursed her lips. "Well?"

Lee picked up his cup and took a long, antagonizing sip of water before setting it back down. "I'm not one for tattling," he said with a shrug. "Why don't you ask Jackie?" He turned to me, and cruel satisfaction flickered in his eyes.

"Jackie?" Katherine said, laughing. She shook her head in dismissal. "Now that's the most ridiculous thing I've heard in ages."

I didn't know what to say to this since the notion of me ripping down someone's shower curtain was, in fact, ridiculously unbelievable, but unfortunately it was also the truth. I couldn't lie.

"I'm so sorry, Katherine," I said, hanging my head.

At the sound of my voice, her head snapped up to look at me. "Jackie?" She paused, clearly confused. Finally, "Why on earth would you do that?"

Her question roused another round of laughter.

"I didn't mean to ruin anything," I tried to explain, "but after my shower, I really needed to, um, cover up."

George narrowed his eyes in suspicion, as if he knew something fishy was going on. "Didn't you remember a towel?"

This was the point of no return. I could either lie, letting Isaac get away with it, or explain the entire story so my actions would be justified. But if I told Katherine and George what really happened, Isaac would most likely be pissed, and that could come back to haunt me. On the other hand, if I rolled over and let it go, the boys might take that as an open invitation to torment me. I risked a quick glance at Isaac. His lip twitched as he stared back, daring me to challenge him. I turned back to George.

"Isaac took it," I said, the accusation rushing out of my mouth. "And my clothes. He took those too."

It took George a moment to react, his jaw clenching and unclenching as he processed my words. "*What?*" he finally roared, his chair flying back as he shot up from the table.

Two seconds later, Benny did the same. "*What?*" he shouted, throwing back his own chair and mimicking his dad. Next to him, Zack started to laugh, while Parker pointed her finger at her cousin and taunted, "Somebody's in trouble."

George ignored all three and turned his rage toward Isaac. "You *stole* her towel? You went into the bathroom while she was showering?"

"Whoa, Uncle G! That's not what happened," Isaac said. From the look on his face, I knew he was starting to regret his actions this morning.

"I swear, boy, if you're lying to me—"

"I'm not. I promise!" Isaac responded, feigning innocence.

I could have kicked him. "That's not true," I said, my voice high. "Isaac said he bet Cole five dollars that I would rather miss school than come out of the bathroom naked. They were going to leave me trapped in there and go without me."

Cole threw his hands up in the air. "Hey, don't drag me into this. I've got nothing to do with it."

Glancing around the table, George gauged everyone's reactions, which ranged from Alex's high eyebrows to Danny's blank face.

He looked like he was physically holding himself back. His hands, which were gripping the edge of the table, had gone stark white.

"George," Katherine whispered softly, putting her hand over his. He glanced down at her contact, and somehow that seemed to calm him down, because he let a breath of hot air hiss out of his mouth.

"With your colorful record, Isaac," he said at last, trying to keep his cool, "I have a hard time believing you."

"He's telling the truth," Lee said, coming to the aid of his brother. It was the first thing he'd said since ratting me out, and I could tell from the look on his face that he was enjoying the chaos he'd caused. "He was in our room all morning trying to get a paper done. I saw him."

"Yeah, right. Isaac doesn't care about homework—" Nathan started, but Lee elbowed him in the side and he shut his mouth.

"Can anyone verify either Jackie or Lee's story?" Katherine asked. Zack and Benny raised their hands, and she sighed. "Can anybody else, someone who wasn't at the dentist, tell me what happened?"

As I looked around the table, trying to find a friendly face, none of the boys would meet my eyes. Even Nathan ignored me. His mouth was pressed tight into the smallest of lines, and he concentrated on stabbing a few stray peas rolling around his plate with a fork.

For the first time since I arrived at the Walters', the house was deadly silent, and I realized no one was going to stand up for me. "Katherine," I said, adopting my father's businesslike tone. "I'd ask Jack and Jordan what they know, or rather, what they caught on camera. I'm sure that will help resolve the issue. If you don't mind, I'd like to be excused."

Without waiting for an answer, I stood up, threw my napkin on the table, and walked out of the kitchen.

When Katherine came to apologize for her boys' behavior later that night, she found me sitting at the windowsill, staring out into the backyard. By then it was dark. I could only see slivers of moonlight reflecting off the pool, and the grass beyond the deck had been swallowed up by the shadows as if it never existed. Half an hour before, I'd heard angry shouts from the kitchen, and judging by George's tone, one of the boys was in deep trouble. Now everything was still.

"It's strange," I told her when she came and stood next to me. "How empty it feels here."

"Empty?" she asked, a look of concern on her face.

I offered her a small smile, knowing that she'd misunderstood me. "Back home, when I looked out my window," I started to explain, "even if it was nighttime, there was always something out there: light from the lampposts that ran along the streets, a stray taxi screeching around a corner, someone walking their dog. The dark is so thick here that when it gets quiet like this, there doesn't seem to be anything out there except emptiness."

"I suppose our nightlife is a bit more subtle," Katherine said, looking out the window with me.

We both fell quiet then, and I focused on the darkness. Every once in a while I could make out the yellow blink of a firefly, but then the glow would vanish like it had never been there, and I was left with the feeling that my mind was playing tricks on me.

"Jackie," Katherine said after a minute, "I'm sorry about how my boys treated you this morning and at dinner. It was completely unacceptable."

There was nothing for me to say back to her, so I nodded my head. Upon my suggestion, Katherine had confiscated the twins' camera and gone through the video clips. Not only had they caught me rushing out of the bathroom in the curtain, but the twins also recorded Isaac picking the lock on the bathroom door and stealing my clothes, so he had been caught red-handed. She apologized again, promising that everyone involved was being punished, and when I told her I would pay for the damage I caused, she laughed. The cost of the curtain was coming out of Isaac's allowance.

She stayed for another fifteen minutes or so and chatted, asking me questions about my first two days of school and how I was settling in. I figured it was her way of checking up on me, making sure that everything was okay.

"I'm fine," I told her. "I swear."

I mentioned that I'd made some new friends and my classes were easy, unimportant fluff to keep her happy. In reality, I was just going through the motions: wake up, shower, go to school, sleep. Colorado was just a bookmark between the pages of my life, the place I had to stay until I was old enough to go home.

Worn out from my long day, I was yawning by ten, so I collected my toiletries and headed for the bathroom. Not surprisingly, when I stepped out into the hall and saw Lee, he scowled at me before sweeping into his room and slamming the door behind him.

I stood in the hallway, taking in his angry attitude. He must have gotten in trouble for lying.

I wasn't bothered by the fact that he'd aligned himself with Isaac at dinner, throwing me under the bus with blatant lies. Lee had made a point of being rude to me since I'd arrived, and I expected nothing less from him. But with Nathan, it was a different story. Notes of a half-formed song drifted down the hallway, fumbling and awkward, and suddenly I felt a rush of irritation push me forward.

The music came from the only open door in the upstairs landing, and I swept into Nathan's room without knocking. Two beds were tucked into the small room. On one side, the walls were decorated with *Star Trek* posters, clothes carpeted the floor, and a stack of video games next to the computer almost reached the ceiling. The other side, Nathan's half, was clean and simple, with only a music stand stationed in the corner to indicate it was his space. He was lying on the bed closest to the door, eyes closed. His fingers slowly passed over the strings of his guitar as he worked out a song.

"Why didn't you say something?" I asked, hurt flooding through me. We'd only known each other for a few days and still I felt betrayed. Nathan was supposed to be my friend in the house. He was the one who'd run with me the past two mornings, his constant chatter keeping painful thoughts of my family at bay, the one who walked me to class so I wouldn't get lost, and the only person who warned me about Cole, his own brother.

Nathan lifted his head and peered at me over the top of his guitar. When he saw me standing in the doorway, he sat up.

"Jackie, I—" he started, as if he was about to give me an excuse. Then he shook his head and started over. "Look, I'll tell you straight up. We have this thing between us kids where we agreed to never tell on each other. If we ratted each other out for every little thing someone did, we'd be grounded permanently, as in forever."

"But how was I supposed to know?" I complained. Were the Walters really upset about some agreement they didn't even tell me about? I felt like someone had punched me in the gut. "Nobody told me the rules. I just didn't want your mom to be mad at me."

"It's stupid," he agreed with me, "but so are most of my brothers."

"So Isaac and them? They're mad at me?" I hugged my arms across my chest, trying to convince myself that everything would be fine.

"No. I don't know, maybe." He pulled his hand through his hair.

A long sigh hissed out of my mouth. "That's completely unfair."

"Trust me, I know."

"So how long do you think they'll be pissed?" I asked quietly.

"I don't know, a week maybe?" he said somewhat uncertainly as he gave me a sideways glance. "I can try and talk some sense into them."

"Thanks, Nathan," I said, tucking a stray piece of hair behind my ear. "That would really mean a lot."

I wanted to tell him that it was stupid that he even had to put in a word for me, but I knew it was no use. If there was anything that I'd learned about the Walter boys so far, it was that they were unpredictable. I couldn't force my tight, neat world where everything made sense upon them. They lived by their own strange set of rules, and somehow I was going to have to learn to work within those boundaries and still strive for perfection.

• • •

Back in my room, I found Cole standing next to my dresser, studying the different picture frames I'd arranged on top.

"Who's that?" he asked, staring down at my sister in the way most boys did.

Lucy was flawless. There was no other way to describe her. She could roll out of bed in the morning, her long, straight black hair looking as if she just stepped out of the salon. I never once saw her put on makeup—she didn't need to. Her skin was always porcelain smooth, with a natural pink blush over her cheeks. But it wasn't just Lucy's beauty that made her so astonishing.

She was a natural when it came to modeling, and for that reason my mother loved her. Lucy always knew just the right way to move her body—a slight turn of the neck or curve of the leg—to create the most dramatic pose. Her eyes always shined as if they were flirting with the camera, and her smile was big and bold. In my mother's eyes, Lucy was a dream, everything a fashion designer could want from a daughter.

We were only a year apart, and still I looked at her in a "you're so big and wise" sort of way, like freshmen do seniors on the first day of high school. Maybe it was because everything she did was so natural, as if she had been born knowing something that the rest of us didn't. Each year after my birthday, we would be the same age for exactly eleven days, and each time I would think, this is it. I'm finally going to feel as old and smart as Lucy. Somehow I would suddenly know the things she did, and then my mom would notice me too. But then Lucy's birthday would come and she would magically skip ahead five years, fifteen going on twenty, always out of my reach.

In my heart, I knew I could never be like my sister—we were just too different. She was like our mom, carefree and personable, while I was like our dad, calculating and serious. I don't remember when I came to the conclusion, but I realized that if I could be as successful as my dad, my mom would start to love me the way she did Lucy. After all, she fell in love with him even though they were opposites.

That was the start of my obsession with being perfect. If I was going have the kind of career that my father did, there was no room for mistakes. I started planning out my life. First, I would graduate as valedictorian of my class. Next, I would attend Princeton University, same as my father, and intern with a top New York corporation. Then I could start working at my father's company, my rightful legacy.

I dropped my toiletries on the desk. "Lucy. She's my sister."

Fully expecting some inappropriate remark about how bangable she was, I was caught off guard when Cole set the frame back in its place and replied, "You look like her."

"I—thanks."

It was the nicest compliment that someone had paid me in a long time. Not because Cole thought I looked like my sister, who was one of the most beautiful girls I knew, but because it made me feel like I was carrying part of my sister with me.

Cole turned to face me, not even noticing how much his words had affected me, softening my aching heart, even if it was only by the slightest bit. But then again, maybe he did know. He was clearly aware of how girls acted around him all of the time, and perhaps he was good at picking up on sudden changes in people, like shallow breathing and twitching hands. Either way, he didn't hint at it.

"Just wanted to check on you," he said, heading toward the door. "Make sure Isaac or Lee didn't kill you or anything."

I nodded my head to indicated that yes, I was still breathing. "Nathan told me about your guys' honor code or whatever he called it," I told him, my voice low. "I didn't know. I only wanted to clarify to your mom what happened, but Isaac just—"

"You don't have to explain yourself, Jackie," Cole said flatly. "If I were in your position, I would have done the same thing."

"So you guys won't be giving me the silent treatment, then?"

"I'm not. Nathan clearly isn't either," he said, heading toward my bedroom door. "You'll be fine. Just remember the rule in the future."

"Okay," I said, nodding my head. "Thanks."

"No, I should be the one thanking you."

"For what?"

"For surprising me."

"Surprising you?"

Cole smiled. "I fully expected I'd have to fork over those five dollars to Isaac. I'm glad you're not as predictable as I thought." He shut the door before I could process what he said. When he was gone, it hit me. Cole had known about the bet all along.

Chapter 6

*J*ackie, save me.

I scrambled up in my bed with a start and quickly reached for the lamp on my bedside table. The darkness in the room was suffocating, and I wasn't able to suck in a deep breath of air until the yellow light met my eyes. My pajamas clung to my drenched skin, and my sister's voice was still echoing in my ears. It was the nightmare, the same one as always. It started the same every time, with us all in the car on a peaceful day, everyone enjoying a ride together. Then an unknown force would rip me from my seat, and I would be helpless to do anything but watch as the earth swallowed up my family.

It was too early to go for a run, but my heart was hammering and I knew that I would toss and turn until sunrise. Pushing the covers back, I decided to go down to the kitchen, hoping that a glass of warm milk with honey would calm my nerves. It was something Katherine made for me when we were in New York. The nerves I had about moving to Colorado made my nightmares worse than normal, and one night I screamed us both awake.

I crept down the stairs quietly. It was even harder than during the daytime, because the lack of light made it impossible to see any of the junk on the steps. The stuff must have bred there—each time I went up or down, there was some new movie or book or game.

When my foot connected with a ball, I sucked in a deep breath as it clattered down the stairs, taking a few other items with it. I held my breath even after it came to a rest; I wanted to be positive that no one had heard the racket. Even though Cole said everything was okay, I knew that some of the boys were probably still mad at me, and I didn't want to make anything worse by waking them up in the middle of the night.

Reaching the bottom without another incident, I made my way down the front hall where a soft, blue glow led the way. When I reached the kitchen, I heard the almost inaudible noise from the TV.

"Hello?" I whispered, moving toward the living room.

When I stepped onto the soft carpet, I saw that TV was turned on to a crime show—a detective was inspecting a bloody corpse on screen. The couch pillows were slopped onto the floor and a bag of chips was sitting open on the coffee table, but the room was empty.

My not-so-subtle descent down the stairs didn't wake anyone, but it did warn whoever was up that I was coming. There seemed to be another insomniac in the house besides myself, and judging from his withdrawn personality, I knew exactly who he was.

• • •

It was the end of the school week, and we were supposed to be finishing up our art project in class. Each group was to present the finished project on Monday, but Heather, Riley, and I were nowhere close to being done. We'd chosen to do a photography collage, but after checking out a camera to use, we didn't make any progress. Heather and Riley were distracted, constantly asking me questions about the Walters.

"Is Isaac a boxer or briefs kind of guy?" Heather asked, pulling her bubble gum in a long string past her lips before letting it spring back inside her mouth.

"How would I know that?" I said, trying to adjust the focus on our camera. I still couldn't figure out how to make everything look less blurry when I looked through the lens. I wanted to scream.

"You live with him," Riley pointed out, as if I spent all my free time at the Walters' house riffling through their underwear drawers. Now that I thought about it, Heather probably would.

"Yes, for like a week," I reminded her. "Can we please focus? I need to get a good grade on this project."

"Relax, Jackie," Riley said in her Southern drawl. "This is art class. Nobody ever gets bad grades in art class. Not ever."

"Unless we don't turn in our project…"

"Don't worry," Heather chimed in. "It will get done."

"When? We have"—I paused to look up at the clock—"exactly twenty minutes to finish ours and we haven't taken one picture."

"I don't know," Riley told me. "We just will."

"Oh. My. God!" Heather cried a second later. "I have the most brilliant idea ever! Why don't we finish the project at the Walters' house this weekend? We could even do a sleepover!"

Riley frowned in disapproval. "I don't know, Heather," she said slowly. "It's kinda rude to invite ourselves over, especially since we just met Jackie."

A jolt of excitement coursed through me. Not only would a sleepover be the perfect solution to our project crisis, but it also could be my chance to cement myself into this group of friends. Even with Lucy's help—she introduced me to everyone she knew at Hawks—it was never easy for me to make friends. Without her now, it was going to be even harder for me to meet people.

I swallowed the lump in my throat as I thought about my sister. Having Riley and Heather over would be a good thing. Maybe I could ask Katherine after school if they could stay over Saturday. It was almost as if Lucy was with me, urging me to bond with these new people.

"No, no, it's fine!" I burst out, looking around at the group. "I'll just ask Mrs. Walter if we can have a sleepover when I get home today. Is Saturday okay with you both?"

Riley studied me for a moment, unsure, so I forced a bigger smile onto my face. "I suppose so," she finally said after a long moment of hesitation. "I'm gonna have to pick out my cutest pajamas."

● ● ●

Later that day, after Katherine had agreed to the sleepover and I called Riley to tell her the good news, I made my way downstairs with the intention of thanking Katherine for letting my friends come over. As I neared the kitchen, I heard an angry voice.

"But, Aunt Kathy, she's only been living here for a week, and you're letting her invite friends into our home?"

"Lee," Katherine said with a disapproving tone, "how can you say such a thing?"

"It's not like it's her house to invite people to."

"Honey, that poor girl has no family. This is her home now, whether you like it or not. I'm just trying to put a little happiness into an awful situation, and you should be doing the same. You of all people should understand that."

I came to a halt so fast it felt like I was on a roller coaster, the safety bar jerking me back as the ride came to a sudden end.

"Come on, Aunt Kathy—"

I didn't stay long enough to hear what Lee said. He was right—this wasn't my home and I certainly would never fit in here. I swept back up the stairs, not caring if I sent a few DVDs flying down in my wake, and hurtled down the hallway toward my room. I was moving with such momentum that when I crashed into something rock hard, I was sent sprawling back on my butt.

"Son of a..." Cole grumbled. He was rubbing his head, his jaw clenched in pain, as we both sat on the floor in a daze. When he glanced over and realized that I was on the ground next to him, he shook his head. "Damn girl, for someone so short, you're like a mini bulldozer."

"Sorry," I replied and scrambled to my feet. My head had that light, whooshing feeling when you stand up too fast, and there were black dots blinking in front of my eyes, but I pushed past Cole, determined to make it to my room.

"Hey, New York! Wait up," he called out. I could feel him stumbling after me, but I didn't stop, throwing open my door with such force that it slammed into the wall, rattling the bookcase nearest it. "Jackie, what's wrong?"

"Nothing," I lied, trying to slam the door shut before he could get in.

"That," said Cole, while sticking his foot in the path of the closing door, "is complete bullshit."

"I don't really want to talk about it right now, okay?" I said, practically begging him to understand. I didn't want to be with anyone at the moment. He couldn't see my tears. Nobody could.

"Was it something I did?" he asked in confusion. I was willing to bet that no girl had ever turned down his shoulder to cry on before. I shook my head.

"Hold on," he said, and there was that look in his eyes, the one I was so afraid of. It was the poor Jackie look. I clenched my fists in anticipation, knuckles cracking as I waited for him to mention my family. But he didn't. "Is this about the whole sleepover thing?" asked Cole.

I blinked back at him. It wasn't what I was expecting him to say, which was a relief, but if he already knew about the sleepover, it meant that gossip spread like wildfire in this house.

"It is, isn't it?" Cole said when I didn't respond.

It's not just about that, I wanted to correct him. It's that my family is dead, and that you know. "Did Lee tell you?" I responded instead. "He doesn't really like me, does he? It was a bad idea anyway. I shouldn't be overstepping."

Back in New York, after my breakdown, I taught myself how to control my feelings. It was vital to my future success because I could never lose myself like that again. So I built a wall inside my mind to keep back my flood of emotions. But here, it was harder to maintain. The Walters' house was like nothing I had ever experienced before: disorganized, rowdy, and unpredictable. Without a proper foothold, some type of steadiness, I was losing myself in the chaos. Lee's comment had put a crack in my wall, and I felt like the whole thing was going to shatter.

"Jackie, you can't listen to Lee," he said in calm, clear-cut voice, the kind people use to convince you of something. "He doesn't know what he's talking about. Just ignore him."

I nodded mechanically as I stared past him. Sure, I understood what Cole was trying to say, some sympathetic form of assurance, but it didn't matter what he told me. It was kind of like when people apologized to me at my family's funeral—it was just words, a script that they all were required to recite. They said they were sorry, but in reality they could never really comprehend what I was going through. So it didn't matter if Lee was only being mean and I should disregard him, because he was speaking the truth.

And then it was almost as if Cole understood what I was thinking. "Hey," he said, putting both of his hands on my shoulders. He gave me a little shake, forcing me to look back at him. "I'm really sorry my cousin is being such a jerk. Let me make it up to you."

• • •

"These are the horse stables," Cole said, holding the door open for me. He'd offered to give me a tour of the ranch, and I agreed. I needed someone, *anyone* to take my mind off things.

I could see the stables from my bedroom window. When I noticed the main building from afar, I presumed that it was just a barn, but now as I stepped inside, I realized that it was much bigger. The first thing that hit me was the smell of animals and hay. It was overwhelmingly pungent—the kind of smell that was so heavy you could feel it in your lungs when you breathed in.

We were standing at the front of a long row, stalls on either side of us. A few were empty, but huge animals occupied the rest, snorting and swishing their tails. They varied in color from dark brown to soft gray, but to me, they were all equally daunting. I could feel Cole directly behind me, and for some strange reason, I found that reassuring.

"Besides the horses," he told me in an easy voice, "the best thing about this place is the loft."

He coaxed me forward, his hand a guiding pressure on my back. As we made our way to the other side of the stables, Cole pointed out the different horses, telling me each of their names. In one of the stalls, a man was brushing down a black mare that Cole called Raisin, and when he heard us, the man glanced up and nodded in our direction.

"Who's that?" I whispered as we continued walking.

"Just one of the stable hands," Cole told me. "My dad has a lot of employees. It takes quite a few people to run a ranch, and my brothers and I can't always be there to help him with the work."

By the time we reached the end of the stalls, I'd counted twenty-four horses in all. Cole had stopped in front of a wooden ladder and I craned my neck, trying to see what was on the second level. Stepping onto the first rung, he started to climb. About halfway up, he looked at me over his shoulder.

"You coming, Jackie?"

I climbed up after him, which was harder than it looked in my pencil skirt. When I reached the top, Cole offered me his hand and pulled me into the loft. The boys had clearly redone the space. I hadn't known what to expect—maybe bales of hay—but instead there was a shabby blue rug on the floor, two couches, an old TV on a coffee table, and one of Katherine's ever-present murals decorating the walls. A pile of board games was stacked in the corner, but judging by the layer of dust on top, the games hadn't been touched in a long time.

"We used to hang out here a lot when we were younger," Cole said as I rotated around the room, taking everything in. One of the beams holding up the ceiling was covered in Sharpie with different ticks, dates, and the boys' names marking their different heights as they grew.

When he saw what I was looking at, he ran his finger over one with his name written next to it. "I remember I broke my leg that day," he said, shaking his head. "Let's add you."

He grabbed a marker. It was hanging from the string that was nailed into the beam, waiting patiently to record a new height. I stepped up against the rough, wooden height chart, and Cole's hands brushed the top of my head as he drew a line. He scribbled my name next to it when I stepped aside, and I realized that the little black mark wasn't just a testament to how short I was compared to most of the Walters, but a memory.

"There," Cole said, glancing over his handiwork after hanging the marker back up. "Now that you've been inducted permanently into the loft, let me show you why it's so awesome." He crossed over to the ledge and leaned over, his hand fishing in the air for a rope that was hanging from the ceiling.

"Cole, what are you doing?" I demanded as he hoisted himself up onto the banister.

"Watch this," he said and grinned. With one big step, Cole swung through the air like some crazy jungle man, shouting at the top of his lungs before dropping into a huge pile of hay.

I rushed over to the edge, hands gripping the railing as I peered over to see if he was okay. At first, I couldn't see him because the pile of hay had swallowed him up. But before I could freak out, Cole popped up, sending pieces of dried grass everywhere. "Your turn, Jackie," he shouted up to me. "Just grab the rope."

"Like hell," I said, backing away. I swiveled to the right, moving in the direction of the ladder. "I'm coming down like a normal person so I don't end up in the ER."

"Oh no, you don't," I heard Cole say below, and before I could reach the ladder, I saw the top of it shake, then disappear, leaving me trapped in the loft. I stared at the empty gap in the banister for a few seconds before I realized the ladder was gone. The sight was strange, like a missing tooth in someone's smile.

"It's not funny, Cole," I finally said, trying to stay calm as I peered down at him. "Please put the ladder back."

"Nope." The ladder was still in his hands, but he was easing it down onto its side, far out of my reach.

"If you actually think I'm going to jump out of this loft, then you're crazy," I informed him, in my best I-mean-business tone. It was a ludicrous idea.

"Come on, Jackie," he responded with a whiny-please voice. "It's not that far of a fall and I promise it's safe. We used to do it all the time as kids."

But I was having none of that. "If you don't put the ladder back up right now—"

"What's the worst that can happen?" he asked, cutting me off. His arms were crossed over his chest as he craned his neck to look up at me.

"I could break my leg," I snapped, remembering what he'd told me a couple of minutes ago as we studied the height chart.

"Jackie," he groaned, his head falling back in annoyance. He rolled his eyes at the ceiling. "I promise that's not how I broke mine."

"I'm sorry, Cole," I told him, firmly planting my hands on my hips. "But I'm not the type of person who takes unnecessary risks."

"Unnecessary risks? You sound like a stuffy businessman. It's not like you're signing a multimillion-dollar contract or something. You're just doing a bit of rope swinging. It's supposed to be fun."

"Like I said before, I don't see the fun in breaking my leg."

"Are you always this stubborn?" Cole asked, muttering more to himself than me. Still shaking his head, he made a point of sitting down, his long legs folding into a cross-legged position. "It doesn't matter. I can hang around all day."

"I thought the point of this tour was to cheer me up," I said, "not to torture me."

There was a pause, and Cole sighed. "I'm trying, but you're making this very difficult," he said, as if I was the one who was being ridiculous. "Seriously, Jackie, just *live* a little."

Hearing this, I drew in a breath.

I had planned to wait him out, sitting up there on the shabby blue rug until my legs went numb. But then he said that one simple word—live. Looking back on it, I'm sure Cole didn't mean much by it; he just wanted me to jump. It got to me, though, hanging in the air like cigarette smoke, thick and unwanted, until I almost choked. Why was I still here breathing when my family was gone, their lives cut short? Would they feel as guilty as me, I thought, if it had been the other way around?

A sudden surge of anger throbbed through my body, and I yanked the blue ribbon that was holding back my bangs out of my hair. Using it like a ponytail holder, I tied my locks back before stepping up to the edge of the loft. It took me three tries to reach the rope, my stomach pressed into the railing as I leaned out into the open air, fingers stretching. When I finally had the rope in my hand, I carefully swung my legs over the side and took a deep breath.

"You got this, New York," Cole was saying now, but I couldn't see him because my eyes were closed tight.

This was stupid, so unbelievably stupid, and yet, I did it anyway. With one huge push, I kicked away from the banister and sliced through the air with a whoosh.

The momentum that pulled me back and forth managed to drag a string of curse words out of my mouth, and I rounded it all off with a massive, "Walter, I officially hate you!" Finally, the swinging rope slowed, but not before I lost my grip. The ground rushed up around me, and I plunged into a sea of hay.

"See?" Cole said, wading through the hay toward me as I stood up. "That wasn't so bad." He was clearly pleased with himself, but my stomach was still up in my throat and the scratchy, dry grass was clinging to me in a million different places. There was still some anger running through my veins, and I slammed my palms into Cole's chest, shoving him away from me.

At least, I tried to. He barely budged. It must have been the adrenaline that made me do it.

"Don't you ever do that to me again," I said, my tongue sharp, trying to make up for the fact that I probably wasn't too intimidating after the failed push. "Not ever."

Startled by my outburst, Cole stared at me momentarily, his mouth half open. I narrowed my eyes and glared at him with as much menace as I could muster, fully expecting an apology, but then he was laughing and it wasn't just a tiny chuckle, more of a full-bellied, hands-on-your-knees kind of laugh.

"Quit it!" I said, when he didn't stop.

"Oh God," he gasped, wiping away a few stray tears. "That was priceless."

"I don't find anything about this funny."

"Yeah, because you couldn't see your face. You were all 'Grrr' and it was adorable."

I choked on the words that were poised on my tongue in response. *Adorable.* Cole Walter had just called me adorable.

"Hold up," he said, stepping forward and reaching toward me. I reared back, but Cole kept coming, his hand reaching toward my hair. When he pulled away, there was a piece of hay between his fingers. "Got it," he whispered.

We were so close now that I could see the tiny scar on his forehead, a small L-shaped nick just above his left eyebrow. As he stared down at me, his eyes glossy with an intense, unreadable expression, it was nice to focus on that one imperfection. Knowing that he wasn't completely flawless made holding his gaze a little easier.

Except for the soft rustle of the horses, it was silent. It felt like one of those romantic movie moments when a guy and a girl are standing close together, just taking each other in. The room goes silent in an electrifying way, and then he starts to lean in, hesitating for a second to build the suspense. Then, in one quick moment, he closes the gap between their lips and sweeps the girl off her feet. Standing next to Cole was just like that, except for the kissing part.

"Oww!" I yelped, as an abrupt pain stung my foot. "What the hell?"

Cole looked disoriented from our near kiss, blinking at me in confusion as I hopped away from him, but when a dog with floppy ears emerged from the hay, Cole started laughing again.

"That's Bruno—mighty hunter of mismatched socks and smelly tennis shoes."

"He bit me," I said, looking down at the dog. In reality, it was more of a nibble, something that didn't hurt, but the sudden nip had been so unexpected that my heart was thumping away.

"You're joking, right?" Cole said, squatting down to scratch the mutt behind his ear. "Bruno wouldn't hurt a fly. Probably just thought your foot was an old shoe."

On further inspection, Bruno did look quite harmless. He was a brown dog, yet the fur on his muzzle was white with old age. He was probably a grandpa in doggy years.

"He'd be sorta cute if I wasn't allergic," I said, backing away as Bruno looked up at me, tongue hanging out of his mouth.

Standing up, Cole took my hand and led me over to a section of stalls that I hadn't noticed before because they were tucked away in the farthest corner of the stables. They were much bigger, and so were the animals within. "Are you allergic to horses?" he asked, stopping in front of a stall with a stunning gray horse. Under the light of the stables, its hair almost looked blue.

"Not that I know of," I replied and took a step back as Cole unhooked the latch. "What's his name?"

"You mean her name," he corrected, stepping inside. "Athena is a girl." At the sound of her name, Athena shook out her mane before nuzzling Cole's forehead.

"She's so…huge." Now I was inching away as stealthily as I could. Growing up in the city, I didn't have much experience with animals, but I didn't want to admit that I was frightened of Athena.

Cole didn't notice. "You wanna go for a ride?" he asked, his voice jumping up. He didn't wait for a response; he was already pulling a saddle off the wall.

"No way!" I was backed up against the opposite wall, as far away as I could get. Nothing could get me on that thing—not even a super-cute boy.

"Jackie," he said as he arranged the saddle on Athena's back. "Remember what I said about living a little?"

"Yeah," I shot back. "Remember what I said about hating you?"

It took a bit of coaxing, but Cole succeeded in getting me on his horse. I was so set in my refusal that Cole attempted to trade five of his morning bathroom minutes to me, but I told him there was nothing that could entice me onto Athena. I, of course, was wrong. There was something worth the uncomfortable feeling of sweaty palms and a jittering heart. After promising that he would get Jack and Jordan to stop following me around with their video camera, I let Cole boost me into the saddle.

For the first ten minutes, I kept my eyes shut tight. My every nerve was prickling, and all I could focus on was the horse moving below me. But then I started to notice other things, like the feeling of Cole's body pressed against mine and the warm spring sun on my face.

Cole took things slowly. He walked Athena through the fields, and the wind rippled the grass around us. I was finally settling in, enjoying Cole's arms around me as he gripped the reins, when the meadow met up with the forest, the long, waving grass transforming into strong trees. Giving the reins a quick tug, Cole slid out of the saddle. After tying Athena to the nearest tree, he helped me down and we started into the forest, following a well-trodden path.

"You're going to like this," he said. Glancing back over his shoulder at me, his face lit up with excitement.

And he was right.

It only took five minutes to reach the clearing, but I knew when we were there. The world around me belonged in a fairy tale. Above us, a forest river ended in a tiny waterfall, the pool at the bottom forming a crystal-clear swimming hole. The sun shone down on the water, making it glimmer like glass, and the greenery around the edge was covered in water droplets sparkling like little emeralds.

The Walters had created a beach entrance with pure white sand, and the water lapped at the shoreline like we were at the ocean. There were two blue beach chairs pushed into the sand, positioned just so, and behind them, a picnic table in the shade. A tree near the water's edge had wooden planks nailed into it so people could climb to the thick branch that hung over the water. Cole smiled, took off his shirt, and shuffled up the tree like a little boy.

"Now what are you doing?" I asked him, even though I knew.

Cole let out a holler, which was followed by a splash as he cannon-balled into the water. "How'd I do?" he asked when he resurfaced.

I shrugged. "Eh, I'd give it a four and a half."

"Out of five?"

"Ten," I replied, watching him tread the water.

"Fine, Simon Cowell," he said, sloshing back up onto the beach. "Let's see you do better."

Kicking off my sandals, I dipped my feet in the water to test the temperature, only to hop back instantly. "Are you crazy?" I asked, surprised there wasn't a thin sheet of ice over the pool.

An alarming grin crept onto Cole's face. "Maybe a little," he admitted, before darting forward and locking his arms around my waist.

"Cole! Cole, no!" I shouted, kicking my legs wildly, but he scooped me up in one swift motion and tossed me into the water.

It took less than three seconds for the whole thing to happen, but my body reacted instantly, all of my muscles tensing up in prepara-tion as I soared through the air. At first, when I hit the surface, I felt nothing. An instant later, as my body plunged into the icy pond, the pins-and-needles feeling rushed up my limbs like a chain reaction. I was so caught off guard by the whole thing that I managed to suck down a mouthful of water. I came up coughing, my lungs feeling as if they were frozen solid.

"Your entry was shaky," I heard Cole saying. "I'll give you a two, and that's me being generous."

"I h–hate you!" My teeth were chattering so badly that I nearly bit my tongue.

"Yes," he agreed, nodding his head. "I think you've already pointed that out today."

If I wasn't shivering in big, violent jerks, I wouldn't have let his cheekiness go unchecked, but I could literarily only concentrate on one thing: "This water is freezing!"

"Yeah," said Cole as he floated on his back, his hands sculling back and forth to stay afloat, as if he were in the Caribbean. "But it's great during the summer when it's piping hot."

"Really?" I said, not believing him. "I feel like I'm going to get hypothermia."

"Stop being a baby," Cole said before diving under the water like a penguin. The Walters must have polar bear DNA, I thought as I took a few strokes toward land. I was positive that I was turning blue.

A hand wrapped around my ankle, and I was yanked under the water. I let myself sink for a second before returning to the surface, choking up more water.

"You okay, New York?" Cole asked, laughing. "Or are you going to need some mouth-to-mouth?"

"That was not funny, *Colorado*."

Cole raised an eyebrow. "Wow, where did that sass come from?" he asked.

"Maybe from the fact that you tried to drown me," I said.

"I did *not*!" he defended himself.

Instead of responding, I sent a wave of freezing water in his direction.

Cole stared at me in shock as droplets trickled down his face. When he recovered, he wiped them from his face. "Oh, this means war!" he said, splashing me back.

We played in the water, splashing each other and laughing, for a long time.

"So besides the fact that my cousin is a total asswipe," Cole finally asked when we stopped to catch our breath, "what do you think of Colorado?"

We were floating on our backs, looking up at the sky, and by now my body was numb to the cold.

A long sigh escape my lips. "It's fine," I said.

"But?" Cole asked.

"But what?" I said back.

"Normally when people sigh like that, there's a 'but,'" he said.

"I guess…" I trailed off. I didn't know exactly how to phrase what I was thinking. Cole remained silent, giving me a moment to think. Finally I looked over at him and said, "Everything's so different, you know?"

"I've never been to New York, but I can imagine."

"Yeah, I miss it a lot."

Cole didn't say anything to that, choosing instead to gaze at me.

The water was still for a moment, and I felt like everything around us was holding its breath, but then Cole let himself slip under the surface, his head disappearing with a splash.

"We should probably head out," he said when he came back up for air. "My mom is going to be pissed that we skipped dinner, and besides, I don't want you to miss the sunset."

"Sunset?" I asked, but started swimming toward the beach.

"Yeah," Cole said, shaking his hair out. "It's one of my favorite things about living here. After a long day of work, watching the sun set over the meadows is just about the most peaceful thing I have ever seen."

The walk back to the fields where we had left Athena was even colder than the water, but by the time we were back, I had started to dry.

"Remind me to bring towels next time," Cole said, helping me up into the saddle again.

"Next time?" I asked, a little surprised.

"Yeah, loser," he said, swinging up next to me. "This is *the* spot. Everyone comes here to hang in the summer."

"Oh, right," I said quietly. Some small part of me couldn't help but feel disappointed. I'd thought he meant just the two of us. Then it suddenly registered in my brain what I was thinking, and the warm feeling of shame rushed into my cheeks. A shiver passed up my spine, and I was suddenly aware of how close Cole was behind me. His hard chest was pressed against my back as his arms caged me in. I sat up straighter, trying to put some space between us.

"Come on, Athena!" Cole said excitedly, digging his heels into her sides. He didn't seem to notice my sudden change in attitude. "Let's show this city girl why Colorado is amazing."

The horse jumped into action, and we rode back toward the house through the grassy meadows. The setting sun cast a warm glow around us. When the house came into sight, Cole stopped and turned back toward the sun. Together we watched the orange ball sink below the horizon, pulling with it a rainbow of colors.

Chapter 7

I have *never* been so jealous of someone," Heather announced. It was Saturday night and we were all lying in my bed, our elbows pressed up against one another. It was cramped on the single mattress—Heather had brought Kim along without warning me—and squishing four bodies onto the limited space was difficult.

I'd just finished telling them about the tour of the ranch Cole gave me yesterday, something I promised to divulge only after we finished our art project. Kim was surprisingly helpful; she knew exactly how to rein in her friends and refocus their attention when they got distracted. Even so, my gossip seemed to work as perfect motivation for Heather and Riley.

"Oh, good God," said Riley. Untangling herself from the rest of us, she grabbed a pillow from the head of my bed, tossed it on the floor, and situated herself on top of it. "Why can't one of the Walter boys take *me* on a date?"

"It wasn't a date. It was a *tour*," I said, correcting her. "Which, I might add, Cole only gave me because Lee was being a jerk."

"You went horseback riding and watched the sunset together," Heather said, sliding down next to Riley. There was a half-finished bowl of popcorn abandoned few feet away, and she scooped up a handful. "That's a straight-out-of-a-book example of a romantic date."

"What do you think, Kim?" Riley asked, holding her hands out to inspect her nails. The bright blue polish was chipped on every finger.

"About what?" Kim asked without looking up from the pages of the comic book spread out in front of her. During our boy gossip, she stayed quiet and stuck to reading. Riley tried to pull her into the conversation with occasional questions, but Kim had a knack for dismissing them immediately. She would offer a few quick words and wave her hand for effect before returning to her comics. It was a talent I had yet to master, because whenever I tried to wiggle my way out of a question, I dug myself into a deeper hole.

"You think the tour counted as a date?"

"Jackie was the one who was there," Kim said. "She would know best."

"That is such a lame answer," Riley said. "Jackie, do you have any nail polish?"

"Sure." I jumped up from my bed, glad for the change of subject. "Do you need remover too?"

"And some cotton balls."

I opened my closet, looking for the heavy box that I knew was inside.

"Whoa," Heather said, as I pulled back the door. "What's with the rainbow?"

She was referring to the fact that all my clothes were hung color coordinated, from shades of red on one end to the purples on the other.

My cheeks got warm. "Just a habit," I said, locating the nail polish.

After sliding the box out with some difficulty, I dumped it next to Riley, making the bottles inside rattle together. Everyone was silent as they looked down at the huge, cardboard moving box that was filled to the top with every color imaginable.

Eyes big, Riley looked up at me. "Is that all?" she asked sarcastically, air puffing out of her mouth in disbelief.

"For real," Heather added, sliding next to Riley so she could get a better look. She dug her hand into the box and plucked out a bright red. "Planning on dropping out of school and starting your own salon?"

I shook my head. They weren't mine. Lucy had been obsessed with painting her nails the way Heather was obsessed with the Walter boys. She put on new color every day to match whatever outfit she was wearing. Her collection of polish was always scattered about the house, stuffed in drawers and cabinets or whatever space she could find. It got to the point that my mom had to set up a vanity in Lucy's room specifically so she would have a space to do her nails. Regardless, bottles would pop up every now and then, tucked between the couch cushions or under a bookshelf where they had rolled and been forgotten.

She was always trying to paint my nails too, but I didn't like the way the polish chipped after a few hours, making my fingers look unkempt. "Jackie," she would tell me, "doing your nails is like making a personal statement. Each color can say something different about you and your mood."

I always thought it was silly—blue was blue, and pink was pink.

Not tranquil or melancholy or cheerful. Even so, when Katherine helped me pack my belongings, I couldn't leave the nail polish behind. I swiped all of the bottles off the top of her vanity into a box so I could take some of Lucy with me to Colorado.

"I don't really use them," I said, showing off my plain fingers. "They were my sister's." The statement slipped off my tongue casually, but everyone went silent. When I realized what I had said, the meaning behind my words, my shoulders went stiff.

"Well," Riley said slowly as she selected a dark purple, "this is quite the impressive collection."

"Definitely," Heather agreed, shaking the bottle against her palm. "Want me to do your nails, Jackie?"

She unscrewed the cap, and I realized what I liked so much about these girls. They knew about my family, that much was evident from the first time I met Heather, and they loved to gossip, yet they never once broached the subject. It had come up through offhand comments that I didn't realize I was making, but these girls maneuvered around them gracefully, as if I hadn't said anything.

"Why not?" I told Heather, dropping down next to her and tucking my legs underneath me.

"So," she said, starting to apply the bright red liquid to my pinkie, "can you tell us a little more about that near kiss?"

I made a face. "Not this subject again," I said, but I couldn't pull away. Heather was bent over my hands, the tiny brush moving carefully. "I thought we were done talking about Cole."

"Please, Jackie?" Riley begged. "Don't you know how amazing

this is? One of us has actually been near enough to Cole Walter to kiss him."

I didn't want to recollect that particular experience—I was embarrassed that I let it happen—but I knew they wouldn't stop interrogating me until they heard every last detail. On the upside, the way Riley said *us* made me feel special.

"Okay, all right," I groaned, giving in quickly. It was easier that way, just getting it over as fast as possible. "What do you want to know?"

Their questions came at me faster than I could answer.

"What did he smell like?"

"Was he holding your hand?"

"How close did your lips get?"

"Did he tuck your hair behind your ear?"

It was suddenly quiet, as both girls waited for me to say something.

"Um?" I answered, looking back and forth between the two.

"How about this," Riley said in a serious voice, as if we needed to resolve some huge issue. "Why don't we ask Jackie one question at a time?"

"Me first," Heather said, looking up from her work. "On a scale of one to ten, how bad did you want him to kiss you?"

"Oh, that's a good one," Riley said, nodding her head at Heather.

"Ahhh?" I said with a frown.

Truthfully, I hadn't the slightest idea. I mean, it wasn't like I was staring at Cole's lips, waiting for the moment he would kiss me. Everything just kind of happened. We were standing there, we were close, and something—an energy of some sort—was moving between us. I didn't even know what was happening until it was all over. How was I supposed to rate a feeling like that?

"We're waiting," Riley said.

"I guess a five?" I said, hoping that wasn't creepy high.

"Only?" Heather said, looking disappointed. "I would have thrown myself at him."

At that moment, my bedroom door slammed open.

"Jackie wants to kiss Cole!" Benny shouted at the top of his lungs. My heart stopped when I saw him. How long had he been listening?

Alarmed, I shot to my feet. "That's not true, Benny," I said slowly. "Why would I want icky boy germs?" There was no way he was leaving my room shouting something like that. If Cole heard him…

"Jackie and Cole sitting in a tree. K-I-S-S-I-N-G!" He sang louder and louder, his voice cracking at the end.

"Benny Walter," I said sternly. "If you don't stop this instant—" I lost my words midsentence when I noticed what was on his head. "Oh my God, is that my bra?"

I tried to snatch it back, but Benny was faster, darting away like a minnow. He leaped onto my bed and started jumping up and down.

"I got your booby holder!" he taunted me.

Kim, who was still curled up on my comforter trying to read, glared up at him. "Hey, kid," she said, sternly and forcefully. "You're going to wreck my comic."

Benny stopped jumping, his eyes huge. "Is that the newest Dr. Cyrus Cyclops?" he asked, sticking his face next to hers so he could get a better look.

"It is," Kim said.

With Benny distracted, Riley was able pluck my bra off his head. She handed it to me, and I recognized it immediately as the one that went missing from the bathroom while I was showering. Someone had drawn nipples on each cup with a marker.

"Can I read it with you?" Benny asked, and then he added, "Please?"

"How about this," Kim said. "If you promise to leave us alone and not repeat any of the conversation you heard, I'll *give* it to you."

"Like to keep?" he asked, and Kim nodded her head. "Wow! Cross my heart, hope to die," he said instantly. Benny held out his hand, but Kim didn't hand it over right away. She gave him a look, one of those piercing stares that said, "Don't mess with me." Only when Benny swallowed, clearly nervous, did she relinquish her comic.

He sat on my bed for a moment, holding it in his hand as he gazed down in amazement. Then he bolted from the room as if Kim might snatch it back.

"Nice one, Kim," Heather said, shutting the door behind him.

She shrugged and stretched out. "I try."

"Thanks a bunch." I let out the breath that I had been holding since Benny appeared. "That could have been disastrous."

We all looked at each other for a minute before bursting out laughing.

• • •

"I had fun last night," Riley told me, zippering up the sleeping bag she'd slept in.

"Yeah, me too," I said as I grabbed my own bag to roll up.

It was Sunday morning, and Riley was helping me clean up the mess in my room. Kim needed to be home in time for church with her family, and since Heather was her ride, the two had left before Riley and I were even awake.

We stayed up most of the night talking about all sorts of things, like how Kim was too obsessed with her online gaming—a problem Heather thought could be solved with a boyfriend—and how Riley thought the new American history teacher was cute in a scholarly, Harvard professor sort of way. But most of all, we talked about Cole and the Walters. I spent the whole night constantly trying to change the subject, but it was as if Riley's and Heather's brains were hard-wired to think about Cole every half an hour. It wouldn't have been so awful if they hadn't kept insisting that I liked him, and vice versa.

"It was really cool of Mrs. Walter to let us stay over," Riley added as she shook a blanket out, holding it by two end corners. A few stray pieces of popcorn were launched into the air, but she ignored them and started to fold up the flannel fabric.

"Yeah, Katherine's been awesome to me." I'd moved on to cleaning up the nail polish. Heather had dumped the entire box over in search of the perfect pink.

"You know, you're pretty awesome too," she said. After setting the newly folded blanket on my bed, she dropped onto the floor next to me and helped me with the bottles. "Most people can't put up with Heather and me. We're a little…"

"Intense?" I offered.

"That's a nice way of putting it, but yeah."

I shrugged. "Back home, I have this friend Sammy who reminds me of you both. The girls at my old school think she's weird, but she's just super passionate. You know, the kind of person who comes off as crazy because she cares too much?"

Riley grinned. "Sounds like we'd get along."

"Totally."

A minute passed as we finished picking up the nail polish. When all the different colors were off the floor, Riley sat back on her heels and tucked a strand of bright red hair behind her ear. I was about to pick up the cardboard box and put it back in the closet, but she looked at me then, a strange half-happy, half-sad expression on her face.

"So," she asked slowly. "Are you…settling in okay?"

It was the closest she had come to asking about my family, and in the silence that followed, I realized that I didn't know what to say.

"It's only been a week," I finally replied, even though that didn't answer her question. And then I added softly, "Everything is so crazy here."

"How so?"

"Living with the Walters—I feel like I never know what's going to happen. It's so—" I broke off, not able to think of the right word.

"Unpredictable," Riley said.

"Exactly."

"What's wrong with that?"

Looking down at my hands, I turned them over as if they held the answer that could help me explain how I felt. "I don't know," I told her, still struggling. "It's like I have to keep my guard up 24/7." I glanced back up at Riley to see if she was following me, but the look on her face said she was lost.

"Why do you need to have your guard up?"

"Because," I told her, a discouraged sigh hissing out my nose, "I have to be ready."

"For what? A zombie apocalypse?"

I gave her a look. "No, just stuff. Life stuff."

"Well," Riley said, her eyebrows scrunched together. "That seems like a lot of work."

"What does?" I asked.

"Trying to be ready for everything."

"Not literally everything," I told her. "But life's a lot easier if things run smoothly."

"Sure," Riley said, "but it's also no fun if there aren't any bumps. Not knowing what's going to happen every once and a while makes things all the more interesting."

I was suddenly overwhelmed, the lack of sleep from the past night catching up. "But if you don't know what's going to happen," I said, throwing up my hands in frustration, "if you're not prepared, that's when you make mistakes."

"Mistakes can be good things, though."

I just looked at her.

"Okay, take me for example," she said. "I wasn't prepared, as you like to say, for my first boyfriend. He was older than me, more experienced. We dated for about four months and then he broke my heart."

"I don't see how that's good," I pointed out.

"Okay, well, maybe that wasn't the best example," Riley said, "but if I could do it again, I would."

"Why?"

"Because he was my first love. Those first four months, as quick as they went, were a whirlwind of bliss. Sometimes you have to let your heart take the lead."

"But if I can prepare for things—"

Riley laughed. "You can't prepare for love. It's not like taking your driver's test or the SATs. It's a gift. One that can happen at any moment."

"How did we even get on this subject?" I asked. "I thought we were talking about my move."

"We're talking about it because you're afraid to take a chance."

"On what?"

"Just stuff," she said, echoing my words. "Life stuff." But there was the tiniest crack of a smile on her face, and I knew she was hinting at something more.

"Riley…" I said, frowning at her.

"What?" she asked, shrugging and faking innocence. "All I'm saying is that you're too busy worrying about the future. Sometimes, you just gotta feel."

• • •

Riley's mother picked her up after breakfast. I stood on the front porch and waved until their car disappeared at the end of the drive, but instead of going back inside, I took the wooden steps down onto the front lawn. The fresh spring air was refreshing, so I followed a gravel path that wrapped around the side of the house into the backyard. I was heading in the direction of the tree house, a place I'd wanted to check out ever since Cole pointed it out during the tour of the ranch.

As I neared the oak tree, I realized just how tall it was and how far the branches stretched out in every direction. A canopy of green above me created a pool of shade from the sun. I took the time to count the number of wooden planks nailed into the trunk—there were twelve in all. The house itself looked neglected, and I wondered when one of the Walter boys had used it last. Probably not for a long time, I thought. It would be the perfect place to hide out.

Placing my hands on the wooden step above my head, I started to climb carefully, not wanting to get a splinter. When I reached the top, I pushed open the trapdoor in the floor, and its hinges screeched.

"Jackie?" someone asked as I poked my head up through the floor.

Startled, I let out a scream and my foot slipped. There was a flutter in my stomach as I lost my balance, but my hand shot out and caught the top rung of the ladder before I crashed to the ground.

"Give me your hand," Alex said, his face appearing above me through the hole. I reached toward him, and he gripped my wrist, yanking me up into the safety of the tree house. We both collapsed onto the floor, chests heaving.

"I almost fell out of the tree," I said in disbelief.

"And I almost died of a heart attack," he replied. "You scared the shit out of me."

"Sorry," I gasped, still out of breath. My heart was pounding so hard that my chest hurt. "I didn't know anyone was up here."

"What are you doing here?"

"Being curious," I said. "I've never been in a tree house before."

My heart was finally starting to slow down, and I had a chance to take in my surroundings. The small room was washed in calm, green shade, and despite its lack of air-conditioning, the foliage outside kept the space cool. There were two tiny windows, one of which had a telescope screwed into the sill.

On the wall was what looked like a hand-drawn map of the ranch, but the imagination of a child had clearly created it. The pool was called Poison Lagoon, the Walters' house was the Black Fortress, and the tree house was Woodland Sanctuary. A plastic toy sword was leaning in the corner, and small crates for sitting were arranged around the floor.

"Never?" Alex asked. He propped himself up onto his elbows to get a better look at me.

"I'm from New York City, remember?"

"Don't you have trees there?" he joked.

"There's a potted bamboo tree in our lobby," I said, still examining the map on the wall. "But I don't think it would make much of a tree house." Underneath the drawing of the waterfall, I could barely make out the scribble of words: Mermaid's Cove. A treasure chest was colored onto the sand with jewels dripping out over the edge.

"It's so strange to think that you didn't have a backyard," Alex said. "I mean, I practically lived outside when I was a kid. My dad helped me build this when I was eight."

"Even if I did have a backyard, it wouldn't have mattered," I said, reaching for the plastic sword. I scooped it out of the corner and swished it in the air. "My dad wasn't much of a handyman."

"He was a businessman, right?" Alex asked.

Lowering the toy, I tilted my head to the side so I could get a better look at him. Alex was the first Walter to ask me a question about my family. As I stared at him, his entire body went rigid when he realized his mistake. Instead of being sympathetic, he seemed uncomfortable, more so than me, and for some strange reason that put me at ease.

"It's okay," I told him before he tried to apologize.

He didn't reply for a moment, and I thought at first that he was going to ignore me. "What do you mean?" he asked carefully.

"Alex," I said, pushing myself up into a sitting position. "I can tell by the way you won't look at me that you feel awkward—about my family."

"Oh." He forced himself to look up at me. "I wasn't trying to act weird," he said then. "I just don't know what to say. I mean, I've never known someone who—whose family—" He stopped, unable to finish his sentence.

"Someone whose family died?" It was the first time I'd said it out loud to any of the boys.

"Yeah, that." He held my eyes for a moment before looking away again.

"Most people just say they're sorry," I said, trying to get him to relax. It was a strange feeling. Normally everyone tried to comfort me when my family came up, not the other way around.

"That's a strange custom, don't you think?" Alex asked, which wasn't what I was expecting him to say. He pulled himself into a sitting position and leaned back against the wall.

"What do you mean?"

"Let's say, for example, that it was an accident," he said, and by "it" I presumed he meant death. "Then there's no reason to

ALI NOVAK

apologize since it technically isn't your fault, right? Saying you feel bad makes more sense, but nobody really wants to hear that, do they? Besides, I'm sure not everyone actually feels bad. What if you don't really know the person who died, but you just feel like you have to say something? That's not really genuine."

Alex was in full-on ramble mode.

"Alex," I said, trying to get his attention.

"Maybe people should just give hugs. Physical contact says a lot without actually saying anything, but I guess people give hugs at funerals anyway. And I'd feel awkward giving you a hug since we barely know each other."

"Alex!" I shouted this time and clapped my hands together for emphasis.

"Huh?" he said, shaking his head. When he noticed me staring at him, he blushed. "Sorry, I tend to talk when I'm nervous."

"I can see that," I said, a small grin curling on my lips. It was honestly the worst condolence someone had ever given me, and yet somehow it worked. "Thanks."

When he saw that I wasn't upset, he smiled back. "No problem."

I turned serious again. "You want to know one of the worst things?" I asked, but I didn't wait for him to respond. "When people treat me differently, like I'm going to break or something. For a second there, I was afraid you were going to get all weird on me."

"I'm sorry, Jackie," he said then, since there was nothing more he could say.

"Yeah," I mumbled, more to myself than to him. "Me too."

We were quiet for a while, both lost in thought, until I finally worked up the courage to speak again. "So what are *you* doing up here?"

This question seemed to make Alex more uncomfortable then talking about my family, and I felt him tense up again, his hands balling into fists at his side. When I looked at him, I realized that something was wrong. There were dark purple marks under Alex's eyes, like he hadn't slept all weekend.

"Hey," I asked, "what's wrong?"

His gaze flickered to the left, and when I followed him with my eyes, I spotted something discarded on the floor—a piece of paper or something. Alex didn't move, so I slowly reached for it, watching him the whole time to make sure it was okay, but he didn't indicate that I should stop. When I picked it up, I realized that it was a folded-up photograph, and I carefully smoothed out the crease. I recognized the people in it immediately. There was Alex, grinning at the camera, his arm wrapped around a girl with blond ringlets— the girl from our anatomy class.

"Her name's Mary Black," Alex said without waiting for me to ask. "She's my ex-girlfriend. We broke up three weeks ago."

"I take it you miss her?" I knew it was a lame thing to say. Of course he missed her, but I didn't know how to properly comfort him. It explained the longing look he gave Mary on my first day of class. Alex nodded his head.

"Do you think you guys will get back together?" I asked, trying to be positive.

"I've had a crush on her since elementary school," Alex said instead. "The first time I saw her was in third grade, and I remember holding my breath as she walked by me on the playground. She was wearing this little pink jumper and her hair was hanging down her back in two braids. She couldn't've cared less that all the boys stopped playing kickball just to watch her skip rope with her friends." The words were spilling out of Alex's mouth now, so I let him go on without interrupting.

"I'll be the first to admit, after that day, I think I was in love, but I never did anything about it. Mary was the type of girl that seemed so unobtainable, and I knew I didn't stand a chance. I dated a few girls in junior high, nothing serious, and then at the beginning of this year, she sat next to me in English. On the first day of class, she just popped down next to me and started talking to me like we were good friends, like I hadn't been crushing on her since forever. After a few weeks, I worked up the courage to ask her to Homecoming, and then we started dating."

"So what happened?"

"She dumped me out of the blue for a different guy."

"Ouch. Did you at least find out who it was so you could get a good punch in?" I was only trying to lighten the mood, but I saw anger flash in his eyes.

"I would have, but she wouldn't tell me," Alex said. "So then, imagine my surprise when I come home and see her sitting on the couch watching a movie with Cole."

I gasped. "She broke up with you to date your brother?"

Alex laughed, but it wasn't a nice one. "Cole doesn't date," he said, repeating the same fact that I had already heard multiple times. "For some reason she thought she could change him, but I know Cole better than that. She called me Friday night and told me she's sorry and wants to get back together."

"What did you say?"

"That I wouldn't be her consolation prize," he spat.

"Alex, I don't know what to say," I said uncomfortably. Obviously something was going on between Alex and Cole, and I didn't want to get in the middle of it. "Why are you even telling me all this?"

A long time passed before Alex said anything, and at first I thought he wasn't going to give me an answer. "Look, I know about your family, and now I've told you my secret, so we're even. I know your baggage. You know mine. We can just be normal." He paused there, as if he needed a moment to collect himself. "I should get going," he said, picking himself up and moving toward the trapdoor. "I'll see you later, okay?"

● ● ●

For the rest of the day, I couldn't stop thinking about what Alex had told me. Cole *stole* his girlfriend. How could he be so callous? As I mulled it all over, I sorted through all the material from all my classes. Since starting at my new school, I hadn't had a chance to organize anything because life with the Walters meant there was always some unexpected event that kept me from the task. Each class received its own file in my accordion folder, ordered by period with the syllabus always at the front.

A history assignment slipped from my hands and fluttered to the floor. When I bent down to pick it up, I caught a glimpse through my window of Cole heading toward the second garage. Over the course of the week, I'd noticed that he frequented it every night. Curious, I left the homework on my desk and pulled on a pair of shoes. By the time I made my way across the driveway, Cole had already shut the doors, but I could hear a stream of music from within.

"Cole?" I knocked, but he didn't answer. "Hello?" I called out. I rested my hand on the handle, not sure if I should intrude. I knew he was still inside because I could hear him moving around, but I didn't want to be rude. When I heard the clang of metal on concrete, followed by a stream of swearing, I yanked open the door to make sure he was okay.

The small space was closer to the size of a shed than an actual garage. Along one wall ran a workbench, covered with different wrenches, ratchets, screwdrivers, and other strange-looking instruments. Above the bench were rows of shelves piled high with car parts, making it look like a Transformer had exploded across the length of wood ledges. A huge black car took up the rest of the space, and its hood was propped open, revealing its guts. Cole was crouched on the floor, picking up the gear that had spilled across the floor when a red toolbox fell to the ground.

"Everything okay?" I asked, making him jump.

"God, Jackie!" he exclaimed, glancing up at me and putting both hands on his knees. "Were you trying to scare me?"

"I knocked," I said with a shrug before slipping inside the cramped space. "What are you doing?"

He stood up. "Working." Cole was wearing a plain white shirt and an old pair of jeans, both of which were covered in grease. There was a red rag hanging from his pocket, and he plucked it out to dab across his brow. "Did my mom send you out here to get me?"

"No," I told him as I picked my way around the car. I didn't want grease on my good silk blouse. "You never showed me this place during my tour."

"That's because nobody is allowed in here," he said, his face flat. "It's my space."

"Oh," I said, taken aback by how curt he was being. "Sorry, I didn't know. I guess I'll leave now."

Cole sighed. "No, it's okay. I didn't mean to snap, but Alex has been a dick to me today and I took it out on you."

"What happened?" I asked, trying to sound mildly interested. In reality, my ears were perked. When I made the decision to come down to the garage, it was partly because I wanted to find out if Alex's accusations were true. I knew that the topic would be hard to slip into a conversation, and I hadn't thought it would actually come up, but now that it had, a spark of excitement shot up my spine.

"I don't know," he said, leaning back against the car. "He's been a prick for the last few weeks."

"I see." I couldn't tell if Cole seriously didn't understand why his brother was mad, or if something else was going on. "So are you going to talk to him?"

"I already did, but he never listens," he said as he wrung the dirty cloth in his hands. "Whatever. If he wants to be ignorant, that's his choice." Cole crumpled the rag into a ball and tossed it on the workbench. "Can we talk about something else?"

"Sure," I said, even though I was dying to know more.

"All right. Well, now that you're out here, I might as well show you my baby."

"Huh?"

Cole pulled back the passenger side door for me. "Get in."

"Is it clean?" I asked, squinting inside. There wasn't much light in the garage to begin with, and the lights in the car didn't turn on when Cole opened the door.

"I vacuumed the seats," he said, making his way around the front of the car. "Just get in."

Ducking down, I carefully settled in. Cole yanked his door shut, and I followed suit, sealing us in the musty cabin.

"So this is your baby?"

"It's a 1987 Buick Grand National," he said, running both hands over the steering wheel. "Used to be my grandpa's."

"Am I supposed to be impressed?" I wasn't trying to be rude, but the car was a bit of a clunker.

"This is a *classic* car."

"It doesn't look like much."

"Well, it is. And when I finish restoring it, it's going to run like a dream," he said, sweeping his hand out in front of him as he imagined his car.

"So that's what you're doing? Fixing it up?"

"I'm trying to, but it's expensive," Cole said, his hand dropping back to his side. "That's why I work at Tony's. He pays me with the parts I need."

"When did you learn to fix cars?" I didn't mean to grill him, but this was the first conversation I'd had with Cole where he actually seemed passionate about something.

"I've taken a lot of shop classes in school, but it's always just come naturally to me," Cole explained.

"How long have you been working on it?"

"On and off since the start of high school." He paused and then added, "But I've really made it a priority since last year." Cole pressed his lips together, and his eyes turned dark cobalt as he stared out the windshield.

I took that as a sign not to push any further. "Cool," I said instead.

He was obviously thinking about something, because then he shook his thoughts away. "I'm sorry, Jackie," he said. "I don't mean to kick you out, but I really wanted to take another crack at the engine before dinner."

At first, I didn't understand what he was saying, but then I realized he wanted me to leave. I must have said something wrong. "Oh, okay." I fumbled in the dark to find the handle, and as I did, my face turned red. When my fingers finally found the smooth metal, I yanked it open as quickly as I could and stepped out.

"See you later," he said, but he wasn't even looking at me. His gaze was still focused out the window.

"Yeah, bye."

I hurried out of Cole's garage, but when I got to the front porch, I glanced back over my shoulder. It was hard to spot him in the shadows, but the mop of blond hair gave him away. He was still sitting in the front seat—he hadn't moved at all.

Chapter 8

C ole, catch," said Isaac, throwing the car keys to his cousin as we all trudged down the porch steps. It was Monday morning, and we were all moving slowly, not looking forward to school.

"You drive," Cole said, tossing the keys back to Isaac. "I have my own ride."

"What?" Alex demanded, and we all looked up at Cole. He smirked as a slick, black Porsche turned into the driveway. Everyone stared as the car pulled up, finally sliding to a stop in front of him.

"It's getting a bit cramped in the truck, don't you think?" Cole asked.

The window rolled down, and I recognized one of the boys who sat with Cole at lunch. "Hey, Walter," he said, looking annoyed. "You coming or not? We're going to be late."

"Dude, chill. We have plenty of time," Cole answered, jogging around the side of the car. He opened the door, leaned down, and said something to his friend that I couldn't hear. "Hey, Jackie," he said, glancing back up. "Want a ride too? You don't have to go with the losers if you don't want." He offered me one of his cocky grins and opened the back door as if he expected I was going to say yes.

Danny, Nathan, Isaac, and Lee had already made their way down to the truck and were trying their best to ignore Cole as they piled their backpacks in the bed. Alex, however, was still standing next to me on the front walkway. I could feel him staring at me, and out of the corner of my eye, I saw that he had gone rigid. But he didn't have anything to worry about. Until I knew exactly what had happened between the two of them, I was going to stick with Alex since he seemed like the more trustworthy one of the pair.

"Actually," I said, shouldering my satchel. "I think I prefer riding with the losers."

Cole's only response was to stare at me, surprise evident on his face. Turning back toward Alex, I offered him a thumbs-up before making my way over to the truck. I kept my eyes glued to its rusty red shape so I wouldn't break my resolve and peek at Cole. One glance at those blue eyes and I would crumble. Nathan pushed open the passenger-side door for me and offered me a hand up. As I climbed in, I heard a car door slam and gravel crunching.

"Damn," Nathan whistled, watching the Porsche disappear through the rearview mirror. "Did you see his face?"

"No," I said, buckling my seat belt. "Why, was it bad?"

"He's beyond pissed," Alex said, laughing, as he climbed into the backseat. The grin on his face was huge. "Man, I wish Jack and Jordan could have got that on camera. Cole Walter getting turned down." He was shaking his head in disbelief.

"It was just a car ride," I said, starting to feel a little nervous. "Not a marriage proposal."

"You don't understand." Nathan had a look of pity etched on his face. "I tried to warn you on the first day. Cole doesn't get rejected.

You're a challenge to him now," he said, and Danny nodded his head in agreement.

"What do I do?"

"Just ignore him," Alex said, like it was no big deal. But I knew how hard it was to ignore Cole when he was around. I wasn't good at it at all.

"Pray," Danny muttered at the same time. My eyes went wide.

"Isaac, can we just leave for school now?" Lee demanded. "I don't really care about this stupid soap opera. I've got classes to skip."

"Preaching to the choir," Isaac said as he started the truck. "I was just waiting for Captain Dork to get in."

Alex rolled his eyes but otherwise disregarded his cousin's insult. The purple marks were still present under his eyes, but unlike yesterday, he looked positively cheery. The truck lurched backward and started down the driveway, and I stared out of the window into the right side mirror. Unfortunately, I thought, as I caught a glimpse of my face, I don't look nearly as happy as him.

Twenty minutes later when we arrived at school, my stomach was still a knotted mess. It didn't help that when I climbed out of the truck, the skin on the back of my neck prickled and I knew that I was being watched. Looking around, I spotted Cole sitting on the front steps with a flock of girls around him, but he wasn't paying them any attention. He was staring across the parking lot at me. I knew that I would have to face him in math class, and the thought made my fingers tremble.

"Hey, Alex," I said as we walked toward the school. "Where do you normally eat lunch?"

"I don't really eat lunch," he said, his cheeks going pink. "Normally, I—um, go to the computer lab to get a quick round of *Gathering of Gods* in."

"That's the online game you play with Kim, right?" I asked.

"Yeah, you play?"

"No, but I was wondering if you wanted to take a break today and eat lunch with us."

"You and Kim?"

"And our other friends, yeah." He looked like he was about to say no, so I quickly added, "Pretty please?"

He was clearly confused but nodded his head anyway. "Sure, I guess."

"Perfect," I told him as we walked into anatomy together. "Pick me up by the math room. We can walk down together."

As we sat down, I smiled to myself. I'd decided the best way to fight off one Walter boy was with another. And my plan worked perfectly. Later that morning, I turned up at math just before the bell rang so Cole wouldn't have the opportunity to talk to me. Then, when he saw Alex waiting for me after class, he swept out of the room without a backward glance.

"Hi," I greeted Alex cheerfully. Kim was standing next to him, an impressed look splashed across her features.

"How'd you do it?" she asked.

"What?"

"Get him out of the computer lab for lunch. I've been trying for ages."

"I just asked nicely."

"That's a neat trick," Kim grumbled. "You'll have to show it to me someday."

"I'm not a dog, you know," Alex shot back. But we knew he wasn't really angry, and the three of us made our way to the lunchroom laughing.

• • •

Despite Nathan's warning, my next two weeks in the Walter house were Cole free. I avoided him as best I could, and in turn, he stayed out of my way. The most interaction we had was one-way—from my window, I could hear everything that went on in the pool below. Swimming was Cole's entertainment of choice when he brought one of his hookups over to the house, and in the past few days, there had been a revolving door of girls in bikinis.

My plan seemed to be working. Because I was hanging out with Alex, Cole left me alone. Alex and I became friends quickly, and now he was eating lunch with me and my friends regularly, not to mention that we always did our anatomy homework together. He had been right—knowing part of his past made it easier for me to open up around him. He was like the brother I'd never had.

I was on my way down to his room, my satchel slung over my shoulder, when I heard the fighting.

"Come on, Alex. You've blown me off all week."

The door to Alex and Nathan's room was ajar. At first I thought Alex was fighting with Nathan, but then I recognized Lee's voice.

"I know, dude, but Jackie and I have a huge test in anatomy that we need to get ready for," Alex said back.

"You're ditching me?" Lee demanded. "We always watch the

game together. Screw her!" There was a pause, and when Alex didn't answer, Lee continued. "Oh, I get it," he said. "That's exactly what you want to do, isn't it?"

"No!" Alex hissed, quickly defending himself. "We're just studying!"

"Yeah, whatever," Lee said, storming out of the room. When he saw me standing a few feet away, he shoved past me, his shoulder ramming into mine. "Bitch," he coughed out and kept walking. Two seconds later, his bedroom door slammed shut.

I contemplated walking back to my room after the encounter, but Alex poked his head out into the hall.

"Oh shit," he said, running a hand through his messy hair. "You heard all that, didn't you?"

"Yeah, kind of," I said, looking away from him. "If you want to hang out with Lee, I understand."

"No, Jackie, don't worry about it," Alex said and pushed his door open all the way. "Come in."

I wavered for a moment, not sure what to do, but then Alex took my satchel from me, so I had no choice but to follow him in. His side of the room was just as messy as the last time I saw it, if not worse. Clothes were scattered everywhere, and empty bags of junk food covered his desk. Nathan's half looked like a *Better Homes and Gardens* magazine, but he was nowhere to be seen.

"I didn't really get the chance to tidy up," Alex told me, kicking a pair of shoes out of the way as he led me over to his desk.

I laughed. "Alex, you'd need a SWAT team to clean up this mess," I said, picking my way across the floor and being careful not to step on any dirty laundry.

"I'll take that as a compliment," he said, pulling out his computer chair so I could sit down. On the seat was a moldy plate that had turned so green I couldn't even tell what type of food was on it. Alex looked at me sheepishly before grabbing the plate and shoving it under his bed. "I'll take care of that later," he muttered. "Have a seat."

"I don't know," I said, eyeing the chair suspiciously to see whether or not it was molding as well. "It might be dangerous."

Alex shot me a look. "Funny."

"What?" I said, but sat down anyway. "Can't be too careful."

After dragging a chair over from Nathan's desk, Alex sat down next to me and pulled out his textbook. "So what's our plan of attack?" he asked.

It was just a figure of speech, but Alex had no clue how seriously I took his question. I'd never been one of those really creative kids who could dance and sing or paint a pretty picture. There weren't any doodles in my notebooks at school because I couldn't even draw a stick figure. But the one talent I could brag about was my ability to study. It didn't matter what type of test it was. As long as I had a decent amount of time to prepare, I could ace anything. This anatomy test would be no different. After all, it was my first academic performance at my new school, and I wanted to set the bar high.

"We should start by going over the review sheet and defining all the terms," I said, pulling the important piece of paper out of my organizer. I handed it to Alex to look over since I knew he'd already lost the one we were given in class. "I've color-coded my notes and arranged them by lecture to assist us. If we can't find a specific answer in my notes, which is highly unlikely, we can turn to the textbook as a last resort."

"What about my notes?" he asked, glancing up from the review sheet. He set it down, and I tried not to cringe as the paper soaked up a tiny puddle of mysterious liquid—probably one of the Kickstart energy drinks that I saw him drinking every morning—that was spilled on his desk.

"Don't be ridiculous," I said, snatching the paper back. "The only notes you took was the picture you drew of Mr. Piper where you labeled all the facial bones. And those weren't even accurate."

"Point taken," Alex said, scratching his head in embarrassment.

"All right," I said, glancing at the first category listed on the review sheet. "Let's start with the appendicular skeletal bones…"

Half an hour later, we had only covered the first twenty of the seventy-five terms we needed to know. I was trying to keep Alex focused on studying, I really was, but that was easier said than done. Every few minutes his e-mail would beep, causing him to glance at his computer. By the time I focused his attention back on anatomy, another e-mail would ping and the process would start all over again.

Finally I gave up.

"Just check it," I said with a sigh as another message drew him out of our textbook. Either Alex had a serious problem with junk mail, or someone was really trying to get hold of him—and apparently whoever it was didn't know how to use a cell phone. This was the tenth e-mail in the past five minutes.

"Check what?" he asked, his eyes darting back to the passage he was supposed to be reading.

"Your e-mail. I know you're dying to."

"Sorry," he said, but he quickly pulled up his inbox. He double-clicked on the first little blue envelope, his eyes scanning the message. "My guild is going on a ZG raid."

He'd lost me in one sentence. "Guild? Raid?" I asked. "What's that?"

"It's gamer talk," Alex said, as he went through the rest of his e-mails. "You know, for *Gathering of Gods*."

"Oh, right. I've heard Kim talking about it before," I said absent-mindedly, "but I didn't really get it."

That was possibly the worst thing I could have said to Alex. He turned to me as an unsettling smile crept onto his face. "Put your notes away, young padawan. Much to teach you, I have."

Alex was so enthusiastic about *Gathering of Gods* that he couldn't just explain it to me. He had to show me. And by showing, I mean he forced me to play. After explaining that game play consisted primarily of completing dangerous quests, he helped me create a character, which took quite some time.

"Why does it matter what color my hair is?" I asked, as he clicked through all forty different styles.

"Because," Alex said, as if I were being childish, "you'll never be able to change it. You have to go with something you really love."

When it came to choosing what race my character was, he got even more frustrated. The options consisted of humans, dwarves, demons, and fae, but I wouldn't pick one until I knew which was the most successful.

"It's a completely legitimate question, Alex," I told him. "Which one is the best?"

"One isn't better than another," he tried to clarify. "I personally like the demons because I think they're badass, but lots of people like fae too."

"So I should be a demon?" I asked, moving the curser so it hovered over an ugly-looking creature with horns and scales.

"No, I'm not saying that." Frustration tinged his voice. "Each race has a different skill set, so it all depends on what you enjoy playing the most."

"But how can I know which one I like the most if I've never played the game before?"

Alex took a deep breath, trying to remain patient. "Just pick one, Jackie."

"At least tell me which race will help me beat the game in the least time."

"It doesn't work like that," Alex replied and snatched the mouse from my hand. Then, making my decision for me, he clicked on the human race. "The game is ongoing. It never ends."

"Wait. You can't win?" I said with a frown. "What's the point of playing, then?"

"This isn't like Monopoly or Candy Land—the point of the game is to improve your character."

"Okay, whatever," I said, taking the mouse back from him. I clicked on the fae, a willowy creature with pastel-colored wings. "But I don't want to be human. That's boring."

I wasn't very good at *Gathering of Gods*. Everything moved so fast, and Alex would shout confusing instructions at me such as,

"Employ your fire shield now!" or "Not that fire shield, your other one!" Still, after an hour and a half of struggling, I increased my character's experience level from one to three. I was quite pleased with myself, but Alex wasn't very optimistie.

"Definitely not a natural," he said, as he logged out of the game, "but I'll make a gamer out of you yet."

"I doubt it," I sighed, collecting my anatomy material. I'd wasted a good chunk of my study time trying to learn the game, and as a result, I knew I would be up late reviewing all my notes. "Thanks, though. I had fun."

The door swung open before he could respond.

"Hey, Alex, I want to talk to you," Cole said, strolling into the room. When he saw me sitting at the computer desk, he stopped. "Oh, I didn't know you were here."

"Um, yeah," I replied.

"I guess I'll have to come back later," he said, turning to leave as if I'd caused some huge inconvenience.

"No, it's okay," I said, jumping to my feet. "We were just finishing up anyway."

"Thanks for helping me study," said Alex as he watched me pack up my satchel.

"That didn't count as studying," I told him with a laugh. "I need to spend at least another four hours on this."

"You're crazy," Alex said as he handed me my notebook. "That was the most time I've spent on school, like, ever."

"Then I'm glad I could help," I said, offering him a smile. "See you tomorrow."

"Night, Jackie," he said as I turned to leave.

Cole was watching me from the doorway, his face blank. When I reached him, he didn't move.

"Cole," I said, raising an eyebrow. He stared at me for a moment longer before stepping aside and letting me leave. As I slipped out into the hallway, he slammed the door shut behind me.

• • •

The dream kept me up again. As I slipped downstairs toward the kitchen, I realized that I was addicted to Katherine's warm-milk-and-honey remedy. Whenever I couldn't sleep, I would make a cup and sit at the kitchen table, nursing the drink until my eyelids were heavy. I liked to linger downstairs with my mug instead of going back to my room, because there was always the chance that I would run into Danny.

My ability to creep down the messy stairs improved, but normally he heard me coming and would disappear before I got to the living room. I always knew when I'd scared him off. The TV would be turned on to some late-night crime show, and snack food would be sitting on the coffee table. When the TV wasn't on, I knew he hadn't come down and I would sit in the kitchen with the lights off, hoping to catch him if he appeared.

But tonight was different. When I tiptoed into the living room, Danny was still sitting on the couch, his hand in a bag of potato chips. I stood at the edge of the carpet, staring in disbelief. He glanced over at me for a moment, but his eyes quickly flicked back to the drama on the screen. Not wanting to spook him, I slowly backed into the kitchen before proceeding to make my milk and honey.

After the microwave dinged, I used the sleeve of my robe to pull out my steaming drink and headed in the direction of the TV. I knew that Danny would be gone by now, and I knew I would have to turn it off. To my surprise, he was still there watching his show.

"You going to sit down?" he asked, his eyes never leaving the screen as I hovered at the edge of the room.

"I—um, sure," I stammered, completely caught off guard. I figured sitting next to him on the couch would push my luck, so I took a spot in the big armchair, folding my legs underneath myself as I settled down. We stayed like that for the next few episodes, quietly enjoying each other's company while neither of us said a word.

It was almost four o'clock when I realized that I had dozed off. The TV was dark and Danny was gone, but he must have turned on the small reading lamp for me because the room was bathed in a soft yellow glow. Happy that I was making progress with Danny, I stayed there for a moment, smiling to myself before heading up to bed.

• • •

"New York!" Something poked my face. "If you don't wake up, I'm not going to take you to school."

Groaning, I cracked my eyes open. Cole's blurry outline hovered over me, his finger ready to jab my face again.

"Go away," I told him and rolled over, burying my face in my pillow. It was too early to deal with his crap. "Who said I wanted to go with you anyway?"

"Fine," I heard him say, "but the guys already left, so if you miss your anatomy test, don't blame me."

"I know you think you're so funny, Cole—" I started to say, opening my eyes again to glance at the clock. I'd set my alarm for six, leaving me plenty of time to iron my clothes and shower, but my heart jumped when I saw the neon green digits—7:26. "No, no, no!" I cried, throwing the covers off me.

"I told you," Cole said, backing away as I started to rush around my room.

"This can't be happening." There was no way I would be able to get ready in time. My hair alone took half an hour to straighten.

"Chill, Jackie. Just throw on some sweats and let's roll."

"Throw on some sweats?" I hissed, swinging around to glare at him. "Have you ever seen me wear sweats?"

"Not really. You normally look like some kind of preppie going to a tea party."

"That's because I don't own any! I'm never going to have enough time to iron an outfit."

"Okay, okay," said Cole, holding up his hands to calm me down. "Wait here. I have an idea." He hurried back a few minutes later carrying a pair of jeans and a jersey. "Try this. It's a pair of my mom's old jeans. They might be a bit too big, but they should work."

"I can't wear this to school," I said a minute later as I looked in the mirror. "I look like a slob." The jersey swamped me, so large that it almost reached my knees. I tried tucking the fabric up, but it slipped down a second later. The jeans were even worse.

"Jackie, it's only one day. Nobody's going to care."

"Well, what about my hair?" I said, trying to arrange my usual ribbon. My fingers were shaking because I was so frustrated and my bangs wouldn't lie right. "It's a mess."

"Stop," Cole said, grabbing my hands. "I like the curls. It's natural."

His words came out so softly and easily. Not forced, like he was telling me something just to make me feel better. I opened my mouth, even though I wasn't quite sure what I was going to say, but a horn honked outside, cutting me off.

"We need to go." Grabbing my satchel, Cole pulled me from my room and out of the house. Then we were inside the shiny, black Porsche, speeding toward school.

"Jackie, you remember my friend Nick," Cole said, twisting in the front so he could see me.

"Hey." Nick nodded his head in greeting.

"Yeah, hi," I muttered, as I stared out the window.

For the next few minutes, Cole tried to start a conversation with me, but I responded with one-word answers. I was too flustered. Finally he gave up and turned to Nick.

"So, you coming to the warehouse today?"

Curious, I turned to watch Cole.

"I don't know," Nick said, glancing at me as if this was something I shouldn't be hearing. "Do we have supplies?"

"Plenty," Cole responded. "Kate scored huge last night."

"I suppose," Nick said, still not sounding entirely convinced. "We're not taking my car, though."

"Might be able to snag the truck keys." Cole pulled out his phone. "I'll text Isaac."

We were coming up on Valley View High now. I could see the

building at the top of the hill in the distance. Cole's fingers were punching away, but Nick still looked uncomfortable.

"Don't invite anyone else, okay?" Nick said, his eyes flickering toward me again. "I don't want to get in trouble."

Hearing this, I focused my attention back out the window. I wasn't sure what they were talking about, but whatever it was, it sounded like trouble. I kept my mouth shut until the car was parked.

"Thanks a bunch, Nick," I said, throwing open my door. By now, the parking lot was mostly empty, and only the kids who didn't care if they were late lingered outside. "See you guys later."

I tore across the pavement without waiting for them, and thankfully, I managed to make it to class as the final bell rang. Slamming my bag down on the table, I turned to Alex. He was staring down at his textbook, pretending to cram in some last-minute studying, but his eyes weren't moving over the page.

"What the heck was up with this morning?" I demanded.

"What do you mean?" he said, not bothering to look up.

"You guys left without me," I said as I pulled a handful of pencils from my bag. "I had to get a ride from Cole's friend Nick."

Alex bit his lip. "Cole said you wanted to go with him."

"Are you for real? When did he say that?"

"At breakfast," he told me.

"Unbelievable," I said, gritting my teeth. Cole was in serious trouble.

"Sorry?"

"Alex, my alarm clock didn't go off this morning. Cole must have messed with it, because he didn't wake me up until *after* you guys were already gone."

"Really?" Alex asked, finally looking up at me. When he saw how irritated I was, relief washed over his face. "Thank God. I thought you gave in to him."

"I didn't. And by the way, I'm totally mad at you," I said, half joking. "I didn't have any time to get ready this morning. Do you see what I'm wearing?"

Alex looked down, and his face froze when he spotted the jersey. "Where did you get that?"

"Cole loaned it to me. I didn't have anything else to wear."

"He *loaned* it to you?" Alex asked, as if that was the most insane thing he'd ever heard.

"Yeah. What's the big deal?" I asked. "It's just an old jersey."

"But that's Cole's football jersey. I haven't seen it since..." Alex trailed off, too shocked to finish his sentence.

Suddenly a conversation I had with Nathan came back to me. *He used to be the best receiver in the state until he got tackled wrong and broke his leg...*

"Since the game he got hurt," I finished for him.

"Yeah, how'd you know?"

"Nathan mentioned it to me when I first got here."

"Jackie," Alex said slowly, still shaking his head in disbelief. "The thing you don't understand is that football was Cole's life. After he lost his scholarship, he stopped talking about the game completely. It was like he'd never played at all."

"And?"

"And for him to just give you his jersey..." Alex said. "I don't even know what that means."

MY LIFE WITH THE WALTER BOYS

Neither did I.

Mr. Piper appeared at the front of the room, clapping his hands to get out attention. "All right, everyone, listen up!" he said. "Put everything away. Books and notes under the table. It's time to take this test."

• • •

It was the easiest test I had ever taken. Even though I was distracted by what Alex told me, I was able to get through all the questions in thirty minutes. If that was any indication of what my examinations would be like, these last few months were going to be a breeze. But for some reason, the thought didn't lighten my mood.

As my morning went on, I became more and more self-conscious about wearing Cole's jersey. I almost asked Heather if I could borrow something. I had seen the backup outfits she kept in her locker in case someone showed up wearing the same clothes as her. But if I borrowed something, I'd have to tell the girls about what happened this morning and they would freak out.

Intent on asking Cole exactly why he let me wear the jersey, I arrived at math five minutes early so I could ambush him before class started. As I stood outside the door waiting for him, someone tapped me on the shoulder.

"God," I gasped, spinning around. "You scared me to death."

"Sorry." It was Mary, Alex's ex-girlfriend, and the way her eyes narrowed made it seem as if she wasn't sorry at all. "You're Jackie, right?"

"Um, yes…" I said back.

"My name is Mary Black."

161

"Nice to meet you, Mary," I responded slowly and calmly. "Can I help you with something?"

"I really like your outfit," she said, sarcasm tainting her voice. "Very…cas-chic. Is it part of your mother's new collection?"

"I—what?"

"Oh wait," said Mary, a sick grin appearing on her face. "She's dead, isn't she?" She took a step toward me, her smile transforming into a glare. "Listen to me, new girl. Stay away from Alex. He's mine."

I was so shocked that I just stared, openmouthed.

"You got it?" she snapped angrily when I didn't respond. I nodded my head. "Good." She smirked. "It was so nice to meet you, Jackie."

As she walked away, I could only think of one thing. Not Mary's threat or Alex. Not even how angry I was with Cole, because it didn't matter. All I could think of were those four, horrible words: *She's dead, isn't she?*

Chapter 9

"Whoa, is the world ending?" I heard a familiar voice behind me. "New York skipping class?"

I was still outside the math room, sitting against a row of lockers, but now the hall was empty and class was in progress. Never in my life had I skipped a class, but Mary's words were crippling. It had taken nearly five minutes of heavy breathing just to contain my tears.

Looking up, I saw Cole coming down the hall toward me. At first I thought he was arriving at class late, but then I noticed that his letter jacket was slung over his shoulder and his backpack was nowhere in sight.

"I'm not skipping," I told him quietly. "Just a little bit late."

Cole stared at me for a second before squatting down next to me. "What's wrong, Jackie?" he asked.

"Besides the fact that I'm pissed at you for messing with my alarm clock?" I said, brushing his hand off my shoulder. "Nothing."

"I don't believe you."

"Good for you," I said, burying my face in my hands, "but that still doesn't mean I'm going to talk to you about it." Why did he always show up when I was on the verge of tears?

"If you don't want to tell me," I heard Cole say, "that's fine. But at least let me make you feel better."

"Why?" I mumbled. I wasn't really listening to what he was saying anymore. I was just trying to get through the conversation so he would leave me alone.

"It seems to be my job lately. I should add it to the description next to devastatingly handsome. Cole Walter—professional cheerer-upper and sexiest man of the year."

"I'm not in the mood, Cole," I said, sighing.

"Okay, I'll be serious," he said, swinging the truck keys in his hand. "Just come with me, and I promise that I can help you forget."

Startled by his words, I glanced up. Unlike the last time Cole found me an emotional wreck, this time I knew he was talking about my family. His face was not unkind, and the pity that I was afraid to see wasn't there. It was such a relief that I barely understood the words that came out of my mouth next.

"You mean cut class?" I asked. "With you?"

He nodded. "Why not? You're already twenty minutes late."

I looked at my watch and saw he was right. "I don't know…" I said, not really knowing what to do.

"Come on, Jackie. I promise it will be fun." He gave me a puppy-dog look. *Damn those gorgeous eyes.*

In my right mind I would never cut class, but after what had just happened with Mary, the thought of being whisked away by Cole was a nice distraction. "Fine," I said, climbing to my feet. "Lead the way."

As soon as I spotted the truck and the people sitting in the back,

I remembered the conversation I'd heard between Cole and Nick this morning. Sure enough, Cole's friend was leaning against the tailgate, and I was starting to get the impression that the frown on his face was a permanent feature. Besides Nick, I couldn't remember the names of anyone else, but they were all friends that sat with Cole at lunch.

"Cole, it's your turn to drive," said one of the girls as we approached. She had dirty blond hair with a strip dyed hot pink, and suddenly I remembered that she had come over to the Walters' house this past week to swim with Cole.

"I never would have guessed, Kate," he said, opening the tailgate so I could climb up. "Considering we're taking my car and all." Then he held out his hand and offered me a boost up.

"If you're driving," I said quietly, so the others wouldn't hear, "I'd like to ride up front."

"Of course you would." The satisfied smirk on his face almost made me change my mind, but I didn't want to sit with all the strangers. Walking around the side of the truck, I opened the passenger door and climbed in. The truck felt strangely empty without the rest of the Walters in it, but Cole didn't seem to notice as he got in next to me.

I didn't know what I was expecting, but it definitely wasn't what Kate offered me after she slid open the back window from the bed of the truck.

"Want one?" she asked me, holding out a beer.

"No," I replied instinctively. I didn't even stop to consider it.

"Yes, she does." Cole grabbed it from Kate and dropped it in my lap. "A cold beer always fixes a bad day."

"What are you doing?" I hissed at him as he started the truck.

"Making you feel better." He reached for the radio and cranked up the music.

The thought of unbuckling my seat belt and jumping out crossed my mind, because I didn't want to get in any trouble. But before I could make my decision, Cole put the truck in reverse and we were moving. At first, as we ripped out of the parking lot, I couldn't breathe. What had I gotten myself into? I let a girl I didn't even know affect me with one sentence. I'd spun out of control and now I was in an even worse situation.

But then I turned to Cole. He had the window rolled down, his arm hanging out over the side of the door, and as the song we were listening to hit the chorus, he started to shout the lyrics at the top of his lungs. I heard a few hollers join in from the back, and somehow their mood was contagious. Cole smiled, the warm sun hitting his face just right, and then I was smiling too.

"You gonna drink that?" Cole asked, pointing at the beer in my lap.

Glancing down, I stared at the can. It was melting in the warm air, trickles of cool water raced down the aluminum. Skipping school was bad enough; I didn't need to add underage drinking to my list of crimes. But then again, I was already here...

"I can't believe I'm doing this," I said and popped open my first ever can of beer.

• • •

Sal's diner was near the outskirts of town. Nick insisted on eating lunch there, because he didn't want to get caught skipping school. The service was slow even though we were the only customers, and by the time we finished our greasy burgers, my English class was starting. Next we stopped at Kate's house so she could grab more beer that she had hidden under her front porch. Our final destination was an abandoned warehouse with boarded-up windows, an hour outside of town, and when we finally arrived school was letting out. I didn't know what I was expecting—maybe someone's lake house or hunting cabin, but not somewhere so creepy. Cole assured me plenty of people hung out here when they skipped school, and that a few great parties had even been thrown here.

I didn't discount that. On the inside, the space looked as if many generations of high school students had used it. The first thing I noticed was the layer of graffiti—hearts with initials covered every inch of the walls. There were crates and camping chairs to sit on, an assortment of plastic coolers, and even an old ping-pong table. In the corner of the room was a pile of sleeping bags and blankets, along with a box that had the words "Survival Kit" written across it in Sharpie. Inside was a collection of supplies: batteries, candles, plastic cups, a bottle opener, Band-Aids, and a flashlight.

Someone had taken the time to decorate the place, probably for one of the parties. Streamers hung from the ceiling and Christmas lights lined the walls, but they didn't work because the building didn't have electricity.

I had no idea how long we'd been at the warehouse, but almost all of the sun had disappeared, and a battery-powered lantern in the middle of the floor was our only source of light. The dull illumination cast shadows on our faces, making everyone look sharp and spooky. I'd lost track of how many beers were running through my system, but they were enough to make my head buzz.

"I don't think so, guys," I said slowly, trying to clear my mind and concentrate. It was hard to think when my head felt so heavy.

"Oh, come on," Nick said with so much enthusiasm that he knocked over the row of empty bottles next to him. "You have to play!" He was quite a different person when he was drunk. More friendly.

The group was trying to get me to play spin the bottle, and I felt uncomfortable.

Cole had introduced me to everyone when we arrived—two girls and four guys—but they still felt like strangers. There was Kate, the girl with the pink streak in her hair, and her friend Molly. Then, not including Nick, two of Cole's friends from the football team had come. I couldn't remember their names, maybe Ryan and Jim, but they also could have been Bryan and Tim. Then there was Molly's little brother Joe who had a lip ring and insisted on being called Jet.

Besides the fact that everyone here was older than me, I didn't want to play spin the bottle for one huge reason. I had never been kissed. Did I really want my first one to be some sloppy, tipsy trainwreck with a boy I didn't know?

"I probably shouldn't," I said, shaking my head.

"Sounds like you're thinking too much," Kate said, grabbing me another can. It was her personal mission to make sure that there was a drink in everyone's hands at all times. When I didn't take it from her, she stuffed it into the cup holder on my chair.

"Maybe we should do something else." It was Cole. He was

lounging back in one of the camping chairs, and the way the light from the lantern hit his face, he looked sexy, dangerous.

"Why not? You love spin the bottle."

"I do, but I don't think it's Jackie's kind of game."

"What do you mean, not my kind of game?"

"You're a Goody Two-Shoes."

"Am not."

"Prove it."

In the back of my mind, I knew he was baiting me, but the alcohol made words that I normally wouldn't say come out of my mouth. "Oh, you're so on."

We all sat cross-legged on the floor in a circle and placed an empty bottle in the middle. Kate spun first, and when it landed on Ryan-Bryan, she laughed and spun again.

"Hey!" Ryan-Bryan complained. "You can't do that."

"I'm instigating an ex-girlfriend rule," she said. "I've kissed you enough to know never to do it again."

"What are you talking about? I'm a great kisser."

"Ryan, you're a biter. Seriously, what was with all the tooth action? It's not like my face is a midnight snack."

Jet was up next, and when he spun the bottle, I silently prayed that it wouldn't land on me. When it came to a stop on his sister Molly, they both made a face, and he ended up kissing Kate instead. I was beginning to understand that people just kissed whomever they wanted instead of the person the bottle actually landed on.

Then it was Cole's turn, and the bottle landed on Nick.

"Ah, hell no," Cole said, looking at his friend in disgust. Everyone laughed. "I'm going again," he said, giving the bottle another spin. It twirled on the floor in front of us, and I felt my pulse quicken. Did I want Cole to kiss me? Sure, he was attractive. There was no denying that, but I just couldn't figure him out. What if everything Alex said about him was true? Even worse, what if I was falling for him anyway? What did that say about the kind of person I was?

When the bottle started slowing, making one last circle, I realized that it was going to land on me. However, just as the nose pointed in my direction, the bottle wobbled one last time and finally stopped between Molly and me.

"Well, now what do you do?" Jim-Tim asked Cole as we all stared at the bottle. It was quiet for a moment, but then Cole answered.

"I get to pick," he said, before sweeping across the circle with a quick step and crashing his lips onto mine.

For one small moment I let him kiss me, his body pressed up against mine, and a wave of heat washed over us. Then my dulled senses kicked in. I could hear Riley's voice in my head: *That's boy's gonna eat you alive, and you won't see it coming...*

Frightened, I shoved Cole away. "Get off," I said, wiping my mouth with the back of my hand.

Cole laughed and moved back to his spot across the circle. "It's okay, Jackie," he said, winking at me. "I got what I wanted."

It was quiet. Everyone looked back and forth between Cole and me as the boom box crackled in the background.

"God, Cole," Kate said, breaking the silence. "You're such a pig."

"That's not what you were saying the other night," he shot back, without looking away from me.

"Dammnnn!" Nick jeered, covering his mouth with his hand. All of the guys were snickering.

Kate said something back, but it was like my ears had popped, and I could hardly hear what she was saying. Cole was still watching me with a look that I couldn't figure out, at least not with how my head was spinning. I needed fresh air. With some difficulty, I pushed myself to my feet.

"Jackie?" someone said, but the words were muffled, barely there.

Standing up, I realized that I was drunker than I'd originally thought. My head was throbbing as everything around me reeled. I made it to the door without falling over, even though my steps were unsteady at best. Turning the rusty handle, I pushed open the heavy door to the warehouse and stepped outside.

The pavement was uneven, broken up in chunks. As I made my way to the truck where I planned to curl up until everybody was ready to leave, I stumbled on a crack. Suddenly it was as if the earth had moved, slamming into me as I stood still, not the other way around. Laying face-first on the ground, I could taste a trickle of blood where I bit my lip, but I was too dizzy to feel the sharp bite. I rolled over onto my back and gazed up at the sky. The sun was lingering just below the horizon and the sky was royal purple, but the stars had already come out for the night. Never in my life had I seen so many clear, sparkling dots against the dark canvas.

It was then that I finally let the tears flow. I wasn't crying because my knee was surely torn up and bloody. I wasn't even crying because of Cole. The tears were for the people I missed. I wanted to hear my sister laugh at this horrible situation, my mom to yell at me for my bad behavior, and my dad to hold me tight as I cried.

The warehouse door slammed shut as someone followed me outside. The crunch of the gravel warned me of their approach, but I continued to stare up at the sky, water slowly leaking from my eyes. For the first time since arriving in Colorado, I didn't care if someone saw me cry. I was too worn out.

"Jackie, are you okay?" I couldn't see him since he was standing behind me, but I knew it was Cole.

"The sky looks like diamonds," I said instead.

"It does," he answered. His hand appeared above me, held out to help me up. I tried to lift my own hand to put in his, but it was just too heavy and my head was really spinning now. The diamonds above me were a blur.

"I like it down here," I told him, letting my hand fall back down at my side.

"Okay." Cole sat down beside me, and then, when we were closer and he could actually see my face in the dark, he added, "Is that blood?"

I winced in pain as he brought his sleeve up to my face and gently wiped the trickle away.

"Tripped," was the only word I could get out.

"I'm sorry, Jackie," Cole said then. He gently pulled me close to him, cradling my head in his lap.

I didn't know exactly what he was apologizing for. It could have been for convincing me to skip school and drink, something I had never done before. Or it could have been for kissing me. Whatever the reason, it didn't matter.

"I want to go home," I said softly.

"All right," he said, pushing back my hair. "I'll take you."

But he couldn't. Not really.

• • •

There must have been a pothole in the road, because the truck lurched forward and I fell off the backseat, snapping awake.

"Shit!" I heard Cole say from the driver's seat. "Knew I should have buckled you in."

"It's like a roller coaster," I giggled as I let my head roll back.

"Jackie, can you do me a favor and just stay right there on the floor? I don't want you getting hurt."

"Coley, don't worry about me," I told him. "It's really comfy down here."

The windows were rolled down, letting in the cool nighttime air and a chorus of chirping crickets. My toes and fingers tingled, and I smiled to myself. I was trying to remember how everything ended up so dizzy, but I only saw flashes of strange faces, an old building, and…a kiss?

The truck hit another hole, making my stomach jump.

"You good?" Cole asked.

No. My happy feeling was without doubt gone. "Nuh-uh," I said, as my insides turned. "I think I might throw up."

A few choice words hissed out of Cole's mouth, but he pulled over to the side of the road. I heard the car door slam and then Cole was helping me out. As I emptied my stomach into the bushes, he held back my hair.

"Is that it?" he asked when I stood up and wiped my mouth. "There is a strict no-puking policy in the truck."

"All better," I told him, before trying to stumble back to the truck.

"Well," Cole said, "your stomach might be empty, but you're definitely not sober."

After I got back inside and lay down on the backseat, we were quiet for a long time.

Finally Cole spoke. "We are so grounded," he said as he pulled off the road and into the driveway.

"I've never been grounded before," I told him with a yawn. I should have felt a sense of panic, but my head was too empty and exhaustion was starting to take over.

"You're in for a treat," he said, as he parked the truck. It took a moment for him to climb out and shut his door quietly, but finally mine clicked open and he helped me as I pushed myself up into a sitting position. "I need you to be quiet when we sneak in, okay?"

"Shhh!" I said, putting my finger to my lips, which were tugging up in a sleepy grin.

"Exactly," Cole said. "Now how about I help you outta there?" He put his hands around my waist, and as he lifted me from the truck, his finger brushed underneath the jersey on my bare skin.

"My legs feel funny," I said when he set me down. My knees buckled as I tried to take a step.

"Whoa there," he said, and suddenly my world tilted as Cole scooped me up in his arms. I let my eyes flutter shut as he carried me up the front path, his strong arms supporting me easily. It was a bit tricky for Cole to open the door while I was in his arms, but finally he managed to jiggle the handle enough for it to turn.

The hall light flipped on. "Care to explain what's going on?"

"Ah hell," Cole mumbled, and I opened my eyes.

"'Ah hell' is right," Katherine said. She was standing at the bottom of the staircase in her robe. It looked as if she had been waiting for us.

"Hi, Katherine," I said, lifting my head so I could smile and wave.

"Is she…?" Mrs. Walter said, trailing off in disbelief.

"Drunk?" Cole finished for her. "Yeah."

Katherine just stared at the two of us, mouth hanging open.

"Mom? What's going on?" Alex asked, appearing at the top of the stairs. Katherine closed her eyes and put a hand to her forehead in frustration. "Hello?" Alex asked again when nobody answered.

"Alex, help Jackie to her room, and then go back to sleep. Okay?" Katherine said in a non-negotiable voice.

He nodded and took me from Cole. I closed my eyes and snuggled closer to Alex, taking in the smell of his body wash.

"You stay where you are," I heard Katherine say. Cole must have tried to follow Alex up the stairs.

"Aww, come on," I heard him complain. "I was the responsible designated driver."

Alex turned the corner and headed toward my room, cutting off Katherine's response. He pushed my bedroom door open with his foot and then rubbed his back up against the wall for the light switch. Once it was on, he gently laid me on my bed and reached over to take off my shoes.

"You're only in your boxers," I said, giggling at him.

"What? Oh yeah," he said, looking down at himself as if he'd just noticed the lack of clothes. He blushed but continued to untie my laces. "Do you need a glass of water, Jackie?"

"No," I said and yawned, "but I'd like a kiss."

"Go to sleep, silly," he said before quickly pecking me on the cheek.

"Night, Alex," I told him as he turned off the light.

"Night, Jackie," he responded and shut my door.

• • •

I quickly learned that Mr. and Mrs. Walter were not afraid to punish me. The next morning I woke up to a wicked hangover and Katherine sitting on the edge of my bed.

"How are you feeling, Jackie?" she asked, offering me a Tylenol and a glass of water.

"Um, I've been better," I replied, slowly pushing myself up. My head was pounding, but I was more uncomfortable with the fact that Katherine was smiling at me.

"I don't doubt," she said with a knowing look as I popped the medicine into my mouth. "But school starts in two hours, so you need to get ready."

"Thanks," I said, nodding my head nervously as she stood up. Katherine should be yelling at me, not helping me nurse my headache.

"Of course, dear," she said, crossing my room. She dropped the bomb when she reached the door. "Oh, and, Jackie, honey? You and Cole are both grounded. Three weeks."

It meant we were restricted to the house with the exception of school, no watching TV or playing video games, and absolutely no friends. Truthfully I didn't mind that much, as I figured it would give me time to refocus my priorities. My real punishment was the guilt. I could feel it in my lungs and chest, and in the heat of my blush. Something about skipping school with Cole had been so fun, so...liberating. For a few hours, I'd forgotten about my family and what Mary had said. That thought alone was terrifying.

How could I possibly have forgotten feelings that were so painful that they felt like a permanent scar? Although spending time with Cole gave me this new, thrilling feeling I couldn't quite explain, I never wanted to forget again. My family was the force that drove me forward. I needed to refocus my attention on grades and my Princeton application.

The ride to school was awful. Every bump the truck hit was a hammer to my temple, but it wasn't just the pain that was bothering me. Most of the guys weren't angry that Cole stranded them yesterday after school, as they evidently were used to it. Isaac was bummed that Cole didn't invite him along, but when I told him how long we were grounded for, he changed his mind. Alex, however, was avoiding me. He didn't say a word to me during the drive, and when we got to school, he rushed inside without waiting for me. I knew he was mad, but he would have to face me in anatomy.

When I walked into class, Alex was sitting in our usual spot, his face blank as he stared straight ahead. I took a deep breath before crossing the room, and when I sat down, he didn't move or acknowledge my presence. Up close I noticed that his skin was pale and glistening—maybe he was nervous about getting our test back?

"So," I said after an awkward silence. "How long are you going to ignore me?"

His lips pursed, but he didn't say anything.

"Okay, fine," I said, scooping my stuff up into my arms. "If you're going to be like that, I'll sit somewhere else."

"I can't believe you skipped school with him," he said.

"It wasn't like I planned on it, Alex. It just happened."

"That's kind of hard to believe coming from Ms. I Need a Schedule for Every Second of My Life."

Okay, I was so done with this damn sibling rivalry war or whatever it was. "Alex, I know you have issues with Cole, but don't take it out on me. You can't expect me to never talk to him, and he was only trying to cheer me up."

"There's a difference between talking to him and getting drunk with him!"

"You know what, Alex?" I snapped, sick of how unfair he was being. "Maybe if your damn ex wasn't such a bitch, I wouldn't have ended up in that situation to begin with." The words tumbled of my mouth out before I realized I didn't want him to know about my confrontation with Mary.

"What?"

"Nothing. Never mind."

"No, I want to know what she said to you."

"Well, I don't want to talk about it, so just forget it."

Alex looked like he was going to argue, but then Mr. Piper appeared at the front of the room.

"Who's ready to see their grades?" he called cheerfully. Everyone groaned.

For the next fifty minutes, I barely listened to the lecture. It wasn't that I didn't try to, but I could practically feel the anger pulsing off Alex in waves, and it made me so tense that I couldn't think. When the bell rang, he shot out of his chair, not waiting for me to pack up my bag. The rest of my morning went just as terribly, and by lunchtime, I was desperate for the break.

"How you feeling?" Cole asked me as we walked out of math.

"Like shit," I grumbled, adjusting the strap on my bag so it wouldn't slide off my shoulder. "I'm never letting you talk me into doing something so stupid again."

"How about I buy you lunch to make up for it?"

I sighed. "Look, Cole, that's really nice of you. It's just…"

"Just what?"

"Alex and I are really starting to get along. He hangs out with Kim and likes the rest of my group of friends, and it just kind of makes sense, you know?"

I don't know exactly when I made up my mind to distance myself from Cole, but I think it had something to do with my fight with Alex. When I was with him, everything was so different. He didn't make me feel like that strange, adventurous girl that emerged through my cracks when I was near Cole. With Alex, I felt comfortable, not anxious. Calm, not restless.

"So what exactly are you saying?"

"It's no big secret that you guys have issues. I just think that we should, I don't know…chill out?" It was half true, but I wasn't going to tell Cole the real reason that we needed to keep our distance. The part about how being with him was so exciting that it scared me.

"Chill out?" he repeated as if he couldn't quite hear me.

"Yes, does that make sense?"

"Oh. Um—yeah, sure."

"Cool, so I'll see you later, I guess."

"Yeah, later."

• • •

I should have asked Cole for directions to the computer lab. Alex always picked me up after math class and we walked to the lunchroom together, but today he didn't show. He was probably sulking and playing *Gathering of Gods,* and I really wanted to smooth things over between us. If I didn't, I would be pissed at myself for letting a drinking mistake ruin our friendship.

Some teacher tried to point me in the right direction, but I was definitely lost. There was a wide set of double doors in front of me, which I was positive didn't lead to the computer lab, but I pulled them open anyway, not knowing what else to do. The room was huge, with rows and rows of red theater chairs. The space was dark, except for a spotlight on stage, and I realized that this must be the auditorium. I was about to turn back around when I noticed someone pacing back and forth down below.

"'O, speak again, bright angel! For thou art as glorious to this night.'" It was Danny, and he was reading from a script I knew by heart. "'Being o'er my head as is a winged messenger of heaven…'" He trailed off, leaving his line unfinished as he pulled his hair in frustration. From the way he spoke, I knew that he had every word memorized, so it must have been his line delivery that was upsetting him.

"'O Romeo, Romeo! Wherefore art thou, Romeo?'" I called down Juliet's next line, hoping to inspire him. Danny's head snapped in my direction, and he stared at me as I made my way down to the front of the stage. "'Deny thy father and refuse thy name. Or, if thou wilt not, be but sworn my love. And I'll no longer be a Capulet.'"

"'Shall I hear more,'" Danny whispered Romeo's response, "'or shall I speak at this?'" He sounded breathless—my sudden appearance was clearly a surprise.

I clapped my hands, a huge smile on my face. "*Romeo and Juliet*, huh?"

"Yeah, it's this year's spring play. I didn't know anyone else was in here with me."

He looked away from me, and I took the opportunity to study his face. He had all of the beautiful Walter facial features, but in more of a rugged way with the usual scruff covering his face. He was just as good-looking as Cole, but it was subtle—something I had to study to notice. It was a silent, softer beauty.

"Sorry, I didn't mean to interrupt," I told him as he shuffled his feet. "I was trying to find the computer lab."

"That's on the other side of the building."

"Figures," I said with a sigh. "So you're the male lead? That's pretty cool."

Danny shook his head. "Not yet. Callbacks are next week."

"Oh, I'm sure you'll get the part," I told him, as I pulled myself up onto the platform. I sat on the edge and let my feet dangle over the side. "It sounds like you have everything down."

"I don't know," he said, sounding agonized. "Something is off. I'm having a hard time getting into character and this part…" He sighed. "This is the most important play I've ever auditioned for."

"Is it your favorite or something?"

"No, but our drama teacher told us that one of his friends is coming here to watch it. She's a talent scout."

"Maybe you just need someone to read lines with," I said, trying to look casual. This was by far the longest conversation I'd had with Danny since moving in with the Walters, and I wanted to see how far I could take it. "I can help if you want."

Danny looked unsure, as if he thought I would rather give myself a paper cut. "You'd do that?" he asked.

"Well, *Romeo and Juliet* isn't my favorite Shakespeare play," I said, giving him a hard time. "But I suppose I could spare some time."

It took Danny some time to warm up to me. At first, when he spoke, his lines were clumsy. But after one run-through of the famous balcony scene, he forgot I was standing there with him. He transformed into Romeo and I was Juliet.

The bell rang, signaling the end of lunch period, and Danny shook his head as if waking from a daydream. I could see why he was the president of the drama club. Danny didn't just act out a role; he submerged himself in it until he believed he was the character.

"That went well, don't you think?" I asked, hopping off the stage.

Danny followed me down and walked me to the auditorium door. "It did. You're pretty good. Ever considered acting?"

"Heck no," I laughed. "I get way too nervous in front of crowds. I don't understand how you do it."

"What do you mean?"

"I don't know…" I said, unsure of how to verbalize what I was thinking. "You're just so—"

"Shy?" he said bluntly.

"Yeah, that."

"Most people think I'm unfriendly," Danny explained, shoving his hands in his jean pockets, "but I just have a hard time talking to people I don't know."

"Me too," I told him.

Danny gave me a look. "That's not true. You talk to everyone."

"It's not like I have much of a choice. I don't know anyone here," I said. There was a distinct note of grief in my voice, so I quickly changed the subject back to Danny. "If you have such a hard time talking to people, how do you stand up there in front of so many of them?"

"That's different."

"How?"

"For starters, I don't have to interact with them," he told me. "But also, there's something about playing a character, slipping into a different skin, that gives me this rush of confidence. It's like I know that the crowd can't judge who I am because I'm just per-forming. The person I'm pretending to be isn't really me."

"That makes sense," I said, "but why do you care what people think?" He made it sound like everyone would hate him if they got to know the real him.

Danny raised an eyebrow. "What about you?"

"Me?" I asked. "What's that supposed to mean?"

Yes, I liked to make sure I looked presentable and I was a little uptight about my grades, but those were both key ingredients in becoming a successful person. It wasn't like I avoided talking to people.

For a moment, Danny held my gaze, staring at me as if he was trying to figure something out. "Nothing," he finally said and looked away. He pushed the auditorium door open a crack, and a beam of light poured into the dark room like molten gold. "Anyway, thanks for helping me out today. It was super cool, but I should probably get to class."

"Right," I said, confused. Why was he suddenly clamping down?

"See you at home," Danny said. He slipped out into the hall, the door swinging shut behind him, and then I was alone.

Chapter 10

It was Saturday morning, and I was finally starting to feel the effects of my punishment.

"What do you mean I can't go?" Cole shouted.

Nathan and I had just gotten back from our morning run and were stretching out on the front lawn. A moment ago, Cole came storming out of the house to find his dad loading the truck with supplies: tents, sleeping bags, a box filled with pots and pans made for cooking over a fire, and other outdoorsy things.

"I didn't say you couldn't come," George replied, looking up from his work.

Danny and Isaac, who were busy strapping a canoe to the top of Katherine's van, glanced at Cole and snickered.

"Dad, I can't miss the camping trip," Cole said, his tone unyielding. "We always go—as a family."

If he thought playing the sentimental card would work, Cole was mistaken.

George snorted. "Cole, if you want to come, then come. I'm giving you a choice, so I don't see what the problem is."

The problem was that Cole didn't like either choice.

When I got home from school Friday afternoon, I found out

that Alex hadn't ditched me at lunch. He went home sick with some kind of stomach flu, although he still wasn't talking to me. The Walters were going on their annual camping trip, but since Alex was ill, Katherine wanted someone to stay home with him. If we chose not to go on the camping trip and took care of Alex, we would be released from our grounding after the weekend. On the other hand, if we decided to go on the trip, our grounding would stay the same—two more weeks of solitude.

For me, the choice was easy. I hated the outdoors and the thought of sleeping outside with bugs and the cold made me cringe. Staying home was a win-win. Cole, however, was pissed. His and Danny's birthday was in two weeks and he wasn't willing to give up his social life, family camping trip or not.

"This blows," he complained as we watched his family back out of the driveway, both cars packed full.

"Sorry," I said.

"No, you're not," he snapped, looking away from the window. "You didn't even want to go."

I knew he was only taking his frustration out on me, but it still made me flinch. "It's not like this is my fault."

"Maybe if you hadn't been so drunk…" he whispered under his breath.

"Don't you *dare* blame this on me," I hissed. "You were planning on skipping school whether or not I came."

"Whatever," he said, storming out of the room. When I heard the front door bang, I knew he was heading out to work on his car. For the rest of the day, we all avoided each other. Alex stayed in his room playing *GoG,* while Cole stayed shut up in the garage. I tried to work on some homework, but I couldn't concentrate. Instead, I camped out on the couch watching reruns of a soap opera that my mom had been addicted to. I tried to find Danny's crime show, but it must have only been on at night.

Later, Cole came in to make himself dinner. After his frozen pizza was done cooking, he plopped down on the cushion next to me.

"Sorry I blamed you before," he said. "I was pissed at my dad." Then he shoved half a slice of pizza into his mouth. A few hours of cranking on his car must have cleared his mind. That didn't mean I wanted to forgive him, though. Cole had a bad habit of taking his anger out on me, and I didn't like it. I stayed silent. He finished chewing and set down his plate with a sigh. "I was a jerk, Jackie. What else do you want me to say?"

I thought for a moment. "Give me a slice of that pepperoni. Then we're good."

After eating, we decided to watch a movie. While Cole turned on the TV, Alex wandered into the kitchen in search of dinner. He glanced at the last piece of pizza longingly before opening the pantry.

"Hey, Alex," Cole said as he sat back down on the couch. "Wanna watch a movie with us?"

I glanced up, eager to hear his response, but when Alex caught me looking, he scowled. "I'm kind of busy getting eaten by scorpion trolls at the moment, but thanks." Grabbing a bag of potato chips, he disappeared back upstairs.

Cole shrugged when we heard a door slam. "His loss. This is a great movie."

His idea of a great movie was a slasher film called *Crazy Jack*, and I knew I wouldn't be able to sleep later. I tried to tell him nonchalantly that horror movies weren't really my thing, but he called me a chicken until I reluctantly agreed. And that was how I ended up stuck on the couch with my face buried in Cole Walter's shoulder on a Saturday night, as I tried not to scream my head off. He laughed at the gore and kept hinting who was going to die next, and I tried my best to hide behind a blanket. It didn't help that a full-on thunderstorm was assaulting the house.

I peeked over the edge of the fabric. "Don't go outside!" I yelled at the stupid girl who was slowly opening the front door.

"Is Jackie scared?" Cole asked, poking me in the side.

"No," I told him, but my voice was shaky and I knew it sounded unconvincing. The rain was pounding on the window behind us.

"Yeah, you are," Cole said and chuckled. He turned his attention back to the screen just in time to see the stupid girl step outside into the dark night. Then the TV and lights flickered out.

"Oh my God! He's coming for us," I screamed and buried my face into the closest available shoulder, which happened to be Cole's.

"Not scared, huh?" he asked.

"Um, maybe a little?"

"Don't worry." He stood up from the couch and in the process pulled my protection—the flimsy blanket I had been hiding under—away from me. "The power always cuts out during big storms. Dad's been trying to fix it for years."

"Guys?" I heard Alex call out. He appeared in the kitchen, using the light of his phone to guide himself through the dark house.

"Alex, over here," Cole said. "I'm going to go see if I can get the backup generator working. Can you go find some candles in case I can't?"

"All right," Alex said and turned back around as Cole made his way to the back door.

"Wait, guys," I cried, shooting out of my seat. "Don't leave me alone."

Alex paused and glanced over his shoulder, which I took as a sign to follow him. When I caught up, he headed for the basement door. A bad feeling formed in my stomach.

"Alex?" I asked, trying not to sound nervous.

"Yeah?"

"The candles aren't in the basement, are they?"

"Yup."

"I think I'll go with Cole."

"That's fine," Alex said. "But just so you know, the backup generator is in a shed outside."

"Basement it is," I mumbled as we headed toward our doom.

• • •

"We're going to end up like the girl in the movie Cole made me watch," I told Alex as we descended into the basement.

"Did she die?" Alex asked, continuing down the steps.

"Well, not yet," I said, "but I know she will."

"So?"

"That's my point. We are *so* going to end up dead."

Alex stopped on the stairs. "Jackie, it's just the basement. Do you think we keep monsters down here?"

"No, it's just that…" I trailed off.

"You're afraid of the dark?" Alex finished for me.

I sighed. "Yeah, I guess so." I didn't used to be, but since the nightmares—I just couldn't handle the dark anymore.

"Once we get the candles it won't be as dark, okay?"

"Okay," I mumbled, not really feeling better.

When we reached the bottom, Alex grabbed my hand and pulled me to the left. I followed behind him in astonishment. This was the first real conversation we'd had since our fight, which was why his sudden contact was all the more surprising. We fought our way through a maze of cardboard boxes, and when Alex suddenly stopped, I ran straight into him.

"Sorry," I muttered.

"This is my dad's workroom," he said in response, holding his phone up so I could see. There was an outline of an open door, and then nothing. "There are always candles in here."

Alex went in, and I hesitated outside for a moment, but only until I heard an awful banging noise from somewhere else in the basement.

"Hey, Jackie, just make sure you don't—"

"Oh my God, what was that?" I burst out, before dashing inside and slamming the door behind me.

"—shut the door," Alex finished.

"What?" I squeaked.

"Don't shut the door," he repeated with a sigh. He rattled the handle, but the door wouldn't budge.

"Are we locked in?" I asked, horrified.

"It looks like it," he said. "It's been broken for as long as I can remember."

"What are we going to do?" I asked.

"Hold on a sec," he said.

He shuffled around the room, opening and closing cabinets until I heard him strike a match. A candle came to life, filling the room with light.

"Much better," Alex said.

"Now what?"

"Texting Cole to come get us out," he said, walking around the small room while holding up his phone. "Crap. I can't find any service." He snapped it shut and shoved it back in his pocket.

"I left mine upstairs," I said, feeling guilty.

"It's okay. You didn't know."

"So what are we going to do?" I asked.

"We'll have to wait until Cole finds us, but in the meantime..."

He grabbed a wooden barrel and placed it in the middle of the room. The candle was put in the center, and he pulled two chairs up, making a table for us to sit at. Then he went over to one of the cabinets and started searching through the shelves.

"Now what are you doing?" I asked him, carefully sitting down on the rickety folding chair.

"Looking for these!" he said, grinning like he'd won the lottery. In his hands was a beat-up deck of cards. He came back over to the table, pulling them out of the flimsy cardboard box as he walked. "I use to sit in here and watch my dad fix things when I was a little kid. When he got frustrated with something he couldn't fix, he would pull these out and teach me to play different card games."

"So your dad fixes stuff but never thought to repair the lock on the door?"

"He's tried." Alex sat down, and the candlelight made shadows flicker across the angles of his face. "I never said he was good at it, and the man's way too stubborn to replace the handle, so more often than not, we just ended up playing cards."

"That's nice," I said, cocking my head so I could see the image on the back of the cards. It looked familiar, and sure enough, when Alex held them up for me to examine, the New York skyline was plastered there. The reminder of home was so unexpected that my chest went tight. "I wish my dad could have taught me stuff like that when I was little."

"Why didn't he?" Alex asked. He was shuffling now, his hands moving back and forth as he blended the deck together.

I gripped the edge of the barrel, trying to think of the best way to answer. In all honesty, my dad didn't have much time when I was growing up. Sebastian Howard was a busy man with lots of work, and whenever he came home, it was only to lock himself in his office. I looked away from Alex. I wanted nothing more than to be sincere, but the last thing I needed was to give the Walters another reason to feel sorry for me.

I shrugged and said, "We weren't much of a game family. Watching movies was more our thing."

Alex leaned in. "I'll teach you something," he said.

He dealt quickly, explaining the rules as he went. Picking up my hand, I decided that the cards were older than I'd originally thought. Each one was bent and grubby. The ace of spades was sticky with what looked like grape jelly, and I could feel the grime on my fingers.

For my first few turns, I concentrated on grasping the rules and nothing more. Occasionally I would ask Alex about one of his moves and he would answer, but other than those few words, we played silently. He won the first round, but by then I'd caught on to the strategy and was confident that I could beat him in the next round. This time I dealt, and after arranging my hand, I asked Alex the question that had been bothering me since this morning.

"So, are you still mad at me?" I asked as he reached for the top card from the remaining deck. He paused and looked up at me. "Because if you are, now's a pretty good time to talk about it."

"I guess not," he said. Then, after a long moment, "But I would really like to know what Mary said to you."

"This is about you and me, not her."

Before anything more could pass between us, I heard a distant shout.

"Where the hell are you guys?" It was Cole from somewhere in the basement.

Alex rushed over to the locked door. "Over here," he shouted.

After a few minutes of searching in the dark, Cole found the key his dad kept on a hook outside the workroom and unlocked it. His hair was still dripping from the rain and his shirt clung to his shoulders, revealing the definition of muscle beneath, but he hadn't been able to get the power back on.

Much to my annoyance, as we headed back upstairs with a few candles in hand, Alex told Cole how I'd locked us in the workroom.

"Don't worry, Jackie," Cole said, still laughing at me as we stepped into the kitchen. "We'll protect you from all those scary monsters."

"Oh yeah?" I said, a little grumpy. "What are you going to do? Stand guard outside my room all night?"

"Nope." He pointed to the living room. The floor was covered with sleeping bags and piles of blankets and pillows. "I thought we could all sleep down here since the power is still out."

Alex turned to Cole, grinning from ear to ear. "Good idea."

Cole's signature smirk was plastered across his face. "Yeah," he said, "I know."

"Awesome," I said, trying to keep my voice steady. On a scale of burned toast to global warming, this was a disaster. In my head, I could picture Heather melting to the floor in joy, but after a month of living with the Walters, I knew better. These boys were pure trouble.

In the end, I managed to snag the couch. Cole and Alex fought over the love seat, and it was no surprise when Cole came out victorious, leaving Alex to make himself comfortable on reclining chair.

I had just finished arranging my pillows when Cole started to unbuckle his belt. "What are you doing?" I hissed, and averted my eyes.

"I sleep in my boxers," he said, stepping out of his pants as he bit back a grin. Next he tugged off his shirt, revealing his photo-shopped abs. "It's okay if you stare," he said, plopping down on the small sofa. He stretched out, and his long legs dangled over the edge of the armrest. "I don't mind."

"I was not staring," I snapped at him.

"Yeah, Cole," said Alex, who, after watching his brother for a few hesitant moments, made the decision to yank off his shirt as well. "Not every girl is obsessed with you."

"All I'm saying," Cole said, wiggling down into the cushions, "is that Jackie wasn't looking at your scrawny self when you pulled off your shirt."

"Would you both be quiet?" I said, thankful for the cover of darkness that hid my blush. And for some amazing reason, the boys actually listened to me, both falling silent as we settled into our makeshift beds for the night.

My muscles were tired from the long day, and I thought I would drop off instantly, but I lay there wide awake, unable to close my eyes. I was exceedingly aware of Cole and Alex, one on either side of me. I was so tense, that when a drop of water hit my forehead, I nearly screamed.

"Jackie?" Alex said, his voice sleepy. "What's wrong?"

"I think the ceiling is leaking," I said, holding my hand out in the air. Sure enough, after a few more seconds of waiting with my palm outstretched, I felt a cool splash against my skin.

"I'll get a bucket," Alex said. With a yawn, he scooted off the chair and made his way into the kitchen.

"Here, Jackie," Cole said, standing up. He picked his pillow and blankets up off the sofa.

"Don't worry about me," I told him as I spread my blanket out on the living room floor. "I'll be fine."

Not surprisingly, he didn't listen, and soon he had a bed laid out on the ground right next to me. He flopped down, and I could practically feel him lying there, his arm inches from mine. *Can you please move over?* sat on the tip of my tongue, but I refused to say anything, not wanting to admit that he had an effect on me.

"What's going on?" Alex asked when he came back from the kitchen with a mixing bowl in his hand.

"Couldn't let the lady sleep on the floor by herself," Cole responded. "Not with all those psycho murderers on the loose."

"Dang it, Cole," I said, hitting him with a pillow. "It's not funny." I'd managed to forget about the movie until he brought it up again. Now I would never get to sleep.

Alex paused and glanced between his bed for the night and the empty carpet on my right-hand side. "Oh," he said. He arranged the bowl on the couch to catch the leak before returning to the recliner.

From the floor, I had a full view of the raging storm through the window. There wasn't much to see, but every time lightning flashed, I expected to see Crazy Jack standing there with a meat cleaver. I told myself to close my eyes, but I couldn't look away as my chest pounded.

"Cole?" I finally asked, my voice squeaky.

"Uh-huh?"

"Could you close the blinds?" I was past caring if he made fun of me.

"Sure," he said, getting up slowly. He pulled on the curtain cord but had to yank it around a few times before the shades tumbled down. Once they settled in place and I could no longer see outside, I finally let out the breath I was holding.

"You know," Cole said, as he lay back down, "I think the only reason you wanted me to get up was so you could see my perfectly toned abs again."

"Cole," Alex and I said at the same time, "shut up."

He chuckled, but then it was finally silent again. So quiet, in fact, that I could hear the ping of water droplets as they fell into the bowl on the couch. Next to me, Cole had already dozed off, a soft wheezing sound escaping his lips as he breathed in and out. There was a creak of springs as Alex moved on the recliner, but then I saw his shape moving around in the dark.

"What's wrong?" I whispered. He dropped his blanket to the floor.

"The chair's uncomfortable," he responded. I could tell from the way he stood there awkwardly that he was waiting for permission to lie down.

"Okay," I told him.

That seemed to be enough, because a second later Alex was stretching out next to me, and not long after that he was out. In their sleep, both boys kept moving closer to me, and when I finally drifted off, there was one arm wrapped around my stomach and one hand intertwined with mine.

• • •

Sunday passed quickly. The boys called Will in the morning and he came over to fix the power. Once it was back on, Cole spent what little time he could watching ESPN before his parents got home. Alex tried to tempt me into playing *GoG*, but I wasn't willing to break Katherine and George's rules. I stayed in my room reading until my phone rang.

"Sammy?" I asked, picking up immediately when I saw her name on the caller ID.

"Hey, girly," she said. "What you up to?"

"Not much," I said, pushing away from my desk and moving to the bed. I collapsed on the comforter and switched the phone to my other ear. "Just doing some anatomy homework for next week."

"Ugh, typical Jackie," Sammy criticized. I could practically see her sitting on the fuzzy pink rug in our dorm room, painting her toenails. "You're living with a bunch of hot guys, and instead of finding Cole and experiencing some real-life anatomy, you're shacking up with a textbook like a pariah."

"It's not like I never see him," I told her. "I mean we did sleep together last night."

"*You what?*"

"Okay, wait," I said, backtracking. "That came out all wrong."

But Sammy was already in full-on rant mode. "My best friend went and got herself de-virgin-fied and you didn't think to call me, like…this morning? Seriously, you moved away and poof! I don't hear from you until five years later and—"

"Oh my God, no!" I said, shouting into the phone.

"'No' to what? The five years part, because it's honestly starting to feel like that. The next thing you know, I'll be stalking your Facebook just to see if you're still alive."

"Would you stop being such a drama queen?"

"Are you kidding me?" she said, clearly upset. "This situation is totally eligible for full-on drama status!"

"Sammy," I said, lowering my voice so nobody could hear me. "Can you just chill out? I didn't de-virgin myself or whatever."

"Sex, Jackie. We're talking about sex!"

"Yeah," I said. "I know what we're talking about, and I didn't do that."

"Oh," she said after a long pause. "Then what *are* you talking about?"

"When I said 'slept,' I meant we fell asleep in the same vicinity."

"Well, that is totally less newsworthy. Mr. Elvis sleeps with me when he can't get comfy on his doggy bed, and then he makes these little farts that stink up the whole room, but you don't hear me blabbing on about it."

"I'm not the one blabbering," I said. "And I don't know, it just—it feels kind of big to me. I don't know what to do about him, Sammy."

"It's not what you do *about* him. It's what you do *with* him. Grab him by those big, manly arms that I'm assuming he has, and show him what New York has to offer."

"Okay, can you please be serious for a moment? I'm really confused here," I told her. "I try to ignore him, but then he does something cute like, I don't know, taking me on a tour of the ranch to cheer me up, and I just—argh!" I grabbed my pillow and flung it across the room.

Sammy sighed. "All right, I'm sorry. I got a little excited to finally hear from you."

"A little excited?"

"Do you want to talk about your Cole issues or not?"

"That's the thing. I don't want to have Cole issues. I just want to get through these next few years and come home."

"So for the next two years of high school, you're never going to have a boyfriend?"

"I don't know."

"Jackie, just because you're leaving eventually doesn't mean you can't get to know people."

"I'm not afraid of forming relationships, Sammy—it's just him."

"Why?"

"Because he's a complete chauvinist. When we go to school, it's like he has a different girl to make out with every period." In reality that was just an excuse. The real reason why I was frightened by whatever was going on between Cole and me was too hard to admit.

"Okay," she said, thinking out loud, "so he's a bit of a man-whore. But, honey, trust me when I say that can be fixed. You should focus on the positive things. It sounds like he can be sweet when he wants to be."

"It's not just that. It's…" I trailed off, still struggling to say what I was thinking.

"It's what?"

"How can I even have these feelings?" I asked, squeezing my eyes shut. "That shouldn't even be okay since—"

"Since what?" she snapped. "Since your family's accident? Are you never allowed to love someone again because of that?" The anger in her voice caught me off guard.

"No, I didn't mean it like that, but…" I paused and took a breath. "Don't you think it's too soon?"

"God, Jackie, no!" Sammy gasped, horrified. "It's not like there are rules detailing the right way to mourn. Being in a relationship might be a good thing."

"How?"

"It could help you heal," she said, "And, I don't know…move on?"

I nodded my head and told Sammy, "Yeah, okay," even if I didn't mean it. Why was she acting like I needed to be fixed? I was here in Colorado, living my life. I didn't need a relationship to heal or whatever, and I most definitely didn't need Cole.

• • •

On Monday, we all piled out of the truck when we got to school. Danny and I had to wait for everyone to grab their backpacks because ours were at the bottom of the pile.

"So, how was being grounded?" Danny asked.

It was the first thing he'd said to me since our afternoon in the auditorium. He wasn't ignoring me per se—he'd nodded at me this morning when we ran into each other in the hallway—and I had accepted that Danny was a silent type.

"Good." I was pleasantly surprised that he actually started a conversation with me. We were making progress! "The lights went out, but I got a bunch of homework done," I said. Danny slung his backpack over his shoulder and nodded his head. "How was your weekend?" I asked, trying to keep the conversation going as we made our way into the building.

"I don't like camping."

"Really?" I asked, and my voice pitched up, revealing my surprise. I thought all of the Walter boys enjoyed the outdoors. After all, they grew up on a ranch.

"All those creepy, crawly bugs freak the crap out of me," he said.

I choked, thinking for a moment that he was being serious.

"I'm kidding," he said quickly, but it was hard to tell because his face was so serious. "About the bugs, at least. I'm more of an indoors kind of guy."

"You live in the middle of nowhere," I pointed out.

He shrugged. "My drama class went on a field trip to Chicago freshman year, and it just felt right. I'd rather live in the city."

"Yeah, there's something about all those people, the busy streets, and the movement—it makes you feel alive." Danny was gazing at me now with a look I couldn't quite decipher, so I went on. "If you enjoyed Chicago, you'll love New York."

"New York," he repeated slowly.

"Yeah," I said. "It's the best place in the world."

"I got the part," he said, suddenly changing the subject.

I blinked. "Oh, right," I finally responded, realizing he was talking about *Romeo and Juliet*. "Congratulations, Danny. That's great news."

"Thanks," he said, and then he was gone, disappearing into crowded hallway.

Chapter 11

The next two weeks passed quickly, the days blending together. But today was different. When I got home from school, I went straight for the kitchen, which had been transformed into a bakery since we left this morning. Mrs. Walter was pulling a pan of cookies out of the oven—I had been able to smell them from the front porch—and four whole sheets of warm, gooey goodness were already waiting on silver cooling racks.

"Hi, Jackie," she said, scooping a few cookies up with a spatula. "How was your day?"

"It was good," I answered automatically. "Those smell *amazing*. What's the occasion?"

"Thanks, honey." She placed half a dozen cookies on a plate. "It's the twins' turn to bring a snack to their soccer game tomorrow. Speaking of the twins, can you go find them for me? I haven't seen them in hours."

"Sure," I said. "Which ones?"

"Oh!" Mrs. Walter laughed. "Zack and Benny. Here, take these with you."

She handed me the plate, and I made my way to the monsters' room, glad that I had a peace offering. As soon as I reached the top of the stairs, Zack poked his head out the door.

"Are those chocolate chip?" he asked me.

"Yup," I said, holding the plate over my head and out of reach. I was amazed he hadn't smelled them before now—the entire house smelled like cookies. "Before I give you any, I need to know where Benny is."

"In here," Zack said, grabbing my free hand and tugging me inside his room. "He's here with Parker. Guys, Jackie has cookies!"

In a matter of seconds, both boys and Parker were circling around my legs, demanding baked goods, and I felt like a swimmer swept out into open water.

"Okay, okay!" I said, laughing nervously.

After grabbing a cookie to make sure I got one, I set the plate down and backed away for my own safety. They inhaled everything within minutes, and I was almost surprised they didn't eat the plate.

"So, Jackie," Parker said, licking her fingers clean. "Do you know how to play Mario Kart, or are you too girly to like video games?"

The twins were already gone, probably off to beg their mom for more, and I decided this was the perfect opportunity to get to know Parker better. Since I'd moved in, Parker had made it obvious that she didn't like me. She was always making comments about how girly I was, as if that was some kind of crime, and one time she purposely spilled Kool-Aid on my favorite skirt. If only I could find some common ground between us, I might be able to connect with her. I didn't know much about being an older sister, but I always loved when Lucy let me win at games.

"I think I can handle it," I told her, plopping down in one of the beanbags. "But I want a controller without chocolate on it."

While she was setting up our race, Parker took the time to explain the game to me, pointing out which button did what. Later, when Bowser sped over the finish line just ahead of Princess Peach, Parker punched her hand into the air. "Yes!" she shouted, jumping up in excitement. "I win again!"

"Wow, you're too good at this," I told her, trying to hold back a smile.

"Not really," Parker said as she rolled her eyes at me. "I just don't drive like a girl."

"Parker?" Alex asked, sticking his head in the room. When he spotted her, he said, "There you are. Mom wants you downstairs."

"Fine," she responded, tossing her controller on the floor. "I was getting bored with kicking butt anyway."

We both watched her go, and after she slammed the door shut, Alex turned to me. "Hey, Jackie," he said. "What are you doing in here?"

"Trying to bond," I sighed, twisting the game cord around my finger. "Something I'm evidently not very good at. I don't think she likes me."

Alex considered this as he came into the room. "It's not that she doesn't like you," he said, sitting down next to me. "I just think she isn't used to having another girl in the house."

"You'd think she'd be excited," I said, sinking back into the beanbag in disappointment. "After having to put up with so many boys her whole life, I expected that she'd want to spend some decent girl time."

"If you haven't noticed, Parker isn't really a girly girl." He picked up the controller his sister had tossed to the floor and wiped away a chocolate smear.

I shot him a look. "I realize that, but I want her to like me. We're kind of outnumbered around here."

"Well, that's never going to change, no matter how close you two get," he said. "Just let it go. She'll get used to you eventually."

"Yeah, I guess."

"How about we play a quick race and you show me what you got?"

"All right," I told him, sitting back up. "But don't go easy on me."

"I would never," he said, twirling the controller in his hand. "I want to beat you fair and square."

"Good luck," I told him, as we both chose our characters.

"Don't need it." His forehead was scrunched up as he focused on the TV.

The game started again to the sound of twirls and bangs, and unlike last time, my kart was the first to cross the finish line.

Alex chucked his controller. "Unbelievable!" he yelled.

I winked at him. "Told you you'd need some luck."

He narrowed his eyes, suspicious of my newfound racing skills, and asked, "Go again?"

"If you want to lose a second time."

"You're so going down," he said, a determined look on his face.

Unfortunately for Alex, I was the champion of Mario Kart. For the next thirty minutes, I beat him using every single character. It was too easy—Lucy had been obsessed with the game when we were kids, and we spent every day after school racing.

"You know, I was just letting Parker win to be nice," I told him, when he finally gave up.

"I realize that," he said, his pride damaged. "You're not allowed to tell anyone."

"Says who?"

"Me. That's confidential information."

"Does it matter that much?"

"You don't understand," he tried to explain. "I'm the king of video games. Nobody beats me, not ever." Alex shook his head in disbelief.

"You've been dethroned," I said, wiggling my eyebrows at him. "And I did it all with Princess Peach."

As if in a daze, he shook his head and looked up at me. For a second I thought he was mad, but then he said, "You know you're adorable, right?" Then, he clamped his hand over his mouth as he realized what he'd said.

I smiled. "You're not so bad yourself."

Alex was blushing now, and he looked away, his lips mashed together in a small line, clearly upset with himself. I thought he was going to leave, but then he took a deep breath and did something I never expected him to—he kissed me.

It started out slow and gentle, his lips soft. It took me a moment to react, but when I did, I wrapped my arms around him and wove my fingers into his blond hair. I could hear my pulse roaring in my ears—I was kissing Alex! I'd never thought about kissing him before because he'd always seemed like just a friend, but there was a warm feeling in my chest that bloomed, twisting its way down my arms and legs like a vine, indicating otherwise.

Sammy had told me horror stories about kissing. She referred to one ex-boyfriend as the Snake. He liked to flick his tongue out like a whip, jabbing her repeatedly in the mouth when they made out. Then there was the fling who was so sloppy, she said, that it was like making out with an overripe pear. Since then, I was terrified of my first real kiss. What if whomever I was kissing thought something bad like that about me? But now, in the moment, those thought melted away. Alex's lips against mine, his hand cupping my face, felt good.

He pulled away to look at me, and I saw that his blue eyes were filled with doubt. I offered him a reassuring smile, and a cheesy grin crept onto his face before he pulled me into another kiss. This one was less careful, more eager. Looping his arm around my back, he pushed me down into the beanbag and pressed his body to mine.

"Hey, Jackie?" Cole asked, opening the door, "Parker said you were in here—"

Alex leaped away from me, but Cole still stopped to gape at us.

For a moment, nobody said anything.

Then Alex scrambled to his feet. "I can leave if you two need to talk," he said, scratching the back of his head in embarrassment.

"Don't bother," Cole said flatly. "You two are clearly busy." He looked at me one last time before slamming the door.

• • •

Breakfast the next morning was interesting, to say the least. Cole glowered at me over his cereal bowl, making it difficult for me to concentrate on spreading jam on my toast. I dropped the knife to the floor, and a glob of strawberry goo splattered on the linoleum.

"You okay, Jackie?" Nathan asked, bumping his hip against me to get my attention. We were standing next to each other at the counter, me with my breakfast, and him with a brown paper bag he was packing for lunch.

"Yeah, just a bit tired." That was a lie, but I wasn't going to tell him the truth with Cole listening. The fact was, I was wired. Last night, I hadn't been able to sleep at all, yet I felt like I had chugged a whole pack of Alex's Kickstarts. I couldn't stop thinking about my kiss with him, and what it would mean for our friendship. What if Alex suddenly got weird and didn't want to hang out with me anymore? I didn't want to lose him as a friend, not to mention that seeing him every day around the house would be awkward. Our spur-of-the-moment make-out session was suddenly starting to feel like a bad thing.

"Okay, just make sure you don't forget that after school my mom is picking us up."

"What?" I asked, looking up sharply. "Why?"

He glanced at Cole before quickly looking back to me and whispering, "Birthday shopping, remember?"

"Oh."

After what happened the previous night, I'd completely forgotten that tomorrow was Cole and Danny's birthday, and I needed to get them both a present. But as we left for school, I had a feeling that Cole didn't want anything except for me to keep my distance. Normally he made a point of offering me a ride with Nick, and in turn, I always said no. But today he shoved past me as everyone made their way out the front door, not even bothering to look in my direction. He was gone before I could even move off the porch steps, Nick's black Porsche snaking down the driveway.

All day long during class, I tried to think of something good to get him, something that would fix the problem between us. But in all honesty, what could I possibly buy that said, "Sorry you saw me kissing your brother"? The more I thought about it, the more upset I got. Cole had no right to be mad with me. It wasn't like we were dating.

Besides, I convinced myself as I emerged into the sunlight after my final class period, I didn't have time to deal with Cole. Something was definitely going on between Alex and me. We didn't talk about it in anatomy because I was too nervous, but he offered me a huge smile when I walked into class. Hopefully that meant things hadn't changed between us, and we could forget about the whole kissing thing and just go back to being friends. Then I could pretend it had never happened.

"Hi, kids," Katherine said, rolling down the window as I walked up to the van. Looking over my shoulder, I saw that Alex, Nathan, and Lee were right behind me, backpacks slung over their shoulders.

"Shotty!" Lee called, pushing me out of the way as he yanked open the front door and hopped inside.

"That was rude, Lee," Katherine told him, but her nephew wasn't listening. Lee was already fiddling with the radio, flipping through the stations until he found something he liked.

"It's okay," I assured Katherine, and slid open the back door. "I'm fine sitting wherever."

Alex and I ended up in the middle seats, while Nathan took the far back. Like usual, Isaac was a no-show. Once we were all buckled in, Katherine pulled out of the school parking lot, turning in the direction of the highway. It was a fifteen-minute drive to the mall, and as everyone piled out after parking, Katherine gave us some instructions.

"Remember, kids, Zack and Benny have a soccer game tonight so we have to be quick. Everyone needs to be back here in half an hour with your gifts or you're walking home. And please," she said, sighing, "no inappropriate presents this year."

Lee was gone before Katherine even finished speaking, and Alex hurried off so he had time to stop at his favorite video-game store after picking out his brothers' gifts. Not knowing the layout of the mall and still clueless about what to get Cole, I followed along with Nathan.

"In here," he said, strolling into an electronics store. He led me through the rows of TVs, computers, and other gadgets with purpose, as if he knew exactly where he was going. He did. We came to a stop in front of a sleek, voice-controlled radio.

"Cole's been eyeing this all year," Nathan said. "He wants to install it in the car he's been restoring." He turned over the price tag. "Dang. I was hoping this would go on sale since the new version came out."

"How about we go in on it together?" I suggested.

"Jackie, I can't even pay for half of this," he said. "Besides, I still have to get something for Danny."

"Don't worry about it, Nathan," I said, thinking of the credit card in my wallet. "Just pay for what you can."

He shook his head. "I can't do that, Jackie. That's not fair."

"I have more than enough," I told him. When he still didn't look convinced, I added, "Besides, you're totally helping me out. I had no clue what to get for Cole when we got here today. I can't take all the credit."

"Are you sure?" he said, glancing back down at the price tag.

Grabbing the box off the shelf, I nodded my head. "Absolutely."

• • •

The next morning, someone knocked on my door before my alarm went off.

"Come in!" I called, sitting up in bed.

"Morning, Jackie," Nathan said, stepping inside. In his hands was the present we'd bought for Cole, already wrapped up in blue wrapping paper.

"Morning, Nathan, what's up?" I asked.

"I just came to tell you that I'm not running this morning. My mom always makes blueberry pancakes when it's someone's birthday, and we watch them open their presents."

"Presents in the morning?" I asked, jumping out of bed.

"Yeah," he said with a frown. "Still don't have something ready for Danny?"

Yesterday, after we purchased the sound system for Cole, Nathan bought Danny the first season of his favorite crime show, *The Blood Trails*, which I recognized from the nights we both couldn't sleep. But the gift that I wanted to get for Danny was something I couldn't buy at the mall, and I had planned on arranging it after school.

"No," I told him, throwing open my closet. "Is there a printer somewhere that I can use?"

"Sure, there's one in my room," Nathan told me. "See you at breakfast."

I rushed about the room changing out of my pajamas and packing my bag for school. Then I turned on my computer and waited for it to wake up. Once it had, I pulled out my credit card and bought Danny's gift before rushing to Nathan's room to print it out. There wasn't time to make a birthday card and I didn't have a gift bag, so I folded the piece of paper in half and headed down to the kitchen.

"Good morning, Jackie," Katherine greeted me as I came in. She was standing at the stove flipping pancakes and directing George on how to squeeze fresh orange juice. By the looks of it, he was successful at getting more juice on the counter than in the pitcher.

"Morning," I said back.

Danny and Cole were already sitting at the table, a pile of presents in front of them. Standing right next to them were Zack and Benny, fingers itching to tear open the gifts.

"Happy birthday, guys," I said offering them both a smile.

"Thanks, Jackie," Danny said and grinned at me for the first time ever. Cole merely nodded his head.

Mostly everyone was already sitting at the kitchen table except for Jack and Jordan who were setting up their camera so they could film the opening of presents. I was surprised to see Will leaning against the counter and even more surprised to see a girl standing in his arms, her head resting against his chest.

I sat down next to Nathan as Katherine brought a huge plate of bacon to the table. "Is that Haley?" I whispered in his ear, looking over at the girl who had black hair and big, round eyes.

"Yeah, Will's fiancée. They go to school together."

"That's what I thought," I said. Since moving in with the Walters, I had heard lots of talk about the upcoming wedding.

Once everyone was stuffed to the brim with Katherine's wonderful cooking, the boys started unwrapping their gifts. Cole went first, and when he got to Nathan's and my present, he looked up in amazement.

"You got this for me?" he asked Nathan in shock. "I've been wanting it for ages."

"Jackie and I got it," Nathan said, correcting Cole. "You're welcome."

Hearing my name, Cole hesitated, but then he nodded his head at me. "Thanks."

"No problem," I said.

Then it was Danny's turn. He unwrapped all the boxes, which turned out to be mostly clothes, except for the homemade coupon for one free wet willy, courtesy of Jack and Jordan.

"What's a wet willy?" I asked as most of the guys laughed at the joke I'd clearly missed.

Jack's lips curled up into an evil smile. "Let me show you." He stuck his finger in his mouth and then, as quick as lightning, stuck it in my ear.

"Oh God, gross!" I complained, shoving Jack away from me.

All the guys laughed as Katherine scolded her son and I tried to get Jack's spit out of my abused ear.

"Wet willy," Isaac said, grinning at me. "A prank where a finger moistened with spit is inserted into an unsuspecting victim's ear, accompanied by a twist."

"That's disgusting," I said. Then I handed over Danny's gift, still cringing. "I promise that I didn't get you something as awful as that."

"Jackie, you didn't need to get me anything," he said, but he took the folded piece of paper anyway. He opened it, and I kept my mouth shut as his eyes slid over the words.

"Are you serious?" Danny asked when he finally looked up at me. I nodded. "Totally."

"Wow," Danny said, shaking his head in amazement. "Thank you so much, Jackie."

"What is it?" Cole demanded and pulled the sheet of paper out of Danny's hand. When he read it, his mouth dropped open. "Whoa."

"Let's see," Isaac said, grabbing it away from Cole. Then, "A plane ticket?" he asked, looking up at me.

"Well, not exactly. It's a voucher for a plane ticket. Danny said he likes the city, and he's never been to New York, so I figured he could come with me when I go home for a visit this summer. You know, maybe go to a few Broadway shows."

Katherine gasped in surprise. "Jackie, honey," she said, clucking her tongue, "that's too much money to spend on a birthday present."

"Mom," Danny said, giving her a look.

"Really, it's not a problem," I told her.

"Are you sure?" she asked, but she knew that the money wasn't an issue.

I nodded my head and noticed that everyone was staring at me. "What?" I asked.

"My birthday's tomorrow," Isaac responded.

"Liar," Jack accused, crossing his arms.

Isaac elbowed his cousin but grinned. "I never lie, and you best get me something good. No slimy spit finger in my ear, okay?"

"Maybe we can arrange for some bleach to end up in your shampoo," Jordan said. "I always thought you'd look good as a blond."

"Boys," Katherine cut in, giving her sons a warning glare.

"Hey, Jackie?" someone said, pulling on my sleeve. I looked down to see Benny staring up at me.

"Yeah?" I asked.

"Can you get me a puppy for my birthday?" he asked. Everyone laughed.

. . .

"That was such a cool present," Alex told me when we were sitting in anatomy.

"Thanks," I said quietly.

The ride to school had been slightly uncomfortable. For once in his life, Danny couldn't shut up. He wouldn't stop talking about how awesome his present was, and everyone seemed jealous of him. I was starting to think that maybe the ticket had been too much after all.

"Truthfully," Alex whispered excitedly, "besides the Xbox we all got for Christmas last year, that was best thing anyone has ever gotten."

"Really?" I asked, feeling even guiltier. I didn't want Mrs. Walter to be mad at me for getting her son a better gift then she could afford.

Alex nodded his head. "Flying to New York is going to be so fun."

I finally giggled. "What's so fun about flying?"

"I don't know," Alex said, grinning at me. "I always thought it would be fun."

My smile dropped. "You've never been on a plane before?"

"Nope."

"Don't you guys ever go on vacation?" I asked.

"Yeah, we go camping all the time. Oh, and last year my parents saved up enough money to go to Florida for their twenty-first anniversary, but they drove down."

At the moment, I felt unbelievably spoiled. Back home in New York, when it got really cold, my mother would take me to Miami for the weekend to soak up some sun. I never even considered Florida a vacation.

"Why? Where did your family go on vacation?" Alex asked me.

For a second I didn't say anything. I didn't want to tell Alex that I had been all over Europe, South America, and even China.

"Oh, you know, just around," I said, shrugging my shoulders.

"Oh, come on. Tell me," Alex said and elbowed me in the side. When I didn't answer, he frowned. "What's wrong?" he asked.

"I guess I just feel awkward. I didn't know this was going to be such a big deal. Everyone seemed kind of jealous." And I don't know how to act around you anymore, I wanted to add, but I kept my mouth shut.

"Jackie," Alex responded, staring at me seriously, "what you did for Danny was thoughtful, and sure, some people are probably jealous, but that's not a bad thing."

"You sure?" I asked, looking up at him.

"Yup," he said. "It also means that I expect something cool for Christmas."

I laughed. "And what would that be?"

"Just a Darth Vader helmet, dual signature edition."

"What's that?"

"Nerd shit," he said with a laugh. "And only one of the most expensive pieces of Star Wars memorabilia in the world."

"Well, it sounds like you'll have to be awfully nice to me."

"How about I start by taking you somewhere fun tonight?"

My heart almost burst from my chest. He didn't mean like on a date, did he? "Where?" I finally asked him, not bothering to meet his eyes. Instead, I concentrated on my anatomy notebook, flipping to a blank page and writing the date in the right-hand corner.

He paused at this. "I know someone who's having a party tonight," Alex said, trying to sound casual. "We should go together." When he saw the hesitation on my face, he added, "You know, as friends."

I thought that hearing those last few words would help me relax around him, but when my stomach dipped, I realized that maybe that wasn't what I wanted after all. What if I just needed to give Alex a chance?

I was about to say yes, that I would go with him, but there was something about the way he was avoiding my gaze that made me suspicious. "Whose party is it?" I said instead.

"Mary's," he said in a rush. "But I thought that if you told me what she said, we could work everything out."

I shook my head. "Sorry, Alex, but no." Maybe I needed to

stop thinking of all the bad things that would happen if there was something more between Alex and me, maybe I needed to give him a chance, but I wouldn't do it at *her* party. Not after what she'd said, how she'd hurt me. There was nothing Alex could do to get me to go.

"Please, Jackie? I don't get why you're making such a big deal out of this."

"If I tell you what she said, will you drop the subject?" I snapped.

"Of course," he said eagerly.

"She shoved my family's death in my face."

"What? Why would she do that?"

"To hurt me," I said, "because I'm friends with you."

Chapter 12

After school, Katherine had a meal waiting for us. We all sat down and ate together, no snakes included.

"Someone want to get me some more milk?" Isaac asked, holding up an empty cup.

George raised an eyebrow. "What happened to your legs? No one here is your butler."

"Jackie?" Benny asked me then. "Did you have butters to serve your food at dinnertime?"

Isaac, who was trying to chug from Cole's glass before he noticed, spit milk all over the table in laughter.

"No, Benny," I said. "We did not have any *butlers*."

"Hey!" Cole complained, noticing his empty glass in Isaac's hand. "That was my milk!"

"And this was your roll too," Isaac said, shoving half of it in his mouth. "Mmmm, tasty."

When everyone was done eating and the table cleared, I headed up to my room to do homework. It was going to be a very boring night since most of the guys were going to Mary's party, but maybe later I could watch a movie with Jack and Jordan.

It was loud in the hallway as everyone got ready, and the smell of Axe seeped under my door. Finally all the commotion traveled downstairs, and I went to the window to watch everyone pile into the truck and pull away. Sighing, I collapsed on my bed, ignoring the calculus notebook that was open on my desk. Even though this was my choice, a tiny part of me felt left out. I wished I could spend the night hanging out with Alex and Nathan.

Not long after the thought crossed my mind, my bedroom door slammed open.

"Up!" Cole demanded, strolling into my room.

"Huh?" What was he still doing here? Hadn't he left with his siblings?

"We don't have all night." He yanked me out of my bed and dragged me over to the closet. Throwing it open, he started riffling through my clothes. "No. No. No," he said, pushing aside each hanger as he went. "Don't you have anything hot?"

"What about this?" I asked, pointing to one of my favorite dresses.

"Do you want to look like a couch?" he said, and flipped past it. The dress slipped off its hanger and crumpled to the floor.

"That's a Chanel piece!" I gasped, scooping it up.

"We have a winner," he said, ignoring me. "Here, put this on."

The air froze in my lungs when I saw what he was holding—a black minidress with a silver buckle at the waist. It wasn't mine. Somehow, one of my sister's clubbing outfits must have ended up in my clothing.

"Hello? Earth to Jackie?" Cole said, waving the outfit in my face.

"I can't wear that," I told him, my voice tight. "It's not mine."

"Well, I'm pretty sure it's not Isaac's or Danny's, so it must be yours."

"It was my sister's," I told him. "I don't know how it ended up inside one of my moving boxes."

"Oh," Cole said, dropping his arm. "I supposed you can just go in what you're wearing."

"Where *are* we going?" I asked, even though I already knew what his answer would be.

"The party," he responded, his voice edged with amusement. "You're coming with me."

And that's all it took. There was that feeling again—the one that made me bold just because Cole was standing next to me. It was so overwhelming, irresistible even, that in a daze, I let him guide me out of my room and down to the car.

• • •

When Nick's car pulled onto Mary Black's cul-de-sac, I realized I had gotten myself into another situation. I couldn't go in—the last time I'd let go and taken a risk, it had ended badly. The music from the party was so loud that I could feel it even though the doors were closed. I crossed my arms, refusing to take off my seat belt as Cole popped a piece of gum into his mouth.

"Do I need to carry you inside?" he asked. "Because I swear I will."

Instead of answering, I stared out the windshield with no intention of moving. I was prepared to sit in the car all night if I had to. Not only was it Mary's house, but I didn't want Alex to think I'd turned him down just to show up with his brother.

Cole sighed and yanked the handle and stepped outside. I risked a quick glance at him and saw the breeze ruffle his light hair. When he moved to the front of the car, I smiled, thinking that he had given up. But he was just stopping to say something to Nick. They shook hands, which transitioned into a man hug, a semi-embrace that lasted for a split second and ended with a firm pat on the back. The smile slipped off my face when Cole jogged around the side of the car and opened my door.

"Out now," he said with a serious face.

"Cole!" I said, hearing the whine in my voice. "I told Alex I wasn't coming. He's going to be upset if I show up now."

"And that's my problem?" he asked, reaching over to undo my seat belt. "Just tell him you changed your mind."

How was I supposed to tell him about what Mary said to me? I felt the words perched on my tongue, but I paused too long and lost my nerve. "Seriously," I said instead, "it's not funny."

Cole didn't respond. Instead he grabbed me by the waist, pulled me from the car, and threw me over his shoulder.

"Put me down!" I screamed as he kicked the door shut with his foot.

A few people who were standing on the porch looked up at us. He was laughing now, and I pounded on his back with my fist as he made his way toward the house.

"Cole Walter, I will make sure you die a painful death if you don't let me go this instant," I demanded.

We received more strange looks as he trudged up the steps. "Sorry," Cole apologized to the people standing by the door, beers in hand. "I have a runaway date on my hands."

"I am *not* your date!" I hissed at him.

But Cole was already stepping inside, tuning out my every protest. Once he closed the door behind him, he finally put me down.

"See?" he said, shouting over the music and patting me on the head. "That wasn't so bad, was it?"

"Are you kidding me—" I began, but someone cut me off.

"Jackie?" I turned in time to see Alex emerging from the throng of people. "I thought you weren't coming."

"I wasn't, but your annoying brother—"

"Invited her to the party," Cole said, cutting me off. He wrapped his arm around my waist and smirked at his little brother.

"What are you doing?" I hissed, and tried to push him off me. "Get off." But Cole's grip was strong, his fingers digging into my side.

"You came with him?" Alex said, his jaw clenched.

"Alex, it wasn't like that," I tried to say. But there was a tight, anxious knot in my stomach and I had a feeling that it was too late.

"Really, Jackie," Cole said, bending down to press his lips to my forehead. "You don't have to lie about us. Alex understands. Right, little bro?"

And in that moment, the damage was done. Alex stood there staring at us, and I could sense the tension moving off him in waves. His dark eyes were accusing, and I felt myself bristle.

"How about I go get us a beer?" Cole said. His mouth curled into an almost smile, but there was no warmth behind it. "Be right back, okay?"

He removed his arm from around me, and it was as if he'd extracted my spine, stealing every ounce of energy I had along with it. My knees buckled, but then my hand shot out and I braced myself against the wall. Had Cole ruined everything I had with Alex—whatever that was, friendship or something more—in a matter of minutes? Could he really win that easily?

"Alex," I began. There was no way I would let Cole get away with this. "You have to listen to me. He dragged me here. I didn't want to come."

Nostrils flaring, Alex gave a derisive snort. "You really think I'm going to believe that crap lie? If you're going to sneak around with Cole, at least have the decency to tell me the truth."

"I am telling you the truth," I said, trying to disregard the dread that was seeping into my veins, making my heart beat faster by the minute.

"You know, I believed you the first time," Alex said, his light hair falling into his eyes. I knew he was referring to when I had come home with Cole absolutely drunk. "How does it go—fool me once?"

Attempting to marshal my tumbling thoughts, I took a step toward him. "Please," I started to say, but the rest of the words faded in my throat because Alex was already merging back into the crowd. I stared unseeingly after him, my eyes glazing over.

"What is *she* doing here?" I heard someone say.

I came back to myself with a start and saw Mary standing at the bottom of the staircase, a cocktail in her hand. Her hair was piled up in a bun, giving her the appearance of having a golden halo. The pink skirt that she was wearing was just long enough, and the heels on her feet made her legs a mile long. It looked as if she had been having a private girl session in her room, because there was a flock of friends behind her on the steps. Each of their faces was set in a sneer as they glared in my direction.

By now, lots of people were watching me, some already whispering. Desperate, I glanced around the room hoping to see someone I knew—Nathan or maybe Riley, even Isaac would do—but all I saw were strangers.

"I said, what are you doing in my house? You weren't invited." Turning back around, Mary was standing in front of me with a hand perched dangerously on her hip in outrage.

"I–I…" I tried to say something, but nothing else came out.

The entire room was staring at me, and my throat got tight as I saw people turn and start to whisper to one another. My vision was starting to tunnel, and I could hear my blood rushing in my ears. Panic gripped me, and I swung around on my heels and flew out the door before Mary could say anything more.

Once outside, I pushed past the people on the porch and started running. The cold night air burned my throat and soon I was gasping for air. For some reason, the oxygen wouldn't fill my lungs, but I kept pushing. I didn't know where I was going, but anywhere was better than this place that seemed to suffocate me.

When I reached the end of the neighborhood, I spotted the welcome sign: *West Walnut Hills Welcomes You to Evansdale, Colorado!* There I let up, gripping my knees as I caught my breath. Tears streamed down my face in hot tracks, and I could feel my arms shaking.

"Argh!" Rage pulsing through me, I swung my foot at a pebble on the road. It hopped across the pavement as a strong breeze started to whip around angrily, sensing my pain. "I hate it here!" I screamed. "Why can't I just go home?"

Only the wind answered me.

• • •

Nathan was probably the only Walter boy who didn't hate me.

When he woke me up the next morning for our run, I was completely caught off guard. After what had happened the night before, I expected everyone to ignore me, so I planned on staying in bed all day. I was going to tell Katherine that I didn't feel well. She had picked me up from the party last night when I called her nearly in tears, and even though she repeatedly asked me what was wrong on the drive home, I refused to tell her.

"What are you doing in here?" I grumbled at Nathan, pulling the covers back over my head. "Didn't you hear what happened last night?"

"Naturally," he said, yanking them off again. He was dressed in his workout clothes—athletic shorts and a cutoff tee—and was bouncing on his heels, ready to go.

"Why aren't you pissed at me?"

"I'm not an idiot, Jackie," he said, his voice edged with amusement. "I know both of my brothers well enough to have put two and two together when I heard the stories. You did absolutely nothing wrong."

Wrapping my arms around my chest, I hugged myself and refused to look at him. "How am I going to fix this?" I asked.

"Well, you can start by getting out of bed and going for a run," he told me.

It was nice to know that at least there was one person on my side. However, I wasn't in the mood and I let him go without me.

How was I going to survive living here now? It was hard enough in the beginning when I first arrived, but now? The school year was almost over, and I would be stuck on this stupid, isolated farm with a bunch of guys who wouldn't even talk to me for the whole summer.

I glanced at the clock. By now there should have been some movement down the hall as people woke up, but the house was eerily silent. Groaning, I kicked off my remaining sheets and quietly put my feet on the floor. I didn't want to make any noise. Wincing as the floorboards groaned, I crept to my door and peered outside. Every door down the hall was shut. Strange, I thought, stepping back inside.

When she tucked me in last night, Katherine had opened my window so the room wouldn't get stuffy. It was how I heard the shouting down below. It came out of nowhere, an alarming call that broke the silence of the morning. I ran over to the window to see what was going on and saw Cole emerging from the fields carrying a bundle of something in his arms. He was dressed in work clothes and I knew that he was doing his morning chores.

"Isaac, help!" Cole shouted. It was then that I noticed Isaac standing on the back deck in his boxers, trying to sneak a morning smoke in. "Nathan's in trouble!"

Hearing Nathan's name, I squinted at Cole to see better, and the air froze in my lungs. In his arms was Nathan's limp form.

"Aunt Katherine!" I heard Isaac call inside, his voice filled with panic. "Something's wrong with Nate. I think we need to call an ambulance!"

I was moving then without having to think. I threw on a pair of pants and a shirt before racing out of my room. Down in the kitchen, Isaac was helping Cole get Nathan through the back door. The wait was nerve-racking, and by the time the white van sped up the driveway, sirens wailing and lights flashing, mostly everyone was down in the kitchen.

"What's going on?" Danny asked as we watched the EMT load Nathan into the back. "Is he okay?"

"I don't know," I said, as the bile rose in my throat. "I heard shouting—Cole was carrying him—and, oh God!" I stumbled back into one of the kitchen chairs and let my head fall between my knees as I gasped for breath. My thoughts were reeling, back to the day of my family's accident, and now all I could see were their faces blinking by in my vision, Nathan's included.

This wasn't happening. Not again.

"Come on, Jackie," Danny said, gripping my shoulder and giving me a shake. "Isaac has the truck running. We're going to the hospital."

Despite the fact that my head was spinning, I let him pull me from the house without a fight. My thoughts were in a different place, miles away. Not once during the ride to the hospital did I think about how awkward I should be feeling sitting next to Alex. It didn't matter. All I could think about was the fact that I might be losing another person I cared about.

Nobody knew what was wrong. All Cole said was that he went

out to the barn this morning and found Nathan unconscious. The only guess that I could make was that he must have tripped while he was running and knocked himself unconscious. But even that theory sounded absurd.

Isaac's lead foot got us to the hospital almost faster than the ambulance. Before he could even park, the truck doors flew open and everyone piled out. We tore across the parking lot and flooded the front lobby where a startled nurse directed us to the ER.

After so much rushing and panic, time passed slowly in the waiting room. No one spoke as we sat in the uncomfortable chairs, hoping to hear news from the doctors about Nathan. Cole was pacing the length of the room. Katherine was silently crying, her head resting on George's shoulder, and Isaac was tapping his foot so hard that I was surprised he didn't put a hole in the floor.

Finally, a man in a white coat appeared.

"Katherine Walter?" he asked, looking up from his clipboard.

She shot up out of her chair. "Yes?" she asked, her voice cracking. "That's me."

After introducing himself as Dr. Goodman and going through all the pleasantries that nobody cared to hear, he told us the news that we were waiting for. "Your son Nathan has just woken up, and it looks like he is going to be fine," he said, offering her a smile.

Everyone breathed a sigh of relief.

"Oh, thank God," Katherine said, putting her hand to her heart. "When can we see him?"

He paused. "Nathan is in stable condition," he started to say. From the way he was looking at Katherine, I knew he had more news, but was choosing his words carefully. "But there is something we need to discuss first. Your son suffered a severe concussion. We still have to do some more tests, but our initial diagnosis is that Nathan fell and hit his head after suffering a seizure," Dr. Goodman said.

"A seizure?" George echoed in astonishment. "How is that even possible?"

Dr. Goodman explained to the Walters that Nathan's seizure was a result of excessive neuronal activity in the brain, a common chronic neurological disorder known as epilepsy. He also explained that while about fifty million people worldwide suffer from epilepsy, a good portion of those people only experience one seizure in their whole lifetime.

"May we please see him now?" Katherine asked once Dr. Goodman finished explaining the condition.

"Of course," he said, looking around the waiting room. As he noticed our huge group, he added, "But family only."

Everyone stood up and followed the doctor. I trailed after them slowly, not knowing what to do. Would I be allowed to see Nathan? As I watched everyone disappear into a hospital room, I decided I didn't care what the doctor said. One more person wouldn't hurt. Just as I was about to duck in, Lee stepped out into the hall to face me.

"Where do you think you're going?" he asked me with his usual scowl on his face.

"To see Nathan," I told him with a determined look on my face.

"Didn't you hear the doctor?" he asked. "Family only."

"Lee, come on," I responded, and I could hear the hurt in my tone. "I live with you guys. I count too."

"Jackie," he said slowly, a cruel gleam in his eyes. "You could live with us for the rest of your life and it wouldn't matter. You will *never* be part of our family."

I turned away from him, letting the words sink in. He was right. I didn't belong.

"Besides," Lee said, hissing at me, "why should you get to see him when it's your fault he's in here?"

"What?" I squeaked, not believing my ears. I turned to face him, in spite of the fact that my eyes were starting to water. His gaze locked with mine, his expression venomous.

"You heard me," he drawled. "This never would have happened if you'd gone running with Nathan. But you were too busy sulking in your room, weren't you? All because Alex doesn't like you anymore."

It was as if he'd slapped me. "No," I said, shaking my head, but I was already reeling from his implication and I took a step back in horror.

Lee's lips curled in disgust. "Just go away, Jackie," he told me. And I did.

• • •

It was the last place anyone would ever look for me. I didn't know how I ended up there, but Will had always been nice whenever I saw him. He rented a small one-bedroom apartment in town that was only a fifteen-minute walk from the hospital.

I'd been to his place once before when Katherine asked Cole and me to drop off a box of invitations that she wrote out for Will and Haley's upcoming wedding. That was over a month ago, and I was afraid I'd forgotten how to get there. But the apartment complex was right off the main road, and when I spotted it, I let the air pent up in my lungs slip passed my lips in relief.

Nobody answered when I first knocked. I was afraid momentarily that he wasn't home, but when I pounded for the second time, Will pulled open the door, still half asleep.

"Jackie?" he asked, his eyes squinting in the daylight. His usual ponytail was missing, and his blond hair fell down to his shoulders. "What are you doing here?"

"Sorry, Will. I didn't mean to wake you," I said, wringing my hands behind my back. "It's just that, when we first met, you told me that if I ever needed anything I could talk to you."

"Oh," he said, pulling open the door. "Come in."

The inside of Will's apartment was a cave. There was only one window in the main room, and the black curtains were drawn closed to keep the space dark.

"Make yourself comfortable," he said, shutting the door, which cut off the room's only source of light.

I carefully made my way toward what looked like the outline of a couch, and I managed to get there only banging my toe once.

"Would you like some coffee?" Will asked.

I could hear him navigating through the darkness like an expert, guided by the numbers on the microwave's digital clock like a sailor with the night constellations.

"Please," I told him.

Will reached the tiny kitchen and flipped on a light switch. As he shuffled back and forth, turning the coffeepot on and grabbing mugs, I inspected the room around me. Besides the couch and the table I'd stubbed my toe on, the only other furniture was a reclining chair that looked like it was going to fall apart the next time someone sat down. There was also a bookshelf that was almost empty except for a small collection of tiny, potted cacti. Compared to the old furniture, the only thing in the room that looked new was the flat-screen TV hanging directly in front of me on the far wall.

"Cream, sugar?" Will called.

"Just cream."

There was the distinct clanking of a spoon being stirred and the fridge door slamming shut, and then Will came out of the kitchen with two steaming cups. He handed one to me before taking a spot on the recliner. Amazingly, it didn't collapse.

"So," Will said. "What's wrong?" He hadn't taken a sip of his coffee, yet he was starting to look more awake than when I'd first found him.

There was no point in beating around the bush. "Nathan's in the hospital," I told him as calmly as possible.

"What?" It was a good thing that Will had already set his coffee down, because if he hadn't, I think he would have dropped it in his lap. "Was there an accident on the ranch?"

"Not exactly," I said. "He had a seizure." When I saw the dread on Will's face, I added, "Don't worry. The doctor said he should be fine."

Will was shaking his head in disbelief. "But how did this happen?"

I paused. "They said he has epilepsy."

"But—he's so young."

"I don't think age has anything to do with it."

"I know, it's just…" He trailed off, burying his face in his hands.

"I'm so sorry, Will."

He was still for such long time that when he suddenly stood up, making the recliner screech in protest, it startled me. "Is everyone still at the hospital?" he asked.

"Yes, I think so."

"All right." He snatched a pair of keys off the table. "I just need to put on a different shirt and then—wait," he said, stopping to stare at me. "Why aren't you there? How did you even get here?"

I flinched at his questions. "I–I walked here."

"Why did you do that?" he asked. Glancing away, I didn't say anything for a long time. There was no way I was going to tell Will what Lee had said to me. "Jackie, are you okay?"

I sighed. "I left the hospital because I couldn't handle the thought of Nathan being hurt," I told him. "It reminded me of, of—"

"The accident," Will finished for me in a whisper.

"Yeah." It wasn't a lie. When Cole had brought Nathan to the kitchen unconscious, I was overwhelmed by the fear of losing someone else I cared about.

"Oh God, Jackie. I'm so sorry."

Then I was crying, big heaving sobs that made my chest tight and throat sore. I was crying because of so many things: the blank, uncaring look I saw in Cole's eyes at Mary's party, and the crushed look in Alex's when he saw me with his brother, Nathan's accident,

Lee's cruel words, the loss of my family and home. And I was crying because I knew I shouldn't be. Will was the one who had just found out his brother was in the hospital, but still he sat by my side, trying to comfort me.

"Shhh, it's going to be okay, Jackie."

But I didn't know if it would be.

• • •

I must have cried myself to sleep. When I opened my eyes, I could feel the dried tears on my cheeks and the hair plastered to the side of my face. My neck was stiff from lying on the couch. I knew I was still at Will's, but the apartment was dark again and I couldn't see anything.

"Will?" I called out, my voice groggy.

"He's at the hospital."

The lamp next to the couch clicked on to reveal Cole sitting in the recliner. There were circles under his eyes and his hair was sticking up in the back, as if he had been trying to sleep in the chair but couldn't get comfortable.

"What are you doing here?" I demanded. Seeing him made me feel sad all over again.

"Will wanted to go see Nathan, but he didn't want to leave you alone, so he called me."

I lay back down on the couch so I wouldn't have to look at him. After falling asleep, Will must have tucked a blanket around me and I pulled it up to my chin now for protection. "But why are *you* here?" I asked, rephrasing my question.

"Because I was worried about you."

I forced a laugh. "Please, you don't need to lie."

"Why would I lie to you?"

"Cole, stop pretending like last night and *everything* that went down at the party didn't happen," I said. "I'm not in the mood for your bullshit right now."

He sighed. "I know."

"Good. Then you'll understand that I want to be alone."

"Jackie, please listen to me," he said, ignoring my request. His voice was barely audible, almost as if he was hurting just as much as me. I gritted my teeth together and ignored him. "I came here to apologize. And to take you home."

I remained quiet a moment longer, still thinking. Could I really call the Walters' house home? For a few weeks, it had started to feel something like that, but after what happened at the party and with Lee, I knew it wasn't.

"Jackie, please say something."

"Why should I go anywhere with you?" I said in response. "The past two times I've done that, it's ended terribly."

"Okay, I know I might have hurt your feelings, but—"

"Might?" I demanded, sitting up to glare at him. His words put fuel in my system, like someone struck a match inside my chest, and I narrowed my eyes, trying not to explode. "I lost my family, moved across the country to live with strangers, and was then treated like crap by the likes of you, and you think it *might* have hurt my feelings?"

Instead of lashing out like I thought he would, Cole hung his head. "I'm sorry," he mumbled.

"What?" I asked, putting a hand to my ear. "I can't hear you."

"I'm sorry. I was a jerk."

"Oh, a jerk?" I snapped. If this was his apology, he was doing a lousy job. "Don't be so hard on yourself, Cole."

Cole's nostrils flared, but he didn't show any other signs of his rage. "Hey, I'm trying to apologize here, okay?" When I didn't respond, he took a deep breath. "I suppose I was jealous," he finally said, looking down at the shaggy carpet.

"Jealous?" I echoed.

"Yeah." He sounded hesitant, as if he wasn't sure of his answer. Then he continued, "Of Alex."

"What about Erin, Olivia, all those girls?"

"That's just it," Cole said, his fists clenching in frustration. "I don't like any of those girls. It's just—I don't know. I feel like my friends have this expectation of who I am and how I should act. And then there's Alex, and things just come so naturally to him."

I laughed. "Things come natural to nerdy Alex, but not to superstar Cole?" I said bitterly.

"Yeah," he said, looking right at me. "When it comes to relationships they do. He just acts like himself and everything goes so perfectly."

"Perfectly?" I said. "You mean like with Mary?"

"Listen," Cole said, holding up his hands. "I know that I can be a dick, but I swear, I would never do something like that to Alex. She told me that *he* dumped her. As soon as I found it was the other way around, I told her to get lost."

I didn't know what to say to this.

"Jackie," Cole continued. "I shouldn't have dragged you and your feelings into this, but I saw how close you and Alex were getting, and I just didn't want to—" He paused, trying to think of the best way to phrase when he was saying. "I was selfish and afraid of being—"

"Alone?" I finished for him.

"Yeah," Cole said, nodding his head. "I was afraid of being alone."

"Welcome to my life," I told him sadly.

Chapter 13

It took Cole half an hour of coaxing before he convinced me to leave Will's. On the ride back to the ranch, I asked how Nathan was doing.

"He's okay," Cole said, taking his eyes off the road to glance at me. "He was asking for you."

I didn't respond to that. I felt guilty that I hadn't been there for Nathan.

"I can take you to see him tomorrow if you want."

"Sure," I said curtly, and after that, Cole got the message that I didn't want to talk. I was still furious with him, but I didn't have the energy to fight anymore. When the truck was finally parked in the Walters' driveway, I opened the door and shot out.

"Wait, Jackie!" Cole called, but I was already rushing to my room.

Part of me wanted to go to Alex and Nathan's room. Over the past month, the half-messy, half-clean space was where I spent most of my time. It had become a type of retreat, a place where I felt comfortable, and the posters on the walls were as familiar as the mural in my own room. But Alex would be there. Not only that, but he was probably still mad at me, and all I wanted was to be alone.

For the most part, the Walters let me be. Everyone except

Katherine came home from the hospital at lunchtime, yet the house remained calm. Still reeling from the shock of Nathan's accident, none of the kids were their usual rambunctious selves. At one point in the afternoon Parker knocked on my door looking for Jack and Jordan, but even she wasn't in the mood to give me one of her signature sneers.

I didn't go down to the kitchen for lunch or dinner, but at seven someone knocked on my door. Alex nudged it open with his shoulder. He was carrying a tray with a bowl of tomato soup and a grilled cheese sandwich.

"You hungry?" he asked, gesturing down at the food.

Even though I was surprised to see him, I barely moved from my spot on the bed. The day's events had left me mentally drained, and all I could manage was a shrug. My stomach felt empty, but not because I needed food.

"Well, can I come in?"

"I suppose."

Alex crossed the room carefully so he wouldn't spill the soup, and after setting it down on my desk, he stood at the side of my bed with his hands shoved into his pockets. His mouth opened as if he was going to say something but closed again as he changed his mind. I knew he was looking for the right way to start a conversation, but I wasn't going to help him. I remained silent, watching him patiently.

At last he said, "Jackie, I'm super sorry." Alex looked just as worn out as I felt. All the usual color was drained from his face, and for some reason that made me believe him. I wasn't any less stunned, though.

"Two apologies in one day?" I asked, also referring to Cole. "Who's the miracle worker around here?" The sarcasm came out accidentally, but it was warranted. Both boys were being bipolar, like Jekyll and Hyde. Yesterday they hated me, and now they wanted my forgiveness.

Alex's shoulders went stiff. "Nathan," he answered.

"Really? Do tell." I had a hard time believing that, considering he'd just had a seizure.

"When he realized you weren't at the hospital, he got angry. He asked to speak with Cole and me alone, and then he yelled at us," Alex said. "Like, really loudly. I swear, one of the nurses nearly had a panic attack when she heard him shouting."

It was hard to picture Nathan in a hospital bed with an IV in his arm while he reprimanded his older brothers, but the thought made my lips curl in satisfaction. "And what did Nathan say?"

By now, Alex's face was a deep red. "That I was a complete idiot if I actually thought you were trying to hurt me," he mumbled.

"Pretty accurate for someone with a head injury," I said. At that point, I was past being polite. The fact that Alex had so willingly believed Cole's performance upset me all over again. Did he really think I was that cruel?

"I'm sorry." He hung his head. "I know it's not a good excuse, but I was *really* upset that you didn't come to the party, and on top of that, I was drinking. Then all of a sudden you showed up with him, and I just couldn't think straight."

"You know the only thing on my mind when Cole dragged me into that party?" The truth was flying off my lips before I even thought about what I was telling him.

"No," Alex said tentatively. "What?"

"What is Alex going to think?"

"Are you trying to make me feel worse?"

"No," I said, softening the tone of my voice. "I just want you to know that I was."

"Was what?"

"*Thinking* of you."

The truth was, ever since our kiss, the thought of Alex made my stomach flutter. The frustrating part was that I couldn't work out *why*. There was no denying that Alex was good looking—he had one of those adorable smiles that could make anyone grin—but I never felt that whole body-on-fire thing around him, like I did when I was near a certain someone else. At the same time, Alex was caring and dependable. I felt like he was someone I had known for my entire life, like I was home.

"I was horrible," he said, shaking his head like he couldn't believe it himself. When I didn't respond, he looked up at me. "Do you think you'll be able to forgive me?"

"I do forgive you, Alex. I understand that you weren't purposely trying to be mean to me. You saw Cole and me together, and you thought that whole thing with Mary was happening all over again."

At this he said, "But?"

"But it happened yesterday. The wound is still a little raw."

"Right," Alex said, biting his lip. We were both quiet for a moment, but then he perked up. "Can I try to make it up to you?"

"It depends," I responded with the smallest of smiles. "What's the proposal?"

"Well, once we got back from the hospital, I went to the library," he said, grabbing a movie case off the tray that I hadn't noticed until now. "After the party last night I couldn't sleep, so I finished reading *A Midsummer Night's Dream*. I rented one of the film adaptations thinking maybe we could watch it together."

It was so thoughtful that I finally let myself grin. "I guess that wouldn't be too painful," I said, pretending to be indifferent.

"Awesome, where's your laptop?"

It didn't take long for Alex to set up the movie and settle onto my bed. When the opening act began he was still tense, and his whole body went stiff when I accidentally bumped his shoulder, but once the action of the play started, he relaxed. By the end of the movie, my head was resting on his chest.

"So what'd ya think?" I asked, when the credits came on.

"Hmm?" Alex's fingers were running through my hair, and every time he took a breath I felt his chest rise and fall.

"Did you like it?"

"Honestly," he said, his hand coming to a rest, "I didn't pay much attention."

"What?" I sat up so I could look at him. "Why not?"

"Because something else was distracting me," he said. Before I could ask him what, he went on. "Can we talk about something?"

A worried expression covered his face, but his hand reached up again to touch my hair and he tucked my bangs behind my ear. I felt the calluses on his fingers as they glided over my skin and I shivered. It was like part of me knew what he was going to say, and as I nodded, my heart started to pound in my chest. The room was so quiet that I was positive he could hear it.

"Jackie," he began, and his voice was serious, as if he were giving an important speech. I watched his lips move as he said my name. In the light of my room, they looked smooth and sculpted, and they left me thinking about that day on the beanbags. "I know this is going to be a stupid question, but I have to try anyway. At that party, when I saw you standing with Cole, the reason I was so pissed wasn't just because of the whole Mary thing. I was mad at myself for being too late. I thought Cole beat me to it."

"I don't understand the question."

"Hold on, I'm getting to that." At this, he took a breath. "What I'm trying to say is that I should have asked you this the other day—you know, after we played Mario Kart." He paused again, his face going red. Then in a rush he said, "Jackie, will you be my girlfriend?"

There it was, the question I'd feared since our kiss because I didn't know how to respond. But now that I heard it, I suddenly knew what my decision was. There was something so comforting about being with Alex. He was someone I could let my guard down around. Last night at the party I thought I had lost that, and now I wasn't going to give it up again.

I answered him with my lips.

• • •

I was almost positive that Parker was stalking me the next morning. Normally she made an effort to avoid me, sometimes even leaving a room if I came in, but at breakfast she sat down right next to me. While I was in the bathroom straightening my hair, she came in and spent ten minutes brushing her teeth. Later that day, I opened my bedroom door and found her lingering in the hallway.

I crossed my arms and raised an eyebrow. "What are you up to, Parker?"

She smirked, and two dimples appeared on her cheeks. "Waiting."

"For what?" I asked.

"The wrath of Cole," was her only response, and I had no clue what she meant until I heard the fighting. "Oh man," Parker complained when she heard the angry shouts. "I was hoping he was going to go all Hulk on you, not Alex."

She rushed down the stairs toward the sound of the voices, and I followed quickly after her, but by the time we reached the living room George was already pulling Cole and Alex apart.

"What is wrong with you two?" he demanded, glaring at both of his sons. He had a tight grip on both of their shirts as he held them away from each other. Alex was sporting a bloody lip but had a smug smile on his face, while Cole looked like he was going to explode.

"He started it," Alex said. "Went all crazy and just attacked me out of nowhere. No clue what I did to piss him off." From the pleased tone of his voice, I knew Alex wasn't telling the whole truth.

"Well?" George asked, turning to Cole. "Is that true?"

"He was being a punk."

"And that counts as a good reason to punch your brother? God, Cole, I don't know what's gotten into you lately," George said and shook his head. "If this happens again, you're going to be mucking the horse stalls for the next month. You hear me?"

Cole nodded his head and George released both boys. When he was gone, Cole got right back up in Alex's face. "You think you're so cool now, don't you?" he hissed. "Just remember, you only took the first round. We both know from experience that I always win."

The grin on Alex's face faltered, and I saw something dark flash in his eyes.

"Guys?" I asked hesitantly, but as soon as Cole heard my voice he was gone, storming out of the room without another word.

"Dammmnn," I heard Lee say.

Turning around, I found that most of the boys had gathered behind me to watch the scene.

"Shit," Isaac hissed back. "Wasn't expecting that."

"You lose," Lee told his brother. "Pay up."

Isaac dug into his pocket for his wallet. He pulled out a twenty and slapped it into his brother's hand with a scowl. Danny was standing next to him, and I noticed that his usually blank face was covered in surprise. It gave me the feeling that this fight was somehow my fault, and as dread started to lace my veins, I went over to him.

"What the heck just happened?" I whispered.

Danny shook his head, and I thought that he wasn't going to tell me, but then he grabbed me by the elbow and pulled me out onto the deck where we wouldn't be overheard. He explained that last night, Alex had bragged about me being his girlfriend to everyone except Cole. It was like he was purposely trying to entice his older brother, and when Cole found out in the morning, Alex got the reaction he was looking for.

Cole was furious, and he spent the rest of Sunday out in the garage, working on his car.

The next day at school, Alex was no better. When class ended and we walked out of anatomy together, he pulled me against his locker and kissed me hard, his hand weaving behind my back so he could hold me against his body. In the moment, I thought he was being romantic, but when he pulled away, I caught him glancing over my shoulder. Following his gaze, I saw Mary standing with her group of friends, a killer glare on her face.

Lunchtime was a headache. Riley, Heather, and Skylar bombarded Alex and me with questions the moment we sat down. They grilled us for the entire thirty minutes that we had to eat, and while Alex didn't seem to mind, I just wanted the news of us dating to die down so things could go back to how they used to be. Kim, the only one I could count on to act normal, never showed up.

By the time school was over, I was so exhausted that I took a nap, something that I never allowed myself to do. I ended up sleeping for so long that when it was time to actually go to bed, I couldn't fall asleep. That's why, even thought it was well past midnight, I sat straight up in bed when I heard the knock on my door.

"Jackie, you still awake?" Alex whispered, peeking in.

"Uh-huh," I answered.

"Can I come in?" he asked again even more quietly.

"Yeah, sure," I said, sitting up. "What's up?"

He closed the door quietly and tiptoed over to my bed. I looked at the clock. It was already midnight.

"Do you have any black clothes?" Alex asked me.

"Somewhere in my closet," I said, nodding my head. "Why?"

"You're going to have to dig them out," he said, a grin spreading across his face.

"What for?" I asked, but I headed over to my closet anyway. I searched through a few long-sleeved shirts until I found my old Hawks sweater with my name stitched into the pocket.

"The guys all voted, and we decided to let you come along on our little end-of-the-year tradition."

"And that is?" I asked, pulling on black pants.

"We always toilet-paper the principal's house."

• • •

"Shhhh," Isaac whispered as everyone crowded into Lee's and his room later. Alex explained that his cousins' room was the best for sneaking out because of the giant oak tree right by the window.

"All right, does everyone have their roll of toilet paper?" Cole asked, looking around at everyone—everyone except me.

"Yup," Danny answered, holding up a roll. "I also grabbed that box of plastic forks that Mom was going to use for our graduation party so we can fork the yard."

"Awesome!" Lee said, high-fiving his cousin.

"Hey, Jackie, what the heck is on your face?" Alex whispered, looking at me.

"War paint," I answered him, pulling a pencil of black eyeliner out of my pocket. "Want some?"

"Heck yes," he said, grinning. I pulled the cap off with a pop and slowly began to draw two black lines, one under each of Alex's eyes.

"Hey," Isaac said, looking at us, "I want some too!"

"Okay," I said, smiling. "Anyone else?"

Everyone nodded their heads yes and waited for me to add the war paint. The only person who didn't want it was Cole.

"That's so lame," he said when I asked him if he wanted some. Hurt, I shoved the pencil back in my pocket and turned away from him.

"All right, everyone," Isaac said, trying to fill the awkward silence. "Down the tree and out to the truck."

Danny nodded his head and pushed open the window before climbing out and down the tree.

"Watch how he does it," Alex said, pointing out where his brother placed his feet and hands to climb down.

"Okay, next!" Danny half shouted, half whispered when he was down.

Cole quickly scrambled out the window, followed by Lee, then Isaac.

"Ready?" Alex asked me as I stepped up to the windowsill. I could feel the chilly night air drifting in, and I buttoned my sweater up for warmth.

"I guess," I said nervously.

"Don't worry. It's easy," he told me. Nodding my head, I hiked a foot up and out the window. Then I pulled myself up and carefully grabbed onto a branch. "It's okay. Keep going," Alex said.

Taking a deep breath, I scooted off the windowsill and clung to the tree. Slowly I lowered my left foot onto the thick branch below it.

"We don't have all night," someone grumbled from below. It sounded like Cole.

"Don't worry about him," Alex whispered. "He's just being pissy."

Alex helped me down the tree by telling me where to put my feet. When they finally hit the soft grass, we headed over to where the rest of the guys were standing.

"Took long enough," Cole said when Alex finally dumped the bag of toilet paper into the back of the truck.

"Just shut up, Cole," Alex said with a scowl.

"Can you two both chill for a minute?" Isaac said to them. "You guys can have this argument when we get back, but I'd like to get out of here without getting caught."

Cole and Alex glared at each other, but both stayed silent.

"We need to push the truck to the road," Danny said.

"Push it?" I asked, surprised. It was going to be so heavy.

"Yeah, Mom can hear everything," he said. "So, if we want to get out of here, we can't start it until it's on the road."

Everyone got behind Fox, the name the guys had dubbed the red truck.

"Fox?" I asked, raising an eyebrow.

"Yeah," Isaac said with a grin. "Our truck is hot, like Megan Fox."

I rolled my eyes as most of the guys tried to hold in their laughter.

"All right, guys. One, two, three!" Cole instructed. Everyone pushed, and it only took us a few minutes to get Megan down the Walters' long driveway.

"Whoo!" Alex shouted once the truck was on the street. "Let's go."

Everyone climbed in, Cole started the truck, and then we were off into the night.

• • •

"All right, Isaac, Danny. You take the backyard," Cole said, throwing the black duffel bag on the ground. He quickly unzipped it and threw them both rolls of toilet paper. We were all standing outside Principal McHale's three-story house. It was a good distance from the road, and there was lots of tree coverage, but Cole had parked the truck a block back just in case.

"It's huge," I whispered to Alex who was standing next to me. "There are so many trees."

Alex nodded his head with a smile. "It's perfect for a good TP."

"You guys are being too loud," Cole hissed, looking at me.

"Fine, Mr. Boss Man. Give me a job to do," Alex said.

Cole tossed him the box of forks. "Someone has to fork the lawn," he said.

"I'll go too," I said, linking arms with Alex. I didn't want to be left alone with Cole and Lee.

"I don't think so," Cole said, grabbing my arm as we started to head away. "I have the perfect job for you."

A few minutes later, I stood staring up at the back balcony.

"No way in hell am I doing that," I said, crossing my arms. "You're crazy."

"We need someone light to do it," Cole said. "Nathan normally does, but considering he's temporarily out of service…"

"Oh fine!" I said and snatched the roll from him.

"There's a good girl," Cole said, pinching my cheek.

"Screw you," I told him before spinning around and grabbing the rose trellis.

"Just be careful it doesn't break," Cole told me as I tested my weight on the lowest wooden beam. When I was sure it wouldn't, I began to pull myself up. It was like climbing a ladder.

"Ouch!" I yelled as I pricked my finger on a rose thorn.

"Shut up!" Cole hissed from below. "Do you want to be caught? That's their bedroom patio up there."

"Yeah, I know. You already told me like fifty times," I whispered, sucking the little drop of blood from my finger. "It would have been nice if you'd given me gloves."

"Stop being a baby and start climbing," he shot back at me.

I gritted my teeth and held back my response. When I finally made it to the top, I quietly hauled myself over the railing. The sliding glass door to the balcony had a curtain covering it, but my heart started to pound. I felt like everyone inside the house could see and hear me moving around, so I rapidly started to throw the white paper everywhere.

"Make sure you weave it in and out of the railing," I heard Cole call up to me.

"Yeah, yeah," I muttered to myself. If he was going to be so demanding, he should have come up here and done it himself.

"Jackie? Did you hear me? Do the railing."

Glancing back down, I saluted him mockingly.

After wrapping the railing, I moved back to admire my handi-work. As I did, I tripped over the extra roll of toilet paper and fell back into the balcony door. I scrambled back up to my feet as my heart leaped in my chest. I held my breath from a moment, wait-ing to see if anyone had heard me. Principal McHale was probably inside right now, a few feet away sleeping.

When nothing happened, I let the air hiss out of my lungs, but it was too soon. A siren filled the night air and my eyes bulged. The house had a burglar alarm. For a moment I was frozen still, until I heard yelling on the lawn.

"What the hell, Cole?" Lee shouted. "What is she doing up there?"

"Jackie! Get down!" Alex yelled over the sound of the alarm. It helped unfreeze my mind, and I quickly vaulted over the balcony railing and onto the rose trellis.

"Come on, faster," someone shouted.

I was almost to the ground when I heard a rip. My sweater was caught on the trellis by the sleeve.

"Jackie, we need to go now!" Isaac said.

"I can't. I'm stuck!" I cried, trying to pull my sleeve away.

"Who's out there?" a deep voice called from the patio door.

"Just take it off," Alex said.

I tried to shrug out of it, but I was shaking too hard. Suddenly Cole was by my side, and he yanked me from the fabric.

"Come on," he said, jumping down to the ground.

"But my sweater," I said turning back to the rose trellis. "It's still stuck."

"Leave it. I'll buy you a new one." He grabbed my hand and pulled me into the cover of the trees.

"Damn kids!" someone yelled into the night.

Everyone ran as fast as they could back to the truck. When we got there, I was gasping for air.

"What the hell were you thinking?" Alex demanded and shoved Cole into the side of the truck. "You did that on purpose. You wanted her to get caught, didn't you?"

"But she didn't get caught, did she?" Cole asked. There was a smug smile on his face.

"She shouldn't have been up there in the first place!" Alex yelled. "Just because you're jealous doesn't mean—"

"Wait!" I said, cutting them off. I could feel my heart sinking. "You don't normally toilet-paper the balcony?"

"Are you crazy?" Isaac said as Danny shook his head. "That's insane. We don't want to get caught."

But I wasn't really listening to him. My eyes were on Cole, watching the way he reacted. His forehead was bunched together in a frown as if he thought everyone was blowing the situation out of proportion.

"Why would you lie to me?" I asked him. I spoke softly and slowly to keep my voice from cracking. But it didn't matter—my question was filled with the ring of betrayal. If Principal McHale had seen me, it could have been the end to my Princeton dream and everything that followed after. Cole knew the importance I placed on school and my future, yet he purposely jeopardized it. I could feel the anger building up inside my chest, but then I made a terrifying realization. Tonight, I risked my future just as much as Cole did. Nobody forced me up the trellis. I climbed up all on my own. What had gotten into me lately? Never in my life had I ever been so reckless.

Cole crossed his arms. "It was just a joke," he said. "Stop acting like someone died."

Beside me, I heard Danny gasp. I didn't turn to see the other boys' reactions—I was focused on Cole, searching his icy gaze to see if he'd purposely meant what he said. How could he be so insensitive?

"That was totally out of line," Alex said, breaking the silence as he stepped in front of me to face Cole. "Apologize to Jackie."

"Oh, piss off," Cole said, dismissing his brother with the wave of his hand.

"*Apologize*," Alex said again.

"And if I don't want to? What are you going to do?"

"This," Alex told Cole before slamming his fist into his brother's nose.

Cole stumbled back, crashing into the side of the truck. Alex rushed after him, but Isaac reacted quickly, jumping in to grab Alex's arms before he could land another hit. Before Cole could regain his focus, Danny stepped in and wrapped his arms around his twin to hold him back.

I should have seen the punch coming. It was long overdue. Alex and Cole were fighting before I arrived in Colorado, but I was a catalyst that instigated a full-out war.

"What the hell?" Cole roared, trying to break free from Danny.

It took a while for everyone to calm down, especially Cole. The other boys seemed just as mad at Cole as he was at us, and they voted to make him walk home. Thankfully, I convinced them to change their minds. I was upset about what Cole said, his words a slap across the face, but I knew things would get worse if we let him fester in anger. We all piled back into the truck, Danny taking the wheel. Cole sat in the front seat nursing his injury and swore at anyone who talked to him. I was in the back, sitting as far away as possible.

"That was awesome," Isaac said, still laughing. "I mean really, it was the best part of the night. I've never seen Cole get decked so hard."

"Yeah," Danny agreed. "I wish I had Jack and Jordan's camera."

"You better shut your mouth, or you're going to wish you never said anything at all," Cole grumbled. Everyone laughed except me.

"Hey, Jackie, you all right?" Alex whispered in my ear. I shook my head no. "What's wrong? I probably shouldn't have punched Cole, but didn't it make you feel a little bit better?"

"My sweater is back there," I said, trying not to cry. After climbing into the truck, I couldn't stop replaying the entire night in my head. I had remembered something incredibly important.

"So?" Alex said, shrugging, "It's just a sweater."

I turned to Alex with watery eyes. "It has my name on it."

Chapter 14

The sun was pouring through my windows in the morning, and I rolled over with a groan. Every part of my body was sore, and I'd only gotten a few hours of sleep.

My alarm was going off, but I let it screech as I tried to remember why I was so tired. When I spotted my muddy shoes on the floor, everything came rushing back to me and I slapped my clock off angrily. Getting out of bed was the last thing I wanted to do, but I let my bare feet hit the cold wooden floor and I padded down to the bathroom.

Frustrated with Cole, myself, and everything else, I squeezed the toothpaste tube a bit too hard and blue goo shot all over, squirting over the side of my brush.

"Damn it," I said grumpily as I flicked the excess toothpaste off into the sink.

As I brushed my teeth, I thought about the day to come. I bet I would be called down to the office during the day. All the receptionists would glare at me with disapproving looks. Then I would be led back to the principal's office where he would be waiting behind a big wooden desk, my black sweater in hand. My future was ruined.

I'm sorry, Mom, I thought to myself.

Sighing, I spit out the toothpaste and quickly splashed some water on my face. After grabbing my robe, I turned off the lights and headed back to my room. When I stepped inside, I gasped in surprise. Sitting on the end of my bed was my sweater.

I rushed downstairs and flung my arms around Alex. "Thank you, thank you, thank you!" I kissed him on the cheek.

"You're welcome?" Alex answered, somewhat confused.

"You don't understand how relieved I feel," I told him.

"Relieved about what exactly?" Alex asked me.

"My sweater," I said, holding it up. "I just can't believe you went all the way back out there to get it for me." Alex stared at me and didn't say anything. "You did go get it, right?" I asked him.

"Well, now I'm really wishing I'd thought of that," he said, sounding disappointed in his answer, "but no, I didn't."

I turned my head to the other boys in the kitchen. My eyes searched Cole's face for an answer, but he raised his eyebrows, as if to say retrieving my jacket was the last thing in the world he would do.

"Danny?" I asked. He looked up from the morning paper with an apologetic look and shook his head no.

"You?" I asked, turning to Isaac.

"Sorry, Jackie," he mumbled through a mouthful of cornflakes.

"Then who?" I asked out loud.

"Isaac," Katherine said, coming into the kitchen with a coffee mug in hand. "Can you wake up your brother? I can't believe he's still sleeping."

"Sure thing, Aunt Katherine," he said, getting up and putting his cereal bowl in the sink.

"Lee?" I wondered out loud.

"No, dork," Isaac said and rolled his eyes. "My other brother."

During the car ride to school, all the guys chatted about the end-of-the-year party they always hosted. They planned on having it this weekend when Katherine and George were out of town. I listened quietly and watched Lee from my spot in the backseat, trying to understand why he, of all people, went back to get my jacket. Lee was the only one who didn't seem excited about the party. Maybe it was because he had his face pressed up against the passenger-side window, half asleep.

"All right, everyone out," Cole said when we pulled into the parking lot. I quickly opened the door and grabbed my bag from the back.

"Ready?" Alex asked me when he retrieved his.

"Just go without me," I said, still watching Lee slowly unbuckle his seat belt. "I'll catch up later. There's something I have to do."

"Okay," Alex said before kissing me on the cheek and heading into school.

As I expected, Lee was the last person out of the car, being as tired as he was. By the time he grabbed his backpack from the truck bed, the rest of the guys had already gone. He didn't even notice me leaning against the back of truck as he slung his bag over his shoulder.

"Lee," I said as he started to walk away. He stopped for a second but then continued to walk. "Lee!" I called again. When he didn't turn around, I ran after him and grabbed his arm. "I know you heard me." I spun him around.

He just stared at me with a blank look.

"Well?" I asked him, hoping he would spill the answer to my unasked question.

"Well, what?" he said, shaking my hand off his shoulder.

"You know," I told him.

"No, I don't," he said before turning and walking away.

I stood rooted in my spot for a moment, shocked. What was his deal? Why would he do something nice for me and then pretend he didn't?

"Lee, why did you go get my sweater for me?" I shouted. My question made him stop. For a moment he just stood there, his back to me, and then I realized he was waiting for me to catch up. "Why?" I asked again when I was standing right next to him. "I know you don't like me."

"Jackie," he said, looking right at me. "Just pretend it never happened, okay?"

The bell rang, signaling we needed to head to first hour.

"No," I said sternly. "I want to know why you did it."

"We're going to be late for first period," he said, starting to climb the steps.

"I don't care," I told him, surprising myself. "I know you don't either."

"Fine," he grumbled. Lee led me to the back of the school and over to a cluster of trees that couldn't be seen from any of the building windows.

"Is this a part of some secret plan to kill me?" I questioned him as I looked around. We were completely alone.

Lee glanced over his shoulder to glare at me. "This is where I normally come when I don't feel like going to class."

"Oh..."

"Has anyone told you about my parents?" he asked me then.

"Your parents?"

"Yeah, the reason why Isaac and I live with my aunt and uncle."

"No," I said, not knowing where this conversation was going. I'd always wondered what happened to their parents, but truthfully, I was too afraid to ask.

"My mom left right after I was born," he told me. "I never even met her." I kept my mouth shut, waiting for him to continue. "Her leaving messed my dad up pretty bad. He's an Army officer, and instead of raising Isaac and me, he dumped us with his brother and went overseas. We only see him every few years."

I put a hand to my mouth to cover my surprise, but Lee wasn't looking at me. His gaze was focused on the sky. What he was telling me was almost worse than what happened to my family. Even though they were gone, at least I knew that they loved me.

We sat in silence for a while and the almost-summer sun warmed my skin. "Lee, I'm so sorry," I finally said.

"You know? You're probably the first person to actually mean that," he said.

"Really?" I asked him.

"I've heard so many people say 'sorry' to me, and it's all fake. They don't really know what it feels like to not have a family."

I nodded my head. "You know the worst part, though?" I asked him. "When people look at you differently. I'm no longer Jackie, daughter of the Howards. I'm Jackie, the girl with dead parents."

"Better than Lee, the boy whose parents couldn't care less."

"Why do you hate me?" I said then.

"I don't hate you. It's just…" Lee sighed and ran a hand through his curly hair, trying to find the right words. "Let's just say I have mom issues. I never knew mine, and Katherine—it's hard enough for her to pay attention to all twelve of us. And then you showed up, and my aunt felt so responsible for you that she gave up her studio. I felt like you were stealing the little time I had with her away from me."

"I don't know what to say," I told Lee.

"I wasn't asking you to," he said. "I went back and got your sweater because I finally realized that unlike me, you don't have anyone." I could tell that he was struggling for the right words. "I was too jealous to understand that you were in just as much pain as me. I was a dick."

Sighing, I grabbed Lee's hand. As angry with him as I was for everything he'd put me through, at least he was telling me the truth. "Yeah," I said, agreeing with him. "You totally were."

Lee cracked a smile.

• • •

Nathan never made me nervous. There was something about our friendship—something so natural and easy—that I didn't have with any of the other Walter boys. But today as I walked down the hall toward his room, I had to wipe my hands on the back of my skirt and push away the urge to flee.

Katherine had picked him up from the hospital after we left for school, and when we got home at four o'clock, all the boys rushed up to visit him. He had been required to stay in the hospital for the rest of the week, so most of the guys hadn't seen him since Saturday. I hung back, patiently waiting for my turn so we could talk in private.

We hadn't spoken since the morning of his seizure, and I could feel my stomach sloshing back and forth in anticipation. What Lee said to me in the ER was still lodged in the back of my mind. Yes, Monday morning we talked through our issues, but I couldn't help but think in *what if* terms. If only I had pulled myself out of bed when Nathan asked me to go running—swallowing my shame and fear of seeing the other boys—then maybe I wouldn't feel so guilty right now.

Outside his room, my knuckles were poised above the door, but then, losing my nerve, I dropped my hand back down to my side. Gentle notes of a new song were being teased out of his guitar, and I could picture Nathan sitting on his bed, eyes closed with the instrument in hand. Maybe I could come back later, sometime when my stomach wasn't so jittery.

"He's in there," someone said as I turned to leave. "You should go talk to him."

Knowing who it was, I took a deep breath as I looked up. Cole had paused in the middle of the hallway, his face arranged in a tight mask. The bruise around his eye had just started fading to yellow-green.

It was the first sentence had Cole spoken to me since Alex

punched him, and in reaction, a flare of resentment danced inside my chest. In truth, I was more ashamed of myself than angry. I couldn't help but notice the way Cole's shirt clung snuggly around his biceps, and how, in this moment, his eyes looked bluer than I had ever seen them.

After everything he'd done, how he'd purposely hurt me, I still felt that same flutter inside my chest, the one I'd been trying to figure out since I first arrived in Colorado. It was some type of invisible force, as if he were the sun and I was a tiny planet being reined in by his all-consuming gravity. What had Heather called it? The Cole effect.

"Oh—right," I said back, as if I hadn't known. It was all I could manage because suddenly I felt like crying. This feeling was so unfair, unwanted.

Nathan's song stopped, and I knew he could hear us. Cole's loud voice had given me away. However, in that moment, my anxiety about seeing Nathan evaporated. I pulled open the door without knocking and slipped inside. Anything to get away from Cole and the way he was making me feel. Hands wrapped around the doorknob, I leaned back against the wood and took slow, calming breaths.

"Jackie?" I heard Nathan ask.

My eyes snapped open. He was sitting up in bed, a concerned look splashed across his face. And then, as I stared back at him, I realized that it had been completely stupid of me to be nervous.

"Hey, Nate," I responded, and the feeling of relief cooled my flushed skin.

"Are you okay?" he asked, his eyebrows wrinkling together.

After another lungful of air to calm myself—in through the mouth and out the nose—I responded. "I should be asking you the same thing." Pushing away from the door, I straightened out my skirt before moving toward his bed. As I sat down, I noticed the square bandage on his forehead from where he hit his head and the dark circles beneath his eyes. "Oh, Nathan," I said, brushing aside his bangs so I could see the injury better.

"I'm fine," he said, pushing my hand away. I got the message loud and clear—he didn't want to talk about what had happened to him.

"You scared everyone pretty badly," I said anyway. He needed to know that even though I didn't visit him at the hospital, I was still worried, so I added, "Especially me."

He was quiet at this, his lips forced together into a line.

"Nathan?" I asked. My voice cracked, revealing the sudden return of my nerves. Maybe he *was* mad at me.

Finally he looked up. "Did I do something to make you mad?" he asked, a complete mirror of my own thoughts.

"What?" I said, shifting on the bed so I could get a better look at him. "No. Why would you think that?"

"Because I haven't seen you since…" He paused. "Well, since it happened."

I reached out again, this time putting my hand on his arm. "God, I'm so sorry, Nathan. It's just—I couldn't—" I stopped there, not knowing how to explain. I gave myself a second before slowly saying, "When the ambulance came, I felt like it was happening all over again. You know, losing someone I cared about. I panicked."

"Yeah, Cole told me you went to Will's apartment."

My head shot up. "He mentioned me?"

Nathan nodded. "We had a conversation today," he said, setting his guitar down so he could move closer to me. "It was strange," he said, and seeing my puzzled look, he went on. "Not having a conversation, although that was unusual. It was like—I don't know, he seemed disappointed about something. Confused, even."

"Confused? About what?"

"I'm not sure exactly. He was careful with his words. Wouldn't say too much of anything—and that reminds me. Do you know what happened to his eye? I couldn't even get that out of him."

"That's no mystery," I said, my cheeks going pink. "Alex punched him."

Nathan's eyebrows shot up on his forehead. "He *what?*"

"Trust me," I said, shaking my head at the memory. "Cole deserved it."

Nathan's laugh was one of being completely impressed. "Oh, I don't doubt, but man… I suppose that's a contributor to why he's so upset."

"If by upset, you mean angry? Most definitely."

"I don't know," Nathan said, tapping his finger to his chin. "I wouldn't call it angry. It was more like he was sad."

"Sad," I echoed, trying to grasp the idea. What would Cole have to be sad about?

• • •

"Oh no," Alex said to me, his voice low. "This looks bad."

The next morning as I peered down the front hallway into the kitchen, I couldn't help but agree. Katherine was hovering over the table with a finger pressed to her temple. Spread out before her was what looked like a year's worth of old bills and receipts.

"Watch out," Isaac said. He was leaning against the counter, eyeing his aunt warily as he waited for a pot of coffee to brew. Alex and I had slipped into the kitchen unnoticed and were standing next to him. "She's on a rampage."

"What's wrong?" I asked, opening the fridge to find the creamer.

"The florist for the wedding called today and said they still haven't received payment," he explained, pulling two mugs out from the cabinet above his head. "She's convinced the check was already sent in, so she's tearing through everything looking for the confirmation slip."

"That's not good," I replied.

But I wasn't just worried about the florist. Katherine and George were supposed to be leaving for the weekend—their twenty-second wedding anniversary was tomorrow, and George had planned a romantic getaway for the two of them. But with Will and Haley's wedding looming, Katherine had been more stressed than ever. From the look on her face, I could tell that going on vacation was the last thing on her mind.

"Not at all," Isaac said, pouring the steaming brown liquid into two cups, one for him and the other for me. "And if you're looking for the creamer, it's behind the ketchup."

With his directions, I located the bottle behind the sugary red sauce, next to the pickle jar. Taking it out, I slid the cream across the counter toward Isaac.

"Grab me a Kickstart, will you?" Alex asked before I shut the door. It wasn't hard to find one of the bright neon cans, and nose wrinkled, I wrapped my fingers around his favorite form of caffeine. Popping the tab, he chugged half of it in one slip. Seriously, he was going to have a heart attack at the age of twenty.

As I was closing the fridge, a magnet holding a piece of paper caught my eye. "Isaac, you said she's looking for a confirmation slip?"

"Something like that," he replied. He was focused on scooping the perfect amount of sugar into his drink.

Upon further inspection, I noticed that someone had arranged a series of alphabet magnets into an insulting sentence. It read: *Cole is a dillhole*. Under the bright orange letter D was a pink slip, and even though the loopy script was hard to read, I could just make out the word *florist*. Tugging the plastic magnet away from the fridge, I took the receipt and went over to the table.

"Katherine," I asked, holding it out for her to see, "is this what you're looking for?" At first, when her eyes glanced over the paper in my hand, I thought she was going to burst into tears. Instead, I was pulled into a tight hug.

"You, my dear, are a lifesaver," she said. Then, taking a deep breath, she pulled out her phone and punched in a number.

"What's going on?" Cole asked, noticing the mess on the table as he and Danny stumbled into the kitchen still half asleep. Nathan wasn't far behind them, a tuft of hair sticking up at the back of his head as he stretched.

"Wedding crisis," Alex responded, crushing the empty Kickstart can between his hands. "It's been averted."

"Doesn't look like it," Nathan said, pulling out one of the barstools and plopping down at the counter. "Hey, Isaac, want to pour me a cup?"

"Since when do you like coffee?" Isaac asked, but he grabbed a third mug anyway.

"I don't, but my earplugs are missing and Alex was up all night playing that annoying game."

"Shhh," Alex said, slapping his brother on the arm as he glanced at Katherine. But his mom didn't notice as she paced the kitchen floor, talking in a fed-up tone.

"Earplugs?" Isaac asked then. "I think Zack might have had a pair shoved up his nose yesterday."

"What?" Nathan said, looking pissed. "Why did he do that?"

His cousin only shrugged. "How am I supposed to know what goes on in that kid's brain? He's a strange one."

"Okay, okay. Thank you." Looking slightly less stressed, Katherine hung up the phone, only to have her moment of peace interrupted by the doorbell. "Oh, they're early!" she exclaimed, patting down her hair as she ran to the front door. Not long after that, she ushered Will and Haley into the room, both with suitcases clutched between their fingers. "You two are sweethearts for coming on such short notice," she said, and started sweeping the pile of papers on the table into a manila folder.

"Mom, don't worry about it," Will responded as he set down his stuff. "It's the least we can do."

At that moment, Jack and Jordan entered the kitchen, and upon seeing Will, they dashed across the floor.

"Will! Will!" they both shouted. "What are you doing here?"

"Spending the weekend. Haley and I are staying over to watch you rug rats while Mom and Dad are on vacation."

Cole, who was chugging out of the OJ container, sprayed a mouthful of juice down his shirt. "What?" he demanded, turning to his mom. "Why does he need to be here? I'm eighteen."

"Cole, did you honestly think I would leave you in charge?" Katherine asked, half distracted. One of the kitchen drawers was pulled open, and she was rummaging through the files inside. "Where is it?" she said to herself. "I swear I put it here."

"Darling," George said, as he slid open the back door. From the sweat glistening on his face, I could tell that he had been doing work around the ranch. "Are you still looking for the florist's receipt? We need to leave soon and you're not packed."

"What?" Will asked, giving his mother a look. "You're not packed? Go get ready."

"Will," Katherine said, not bothering to look up. "I don't think you understand how much I still need to get done for the wedding. It's less than two weeks away, and I don't know if I have the time to go on this vacation."

I didn't doubt it. In the past month, Will had stopped by to help with the arrangements, but since Katherine was hosting the back-yard wedding, she was the one with the most work.

"Then give us something to do," Will said.

"Yes," Haley said a moment later. "We'd love to help."

"That's really sweet of you both, but these are things that I need to get done myself."

"Kitty," George said, sounding exasperated. "Let the kids help. We've been planning this trip for a while."

"And I've been planning this wedding for the past sixteen months! I will not let it be a total catastrophe."

"Mom," said Will, coming up behind his mother to give her a hug. "I think you need to relax."

She shrugged him off. "How can I relax when I have a to-do list that's a million miles long?" she cried, pulling her hair.

"Katherine," I said, trying to get her attention.

She was back to riffling through the drawer, even though the thing she was searching for hadn't been there the first time she looked. "I'm just too busy," she muttered again.

"Katherine!" I said, raising my voice. Everyone looked at me, but I ignored the surprised expressions, choosing to focus solely on Mrs. Walter. She was starting to slip into panic mode, a habit I recognized from my mother, and I needed to calm her down before she broke down completely. Her head turned at the sound of my voice, and as if in a daze, she looked at me with her mouth half open.

"What do you have to do?" I asked her, my voice slow but direct.

"Pardon?" she asked.

I rephrased my question. "What needs to get done so you'll feel comfortable leaving for vacation?"

"Oh well, I don't know if that will be possible. The seating chart has to be arranged and ceremony programs need to be typed up. Honey, I don't understand why you want to know—"

"No," I said, cutting her off. "Just keep talking."

"All right," she said hesitantly. "I still can't find the..." And she dove into a mental catalog of all her different chores.

"Someone pen me," I muttered, holding out my hand as she continued to list the tasks. Nathan responded, slapping the ballpoint from his pocket into my hand. Grabbing the morning paper, I started to scribble a list on the edge of an article. It wasn't as neatly organized as one of my own to-do lists, but it would suffice.

When he realized what I was doing, George directed his wife to one of the kitchen chairs and made her sit down, keeping his hands clamped firmly on her shoulders. Then he told everyone else to sit down.

"Listen up, crew," I said a few minutes later, after reading over everything I'd written down. "This is how it's going to work." I looked from one Walter boy to the next to make sure they were paying attention. "Cole and Isaac—you have yard duty. The lawn has to be mowed, the hedges need to be trimmed, and the garden is in desperate need of weeding. Jack and Jordan, since you're good with editing, you're in charge of putting together the picture slide show of Will and Haley for the reception. No funny business either because I'm going to look over it when you're done. Danny, someone needs to pick up Haley's dress from the boutique, and Nathan, I want you to call all the vendors and reconfirm arrival times."

When I was done talking, everyone stared at me. "Are you all deaf?" I demanded. "Come on. We have work to do."

All the boys scrambled to their feet.

"Amazing," Alex said, once everyone was out of the kitchen.

"That was nothing," I told him. He had never seen me in my glory days, organizing one of my mother's fashion shows or charities.

"Is there anything left for me to do?" Katherine asked, looking uncertain. "I could write out the placeholders—"

"Yes, Katherine," I said, pulling her to her feet and shoving her out of the kitchen. "Go pack. You have a vacation to enjoy."

• • •

"I bet Cole is totally pissed right now," Alex told me later that day. We were in his room, and I was snuggled down into the pillows on his bed. I could smell the detergent that Katherine used to clean the sheets, along with Alex's musky scent. My anatomy book was propped up in front of me, and we were supposed to be studying together. But as soon as Alex heard the garage door close, indicating that his parents had left for vacation, he'd logged on to his computer to play *GoG*.

"How come?" I asked, flipping to the end of the chapter to see how many more pages I had to read.

"We always throw an end-of-the-year party. It was supposed to be tonight, but with Will babysitting, I don't know if it will happen."

"But what about exams?"

"What about them? We have the next two weeks to study."

"Okay. So what's he going to do?" I asked, even though the prospect of a party made me nervous.

Alex shrugged. "I don't know, but he'll think of something. There's no way Cole will turn down a chance to show off."

I tried to go back to studying then. If there was going to be party, I knew Riley, Heather, and the rest of the gang would want to come over and I would get nothing done. After ten minutes of rereading the same passage, I slammed my book shut, unable to concentrate with the annoying music coming from Alex's computer.

"Alex, do you have to play that right now?"

"Yup," he said, grinning at me. Somehow, even though I was slightly annoyed, his smile made my stomach flutter. Alex was too cute for his own good. "And now that you're my girlfriend, you should start playing *GoG* too."

I snorted. "I have no problem with your obsession, but online gaming isn't really my thing."

"But think about how much fun it would be. We could conquer the entire continent of RuWariah together."

"Shouldn't you be more focused on studying?" I didn't have a clue what the RooWar place was, but I knew that I had no desire to conquer it. "Two weeks of studying isn't much." Knowing Alex, he wouldn't even start studying until the weekend before. That would leave him with no time to properly prepare. The thought made me nauseous.

"Jackie, stop worrying so much."

"We only have fourteen days," I pointed out. "Come on, Alex. I saw your grade on the last anatomy test. You're going to need at least a ninety on the exam to even think about getting a B in the class."

"That's okay. I'm fine with a C."

At this, I felt uncomfortable. How could he be so unconcerned about not doing his best? "Well," I said, taking a different approach. "We need to start thinking about where we'll apply for college. If you want to get into a good school, your transcript will need to be polished."

"That's not a problem. I'll just go to the local community college like Will."

"But don't you want to go somewhere more…prestigious?"

"Like where? Yale? Jackie, my parents can't afford that."

"But if you worked hard and got good grades—"

"I'm a geek, not a brainiac. No school is going to give me a scholarship," he said. Three seconds later, "Argh! Damn these undead priests that keep respawning." His fingers were pounding away at the keyboard, his eyes glued to the screen.

I became quiet. I didn't understand how Alex could be okay with settling for less than the best. Snapping my textbook shut, I untangled myself from the bed and stood up. Yes, living with the Walters had taught me how to loosen up, but that didn't mean I was going to let my grades go slack.

"Hey, you okay?" he asked, glancing over his shoulder.

"Um—yeah, fine," I said, picking my way across the littered carpet. "I'm going to head back to my room. I really need to finish reading these chapters before tonight."

Alex swung around in his computer chair. "Are you sure you're all right?"

I offered him the best smile I could muster. "Just nervous about these next two weeks. Don't worry about me."

"Well, are you going to come to the party?"

If I could avoid it, then no, but something told me that wouldn't happen. "Of course," I told him.

"Awesome. See you then."

• • •

Sure enough, four hours later, I was watching my friends get ready for the party.

"Tonight is going to be to die for, y'all!" Riley gushed, sounding more twangy than usual.

She was stationed in front of the small mirror in my room, attempting to do her makeup. As Alex predicted, Cole was able to convince Will to let him have the party. From what I had heard, it hadn't been too hard, considering Will was the original creator of the Walter end-of-the-year bash. Also, Cole reminded Will of how many times he'd covered for his older brother during high school when he had snuck out of the house.

"Have you ever been so excited about something in your whole life?" Heather asked, being her usual dramatic self. She was rummaging through my closet, looking for something to wear. "Jackie, are you planning on wearing this, or can I?"

In her hands was a shirt my mother gave me from one of her fashion shows. The flashy colors weren't my style, and back home it sat in my closet untouched. Like my sister's dress, it had somehow gotten from New York to Colorado.

"Knock yourself out," I told her with a nod. Then I added, "So what's the big deal about this party?" My friends were acting like they had been invited to Cinderella's ball, but it was just another party.

"Oh, Jackie," Skylar said, looking up from a *Cosmo*. He rolled his eyes and dropped it on the ground before getting up out of my computer chair. "Sometimes I forget how little you know."

When I hung out with the girls and Sky, I was always asking questions. They knew so much more about the Walters, and boys in general, which was ironic since I was living with what felt like a million of them.

"The big deal is that we're friends with you," Riley said.

"Okay?" I still didn't understand.

"You live with the Walters," Heather said.

"Yes," I said, starting to feel frustrated. "We've covered that before."

"So, that means we'll get an invite to the VIP party," Skylar explained.

"There's a VIP section?" I asked in surprise. I could see Cole being exclusive and only inviting a select group of friends to a better party, but it didn't seem like something the rest of the Walter boys would do.

"Everyone from school is invited, so a crazy amount of people show up. The backyard fills up until the place is packed. Last year, you could barely move around the deck because it was so full. There's not really room for everyone, so the guys always invite their friends out for a more private event," Skylar told me.

"My older sister, Dee, was friends with Will when they were in high school," Heather added. "She's told me some insane stories about how amazing it is."

"What's to stop people from crashing?"

"From what she said, I think they go somewhere else on the ranch," Heather explained as she pulled the top I'd lent her over her head.

"It's at the waterfall," Kim said suddenly. Like always, she had a colorful comic grasped between her hands. "The guys use four-wheelers to take guests out."

"That makes sense," I said, nodding my head. There was plenty of room on the beach for a small group of people.

"How do you know that?" Riley asked as she spun around in a circle, checking herself out in the mirror.

"Alex took me out last year," she said sheepishly.

"And you never thought to tell us?" Heather gasped, insulted. Kim just shrugged and went back to reading.

A knock on the door interrupted the conversation before Heather and Riley could attack Kim with another round of questions. "Jackie?" Alex asked, sticking his head in.

"Yeah?" I said, looking over my shoulder at the door.

"Oh, I didn't know you guys were already over," Alex said, and he swung the door all the way open.

"I texted you," Kim said, her eyes still glued to the page.

"Sorry, I've been getting ready for the party," Alex said. "I came up to grab Jackie. We need help putting up decorations."

"We'll all help!" Heather said, volunteering the entire group. "What's the theme this year?"

"There's a theme?" I asked.

"Yeah, we all take turns picking one. I wanted to do a super hero costume party, but the guys shot me down," he explained. "This year we're having a luau. Danny just got back from the store with about a million different-colored leis, tiki torches, and a blowup palm tree."

"Bikini party!" Heather giggled.

"Yeah," Alex said, rolling his eyes. "Guess who picked the theme this year?"

I didn't need to guess.

Chapter 15

The clearing was lit up with torches and the trees lined with Christmas lights. The water sparkled as the flames danced across the surface, and the pumping music gave the whole scene a hypnotic feel. As people jumped into the pond, water droplets sprayed across the surface, making it look like they were swimming in diamonds.

"It's beautiful," I whispered.

"Thanks," Danny said, coming up next to me. "Worked on it all afternoon. Had to bribe Jack and Jordan into climbing the trees to wrap the lights."

"It was worth it."

"Good. It cost me two weeks' worth of allowance."

Riley, Heather, and Skylar, who had never been to the water-fall before, quickly stripped down to their swimsuits. Knowing how cold the water was, I decided to skip the swimming and instead found Alex and Kim talking with a group of friends at the picnic table.

"Greetings, magnificent lady," said one of the boys as I approached. His hair was long and hadn't been washed in quite some time. Greasy bangs gleamed in the flicker of the tiki torches.

I looked to Alex for direction.

"Malcolm," Alex said, as he pulled me down onto his lap, "this is my *girlfriend*, Jackie." He made sure to stress the "girlfriend" part. "Jackie, this is Malcolm and the rest of my guild."

Besides Malcolm, the *GoG* guild included two other boys—one with scrawny arms and a long, hooked nose, and another with hair dyed a shocking shade of blue.

"It is an honor to make the acquaintance of our fearless leader's fair maiden," Malcolm said, taking my hand and kissing it.

"Dude, are you trying to embarrass me?" Alex asked his friend, and Kim burst out laughing.

"Could be worse," blue-haired boy said. "At least he didn't greet her in Sindarin."

"Um—it's nice to meet you as well," I told Malcolm, pulling my hand away from him. I had no clue what language Sindarin was, but as I wiped his kiss off on the back of my pants, I knew I already wanted to get away from this conversation. Maybe I should have gone swimming…

"Ah, the lady speaks, and in such a pleasing tone."

"Seriously, man," Alex said, slugging his friend on the shoulder. "If you don't cut it out, I'm never going out in public with you again."

"Want me to go grab some beer?" I asked Alex as I untangled our legs from beneath the picnic table and stepped over the bench. I wasn't going to drink, not after last time, but at this point I was looking for any excuse to get away.

"That'd be amazing."

I was gone before Malcolm could mutter another uncomfortable word. The keg was situated near the edge of the clearing, right at the line of trees. When I finally reached the front of the line, I found Nick running the tap.

"Hi," I said, trying to be as brisk as possible. There was something about him that made me feel uneasy. Maybe it was the fact that he was Cole's best friend, or maybe it was just because most of the time, he was so unfriendly. "I need two."

"One at time," he said, thrusting a single beer in my direction. "House rules."

"Considering I live here and you don't," I said, putting my free hand on my hip, "bending the rules shouldn't be a problem. And the second cup is for Alex who, if you didn't know, also lives here."

The people behind me in line snickered.

"All right, whatever," he said. The air was tense for a moment as I waited for him to fill the second cup, and as soon as he handed it to me, I moved away from the keg without a thank-you.

"Hey, psst!" Someone yanked me into the trees, sloshing beer all over my arm.

"Cole?" I said when I straightened up and spotted him. "What the hell are you doing?"

"Can we talk?" he asked, gesturing behind him with a nod.

"I'm getting beers for Alex and myself," I told him.

"This is important."

"That's nice, but I'm in the middle of an interesting conversation," I lied, glancing back at the table where Alex and his friends were sitting.

"With whom? The Dungeons and Dragons freaks?"

"Do you always have to be so mean?"

"Do you always have to be so stubborn?"

"I am not."

"I just need ten minutes. Is that really so much of your time?"

I thought about Malcolm, who would be waiting at the table when I returned. "Five," I said, grumbling.

"That works," Cole said, grabbing the beers out of my hands and tossing them to the ground. "Let's go."

"Hey!" I complained, glancing down at the now-empty cups. "I stood in line for those."

But Cole wasn't listening. He was tugging me through the undergrowth, pushing tree branches out of the way as he went.

"What's so important that we need to trudge through half a jungle just to talk about it?" I demanded as we quickly moved deeper into the forest.

Ignoring me, he continued to plow through the vegetation until we broke through into a small clearing.

"Wow." It was all I could mutter.

The moonlight poured over the tops of the trees and onto the small expanse of grass, bathing the area in beautiful white light. However, it wasn't the moonlight that made me catch my breath. There were hundreds of little white flowers growing everywhere. I could feel Cole watching me as I took in the sight around me.

"*Dicentra spectabilis,*" he said.

"What?"

"The flowers." He gestured with his head. "The common name is 'bleeding hearts.'"

"They're beautiful," I said as I cradled one in my palm. They really did look like hearts.

"Most are normally pink," he told me, grabbing my hand and directing me to a boulder in the middle of the clearing. "But some types are white."

"Do they always bloom at night?" I asked, tucking my legs in as I sat down.

Cole shook his head. "They like shade, so they normally open near the end of the day. These guys just haven't closed up yet."

"Since when did you become a flower expert?" I asked.

"I know lots of random facts about plants. My mom loves gardening. Just wait until she starts working on her flower beds this summer." He was smiling at me, trying to scoot closer.

"So what did you need to talk to me about?" I asked then, realizing that the five minutes I'd given him were already up. He was quiet at this, looking away as I tried to catch his eye. "Cole, why did you bring me here?" I demanded. I didn't want to play any of his games.

"Jackie…" He scraped his hair back, the look in his eyes regretful, and I knew he was trying to apologize for the night we went TPing.

"No," I said and took a step back from him. "No, no. You can't do this, Cole. You don't get to do this."

"Will you just listen to me?"

"Why?" I asked. "Everything you told me at Will's was a lie."

"That's not true!"

"Bullshit. You gave me this crap speech about being a jerk because you were jealous of Alex, but as soon as we get home, what do you do?"

"Jackie, please—"

"No, Cole," I snapped. "I'm so done with your shit. You don't get a second chance."

"What about Alex? You've given him two!"

"You're right, Cole. I did. But the difference between you two is that what *you* did—that was out of spite. And want to know what I think? I think that you enjoy being an asshole."

"God, Jackie!" he exploded. "What did you expect after I opened up to you? I tell you my feelings, and then you turn around and date my brother."

"What feelings, Cole? You never said anything about your feelings!"

"That I like you, Jackie! I didn't know I had to spell it out, considering everything I've done for you."

"Oh, so now you care about me? If that's true, why would you try to get me in trouble like that?"

"Because you said yes to Alex!" he screamed. And then, as if he was out of steam, he dropped his head. "Why did you say yes?"

He buried his head in his hands, and we were both quiet for a long time.

"Cole," I finally said as a chilly breeze drifted through the clearing, covering my arms in goose bumps. He lifted his head slowly but finally met my eyes. "I don't understand you. One minute you're making out with the entire cheerleading squad, and the next you're mad at me for dating Alex? That's not fair."

"This was not how I imagined our conversation going," he said, ripping a clump of grass from the ground. He started to shred the long green slices into tiny slivers.

"Lots of things don't turn out how we plan," I responded. After everything I'd been through, I'd learned to understand that.

"But I didn't even *plan* for this to happen." He moved his hand back and forth in the foot of space between us, indicating something more. I knew he meant me and him, and this thing going on between us, whatever that was.

"Look, Cole," I said. "Neither did I, but I'm still dealing with it."

And that's when it hit me—about Romeo and Juliet, I mean. I never figured Cole or Alex into my life, just like Shakespeare's most famous couple never anticipated falling in love. The Walter boys were unexpected, but I was still managing just like Romeo and Juliet did. Sure their way was unconventional, but what if that was the best they could do given the circumstance? Maybe I hadn't given them enough credit.

I had been trying to fit my world into a small, safe box for so long. But life didn't work like that. It could move in and out of the lines. You couldn't control everything, because it wasn't all meant to be perfect. Sometimes things needed to be messy.

I got up from the rock. So I couldn't control the fact that Cole and Alex were in my life, making it one confusing mess. But I could uncomplicate it once and for all. Unlike Romeo and Juliet, I was going to take the easy way out of love. I had already made my decision the night I said yes to Alex. Now I had to follow through.

"I need to go back to the party before anyone starts worrying about me," I said then. "You should go too."

Cole didn't move as I made my way out of the clearing. He just let me go.

• • •

The backyard was a sea of red cups, and I had to pick them all up.

Will woke everyone bright and early since we needed to erase the evidence of the party before Katherine and George got home. Impressed with how I took charge during his mom's meltdown, Will employed my skills to organize the cleanup. I quickly split up the chores that needed to be tackled and dished them out to all the boys. I thought I had given myself the worst job, but I could hear Isaac complaining from the deck.

"Too early for this shit," he said as he yanked his shirt over his head. He was responsible for cleaning the pool. Not only was it murky, but two patio chairs were submerged in the deep end and a swimsuit top was tied to the basketball hoop that hung over the water. With one last grumble, he dove in and the cups floating on the surface bobbed like buoys.

Besides Isaac, Danny was putting the house in order. Even though partygoers were restricted to the backyard, somehow the mess had managed to leak inside. Will and Haley were making sure the front yard was spotless, and for obvious reasons, I sent Cole to clean up by the waterfall.

After our conversation the night before, I'd returned to the party and spent the night talking with Alex and his friends. Malcolm was obnoxious the entire time—hitting on me and saying awkward things—until it got so bad that Alex pushed him into the freezing water. I didn't notice when Cole rejoined his friends, but eventually I spotted him, a beer in one hand and his other arm wrapped around Olivia. He kept his distance, but I caught him watching me from across the beach more than once.

This morning was tense. There wasn't much time for breakfast, so we started a toast assembly line. Danny put the bread in the toaster. When it was done cooking, he handed to Isaac who put it on a paper plate and passed it to Cole. He would spread jam on one piece before sliding the plate to me, so I could butter the second piece. Finally, Alex would cut both pieces in half and move the plate to the kitchen table. I don't know how I ended up squished between Cole and Alex, but I could feel how uncomfortable Cole was.

I gave him the waterfall job so I wouldn't have to see him, but as Alex opened his mouth again, I'd wished for a second that I sent him along as well.

"I'm really sorry about last night," he told me for the millionth time. He was standing a few feet away from me with a garbage bag clutched in his hand.

"Alex," I said, plucking a cup off the sparkling grass, which was wet with morning dew. I dropped it into my own bag and caught a whiff of stale beer. "How many times do I need to tell you? Stop apologizing."

"I just feel bad that you had to put up with Malcolm all night."

I knew he was really worried that I was judging him based on his friend, but I honestly didn't care that Malcolm was weird. As long as I didn't have to hang out with him again, I'd be fine. I was anxious about not getting everything cleaned up in time, and if Alex had spent as much time cleaning as he did being nervous, we might be done already.

"He wasn't that bad," I lied. "Let's just focus on getting this done."

"Are you sure?" Alex asked, and I gave him a death glare. "Okay, I get it! More cups, less talking."

It was a miracle, but we managed take care of the party mess before Katherine and George returned. By the time they pulled into the driveway, Nathan and I were already studying for our exams. We didn't have any classes together, but Nathan asked if he could work in my room with me. He was having a hard time focusing in his own since Alex was trying to get in a quick round of *GoG* before his parents got home.

An almost-summer breeze wandered in through my open window, brushing against the back of my neck and cooling my sticky skin. Frustrated with all the different dates I needed to know for my history exam, I closed my eyes and rested my head against the wall. I tried to relax, but it was impossible with Nathan's music. He had headphones in, but I could still hear the heavy beat of some rock song. It didn't really seem like his thing, but his head was bopping away as he flipped through a set of flash cards.

"Hey, Nathan?" I called, trying to get his attention. There was no answer. "Nathan!" I shouted, and he jumped, the cards in his hand slipping to the floor. Jostling his MP3 player, he turned off the music and looked at me.

"What's wrong?"

I laughed. "Nothing, I just wanted to talk. How do you concentrate with all that noise anyway?"

"Oh," he said, kneeling to collect his flash cards. "It's nothing really. I've grown up with so much noise in this house."

"So you can only work with loud, brain-splitting music?" I asked, unconvinced.

Nathan shrugged. "If it gets too quiet around here, something just feels off."

"Gotcha. So where were you last night?" I asked. "I didn't see you at the party."

"I wasn't allowed to go. Will needed someone to keep all the little ones occupied while he was supervising, and he decided I was too young to attend. Lee got to go last year when he was a freshman, but Cole was in charge then."

"Dang," I said, knowing how excited the boys were about the party. "That stinks."

He considered this momentarily. "Not really," he told me. "The party scene really isn't my thing."

"Yeah, same here." As the words left my mouth, I realized how hypocritical they sounded. Since moving to Colorado, I'd been to more parties in the past month and a half than in my entire life.

Nathan must not have been paying attention, because he kept talking. "The only bad part was trying to fall asleep with all the racket outside, and of course the food fight."

"Food fight?" I questioned.

"Zack and Benny got in a fight over who was better: the Green Goblin or the octopus dude. I forget his name."

"Doctor Octopus," I added.

"Yeah, him. Well, anyway, they started throwing popcorn at each other. When they ran out, they used their grape soda. It took forever to pick up all the little pieces and I had to get a mop."

Before I could respond, I heard yelling from the backyard.

"Giddyap, horsey!"

Getting up, I went over to the window just in time to see Isaac rocket off the deck with Parker clamped onto his back. Around her neck was a cowboy hat hanging by a string. On her feet were a pair of worn-out cowboy boots, and clutched in one hand was an orange squirt gun.

The door slammed shut again, and a second later Benny and Zack leaped off the steps, copying their older cousin. They were both wearing swim trunks and had war paint slathered across their chests. The twins began to launch water balloons at the cowgirl and her horse.

"Turn around, horsey!" Parker said, slapping Isaac on the butt to get him moving. "We need to get those Indians!"

I giggled and pushed the window all the way up so I could sit on the sill and watch. As I made myself comfortable, Zack ducked out of the way of the stream of water from Parker's gun. His flimsy headband made of construction paper and neon craft feathers flew off his head.

"Time-out!" Benny yelled so his partner could collect his headgear. Parker didn't listen.

"Hey, no fair!" Zack shouted at his sister who blasted him in the face anyway. "He told you time-out!"

"I don't listen to savages!" Parker announced. A moment later a water balloon exploded on her arm.

"Kids!" George demanded, emerging onto the deck. He wasn't facing me, but from the tone of his voice, I could tell he was frowning. "When I told you to stop using the dog as a horse, I didn't mean for you to bother Isaac. He's supposed to be helping me fix the kitchen sink!"

Isaac's shoulders slumped, his fun ruined, and he let Parker slip off his back.

"Aw, man!" Parker complained, crossing her arms. "Now the teams are unfair."

"Hey, Jackie!" Zack shouted when he spotted me in the window. "Do you want to play Wild West?"

"Of course she does," Parker said, and before I could respond, she blasted me with a spray of cold water from her squirt gun.

"Hey!" I shrieked. She giggled and pumped up her gun for another attack. "Don't you dare!"

She pulled the trigger again, spraying my shirt. Trying to get out of the way, I tumbled to the floor with a loud thump.

"You guys," Nathan shouted from behind me. "We're trying to study."

As I picked myself up off the floor, the bedroom door banged open.

"What's wrong? I heard a crash!" Katherine was panting in the doorway, with a worried look on her normally gentle features. Her eyes searched for Nathan, and when she saw him sitting perfectly fine at my desk, she let out a breath of relief. "Thank God," I heard her whisper.

"I'm fine, Mom," Nathan said angrily.

"I'm sorry. I just thought something bad had—"

"That was my fault, Katherine," I said, cutting in. "I didn't mean to upset you. I was just being clumsy."

She watched us for a moment. "Are you sure?" she asked, still sounding unsure.

"Everything is fine," Nathan said slowly. I could tell he was trying not to yell.

Just then a water balloon came sailing through the window. It exploded at my feet and sprayed everywhere. A stream of laughter followed the attack.

"Kids!" Katherine shouted. The giggling cut off. "What did I tell you about water balloons in the house? Get inside right now!"

Then she stormed out of the room, leaving us slightly stunned and silent. I couldn't tell if her anger was caused by the little kids or by stress from what she thought was Nathan having another seizure. I stayed still until Nathan finally let out the air he was holding in.

"Do you want me to leave?" I asked, even though we were in my room. He looked like he needed to be alone.

"No!" he answered and angrily shuffled through his flash cards. Then he sighed and added, "Sorry, Jackie. I didn't mean to yell at you. I'd just like to go back to studying."

"It's okay," I told him and opened my book again. But as the minutes passed, I couldn't concentrate on the words in front of me. "Do you want to talk about it?" I finally asked.

"I'm fine," he told me. "It's just really frustrating when I can't have any privacy. My mom is constantly checking on me. I'm surprised she hasn't started sleeping on my floor at night."

"She's just worried about you," I said, not sure how to respond. I hadn't the slightest idea of what he was going through. It must be hard to always have someone with you, never alone.

"I know." He sighed and ran a hand through his hair. "But I just want my old life back."

"Yeah," I mumbled, looking down. Then we were both still, lost in our own problems.

The door banged open again. "Hey, Jackie?" Alex asked, beaming like an excited child.

"What's up?"

"Not much. I was just wondering if you wanted to come to my baseball game later today. It's the last one of the year." The corners of his mouth rose in a hopeful smile. How could I say no to that cute grin?

"I'd love to, Alex," I told him, patting the spot next to me on the bed. "But you have to do me a favor first."

"Sure," Alex said excitedly.

"You need to study for anatomy."

• • •

As I washed my hands, I whistled the tune of a song Nathan had been listening to. Somehow I'd managed to convince Alex to go over our anatomy definitions together, and along with Nathan, we'd been holed up in my room for the past two hours. When Alex's attention span finally waned, I walked him back to his room and took a quick bathroom break.

Turning off the faucet, I heard a giggle.

"Who's in here?" I demanded and spun around. Someone tried to suppress another laugh, and I flung the shower curtain back. "Benny!" I cried when I saw him curled up in the tub. "What are you doing?"

"Playing hide-and-seek. Mom took away the water balloons," he explained, a frown of disappointment on his face. But then he smiled and added, "Do you always wear polka-dot underwear?"

I counted to three in my head to contain my anger. "Benny," I said, after taking a few calming breaths, "why didn't you say something when I came in?"

"That's not how you play hide-and-seek," he whispered and put a finger to his lips. "You have to be quiet, duh."

"But I needed to use the bathroom," I said.

The door slammed open. People really needed to learn how to knock in this household. "I found you!" shouted Zack.

"Did I win?" his twin asked eagerly and climbed out of the tub.

"No!" Parker complained, pushing into the bathroom as well. "Zack cheated. He was peeking when I hid!"

"Did not!"

"Yes, huh!"

"You're just a shitty hider!" Zack said, shoving his sister.

"Am not!" Parker shouted back.

"I won! I won!" Benny sang as he danced across the tile in celebration.

"Guys!" I said, trying to break up a fight. "How about we start over? I'll play too. This time, no peeking."

I gave Zack a no-funny-business look, and he flashed me a grin before running back to his room to count. "One. Two. Three," he started slowly. Then, "Four-five-seven-ten!"

Parker dashed out of the bathroom as Zack rushed to sixty, and as I searched for a place to hide, I realized I had acquired a tiny shadow.

"Benny, you can't keep following me around," I told him. "I'm trying to find a spot."

"Can I hide with you?" he asked. His bottom lip was out stuck out in a pout as he looked up at me with big eyes.

"Oh fine," I said, unable to say no to his adorable face. Opening the linen closet, I yanked out a few towels, clearing off a shelf. "Come here, you," I said, lifting Benny up and helping him climb onto the shelf. He pulled his knees up to his chest, and I covered him with the towels. Then I stepped inside and closed the door, throwing us into darkness.

"He's never going to find me," Benny giggled.

"Hey," I whispered. "I thought the rule was you had to be quiet."

We hid in the darkness for only a minute, and I was already starting to get antsy. Even though I had just gone, my bladder was turning tight. It was the one thing I hated about playing hide-and-seek—you always ended up having to pee. Just when I couldn't take it any longer, someone pulled open the door.

Cole jumped back in surprise when he saw me. "Jesus," he shouted, almost dropping the towel that was wrapped around his waist. He must have been heading for the shower. "Why are you creeping in the closet?"

"Peaches, peaches, apple pie. If you're not ready, holler I!" Zack shouted from his room, and I felt Benny tug on my shirt in panic. Crap, we were going to be found first.

"Get in here," I said, grabbing Cole's wrist and yanking him in.

But there wasn't much room. With the door shut, I could feel the shelves digging into my back. And then there was the part where Cole's entire body was pressed up against mine.

"Change your mind about dating Alex?" Cole asked. I couldn't see him in the dark, but we were so close that I could feel his breath on my face.

"What?"

"Well, you just pulled me into a closet nearly naked. I'm assuming you're going to confess your undying love for me and tell me how you made a mistake that night at the party. Then we could have hot, passionate se—"

"Oh my God, no," I hissed at him, as my face went warm. "I haven't changed my mind about anything. We're playing hide-and-seek and you were about to ruin my spot."

"Okay, fine. We can skip over the undying love and jump right to the fun part."

"Cole," I said, stomping on his foot. "Shut up!"

"God damn, woman! That hurt!"

"Can you guys just kiss or something?" Benny complained. "At least then you'd be quiet. I wanna win."

"Holy shit, Benny?" Cole exclaimed, his chest heaving against mine in surprise. "Anyone else hiding in here too?"

"Yeah," I said. "Carmen Sandiego and Where's Waldo. Now please, be quiet!"

Cole listened to me then, and even though he kept his mouth shut, I was afraid that my heart would give us away. It was pounding so loudly that the entire house must have heard it.

Chapter 16

"Ay me! Sad hours seem long. Was that my father that went hence so fast?'" Danny said, raising a hand to his heart. The other was clutching a script.

"'It was. What sadness lengthens Romeo's hours?'" Isaac said in a booming voice, flourishing his hands wildly.

"Thank God you're not in the play," I mumbled in his direction and shook my head in embarrassment.

Danny, Isaac, and I were sitting on the bleachers at Alex's baseball game. The seats were metal and burned in the afternoon light. I was wearing a skirt that forced me to sit on the edge of the seat to keep the skin on the back of my legs from getting scorched. My boyfriend was far out in left field, and I could barely see him since the sun was glaring in my eyes.

"'Not having that which, having, makes them short,'" Danny recited.

When Isaac didn't answer because his attention was focused on a possible home-run hit, Danny elbowed him in the side.

"Oh, um—'in love'?" he said, quickly looking down at his copy of the script. Danny was forcing Isaac to run lines with him so I could watch Alex play.

Danny sighed, embodying the lovesick Romeo, "Out."

Isaac stood up in excitement as the ball flew toward his cousin in the outfield. "Did he catch it?" he demanded a few seconds later. "I can't tell. The sun is in my eyes."

"Huh?" I responded. I was trying to watch, but the humidity was making my head feel heavy, and it was hard to concentrate.

"Never mind," Isaac grumbled and sat back down on the bleachers. "You're not even paying attention."

"Neither are you," Danny told him angrily. "We should be done with this act by now."

"Dude, why do you even need to go over this? You've already had your costume rehearsal," Isaac complained. When Danny glared at him, he sighed and glanced back down at the script. "'Of love?'"

"'Out of her favor, where I am in love.'" Danny said his line without having to look down at the sheet.

"You're out!" the umpire shouted at a player who tried to slide into home.

"Yes!" Isaac shouted, fixing his attention back down on the field. "Was that two or three?"

"Two, I think," I answered absentmindedly, but then Alex's team began to jog back from the field toward the dugout.

Isaac rolled his eyes at me. "Not much of a baseball fan?"

"No, that's not true," I said, pressing a hand to my sticky forehead. "I love the Yankees. It's just that—"

"That she can't stop thinking about Cole. And you," Danny said, jabbing his cousin in the chest, "keep forgetting you're supposed to be helping me practice. God, Isaac, you're a horrible Benvolio."

"*Hey!*" both Isaac and I shouted at the same time.

"I'm not thinking about Cole," I said, defending myself.

"And I'm a great actor. Academy Award winning, thank you very much," Isaac said, shaking his finger back and forth in Danny's face.

"Isaac, if I remember correctly, you were the one who couldn't play a tree in the spring recital without messing it up."

"That was kindergarten," Isaac mumbled, but Danny wasn't listening.

"Jackie, I'm quiet, not blind," he told me. "That dazed look that's been on your face ever since you two came out of that closet says otherwise."

"Say what?" Isaac demanded.

"I wasn't like that," I said. "I swear." Because of his shy nature, Danny might have developed a certain affinity for perceptiveness, but this time he had it all wrong.

"Sure it wasn't," Isaac said.

Okay, so maybe I wasn't telling the truth. Yes, I was thinking about Cole, but not in the way they thought. And that was exactly why I couldn't quite concentrate on the baseball game. When we were playing hide-and-seek, Zack took forever to find us. Ignoring Benny's protest, Cole got impatient and opened the closet door. His shower was running, and he didn't want it to get cold. Danny, who had been looking for someone to read lines with, had seen both of us tumble out of the tiny room. I was worried he would get the wrong idea and tell everyone. What would Alex think if he found out?

"There's nothing going on between me and Cole," I objected. "Danny, you saw Benny climb out of the closet too. Tell him that."

"What the heck was he doing in there with you both?" Isaac said. "That's disgusting and definitely not PG-rated. Poor Benny is going to be scarred for life."

"We were playing hide-and-seek," I said, starting to panic. "Come on, Danny, tell him the truth."

"I don't know, Jackie," he said, his face straight. "Cole didn't even have a shirt on."

Isaac shook his finger at me. "Now that's naughty." He put his hand on my leg and grinned. "Why wasn't I invited?"

"God, you're disgusting," I said, pushing him away.

"Did you rip his shirt off with your teeth?" he asked, wiggling his eyebrows up and down.

"He was going to take a frickin' shower!" I exploded.

A few moms sitting around us turned to frown at me. Both boys watched me for a moment before bursting into fits of laughter.

"Wow, it's fun to watch you squirm," Isaac choked out, and I punched him on the shoulder.

"We were only kidding, Jackie," Danny said, wiping away a stray tear.

"Not appreciated," I grunted, crossing my arms. I stared down at the game, refusing to look in either of their directions.

"Come on, Jackie," Isaac said, putting a hand on my arm. "I was just messing around."

I stuck out my tongue and continued to watch the game going on below.

"Are you going to ignore me for the rest of the day? Because I can be quite annoying if I want to." Isaac started poking me repetitively in the cheek.

Pushing his hand away, I answered. "I sure can. Now be quiet. Alex is up."

All three of us fell silent and watched as Alex hit a grounder. It rolled right between two infielders, and he made it to second base before they could get the ball.

"Go, Alex!" I shouted excitedly, jumping up and down.

"Oh, Alex!" Isaac squealed in a girly voice. "You're so damn sexy that I was making out in the closet with your older brother!"

Danny choked on air as he tried not to laugh. I spun around and whacked Isaac on the shoulder again.

"Dang, Jackie! You're going to bruise my delicate skin," he complained, rubbing the sore spot.

"Good," I said and sat back down to watch the next hitter.

Danny's phone rang. "Hey, Dad," he said in greeting. "Right now?" He paused. "Okay, I'll be there in a few." He clicked his phone shut and turned to us. "I have to go pick Zack and Benny up from their soccer game."

At this, I frowned. There were still four innings left. Danny had driven us, so how would we get home if he left?

"I'm coming too," Isaac said and stood up.

"But what about the rest of the game?" I asked.

"You can stay if you want," Isaac suggested. "Alex rode his bike here. He can give you a ride home on the pegs."

• • •

"You did great today," I told Alex when he found me after the game was over. His team had won by three runs.

He pulled me into a hug. "Thanks, Jackie. I'm really glad you came."

"You're all sweaty," I squealed, trying to squirm away. He was going to ruin my shirt.

"You don't like that?" he asked with a laugh, locking his arms tightly behind my back.

"No! Alex, let go," I said, but gave in with a laugh.

Clouds had rolled in near the end of the game, covering the hot sun, but the air was still humid, making our bodies stick together.

"Where'd everyone go?" he asked, letting his arms hang loose.

"Danny had to pick Zack and Benny up. I wanted to stay, so I was hoping you could give me a ride home on your bike. You're not too tired, are you?"

"A little," he said, slinging his arm over my shoulder. "But it will be my pleasure."

We made it about halfway home when it started to pour. Alex pulled off the road and onto a gravel pathway that led to a small, rundown pavilion as lightning flashed across the sky. I jumped off the back of the bike and ran under the overhang to get out of the rain. Taking a ponytail holder off my wrist, I pulled my damp hair out of my face. After leaning his bike up against the brick wall, Alex pulled out his phone and called home. He had a quick conversation with someone and then sat down on an old wooden picnic table that was covered in graffiti.

"Someone is coming to get us," he said.

I nodded, looking out over a grassy clearing. "What is this place?" I asked.

There was a boarded-up concessions stand, and beyond the structure was a grassy meadow with a large section that was flat and brown. It looked like a dried-up pond.

"It used to be an outdoor ice-skating rink during the winter months," Alex said, following my gaze out to what must have been the ice patch. Alex took one of my hands and rubbed my skin gently with his thumb. "Ever been skating before?"

It was a harmless question, yet I still felt a sudden jab at my heart.

"Yeah," I said slowly. "My family had this tradition where we'd go to the rink at Rockefeller Center on my mom's birthday. I don't remember how it started since my mom wasn't very good, but we did it every year."

Alex wrapped his arms around my waist and pulled me close. "Sorry, I didn't mean to make you sad."

"I'm fine," I told him, resting my head on his shoulder. "It's one of those nice memories. You know, the kind that makes you sad but you smile at the same time?"

I could almost picture my family gliding across the patch of dried-up grass as I stared out at the meadow, and the memory was so captivating that it took me a minute to realize that Alex hadn't answered me. When I turned to look at him, I found that his eyes were already locked on me.

The first time Alex kissed me, it was so unexpected that it made my stomach jump in excitement. At the time, I hadn't known what to think because there was so much adrenaline soaring through me. This time as his eyes fluttered closed and he leaned in, I knew what was about to happen and I could feel the steady beat of my heart.

Everything about the way he kissed reminded me specifically of him. First it was a slow, barely there kiss, so if I rejected him he could pull away and pretend it never happened. But then, when he realized that I was in fact kissing him back, it was excited and sporadic. His hands never stayed in one spot. First they would be in my hair, then grasping my arms, and finally moving to my waist before the whole procedure would start over again. It was a little wet, but I didn't think it was slobbery enough to call it sloppy. At the same time, I didn't have much to compare it to, so for all I knew, Alex could have been a great kisser.

As weird as it sounded, he reminded me of a puppy. Puppies are good, right? Everyone likes puppies. And just like a dog, he had boundless make-out energy. I needed a breath, to stop and surface, but Alex was pushing me down onto the picnic table.

Just as I was running out of air, a car horn honked from out in the rain and Alex quickly jumped back. Standing up, I tugged down my shirt, which had ridden up while we were kissing, and smoothed out the wrinkles. Alex shot me a cheeky grin before grabbing my hand and pulling me to the edge of the pavilion.

"We can finish this later," he whispered before stepping out into the rain to grab his bike.

To shield myself from the downpour, I lifted my arms over my head and sprinted to the truck. When I reached the passenger-side door, I yanked on the handle, but it was locked.

"Open up!" I shouted over the rain, pounding my fist against the window. It was coming down so heavily now that I couldn't even see who was inside. I heard the distinct click of the lock and threw myself into the truck a second later. "God, it's nasty out there," I said, patting down my hair. My shirt clung to my skin, and I could feel the crumbs of someone's morning Pop-Tart sticking to the back of my leg as I sat back.

Nobody answered, and I turned in my seat to find Cole behind the wheel. He was glaring out the windshield so fiercely that I was afraid he would burn a hole through the glass and the storm outside would pour in.

"You okay?" I asked, but there was a sinking feeling in my stomach. When he said nothing, I knew he had seen Alex and me making out.

I waited in awkward silence as Alex threw his bike in the bed of the truck. The air-conditioning hummed softly, drying my damp skin and leaving behind a trail of goose bumps. I could feel the anger pouring off Cole, so I forced myself to concentrate on the radio, repeating the string of lyrics in my head. But he was impossible to ignore, and I found myself wishing I had sat in the backseat. Finally, after three uncomfortable verses, Alex climbed in the back and Cole stepped on the gas, reversing down the gravel path at full speed.

"Whoa!" Alex shouted as he was thrown backward before being able to buckle his seat belt or even breathe. The truck took a sharp left, back onto the main road, and Alex was thrown into the window. "What the hell?"

"Cole, slow down," I said quietly.

He narrowed his eyes at his brother in the rearview mirror but let up.

The rest of the ride home was completely silent, and an uncomfortable tension filled the small, confined space. It didn't help when a love song started to trickle out from the radio, its melody sickly sweet. Thirty seconds into the cheesy lyrics, I leaned over and switched it off. Alex heaved a sigh of relief.

When we pulled into the Walters' driveway, Cole parked at the bottom of the hill. I turned to give him a puzzled look as he yanked the key from the ignition. We were going to get soaked walking all the way up to the house. Why wasn't he parking in the usual spot underneath the basketball hoop? Cole answered my unasked question by pulling out an umbrella and getting out of the truck. He slammed the door shut, and Alex and I sat in shocked silence, watching him make his way toward the house.

"What's his problem?" Alex demanded.

Frowning, I told Alex what I had feared since leaving the ice-skating rink. "I think he might have seen us."

Alex shook his head. "Jackie, I can barely see out the window right now with the rain coming down so hard. How could he possibly have seen us?"

I shrugged my shoulders, not knowing how to answer his question. Even if Cole hadn't caught us, he was definitely mad about something.

"So what do we do now? I can call my mom again and ask for someone to bring us an umbrella," he suggested.

I shook my head no. "I'd prefer not to give Cole that satisfaction. It's only water and we're halfway wet already. Besides, you still smell. A shower would do you good."

"But my cell phone."

"Just leave it in the truck," I said, opening the door. "You're not going to die without it."

As we walked up the driveway toward the house, the rain let up. Giggles filled the air as we approached the front porch, and I looked up to find most of the Walter boys sitting under its shelter.

"What are they doing?" I asked Alex.

"Watching for a thunderstorm," he answered. "Haven't you ever sat outside during one? It's really peaceful."

"I lived on the top floor of an apartment building," I told him as water squished inside my flats. I should have taken them off before getting out of the car, since they were ruined for sure, but the gravel on the driveway was sharp and I didn't want to cut my feet.

"Oh right," Alex said. "Well, we do it all the time."

"Enjoying the weather?" Nathan asked when we reached the house. Alex gave him the finger, and everyone burst out laughing as we trudged up the steps.

"Jackie, you cold?" Isaac asked. "Your headlights are on."

Resisting the urge to cross my arms, I answered him. "Actually, I am. Maybe a hug would warm me up?" I took a step toward him with my arms wide open. Isaac backed away quickly, not wanting to get wet, but Alex ambushed him from the side.

"Dude, really?" Isaac complained. "Now I'm soaking."

"That's what she said," Lee said, making all the boys laugh.

"Not *soaking*," Alex answered Isaac, shaking his head in disagreement. Isaac had splotches of damp on his clothes, but it was nothing compared to us. "Let me fix that for you." With one quick push, Isaac was out in the rain. Danny gave Alex a high five as Jack and Jordan stepped out onto the porch.

"What's he doing out there?" Jack asked as he wiped his already foggy glasses on his shirt.

"We don't like him anymore," Danny said. "He was voted off our island."

"Really?" Isaac demanded from out in the rain. "Who's going to read lines with you then?"

"Definitely not you," Danny said, rolling his eyes. "You're terrible."

Isaac smirked as he climbed up the steps. "'O Romeo, Romeo, wherefore art thou, Romeo?'" he called, descending upon his cousin.

"Stay back," Danny said, jumping up out of his seat. "I don't want to get all wet."

"Too bad," Isaac laughed and pushed him off the porch.

Lee burst out laughing. "Hey, look! Romeo's all washed up," he said, pointing a finger at his cousin. In response, Danny yanked him out into the rain. "What the fudge?" Lee demanded.

Benny, who had been standing next to me quietly, tugged on my hand. "Jackie, can I go out in the rain too, or does someone have to push me?"

I broke into a grin. "If you want to play in the rain," I told him, "go for it. I'll even play with you. First one to jump in a puddle wins?" I asked.

Benny's eyes lit up, and he bounded off the porch in his yellow rain boots.

"Care to join me?" I asked, grabbing Alex's hand.

"It would be a pleasure," he said, grinning at me, and we both stepped back out into the rain.

The cool water felt relaxing as it ran down my back, and I ran my fingers through my soaking hair, lifting the new weight off my neck.

"Jackie! I beat you!" Benny called.

"Did you, now?" I responded, splashing toward him. "Well, guess what? You're it," I said and tapped him on the shoulder. It only took Benny a moment before he was chasing after one of his older brothers in a game of tag.

"You know what this weather reminds me of?" Jack asked his twin. "That pirate movie we watched last night, where there was a sword fight in the middle of the storm."

"You thinking what I'm thinking?" Jordan asked, picking up a broom. He swung it at his brother's face. "En garde!"

Jack grinned and swiped a stick out of the flower bed. The two started to sword fight across the slippery wooden porch, pretending it was the deck of a pirate ship.

"I get to be the captain," Jack called.

"You have glasses," his double said. "That makes you a loser. Captains are never losers." With that, he pushed his brother off the steps with a quick jab of his sword. Jack fell back into a puddle of water and sprayed mud everywhere. When he stood up, his pants were covered.

"Looks like you shit your pants," Lee teased.

"Well, it looks like you shit your face," Jack shot back. He scooped up a handful of mud and threw it at his cousin, splattering brown muck on Lee's face.

"Oh, hell no," Lee said, wiping the mud off. He bent down and grabbed his own handful. "You're gonna regret that." He sent the mud flying in Jack's direction, but he ducked and it sprayed across Nathan.

"What the...?" Nathan said in confusion.

"Mud fight!" Jordan shouted, throwing a goopy fistful at Danny. Everyone joined in quickly.

"Jackie!" Alex called, dark sludge oozing out from between his fingers. "I'm going to get you!"

"Please don't," I said, backing up slowly. "This is a nice shirt. You're going to ruin it."

But Alex was still advancing on me, an evil grin on his face. Spinning on my heels, I dashed off in the opposite direction. Water splashed up to my knees as my feet pounded across the sopping grass. I could feel the exhilaration pumping through my body, and I stole a quick glance over my shoulder to see how close Alex was.

"Jackie, look out!" Danny called.

I turned in time to see Zack standing in front of me. His neck was craned up at the sky, his tongue stuck out to catch the falling raindrops. I nearly crashed into him, but I managed to dig my heels into the ground seconds before we collided. Alex, on the other hand, wasn't so quick to react and smashed right into me. We both toppled over, sending mud in every direction. On top of me, Alex winced.

"Crap, I'm sorry, Jackie," he said.

I chose not to respond as I let everything sink in. The mud had splattered across my face, and I knew that my top was covered in it too, completely ruined. Part of me knew I should be mad because that was how I normally would have reacted, but something about playing in the rain was so completely freeing that, for once, I didn't care.

"Well," I finally said, digging my fingers into the ground. "You'll just have to pay." I smeared a handful of mud on his cheek. He blinked in surprise and then we both burst out giggling.

"This is the most fun I've had in forever," Alex said. He bent down and pecked me on the lips.

"PDA alert," Isaac shouted from across the lawn, making us both glance up. "You two are disgusting. Get a room."

Alex rolled his eyes, and when he turned back to me, I knew he was going to ignore Isaac and kiss me again.

"Oh no." I pushed him off me. He looked confused for a moment, but then he saw me scoop up another handful of brown slime. "Isaac is *so* asking for it," I told him.

"Well," Alex said with a huge grin on his face. He stood up and held a hand out for me. "We should give him what he wants."

• • •

As we filed into the school auditorium Monday night, the lights started to dim. We were running late, as usual, since it was nearly impossible to tear Katherine away from the kitchen. Given that she was such as amazing cook, she'd decided to prepare all the food for the reception instead of paying for a caterer who she said couldn't possibly make as good a meal as her. The result was that, for the past three days, there had been a tiny tornado in the Walter kitchen as Katherine rushed about kneading bread, mixing sauces, and chopping up different roots, vegetables, and fruit.

Occasionally she would run out of an ingredient or realize that she had forgotten an item on her grocery list. Then she'd panic until someone jumped in the truck and rushed off to the store to pick up whatever she needed. The wedding was still two weeks away, but with so many people to cook for, she had to start early.

When we needed to leave for Danny's play, Katherine was still at the sink, unconvinced that her kitchen was clean. Quite the opposite was true; I had never seen the place so sparkling. George was finally able to pull the rubber gloves from her hands and drag her to the car, but as soon as we pulled out of the driveway, Jack and Jordan realized they forgot the tripod for their camera, which they needed to film the play.

Five minutes later, Nathan remembered that he left the iron on and we had to turn back around again. When Parker noticed that she was wearing two different colored socks, everyone groaned in frustration. But this time, George told her to suck it up, and we continued on our way to the high school.

Only the row in the very back of the auditorium had enough empty seats for our entire group to sit, but we had to scoot by a family to get to the middle.

"Ouch, that's my foot," someone hissed as the curtain opened.

I sat down, Alex on one side and Nathan on the other.

"Up," Cole whispered to Nathan.

Nathan leaned forward and saw that Zack and Benny had taken the seats after Cole. He shook his head. "No way, dude, I'm not sitting next to those two monsters."

For that I was thankful. Since the party, Cole was different. Instead of his cocky obnoxious self, he was withdrawn and spent most of his time out in his garage. As a result, the dynamics of the Walter household had changed drastically. Without his outgoing attitude, which was the glue that got all of the guys and their different personalities to stick together, the house was silent. Everyone did their own thing—the days of baseball games and movie nights were fading.

On a rare occasion when I ran into Cole in the hallway, he would smile. However it was never a real smile, because it didn't reach his eyes. I almost missed the smug smirk that was normally on his face. Alex on the other hand, was his happy-go-lucky, clueless self when his older brother was around. He flirted and laughed, acting like life couldn't get any better. I tried to tone down the happy-couple vibe whenever we were around Cole, but Alex seemed to think that since his brother wasn't acting mad, everything was fine.

It was a struggle for me to be around both of them at the same time when I could see so much happiness in one of them and so much hurt in the other. Knowing that I had caused all this didn't help me feel any better. I didn't want to feel the awkward tension of sitting between both boys for the entire play, because I wanted to focus on Danny's performance.

"Too bad. I'm older than you, so I get to pick where I sit."

When Nathan laughed, a woman sitting in front of us turned around. "Would you both be quiet?"

Cole glared at Nathan for a moment longer before giving him the finger and dropping into the only open seat next to Zack.

"Hey, Cole?" I heard Zack whisper. He held his finger an inch away from Cole's cheek. "I'm not touching you."

"Boys!" Katherine hissed at her younger twins. "If you don't behave yourselves, then no dessert at dinner."

They didn't take their mother's warning seriously because as the first actor stepped out onto the stage, I heard the twins' evil giggles.

• • •

"Danny, that was amazing!" I exclaimed, pulling him into a hug. He had joined us outside the auditorium after the show, and he was still in his Romeo costume.

"Truly a heart-wrenching performance," Isaac said, wiping away pretend tears. "Can I have your autograph?" Danny rolled his eyes and gave his cousin a small shove. They both laughed. "Really, dude," Isaac said, getting serious. "It was great."

"Thanks," Danny responded, nodding his head. Doing one of those silly man hugs, they clapped each other on the back.

"Danny Walter?" a woman asked, coming up to our group.

"Yes?" He turned to look at her.

"Hi," she said, extending a business card. Danny took it from her outstretched hand and quickly glanced over the tiny text. "My name is Jillian Rowley, and I'm a talent scout from the Starlight Group. We're a theater company in New York, and I was wondering if you had a moment to spare."

"I—um, yeah!" Danny said, looking back up. His face was neutral, but I had come to learn that Danny was very good at masking his emotions. The small stumble in his sentence said it all: he was ecstatic.

"Wonderful," Jillian said and led him away from our group.

"What was that all about?" Alex asked, joining us. One of Kim's sisters had been in the play, and after it was over, he'd gone to find Kim to talk about the latest *GoG* news.

"Danny told me about a potential talent scout attending the play this year," I explained. "It was why he was so anxious about auditions. He wanted to make sure he got the male lead in case the talent scout came."

He hadn't said it, but I knew Danny thought his future depended on tonight's performance. He hadn't applied to college, not only because his parents couldn't afford it, but also because he didn't want to go. His dream was to be an actor, and even if nothing came out of this performance, he was going to move to New York City and follow his dream. It just meant that he was going to have to do it the hard way—waiting tables while auditioning for everything and anything.

"Jackie?" Katherine called. She and George were standing with the parents of the actress who played Juliet, and the other three were still deep in conversation.

"Yes?" I asked, coming up next to her.

"What was that all about?" she asked, nodding her head in Danny and Jillian's direction. The woman was still talking, and he was nodding his head eagerly to every word.

"I'm not entirely sure yet," I responded. "But she introduced herself as a talent scout for a New York theater company."

Katherine raised an eyebrow. "Well, now," she said, a flicker of a smile playing on her face. "That's interesting news." I could tell she was thrilled but was holding back in case things didn't turn out the way we hoped.

"Did I hear something about a talent scout?" Cole asked, appearing next to his mom. After the play was over, he was charged with taking the younger kids to the restroom. Now Zack, Benny, and Parker were chasing each other about the auditorium lobby, weaving in and out of the crowd, but Cole was done with his babysitting job.

"Apparently the woman speaking with Danny is one," Katherine told him.

"What woman?" Cole asked.

We all turned toward Danny and Jillian, but she was gone and he was making his way across the room toward us with a grin on his face.

"Guess what?" he asked.

"She wants to make you the next A-list actor in Hollywood, and you're going to become so famous and rich that you can buy me a house?" Cole asked. We all shot him a look, but Danny was too happy to care.

"I've been offered a spot in their company's summer training camp. After the program, if things go well, I could be in New York productions this fall!"

"Oh, honey," Katherine said, pulling her son into a hug. "I'm so proud of you."

"Congratulations, Danny," I said, waiting for my turn to hug him. "This is so exciting!"

"Thanks, Jackie. I really owe you," he said, pulling away from his mom to face me. "If you hadn't spent all that time reading lines with me, I don't know if I would have gotten the part."

"That's not true," I told him. "But I'll accept your gratitude anyway."

"So when does this training camp begin?" Katherine asked.

Danny hesitated. "That's the thing. I'd have to leave for New York as soon as summer starts." When he saw the frown on his mother's face, he added. "I am, after all, an adult and the company will provide lodging until I find a place to live."

"Okay, dear," Katherine said. "Why don't we discuss this later?"

"All right," said Danny. It wasn't the answer he wanted to hear, but there was still a huge, excited smile on his face.

"Mom! Mom!" Zack and Benny shouted as they crashed into their mother's legs. "We're hungry."

"Come on, Walter clan," she said, raising her voice so we all could hear her. "Head out to the cars. We have a celebratory dinner to prepare."

Chapter 17

During the last week of school, I stayed locked in my room so I could focus on studying. When it was finally time for exams, they passed in a blur of Scantron sheets, true-false questions, and written essays. Afterward, the Walters spent the first week of our newfound freedom vegging out, their thoughts of school long gone, but all I could think about was getting my results back. I knew I'd aced all my classes because every final had been a breeze, but I needed visual confirmation before I could relax.

"Hey, guys, come here," Nathan said.

I glanced up from my anatomy notebook. For the past hour, I had been sprawled out on Alex's bed, double-checking all my notes to make sure I hadn't missed a question on the exam. Alex was wrapped up in a quest on *GoG* and Nathan had been teaching himself a new song, but now his guitar was gone and he was hunched over his laptop.

"What's up?" Alex called, hardly looking away from his own computer screen.

"Grades are in," Nathan replied.

"Oh!" I scrambled off the bed and over to Nathan's desk. He slid the computer to me, and I quickly logged in to my school account.

"Come on," I muttered as it took forever to load. Finally a new screen popped up.

"A, A, A, A, A, A," Nathan said, reading off my results.

"No shocker there," Alex said.

"You never know," I told him. "Freshman year I got an A- in my history class because my teacher said my final paper was too long. That was horrible."

Alex rolled his eyes. "Heaven forbid," he said, but it didn't bother me.

Finally it was summer. That meant I could relax and maybe even take a trip to New York. The knots in my neck and back loosened at the thought. But before I could go home, there was Will and Haley's wedding, and tonight was the night before the big day.

Katherine had spent the entire morning making cupcakes, which Haley had requested over the traditional wedding cake. The two hundred or so personal chocolate cakes were left to cool on the dining-room table, and the room was strictly off limits to prevent any of the boys from eating them. The rest of the day was dedicated to scrubbing down the kitchen while Katherine kept an eye on the dining-room entrance to make sure no one snuck in.

At one point, I heard her shout at Jack and Jordan. Two seconds later, there was the telltale sign of retreat—the pounding of their feet on the stairs. Now that the kitchen was clean and all her cooking done, the space was off limits. The rehearsal dinner was taking place at a fancy Italian restaurant in town.

"You want to check your results?" I asked Alex, moving away from the computer so he could get a turn.

He grimaced and shook his head. "I'd rather not ruin this weekend's fun. I'll check on Monday morning."

"Kids," I heard George shout from the bottom on the staircase. "Everyone needs to start getting ready. We're leaving in an hour."

It was time for the celebrations to begin.

• • •

I didn't know which was more alarming: the fact that Parker was sitting on my bed with a sleeping bag at her feet, or that she had a bouquet of flowers in her hands. After the lengthy rehearsal dinner, during which Zack stabbed Benny with a fork and Jack and Jordan almost set the tablecloth on fire, we headed back to the Walters' house to get a good night's sleep.

"Um, hi?" I said, not sure what she was doing in my room.

"These were waiting for you," she said and tossed me the flowers. They came at me fast, but I managed to snap my hands up and catch the bouquet in time. Parker's features wilted, almost as if she had been hoping to hit me.

"Who are they from?" I asked, burying my nose in the roses. They were beautiful with huge, deep red petals.

"How am I supposed to know?" Parker shot back as she made herself comfortable on my bed. "But whoever it was, they're a sap. Roses? Come on."

They must have been from Alex. He was so sweet. "I think they're beautiful," I responded, holding them out to admire. A note fell out and fluttered down to the floor. I bent down and snatched it up before Parker could read what it said. Hopefully, Alex hadn't written anything too cheesy or inappropriate.

Jackie, the scribble read, *I'm sorry I keep screwing up and making mistakes. Life didn't come with instructions.* There was no signature. My mouth went dry, and I quickly discarded the flowers on my dresser.

"What'd the note say?" Parker asked, curious about my sudden change in attitude.

I crinkled up the piece of paper and tossed it in the trash. "Nothing," I said. "So what are you doing in my room?"

Parker opened her mouth to respond, but the bedroom door swung open.

"Jackie, I was hoping you'd be here," Katherine said. She shuffled into the room backward, holding the end of a cot. Isaac appeared on the other end, muttering something about slave labor. As soon as they set it down in the limited empty floor space, he was gone.

"Isaac," Katherine called after him. "Remember to bring those blankets and pillows in here."

"Of course, Your Majesty," he called from down the hall. Katherine pursed her lips, but didn't say anything else on the matter.

"What's going on?" I asked.

"Parker will be staying in your room for the next two nights," Katherine explained. "Grandma Green flew all the way out from New York and is staying in her room."

At the rehearsal dinner I'd met some of the Walters' extended family, Katherine's mother being one of them. Since Parker and I were the only girls, it made sense that we would have to share a room for the weekend so an out-of-town guest had somewhere to sleep. I just wasn't sure if my new bunkmate was going to be hostile or friendly.

"Okay," I said, avoiding Parker's gaze. I could feel her watching me and didn't want to appear too anxious. "So what's the plan for tomorrow?"

"I want everyone out of bed by seven o'clock so we all have time to get ready. Knowing me, there will probably be some last-minute chores to complete, things that slipped my mind. I was wondering if you could possibly do Parker's hair tomorrow. With eleven boys, I've never been an experienced hairdresser."

"No, Mom!" Parker complained, jumping up. "I don't want my hair done. Why can't I wear it like I always do?"

Katherine gave Parker a stern look. Her daughter's normal look typically lacked the use of a brush. "Because tomorrow we all have to look presentable. You especially since you're in the wedding." As she said this, a pile of bedding flew through the open door and landed on the floor with a thump. Katherine massaged her temple. "Thank you, Isaac," she said and rolled her eyes. "A-plus effort."

"No probs, Aunt Katherine," he called, already halfway down the hall.

Katherine turned back around when we heard his bedroom door slam, and Parker immediately started to pout. "I never wanted to be the stupid flower girl anyway," she grumbled, kicking at one of the pillows Isaac had slopped on the floor. "It's stupid."

"Remember, you're doing this to make your brother happy," Katherine reminded her.

This seemed to win the argument, but Parker still grumbled and plopped down on the cot, clearly not happy.

"Good," her mother said with a curt nod. "You two should go to bed. It's late and tomorrow is going to be long."

"Good night, Katherine," I said as she moved toward the door. The rehearsal dinner had worn me out, and I had no problem turning the lights off early.

"Sweet dreams," Katherine said to the both of us. When Parker didn't respond, she glared at her daughter.

"Night," Parker mumbled.

After Katherine left, I turned to Parker to tell her that I wouldn't do her hair too girly for the wedding, but the scowl on her face kept me quiet. Gathering my toiletries and pajamas, I decided to go down to the bathroom and get ready for bed, giving her time to cool off. When I got back, Parker had already turned the lights off and was curled up on her cot, clearly in no mood to talk.

I lay awake for a long time, unable to fall asleep. I could sense that Parker was awake as well, even though she didn't move an inch. There was a tension in the room that could only be caused by another sleepless person.

Finally she sighed. "I don't want to wear a dress," she said, her voice coming up out of the darkness.

I wanted to tell her that it would be fun, that the right dress could make any girl feel special, but it was the first time she'd opened up to me, and I didn't want to ruin it. "How come?"

"They're so girly."

"But you are a girl," I said, choosing my words carefully.

"I'm a Walter," she said, as if that meant something different.

"What does that mean?" I asked. "Because you live with a bunch of boys, you're required to act like one?"

She considered this for a moment, and I could see her outline in the dark, twisting her blanket in her hands as she thought. "Yeah, kind of. Being one of the boys makes me special. Everyone at school knows who I am—Parker Walter, the tough girl with eleven brothers who can play tackle football and burp louder than any of the guys in my grade."

I laughed. "But what about at home?"

"What do you mean?"

"Well, if you're just one of the boys, what makes you different from your brothers?"

"I don't know."

"Honestly, Parker, you have the best of both worlds," I said, sitting up in bed. "You can enjoy doing boy things, like watching sports and playing video games. But you can also put on a dress and be a girl. That's something that your brothers can't do."

She was quiet for a long time. "I never thought about it that way."

"Being a girl doesn't make you weak, Parker. It makes you special."

"I guess I can wear the dress, but just this once," she said. "And you have to promise not to curl my hair."

"All right," I told her. "It's a deal."

• • •

Saturday morning did not go smoothly. Since life with the Walters was always unpredictable, I'd set my alarm an hour earlier than needed as I almost expected some kind of tiny disaster to occur. Of course, the extra hour wasn't near enough time when something *did* happen. I was standing at the toaster waiting for my English muffin to pop when I heard a scream.

"Katherine?" I asked, rushing into the dining room. "What is it?"

"The cupcakes," she said, clamping a hand to her mouth in horror. She was standing at the head of the dining-room table, and for a moment, I was afraid they were gone—*how could the boys eat two hundred cupcakes?*—but then, she stepped aside, revealing all of baked treats. "I forgot to frost them."

"Okay," I said calmly. "I have some time. Where's the frosting?"

She disappeared back into the kitchen and I heard the fridge open. "…Just knew something like this would happen. Told George something wasn't right before we went to bed, but did he listen?" A moment later she was back, carrying an armful of supplies. "So the frosting is already mixed," Katherine told me, quick to use my help. "You just need to make sure half of the cupcakes are frosted teal and the other half yellow. I have a few icing tubes with different piping tips you can use. Once they're all frosted, I also have sprinkles that go on top."

And just like that, I had a huge project on my hands. I thought it would be easy, but I'd never frosted two hundred cupcakes before. It took a lot longer than I thought. I was only about halfway done when I looked at the clock and panicked. I still needed to take a shower, get ready, and do Parker's hair.

"Crap, crap, crap!" I said, as the frosting in the tube I was squeezing ran out. Refilling the tubes was the messiest and most frustrating part of the job.

"Jackie, are you okay?" someone asked.

I glanced up to see Cole. His hair was damp from a shower, and he was already dressed in his suit. When he leaned against the table, I realized he was eating a cupcake.

"Can you please not do that?" I snapped.

"Do what?" he asked me through a mouthful.

"Eat those! They're for the wedding." I yelled.

"Sorry," Cole said quietly after swallowing. He looked away from me, and I was flooded with guilt. I shouldn't take my frustration out on him, because none of this was his fault.

"Look, Cole, I didn't mean to snap at you," I said. "It's just that I still have to get ready and help Parker, and this is taking forever."

"Do you need help?" he asked after a second, completely catching me off guard.

"Thanks, Cole, but you're already dressed. I wouldn't want you to get your suit dirty."

"That's no problem." He started to shrug out of his jacket. When that was off, his fingers began working the buttons on his shirt, and I couldn't help but stare. Soon he was down to his dress pants and undershirt. "Okay, boss," he asked, setting his clothes aside where they wouldn't get dirty. "What do you need me to do?"

It took me a minute to regain my composure, but then I breathed a sigh of relief. "Here," I said, handing him the empty icing tube. "If you could fill this with yellow frosting and start on that row over there, that would be amazing."

"Sure thing," he said, taking the tube from me. "And by the way, you have frosting on your nose."

"Did I get it?" I asked, using the back of my hand.

"Here," Cole said, stepping forward. He brought his finger up to my face and rubbed it off. Then he stuck his finger in his mouth and sucked away the frosting. "Got it."

My cheeks went pink, and I turned back toward the table to hide my embarrassment. "Thanks," I said, grabbing one of the sprinkle containers. "We should probably get to work."

"Of course."

I risked a quick glance in Cole's direction. He was already spooning the yellow paste into the tube, his hands quick, but on his face was the classic Cole smirk. We both knew that he had gotten to me.

• • •

"Are you kidding me?" I complained to Nathan when we reached our assigned table. My name card was right between two boys—Cole and Alex, to be exact.

Will and Haley had already said "I do" in a ceremony by Katherine's blooming garden, and cocktail hour had just ended. For dinner, there were two huge tents set up in the backyard, with enough room to seat all the wedding guests.

"This is going to be an enjoyable evening," Isaac said. Rolling his eyes, he pulled back his chair.

I shot him a dirty look and turned to Danny. "Would you mind switching with Cole?" I asked.

Danny quickly sat down. "I'm sorry, Jackie," he said, looking regretful. "I can't."

"Why not?" I asked, still hovering behind my spot. Was it really that hard to move one seat over?

"Well, you see…" He trailed off, almost as if he felt uncomfortable finishing his sentence. Then Danny grabbed the water glass next to his plate and took a long sip so he didn't have to answer me.

"He doesn't want to lose our bet," Isaac said with a grin as he unfolded his napkin and set it on his lap.

"You made a bet?" I asked, whipping around to glare at Danny. Isaac was addicted to gambling, but for the most part the boys knew not to indulge him. This was so unlike Danny that it made me furious.

"I know I shouldn't have," Danny said, hanging his head. "But if I'm going to move to New York, I need some extra money."

Sighing, I yanked back my chair and took my place. "Why didn't you say something?" I demanded. "You know I'd be more than happy to help you."

He shrugged. "I didn't want to owe you anything."

"Apparently he'd rather owe me," Isaac said. "I'm earning a hundred bucks on this."

"A hundred bucks?" I asked in shock. "What's this stupid bet anyway?"

"That Cole and Alex won't be able to get through dinner without fighting over you," Isaac explained.

"And?" I asked, not knowing if I wanted to hear the rest.

"I said they wouldn't last five minutes," Danny responded quietly.

"Wonderful," I said, sinking into my seat. "Just wonderful."

"At least they will both be happy," Nathan said, trying to look on the bright side of things. "Well, for a little bit."

He was right. Cole and Alex would both be happy to find that they were sitting next to me. However, they would quickly get fed

MY LIFE WITH THE WALTER BOYS

up with each other. The worst part was that I was going to be stuck in the middle.

"Well, what about me?" I whined. Didn't I deserve to be happy too?

"What about you?" Alex asked, coming up behind me. Leaning down, he pecked me on the cheek.

"Nothing," I grumbled as he kissed me again.

"Um, barf. Not at the dinner table, please," Cole said, turning up next to Alex. He sat down and let out a large belch. "Man, I'm hungry."

"What a gentleman," I said, shaking my head in disgust.

"Oh, sorry. Didn't know I was in the presence of any ladies," Cole shot back.

"Hey!" Alex said. "Don't be mean to my girlfriend."

"I was just joking. Chill. And do you have to keep calling her that, or are you afraid she might forget?"

"Come on, guys," I said, trying to stop the fight. But it didn't matter; everyone knew it was going to happen. I could already see the anticipation on Isaac's face, and Danny's eyes were glued to his watch.

"What the hell is that supposed to mean?" Alex demanded as his face flushed red.

"Nothing," Cole drawled. "I'm just pointing out that Jackie is a person, not a thing,"

"Boys!" I cried, looking back and forth between the two.

Cole looked calm and under control, but beneath his smooth exterior, I could tell he was aggravated. Alex, on the other hand, looked like a volcano on the verge of activity. Unconsciously his fingers had wrapped around the fork resting on his napkin, and as he squeezed the thin strip of metal, the color drained from his knuckles. I kept an eye on the utensil in his hand, afraid of what might happen if he snapped.

"Just shut up, Cole," Alex hissed.

"Shut up?" Cole snickered. "That's a good one. I'll have to remember it. I bet your girlfriend can't wait for you to defend her in a fight."

"Guys, please stop," I begged.

I risked a quick glance at the head table. Mr. Walter had just stood up with champagne glass in hand. He was about to give a speech about the bride and groom, and all the horrible possibilities of what would occur if Cole and Alex didn't cool down were running through my head. Worst case scenario: the boys get into a fistfight in the middle of their father's speech and ruin Will and Haley's wedding.

"At least I have one," Alex replied, looking smug.

Cole narrowed his eyes at his brother, and I gave up. Alex had officially pushed Cole too far, and there was no stopping either of them now.

"Is that a challenge?" he hissed.

"Suck it!" Danny whispered to his cousin with a smile on his face. "That was exactly three minutes. I want my money in cash."

"Damn," Isaac said, shaking his head and pulling out his wallet. "I've been on a losing streak lately."

Alex didn't respond to Cole, except to flip him off.

"Fine," Cole said, smiling evilly. "But don't blame me when your girl's in my arms."

"Cole!" I shouted angrily before giving him a hefty kick in the shin from under the table, but he didn't even seem to notice my attempt to bruise him. Instead, he and his brother continued their stare-down.

"Well," Nathan said, turning to Danny. "What a great way to start the reception."

"Yeah," Isaac said with a smile. "We haven't even gotten our salads yet."

• • •

As dinner progressed, Alex and Cole became increasingly annoying.

"Jackie, would you like me to get you something from the bar?" Cole asked, turning to me.

"What are you trying to do, get her drunk?" Alex said. Since his fight with Cole, there had been a frown permanently etched onto his forehead.

"No, I was just trying to be nice," Cole said, holding his hands up in defense.

"Is that what happened last time you got her a drink?" he asked, referring to the time Cole and I skipped school.

"Guys, cut it out," I said for the millionth time. I put a hand on Alex's leg to try and calm him down. "A glass of red wine would be great," I told Cole. If the rest of the night was going to continue like this, I needed something to calm *myself* down.

"Classy," Isaac said, getting up to go with Cole. "I like it."

"Anything for you?" Cole asked Danny.

"A beer is fine, thanks."

Alex grumbled to himself as his brother and cousin walked away, but I was beyond caring. As much as I was against drinking since my last experience, I really needed something to take the edge off my headache. When I was little, my mother would always let me take a sip of her wine at dinner, and surprisingly I found it was a bitter taste that I didn't mind.

Everyone waited for Cole and Isaac to return with the drinks, and we munched on our dessert in silence. The wedding cupcakes had turned out beautifully, thanks to Cole's help, and Haley loved them.

"Here you go, my lovely lady," Cole said, setting my drink in front of me. Alex shot him a glare, but before he could say anything, Isaac set a drink down for him as well.

"For me?" Alex asked in surprise. His cousin nodded. "Thanks, dude. What is it?"

"Iced tea, with a little something extra," Isaac answered. "Just be careful with those. They'll creep up on you fast."

I watched Alex as he lifted the drink to his lips and took a swig. "This is great," he said, perking up in his seat. "You can't even taste the alcohol!"

The drink seemed to make Alex less hostile toward Cole, so Isaac kept them coming. But Alex didn't heed his warning and two hours later, he was in the bathroom puking his guts out. After bringing him another glass of water, I collapsed onto one of the kitchen chairs to wait for him to finish. When his stomach was empty, I was going to tuck him in bed so he could get some rest.

Sitting down, I realized just how tired I was, and how much today had sucked. I had been looking forward to the wedding for so long, and although it turned out beautifully for Will and Haley, it hadn't been fun for me. Between the cupcake crisis in the morning, the boys fighting through dinner, and Alex getting sick, the day was pretty much ruined.

"And this will be our last song of the evening," I heard the lead singer of the band announce.

"Dang it," I said, thinking I was alone. "I didn't even get to dance to one song."

"We could fix that." Cole pushed open the screen door and stepped inside. "Jackie, come dance with me," he said, extending his hand to me.

I looked at it reluctantly. Dancing with him would probably only cause more drama by the end of the night, but I had really been looking forward to the wedding reception. "You need a break," he added.

"I don't know," I said, wringing my hands. "I really should look after him," I said, nodding my head in Alex's direction.

"He's a big boy, and you're not his mother," Cole said, heaving me to my feet. "It's just one dance. He won't even notice you're gone."

"I don't—" I started to say, but Cole was already pulling me out the back door and I let him.

He led me out onto the dance floor, where a slow song was starting to play. Couples stood all around us, swaying back and forth to the music. I didn't know what to do—if I should actually dance with him—but Cole made the decision for me by wrapping his arms around my waist.

"You know, you're supposed to put your hands on my shoulders," Cole pointed out. "Otherwise, this is going to get really awkward, really fast."

"I shouldn't be doing this," I said, but I hooked my hands around his neck anyway.

"Probably not," he said softly. "But you want to."

"Cole, don't start this again," I begged. His nearly white bangs were longer than when we first met—now they brushed at the top of his eyes, and his lips were partially open, begging to be kissed. He was perfectly beautiful and I had to glance away. I could feel the blood rushing through my veins.

"Why not, Jackie? Was what I said wrong?"

"Please," I said, avoiding his question. "I just want one dance."

"And I just want one answer."

"Why does it even matter, Cole?" I asked, looking back up at him sharply.

He squeezed his eyes shut for a moment in concentration. "Because," he said, opening them again. They were a dazzling blue. "Loving you just crept up on me, and before I knew it, I was head over heels for you."

I stopped dancing. "Love?" I repeated in shock.

"Tell me you feel the same way, or that you feel *something*." Here, his voice cracked, but he kept going. "I just—I need to know that I'm not alone."

"God, Cole, don't put me in this situation. I can't!"

"The hell you can't!" he exclaimed, ripping his arms away from me. "I've seen the way you look at me when you think I won't notice. But the thing is, I'm always paying attention to you, Jackie. It's like—you're gravity and I'm just a little blip on your radar."

"A blip on my radar?" I asked. The idea was ridiculous. "Cole, you're impossible to miss."

"So does that mean—"

"No," I said, stepping away from him. "I'm not saying it. I'm done with this. With us."

"Every time I try to work things out between us, you run away," Cole said, grabbing my wrist and spinning me back around. "Why do you keep avoiding me?"

"Because!" I finally shouted. "I like you, even though it doesn't make sense, and I hate that I can't control my feelings." I wouldn't let myself love Cole the way he said he loved me. If I did, our love might be ruined by the guilt I felt over my family.

Cole dropped his hand in shock, but I was already turning on my heels. I needed to get away before he recovered from my confession. But when my gaze landed on the back porch, I realized that someone was watching us. Alex was standing on the steps, an unreadable expression on his face.

"Are you happy now?" I asked Cole and shot him one last glare before pushing through the crowds.

• • •

"Jackie, what are you doing up here?"

I slowly pulled my head away from my knees and brushed away a tear. Danny's head popped up through the trapdoor in the tree house.

"Hiding from the world," I grumbled. Danny smiled sadly and pulled himself up into my hiding place. "How'd you find me?"

"No offense, Jackie, but I wouldn't call it hiding. I could hear you crying from a mile away," he told me.

After my conversation with Cole, the one where I confessed my feelings for him and Alex heard, I had needed to get away from everyone. I wanted to go somewhere where nobody would look, and only Alex used the tree house anymore. He was the last person who would come looking for me.

"You know, my brother is looking for you," Danny said, sitting down next to me.

"I don't want to talk to Cole," I said glumly.

Danny was silent for a moment, and he wrapped an arm around my shoulder. "Jackie," he whispered quietly, "you shouldn't feel bad."

"No," I said, wiping the snot away from my nose. "I shouldn't have danced with Cole."

"You can't control how you feel about him," he said, as if it was no great secret that I liked Cole.

I was quiet for a while as I thought about my answer. "But what does that say about me? My whole family just died and all I can think about is him." Admitting the truth out loud to Danny made me feel horrible all over again, and I started to sob.

"Jackie," Danny said soothingly as he pulled me into a hug. "It's okay. Don't cry."

"No, it's not okay," I bawled as more and more tears started to pour out of my eyes. "I'm a horrible person. My mom—I don't know how she'll ever be proud of me."

"I'm not sure what your mom has to do with this," Danny said, "but how could she not be happy for you? With Cole, you found someone who helped take away the pain of losing her."

I had no idea how to respond to Danny, so I gave another excuse. "Really? Even after everything he's done to me?"

"I know it doesn't seem like it, but my brother is a good person. We might be completely different, but we're still twins and Cole tells me everything. He was crushed when Alex stopped talking to him after the whole Mary thing. And he was telling the truth—Cole had no clue that she dumped Alex for him."

"Danny, why are you even telling me this?" It had nothing to do with the struggle going on in my head.

"I don't know. I'm just trying to explain him," he said. "Sure Cole's a player, but he's never been a mean person. Then you came along, and the rift between him and Alex turned into a gaping hole and Cole got all aggressive." When Danny saw the pained look on my face, he quickly added, "There was nothing you could have done, Jackie. It wasn't your fault."

"Is this supposed to be some kind of pep talk? It's not working."

"All I'm trying to say is that I know Cole hurt you, but I don't think it was intentional."

"You honestly believe that? What about the night we went TPing or the time he dragged me to Mary's party?"

"His anger was always directed at Alex, not you."

"It didn't seem that way."

"Look, Jackie, he has a bad way of showing it, but he cares about you. I've never seen Cole fight so hard for something in his life. Not even for his football scholarship."

For a long time, I didn't say anything. "You know, you're making things a lot more difficult," I told him.

"You just need to talk to him."

"I doesn't matter that I like him. I'm still pissed, and I don't think I can handle seeing him right now."

"Not Cole, Alex."

"Yeah, right. He's not going to talk to me."

"*He* was the one looking for you," Danny said. "Not Cole."

"Why would Alex want to talk to me?"

"He isn't as clueless as he seems."

I was quiet for a full minute as his words sunk in. Did he mean Alex had known all along that I had feelings for Cole? Had I even known? "Hey, Danny?" I finally said.

"What?"

"I'm going to make sure you make it to your training camp in New York, whether you want my help or not."

"About that," Danny said, scratching the back of his head. "I know now isn't the greatest time, but I had a conversation with my mom tonight. This wasn't exactly how I was planning on telling you, but she said you could come with if you wanted."

"What?" I asked, taken aback. "Katherine said I could go back and live in New York?"

"Yeah, well, I'm eighteen now, and she knows how much you really want to be at home. It would only be for the rest of summer since you'd have to come back here for school, but your uncle

Richard agreed that we could live in your apartment together. Of course, if that's okay with you."

For a moment I was so excited I could barely contain myself. I was going to get to go home and, on top of that, live with one of the best friends that I had made in Colorado. But then, I thought about all the other amazing friends I met here. What would it be like without daily runs with Nathan, or Riley and Heather's bubbly personalities? How would I feel without Alex and Cole?

"Danny, I would love to go to New York and live with you. You know that's where I want to be. I guess I just have to decide if that's the best thing for me right now."

"I completely understand, Jackie. Take your time deciding. I don't want you to feel like you made the wrong choice."

Chapter 18

The next morning, the house was quiet since everyone was recovering from last night's festivities. I stayed cooped up in my room, trying to figure out what to do. I was conflicted about Danny's proposal. More than anything I wanted to go home, but what about the people I'd come to love here in Colorado?

A knock on the door pulled me out of my thoughts.

"Come in," I called. Alex opened the door, and I could tell from the way he squinted at the bright light of my room that he was still hungover.

"Hey," he said, his voice strained. "Can we talk?"

"Um, yeah. Sit down." It didn't sound good, but I moved over on my bed to make room for him.

Nodding his head, he shuffled across the room toward my bed. As he sat down, the squeal of the springs made the tense silence in the room more apparent.

"So," I started to say when Alex said nothing. "About last night—"

"Jackie, I'm so sorry."

"I didn't mean for you to hear that, but—wait, what?"

"I've been so unfair to you," he said. I didn't understand what he was trying to say, so I waited for him to continue. "After the whole thing with Mary and Cole, I was so hurt. I think I knew deep down that Cole didn't know Mary dumped me, but it just felt so good having a reason to be mad at him."

"Why would you want to be mad at your brother?"

"I was jealous. People always compare us, but he's so much better at everything than me."

"That's not true, Alex. You're good at video games and baseball, not to mention that you're a much better friend then he is."

"That didn't matter back then."

"Back when?"

"When you got here."

"What do you mean?"

"Come on, Jackie," Alex said as if I was being stupid. "You're beautiful. How could any guy not notice you? With Cole around, I knew I didn't stand a chance." He looked up at me. "But then you were in my anatomy class, so we had something in common, stuff we could talk about. I had an excuse to hang out with you, and it made me feel like I had a chance after all. What surprised me even more was that you blew him off like he was nothing. That helped me feel better and forget."

"Forget?" I asked, even though I knew exactly what he was talking about.

"About Mary," he said. Alex paused for a moment and shut his eyes. He was clearly in pain and was having a hard time getting his words out. "It was the weekend that my family went on the camping trip," he said, continuing his story. "The time you, me, and Cole slept on the living-room floor during the storm? That was when I realized that I was going to have to fight him for you. I wanted to beat Cole, to feel like I accomplished something that he hadn't. And I wanted to prove to Mary that I was done with her."

Neither of us said anything as Alex's words drifted through the silent air. I didn't know how to react to his confession, but then I realized what he said *should* have hurt me. But it didn't. All I felt was...relief. Alex had made living with the Walters so much easier for me—my anchor as I adjusted to the storm. He was my comfort, my first real kiss, but most importantly, he was my friend.

It took me a moment to collect my thoughts, and in that time Alex panicked. "Well, what do you feel? Massive amounts of hatred?"

"Alex, I could never hate you."

"Then what is it?"

I hesitated, taking the time to search his face. From the alarmed gleam in his eye, I could tell he knew what I was about to say. "You're not over her, are you?" I asked him.

"Jackie, please don't make me answer that question. I really, really care about you. I know I let my issues with Cole get between us, but—"

"Alex, wait," I said, cutting him off. "I have a confession you need to hear as well." It wasn't just something that I needed to tell him, but also a truth that I had to acknowledge myself. "I know you heard Cole and me talking last night at the wedding, but there's more to the story. When I first got here, I was so focused on proving that I was okay even though my family was gone. I had this messed-up perception in my head that I needed to be perfect, so my mother could be proud of me. Then I met Cole and I knew he was going to be trouble, unpredictable. He could've ruined everything

I was working toward, but you were safe. I started dating you so I wouldn't have to deal with him. I don't know, maybe I'm still confused about my mom, but I know for sure that what I did to you was wrong."

Alex sucked in a sharp breath. "Is this your way of saying you're breaking up with me?"

"I—I think so."

We were quiet for a long time.

Finally Alex said something. It wasn't a protest or angry words, just a simple statement. "Jack and Jordan heard Danny and my mom talking last night. They said you're leaving with him next week."

Then I realized what he was asking. He wanted to know if I was running away from him. "I haven't made a decision yet, but I never considered leaving because of what happened between us. It's just that I miss home so much, but I don't want to leave you all behind."

"You promise it's not because of me?" he asked, holding out his finger so I could pinkie swear.

"I promise."

He nodded his head in understanding. "Well, then I think you should go."

"What?"

At first I thought he was being bitter, but then Alex grabbed my hand and looked at me. "You need this, Jackie," he said. His face was soft but insistent as he tried to convince me. "Go home. Sort everything out. Then, when you're better, you can come back to us."

Alex couldn't have been more right. It was time to leave Colorado and face my past.

• • •

It was supposed to be Cole and Danny's graduation party, but Cole was missing. George was cooking hamburgers and hot dogs on the grill. Katherine made three bowls of potato salad, and Nathan cut up a huge display of fresh fruit. There were a ton of kids from our school hanging out by the pool, mostly people who knew Cole, but a few drama club members had stopped by to congratulate Danny as well.

"Jackie?" Nathan called. "Do you know where Cole is? He's got another check here."

"I haven't seen him in a while," I said, taking the envelope out of his hand. Katherine had me keeping track of the gifts because she didn't want any of the money disappearing. "I can go look for him if you want."

"Sure, tell him he's missing a good time."

Inside the house, I slipped the card on top of the fridge where none of the little kids could get at it and then went in search of Cole. It didn't take me long to find him since he was in the first spot I looked—his garage.

Normally, the doors were shut tight, even while he worked. Today, however, they were thrown open, letting the late-afternoon light paint the small room in a golden yellow.

"You know," I said, stepping up to the car. "There's a party going on out back. Lots of people are here to see you."

Cole looked up from his work in surprise, as if he hadn't expected someone to come looking for him. "Oh," he said when he saw me. "Hi, Jackie."

"Lose track of time?" I asked. Glancing around, I noticed that the workbench looked tidier than normal. Most of the tools and spare car parts were packed away in the shelving unit.

"No," Cole said, slamming the hood of the car down into place. "I just wanted to finish installing this last part."

"So it's ready to run?"

"Yeah, I guess." Something about the way he responded sounded sad, almost as if he didn't want his car to be fixed. Sighing, he pulled a rag out of his pocket and wiped off his hands.

"Hey," I said, moving toward him. "Are you okay?"

"I'm fine."

"You don't seem like it."

Looking down at the car, Cole took a deep breath. "It's just, I don't know what to do with myself now that I'm done restoring the car. I've been working on it for so long."

In the moment of silence that passed between us, I heard laughter from the party. "You mean, since you broke your leg during a football game last year?" I asked then.

Cole's head snapped up. "How do you—?"

"Nathan told me."

He was quiet for a minute. "Did he say anything else?"

"He mentioned something about how you were different afterward."

This time, he stayed quiet for much longer as if he needed to gather all his energy to make his confession. "When I didn't go out for football this year," he started to explain, "most people just thought I didn't care anymore because I had lost my scholarship. I guess I started acting like it too—skipping school, partying, girls."

"And the real reason?"

"Honestly, I'm terrified that it won't be the same. I feel—I don't know. Broken, I guess."

"So this replaced football?" I asked, gesturing down at the car.

Cole nodded. "I can't fix myself, but I can fix this."

I nodded my head slowly. I couldn't agree with Cole because I didn't think he was broken, but I understood how he felt. "You know what, Cole? I have a feeling you'll be okay."

Instead of answering, he changed the subject. "I'm moving into Will's old apartment. He's living with Haley now."

"How come?"

"I'll be closer to work. I have to save up money this summer if I'm going to pay for college." Cole might have lost his football scholarship, but he still planned on going to the same college: the University of Colorado at Boulder.

"Well, once you're all settled in, you should give me a tour," I said with a smile.

"If that's what you want."

"Of course! Now how about you stop moping around and come join the party. I want to grab a hamburger before they're gone."

"You go," he said. He was staring at me, the look on his face unsolvable. "I'll catch up in the little bit. There's one last thing I have to do."

• • •

The next few days went by fast. Danny and I were leaving to go to the airport in the afternoon, and I spent most of my morning making sure all of my belongings were packed. As I looked around my room one last time, I noticed the pair of Katherine's old jeans that Cole gave me hanging over the back of my chair. They weren't on my list of things to bring, but I scooped them up and shoved them in my suitcase anyway. I wanted to bring a bit of Colorado back to New York with me.

Katherine was teary eyed when I brought my suitcases down-stairs, and I knew it was hard for her as she watched Danny and George load the back of the truck. She was losing three of us in the span of one week. During the graduation party, Cole had packed up his car and moved out of the house, leaving only a note on the kitchen counter to explain where he went. When I heard he was gone, I felt like it was my fault. He'd mentioned leaving back in the garage and I should have known he was trying to tell me good-bye, but I didn't realize he was planning to go so soon. I called him twice, but both times it went straight to voice mail.

"Before you all go, I want to show you something," said Katherine. She had been acting mysterious for the last two days.

"You finished the mur—" Isaac started.

"Don't ruin it!" Nathan butted in before Isaac could wreck the surprise.

"Come this way, Jackie. You have to see."

Katherine led us around the side of the house to the barn, with everyone following behind us.

"You have to close your eyes," she told me and covered my face with her hands.

"All right," I giggled, not quite sure what was going on. Someone pulled back the squeaky barn door and guided me inside.

Parker gasped, someone started to clap, and I heard Jack and Jordan arguing about who looked better. I twitched to see what everyone was so excited about.

"Okay," Katherine said, taking her hands away. "Open your eyes."

My eyelids quickly snapped up, and I blinked a few times to see if what I was looking at was actually real. "Oh my God, Katherine!" I gushed, walking forward in astonishment. "This is—I don't even have a word to describe it."

"Don't touch," she warned Zack and Benny. "It's still wet, and thank you, Jackie. I've been working hard on it ever since you decided to leave with Danny."

One wall of the barn was covered in a spectacular mural. In the middle were Katherine and George, surrounded by their children. The little twins were painted wrestling on the ground, Nathan with a guitar in his hand, and Lee with his skateboard. But then I noticed the girl with two arms wrapped around her shoulder. I was in the painting, and Cole and Alex were smiling on either side of me. On the top of the entire mural in Katherine's cursive font were the words: "My Family."

It was then that the meaning behind it really sunk in.

"Katherine, this—this is the best surprise anyone has given me," I said, barely able to get my words out. My hands were trembling as I pulled her into a hug. There was nothing I could say to truly show her what this—having a family again—meant to me.

"I'm glad you like it, honey," she whispered softly. It was almost as if she understood what was going through my head.

"We need to get going," Danny said, glancing down at his watch. All morning he'd been an anxious mess, and I knew he was afraid of missing the flight.

Everyone paraded to the driveway so we could say our farewells.

"I'm going to miss my running buddy," Nathan told me, wrapping his arms around me for a hug.

"Not as much as I'm going to miss you," I replied, burying my face in his shoulder. "But I'll be back in September. There's no way I could leave you forever." I pulled away so I could look at him. More like look up at him. Nathan was so much taller than me now that he could use the top of my head as an armrest. He only had a few more inches to go before he caught up to Danny.

"All right, you two," George said, opening the truck door. "We should hit the road."

After receiving a hug from everyone, including a second one from Katherine, Danny and I climbed into the truck.

"I'll be home for dinner," George called.

After clicking in my seat belt, I focused my attention on all the wonderful people in front of me as the car roared to life. Every one of them had been important in helping me during a difficult time of my life, and I never wanted to forget that. Looking past their sad but smiling faces, I found the window of my room on the side of the Walters' house. If I squinted, I could make out the bright colors that were on the walls, but I had to imagine the image of my bed and desk inside.

As if the weather sensed everyone's depressing mood, the sky had filled with clouds. Danny and I waved out the truck window, and

I felt the mist of a coming rain brush against my skin. By the time we had backed all the way out of the driveway, it was raining.

Reaching back, Danny found my hand and rubbed it softly in a comforting way. I rested my head against the window and stared out into the gloomy weather. Leaving Colorado wasn't just hard for me; I knew Danny was sad as well. Although he was excited about the opportunities that the theater program was going to offer him, he was leaving his family behind.

"What the heck?" George exclaimed from the front seat. My eyes snapped open. Craning my neck to peer out the window, I spotted a car speeding toward us dangerously fast. A horn honked as the car pulled up beside us. It was the newly restored Buick Grand National.

"It's Cole!" Danny said, his eyebrows rising in surprise.

"You're right," George said, sounding just as confused. "What is he doing?"

My phone rang, and I had to tear my eyes away from the road to find it in my purse. "Hello?" I answered, my voice trembling.

"Jackie, it's me. Please have my dad pull over."

"Mr. Walter?" I asked, holding the phone away from my mouth. "Can you pull over quick? I promise this will only take a second."

"All right," he agreed, "but it has to be fast. Katherine would kill me if you two miss your flight."

"I know. Thank you so much," I said as he slowed the car and parked in the gravel on the side of the road.

Cole pulled up behind us, and I ripped my door open and jumped out into the rain.

"I thought you weren't going to say good-bye," I said, launching myself into his arms.

"I know. I'm sorry," he responded and held me tight. "I was afraid. I don't want to say good-bye to you."

"It's not forever."

"It feels like it," he said. Biting my tongue, I tried to hold back the rush of feelings inside me. "I wish things would have worked out between us." His words were regretful. "It's like the timing was never right."

"Who knows?" I said. Lifting my hands up, I cupped his face with my cold fingers. "Maybe it will be."

Yes, I was leaving Colorado. Coming here had helped me forget some of the pain of losing my family, but I needed to stop running from it. Going back to New York was going to be an agonizing process of putting myself back together, but facing it would make me a stronger person. Perhaps then, when I came back, the timing would be perfect.

Cole turned his head to look at the dark sky above us, and I couldn't tell if it was a raindrop or tear that streaked down his face. "Okay."

The truck horn beeped, signaling our time was up.

"Good-bye, Cole," I whispered, nuzzling my face between his shoulder and neck.

"Wait!" he cried out as I started to pull away. "Just one kiss, Jackie. One real kiss, so you can have something to think about when you get home."

I gazed up into Cole's eyes before I let mine flutter closed. His warm lips pressed against mine, as the cold, numbing rain poured down on us. My hand gripped his shoulders tightly as he tangled his fingers in my soaking hair. Our heavy, wet clothes hung to our bodies, making our embrace feel even tighter.

And one kiss was all it was. As soon as his lips touched mine, it felt like they were gone, even though the kiss had probably lasted a good five seconds.

"Thank you," Cole whispered, his forehead pressed against mine.

My heart was begging me to find his lips again and never let go, but the horn beeped again, and my head made me pull away.

"Good-bye, Jackie," Cole called as I turned in the direction of the truck.

"See you in three months," I responded, looking back over my shoulder. No good-byes. This wasn't good-bye. He nodded his head and flashed me a small smile.

With that, I focused my eyes on the truck and didn't look back. It was time to go home.

Acknowledgments

There are many extraordinary people who were involved in getting this story into bookstores. Firstly, I'd like to thank the people at Sourcebooks, especially my editor Aubrey Poole who helped me sort through the rambling mess of an enthusiastic fifteen-year-old, and Dominique Raccah who took a chance on twelve wild boys. Secondly, I'd like to thank the amazing Wattpad team. To Allen Lau for creating the website that shaped me into the writer that I am today, and Eva Lau who made Wattpad feel like a second home. Their generosity is unparalleled. Also, to Seema Lakhani who guided my through my fan-funding campaign.

Then there are the people who nurtured this story when it was only a single chapter. They encouraged me to add a second and a third, until finally I had a novel on my hands. To my beloved fans at Wattpad for helping me bring this story to life. Without their support, I would be nowhere.

Thank you to my little sister, who was the first person to listen to my story; to my mother, for supporting this crazy career path; to my father, whose memory gave me the strength to finish this story even when I didn't want to; and lastly, to my best friend and fiancé Jared, for loving me even though I'm a little bit crazy.

A Special Thanks To...

Alexandra D. (Mimi)
Maja D Jørgensen
Bipasha Peridot
PeridotAngel
Chellsey Bland
Richard Wiltshire
Lauren Wholey
Fiona Hennah
Kelly Hepburn
Sarah Watson
Megan Toher
Sania Henry
Daniela Jáquez
Shez King
black_rose_love
Annette Kinch
Faux Punker
Natasha Preston
Katy Thrasher

Alexis Stambek
Samantha R. Weck
Isabel Jean Brice
Lovectic
Alexa Dougherty
Czarina Sophia
TheOddPersonOut
Lilian Carmine
Colleen H.
Courtney Baysa
Khadija Al Kiyumi
Colleen Bartsch
Alexandra Trakula
Mélina Vanasse
Alondra Cuahuizo
Golbou Makvandi
Megan Faber
Victoria Murphy
Kimberly Ann Berna
Heather Kelby
Rebecka Teves
Candice Faktor

About the Author

Ali Novak is a twenty-two-year-old Wisconsin native and recent graduate of the University of Wisconsin-Madison's creative writing program. She started writing her debut novel *My Life with the Walter Boys* when she was only fifteen. After posting the story online, it received more than twenty-five million hits. When she isn't writing, Ali enjoys reading anything she can get her hands on and watching Food Network shows even though she can't cook.

About Wattpad

You might not realize it, but the book you're holding started as a story on Wattpad, a social reading platform. It was written by someone just like you, someone who might not have necessarily thought they were an author until they shared their story with the world's largest community of readers and writers. Download the Wattpad app today to discover other stories like this one that you can read for free on your phone or tablet, or on your computer at www.wattpad.com.

16 THINGS I THOUGHT WERE TRUE

Janet Gurtler

Heart attacks happen to other people #thingsithoughtweretrue

When Morgan's mom gets sick, it's hard not to panic. Without her mother, she would have no one—until she finds out the dad who walked out on her as a baby isn't as far away as she thought...

Adam is a stuck-up, uptight jerk #thingsithoughtweretrue

Now that they have a summer job together, Morgan's getting to know the real Adam, and he's actually pretty sweet...in a nerdy-hot kind of way. He even offers to go with her to find her dad. Road trip, anyone?

5000 Twitter followers are all the friends I need #thingsithoughtweretrue

With Adam in the back seat, a hyper chatterbox named Amy behind the wheel, and plenty of Cheetos to fuel their trip, Morgan feels ready for anything. She's not expecting a flat tire, a missed ferry, a fake girlfriend...and that these two people she barely knew before the summer started will become the people she can't imagine living without.

RACING SAVANNAH

Miranda Kenneally

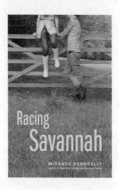

They're from two different worlds.

He lives in the estate house, and she spends most of her time in the stables helping her father train horses. In fact, Savannah has always been much more comfortable around horses than boys. Especially boys like Jack Goodwin—cocky, popular and completely out of her league. She knows the rules: no mixing between the staff and the Goodwin family. But Jack has no such boundaries.

With her dream of becoming a jockey, Savannah isn't exactly one to follow the rules either. She's not going to let someone tell her a girl isn't tough enough to race. Sure, it's dangerous. Then again, so is dating Jack…

BOYS LIKE YOU

Juliana Stone

One mistake. And everything changes.

For Monroe Blackwell, one small mistake has torn her family apart –leaving her empty and broken. There's a hole in her heart that nothing can fill—that no one can fill. And a summer in Louisiana with her Grandma isn't going to change that…

Nathan Everets knows heartache first-hand when a car accident leaves his best friend in a coma. And it's his fault. He should be the one lying in the hospital. The one who will never play guitar again. He doesn't deserve forgiveness, and a court-appointed job at the Blackwell B&B isn't going to change that…

Captivating and hopeful, this achingly poignant novel brings together two lost souls struggling with grief and guilt—looking for acceptance, so they can find forgiveness.

THE SUMMER OF SKINNY DIPPING

Amanda Howells

After getting dumped by her boyfriend, sixteen-year-old Mia Gordon is looking forward to spending the summer in the Hamptons with her glamorous cousins. But when she arrives, her cousins are distant, moody, and caught up with a fast crowd.

That's when she meets Simon Ross. Simon isn't like the snobby party boys her cousins seem obsessed with; he's funny, artistic, and utterly adventurous. And from the very first time he encourages Mia to go skinny-dipping, she's caught up in a current that's impossible to resist.